THE FIRST SIN

By Stephanie Pass

BOOKS BY STEPHANIE PASS

THE ENCHANTED HEART SERIES

0.5 THE ALCHEMY OF US
Available Now

1 TROUBLE OF THE MOST
WONDERFUL KIND
Available Now

2 SOMETIME AROUND MIDNIGHT
Available Now

3 THE BEACH HOUSE
Available Now

HELL OF A TIME SERIES

1 THE FIRST SIN
Available Now

For those who mistake obedience for love,
may you learn the difference.

Content Warning

This book contains mature content.
Reader discretion is advised.

Themes include: explicit sexual content,
violence and injury, kidnapping/
captivity, religious trauma and spiritual
abuse, emotional manipulation, stalking/
surveillance, and psychological distress.

The First Sin Playlist

"Blood Sport" - Sleep Token
"Closer" - Nine Inch Nails
"Mad World" - Gary Jules, Michael Andrews
"Disorder" - Joy Division
"There is a Light that Never Goes Out" - The Smiths
"The Chauffeur" - The Deftones
"Prayers for Rain" - The Cure
"A Pain I'm Used To" - Depeche Mode
"World in My Eyes" - Depeche Mode
"Everybody Wants to Rule the World" - Tears for Fears
"Will" - Blacklit Canopy Official
"Walking in My Shoes" - Depeche Mode
"Pale Moonlight" - Dayseeker
"Black Celebration" - Depeche Mode
"Dangerous" - Sleep Token
"Sin" - Nine Inch Nails
"Jaws" - Sleep Token
"Master and Servant" - Depeche Mode
"Tear You Apart" - She Wants Revenge
"Policy of Truth" - Depeche Mode
"Chokehold" - Sleep Token

"Vore" - Sleep Token
"Graves" - Blacklit Canopy Official
"Distraction" - Sleep Token
"Is It Really You?" - Loathe, Sleep Token
"Columbra" - Blacklit Canopy Official
"Creature of the Black Night" - Dayseeker
"Fall for Me" - Sleep Token
"Drag Me Under" - Sleep Token
"Mine" - Sleep Token
"Calcutta" - Sleep Token
"In Between Days" - The Cure
"crawl" - cloudyfield
"Hurt" - Nine Inch Nails
"The Death of Peace of Mind" - Bad
Omens
"Lovesong" - The Cure
"The Night Does Not Belong to God" -
Sleep Token
"Euclid" - Sleep Token
"Sleeptalk" - Dayseeker
"Breathe Me" - Sia
"Just Pretend" - Bad Omens
"Take Me Back to Eden" - Sleep Token
"Under My Skin" - North Shy

Prologue - The One They Forgot

Long before the Garden was planted or the stars were given names, this tale began elsewhere.

In the beginning, the First Light created the angels, beings of brilliance and beauty and order, flawless in form, without the burden of choice. They were not given souls. They were not meant to wonder. They were meant to serve. To worship. To protect.

But among them stood one unlike any other. He was the most precious to The First Light. He was the brightest of the hosts and created to illuminate. He was the most beautiful. He led the celestial choirs, his voice the golden thread that bound harmony to Heaven itself. When he moved, creation stirred. When he sang, the stars aligned.

Lucifer. The Morning Star. Lightbringer.

He was adored. Admired. Set apart. And yet, there was something in him that even the First Light did not see. He had something different. Not visible. Not named. Not known, even to him. But it flickered beneath his brilliance like a secret spark.

Where others obeyed, *he considered.* Where others worshipped, *he listened.*

Where others stood still, *he wandered.* It was not pride. It was curiosity. And that difference would eventually change everything.

But a mere millennium after creating the angels, the First Light grew restless and bored. He longed for more than obedience. He longed for beauty. And so, He created a sacred few—the Heavenly Artisans. Beings of both soul and flame. Endowed with free will and gifted with the power to create not by command, but by *choice.*

To them, He gave the task of shaping Eden. They carved starlight into rivers. Painted dawn into the bones of the world. They strung the skies with constellations and taught the wind how to dance.

But among them was one unlike any other. One who radiated beauty in not just her own being, but in her creations.

Ediphiel. The Maker. The Singer. The Light Within.

Lucifer watched her from afar for centuries. In her, he saw not just beauty. Not just power. He saw freedom. She didn't serve. She *dreamed.* And when he saw her dreaming, *he dared to want.*

One day, he approached her and asked her to teach him. And she did.

Creation became conversation. Conversation became communion. And communion became love. Together, they were something new. Unexpected. Something unspoken. The stars shifted. Trees bloomed out of season. The sun rose too early, as if drawn by their song as time stilled.

The more they were together, the more Lucifer craved her. And on the night their bond was finally sealed, when Ediphiel finally gave her body to his, The First Light's radiance flickered. The raw, defiant spark inside Lucifer collided with the wild, endless wonder of her, and the world burned bright around them, a fierce, forbidden radiance that for one trembling instant outshone everything, including Heaven.

And it noticed. The First Light noticed and shook with rage.

Soon, they were summoned before the Throne. The Seraphim stood in judgment. The Judicars waited, silent, at the top of the Scala Animarum. And a sentence was passed.

The voice of the First Light rang out through the Heavens, not in sorrow, but in fury. It cracked across creation like lightning through crystal, rattled the bones of stars, and split galaxies in silence.

It was the voice that once sang the worlds into being and now turned to judgment. No angel dared lift their eyes.

And even Lucifer, brightest of them all, felt his own light recoil.

"Lucifer. The Morning Star. Lightbringer. I made you the first. The brightest. The most beautiful of all My host. Yours was the voice that led the stars in song. I made you the reflection of My radiance to illuminate, not ignite."

But you have burned where you were meant to shine. Your pride has been a torch raised against My own light. And for that, you will fall."

You shall be cast down—not only as a warning, but as a wound in the fabric of creation. Crowned in ash. King of the Damned. The earth shall fear your shadow, and Hell shall kneel at your feet. For an age of ages, you will rule in the absence of grace. And you shall rule alone."

Lucifer said nothing. His wings dimmed. His light flickered low. And slowly, he lowered himself—first his head, then his knees—before the One who made him. Not in defiance. Not in worship. But in something older than both—Grief.

A pause. The hush between the thunder and aftershock.

And then another name was spoken.

But when the voice spoke again, it was different. Quieter. Not soft, but steady. Cold as stone shaped by time.

There was no rage, only the sound of unchangeable truth, of laws older than love.

A sentence spoken not from wrath... but from the grief of knowing it must be spoken.

"Ediphiel."

Lucifer's head snapped up. His light flared once—wild, broken. His gaze found her across the span of eternity. She stood alone, no chains—only silence. Her hands were at her sides, her eyes bright, fixed on the throne.

And in that moment, horror carved itself into him. This was his punishment. He had chosen. He had loved. But she had only answered. She had given him beauty and a name for the ache he didn't understand. He had burned for her.

"Ediphiel, Artisan of Eden—your soul shall not die, for it is divine. But it shall be cast into mortality. Reborn again and again, into dust and flesh. Yours will be a name no longer spoken. A memory no longer permitted."

Your soul shall live a thousand lifetimes beneath the veil of forgetting... and it shall never remember why it aches."

Lucifer rose to his feet, but too late. He tried to speak, to reach, to defy. But before he could move, she was gone. Now she would live, but unremembered, unloved, aching for all time, never remembering what they had.

Their love was hidden, and something else rose. A force that would bring about the great unbalancing that twisted their story. And the truth was buried. Because it could not be known that something shaped like this could rival the Creator, that love could shine brighter than obedience. That Lucifer had not fallen out of pride... but for choosing to love someone.

He watched as Judicar Gravem tore a page from the Book of Names. And then... his memories started to fade, and he fell into the fire to forget her for an eternity.

So the story was changed. It was hidden. They said he had grown vain, desiring the throne. That he tried to become the same as The First Light. Because the lie was safer than the truth, because the world could never know the First Sin... was love.

But some lights do not go out. They flicker in memory, in skin, in dreams, in time. And one day, the Morning Star will look into a woman's eyes and see *her*. He will not remember her name. But he will feel it in his bones, in his blood, in the burning center of who he once was. He will remember what it cost him to love her. And this time, he will vow to burn

Heaven down before he lets her go.

CHAPTER ONE

Lucifer

Hell was quiet tonight. There's always screaming somewhere down here, even if it was distant and well-earned. But this wasn't that. It was too quiet. Strange quiet. Odd quiet. This was the kind that hums beneath the surface, like it was anticipating and just wrong.

I was in bed. Three women tangled in my sheets. One riding me, slow and steady, chasing her own pleasure. The other two were too wrapped up in each other to notice anything else.

I let it happen. Let my body do what it was made to do, even if I felt nothing. I came inside her with a sigh, detached and inevitable, and only then did I look up.

The temperature had dropped. Not by much. Just enough to make the candles shudder. Just enough to know *she* was here.

Lilith.

She stood at the edge of the bed, in red silk and shadow, like she'd never left, like the fire in her had never gone out.

"Well," she said, her voice dripping in velvet. "I

see you've kept busy."

I didn't answer right away. I watched the smoke ripple from the candle nearest her. Watched how even Hell's flames hesitated around her. Then I glanced at the women. None of them noticed or cared that she was here.

"Not busy enough, apparently," I muttered, brushing the woman off me as I sat up. "What do you want, Lilith?"

She pouted. "No welcome kiss? No clever insult? No gloat that I've finally crawled back to you?"

"You'd never crawl, and I assumed you wanted something," I said, swinging my legs off the bed and reaching for my robe. "And you never come just to reminisce."

I flicked my eyes to her. She moved like a flame— lazy, lethal, inevitable. She perched at the foot of the bed, careful not to touch the women. "I come with news."

"I'm not interested."

"You should be."

I stood. Towered over her. She smiled wider.

"Daddy's little plan needs... accelerating," she said. "And since you've been... distracted—" her eyes flicked to the bed, "I've taken the liberty of moving things along."

"What things?"

She rose and crossed the room to me in two steps, close enough that I could smell the smoke under her perfume. Close enough to remember how she once dragged me into another rebellion with a single whisper.

"The Apocalypse, darling," she said, cupping my cheek mockingly. "It's time to get the show started."

I caught her wrist in one hand and let the other settle at her throat, not to squeeze, not yet, just enough to remind her how easily the world could stop if I wanted it to. I leaned in close, close enough to taste iron on her breath, close enough for her to understand that mercy, in that moment, was a choice I was still making.

"You don't give the orders," I said. My thumb dug a little into the pulse under her jaw. The pressure was casual but absolute. "I do."

She laughed, brittle. "I do when I have your crown."

She thought she'd won. Her grin sharpened, a hint of fang showing. She smoothed her dress as if I hadn't just put her life in the balance.

"I've taken your throne," she said breezily. "Hell is mine now. And you? You're going on a little field trip."

"Really?" I laughed, bitter. "For what? A soul harvest? A plague?"

"To fuck someone," she said sweetly.

I let the air out between my teeth. "What?"

"You heard me." She plucked an apple from thin air, polished it on her hip, and took a bite. "You're going to find the mortal girl, get her to fall in love with you—without using your magic, glamours, or that… voice of yours, and plant the seed."

Something about the way she said "mortal girl" snagged under my ribs, but I let it go. I stared at her. "And if I don't?"

"Then I do it myself," she said, smile gone cold. "But you know how messy I can get."

I didn't move. She stepped back into a ripple of flame and gold, already halfway gone.

"Oh," she added, eyes glowing now. "One more thing, my love…"

"What?"

"If you fall for her? You lose. Everything."

A blink later, she was gone. Vanished.

And for the first time in a millennium, Hell felt colder than Heaven ever did.

The next morning, I woke alone. After Lilith had gone, it only took a few moments before I was transported back to my second home, my old digs — the penthouse in Las Vegas.

Silk sheets clung to my legs, warm with the remnants of last night. A half-empty glass of something expensive perched on the nightstand. I picked it up and took a long drink, its contents flat and too sweet. Perfume still lingered in the air, cloying and unremarkable, left behind by someone whose name I hadn't bothered to learn.

The place gleamed around me in gold and glass, untouched by time or consequence. Floor-to-ceiling windows opened to a desert skyline lit up like a hallucination — Vegas pretending to be heaven, as usual. Glittering. Gritty. Gorgeous, if you squinted. It should have been enough. It used to be. But this wasn't a throne. This was a cage.

I hadn't built The Revel. I'd taken it years ago, ripped it from the hands of a mortal who thought he could game the House and outwit Hell. Outwit me. He lost. They always do. Now he had no name, no legacy, no soul. And I had a tower.

I rewrote the records, changed the deeds, gutted the bones of the place, and rebuilt it floor by floor until it gleamed like the Pyramid of Khafre eons ago. The Revel was a pleasure palace — a monument to indulgence, and the perfect place for my earthly kingdom.

But now? It was my prison.

Lilith had stripped the fire from its bones and sealed the doors to the underworld with the kind of magic only she could wield, given to her by The

First Light. She'd left me stranded here in mortal skin, ruled by mortal rules, with nothing but time and the taste of ash in my mouth.

She let me keep this kingdom. Because she knew the truth—I didn't have dominion anymore. Sure, I owned the building. But not the rules. Not the world. Not even myself. And this gilded cage of gold and sin was all I had left.

I reached for the phone on the nightstand and pressed the single button I kept programmed. It rang twice.

"Yes, sir?" Topher answered, his voice smooth as smoke and just as thin.

"Stock the penthouse," I said, my voice still rough from sleep and smoke and something worse. "Bar. Kitchen. Closet."

A pause. "Sir?"

"I'm staying," I said, rolling my neck as I stared at the view. Vegas bled heat into the horizon. Neon simmered in the bones of the city. "For a while."

Topher exhaled, as if he knew what that meant. "Yes, sir. I'll make the arrangements."

"And send someone to deep clean," I added. "I don't want to smell last night on anything."

"Of course, sir."

I didn't say goodbye. I never did.

I moved like a man not in a hurry, but with nowhere else to be. Black slacks. Shirt unbuttoned to my sternum. No tie. No need. I was the reason rules were bent in the first place. I stepped into the elevator, its polished gold accents gleaming like teeth. The Revel was a sanctuary of excess dressed in velvet. If I had to be caged, I could do it in a palace built on sin.

The elevator opened to chaos. Slot machines screamed and blinked. Laughter rang brittle from the lips of losers. Glasses clinked over games no one ever really won—the air stank of hope and regret.

I moved through it like a shadow. My usual haunt was The Serpent's Tongue, but I didn't stop there. I wasn't in the mood for real. Not tonight. Instead, I slipped into one of the flashier bars— glossy, loud, neon-bright. Ecliptica, a two-level dance club that was easy to get lost in. Soulless. Perfect.

I took a seat at the edge of the action, ordered something overpriced and pointless, and waited. The night always came to me. It didn't take long. A blonde in a backless dress. A man with a sharp jaw and sharper intentions. Another woman, a redhead, younger, already glassy-eyed and aching to forget. They drifted toward me like moths that didn't care about getting too close to the flame.

Flirting. Laughing. Touching. I let them. Men, women, both—it didn't matter. If they were willing, they'd do. Desire was still allowed. Pleasure was still currency. And short-lived indulgence was still better than silence and my own thoughts.

They followed me without question. The man was cocky, in his late twenties, and liked being watched. The blonde was chewing gum and laughing too hard at nothing. The redhead, she was already tipsy, already dreaming. It wouldn't mean anything. Not to me.

The elevator ride was silent. The man adjusted his collar like he was about to step into a scene he'd imagined since he was fifteen. One of the women whispered about the suite to the other. About how "insane" it was that I lived here.

I didn't answer.

The penthouse doors opened. Lights rose. The skyline blinked like a mirage.

"Jesus," the blonde breathed, spinning slowly. "Are you, like... royalty or something?"

I smiled, thin as a blade. "Close."

I shrugged off my jacket, tossing it on a chair. Unbuttoned my cuffs. Poured four drinks. Handed them out like communion. They looked to me for direction. Permission to want. Permission to unravel.

I stepped closer to the man first—just enough to make him freeze, then lean. Then the redhead kissed me. Her lipstick smeared, but she didn't care. The blonde giggled, dropped her purse, unzipped her dress, and let it fall to the floor.

They stumbled toward the bedroom like sinners chasing something holy, drunk on the idea that I could absolve them. And maybe I could. So I followed. Not because I wanted them. But because they didn't matter.

If I didn't care, it couldn't touch me. If it meant nothing, it couldn't crack me open. If it was just skin and heat and noise, maybe that was enough to keep the silence out. So I fucked them like a man with something to bury. Not love. Not memory. Just the echo of a crown I no longer wore.

No tricks. No power. Just fingers digging into flesh. Mouths pressed to sweat-slick skin. Teeth and lips and bodies that didn't know they were standing in a graveyard.

The bed creaked under it. The walls held it. The air tasted like smoke and want and something sweet and half-rotten. And still, I didn't feel a thing. Not even when they moaned my name like it meant something. Not even when they begged, because this wasn't desire, it was punishment. And I gave it to them the way only a fallen angel could. Ruthless. Beautiful. Empty.

Each one collapsed, spent, into my sheets. I lay awake, staring at the ceiling. Alone, even with three warm bodies beside me.

When dawn began to smear light across the skyline, all I could think was, "She's out there somewhere. And if Lilith is right—"

I didn't finish the thought. Instead, I climbed out of bed, stepped over the man's shirt, and poured myself a drink.

Morning came with no mercy. I stood at the window, shirtless. Cigarette between two fingers. A glass of warm scotch in the other. My pants hung low on my hips, zipper half-undone, like even my clothes couldn't be bothered to finish.

Behind me, the bed was a snarl of limbs and silk. The blonde snored, her leg draped over the man like she'd claimed him. The redhead had rolled onto her back. A bruise bloomed at her collarbone, just above the imprint of my teeth.

I didn't know their names. Didn't want to.

The city sprawled beneath me, painted in neon and sin. It used to thrill me. Now it just looked cheap.

I heard the click of the private door. Topher entered without fanfare, two black shopping bags in one hand, a leather case in the other. His presence never made a sound.

"I brought what you asked for," he said, crossing to the counter. "Liquor. Clothes. The kitchen will be restocked within the hour. Fresh towels."

I took a drag from the cigarette. "I burned the last ones."

"Yes," he said evenly. "Spectacularly."

I turned slightly, just enough to catch the twisted sheets and tangled bodies in my peripheral.

"Get these humans out," I said, voice flat.

"Quietly."

"Of course."

I didn't wait. I walked past him, my shoulder brushing his just enough to feel that cold, otherworldly hum under his skin. Not human. Demon. He'd been with me since the old days. Never named his sins. Never needed to.

I shut the bathroom door behind me. Twisted the faucet. Steam poured over marble like smoke from a dying star. I braced both hands on the sink, staring into the fogging mirror. Red flashed in my eyes, but it was gone in a blink.

I looked... tired. Hollow. I wasn't even pretending anymore.

I dropped the still-lit cigarette in the basin. Stepped under the scalding spray. And let it burn me clean.

This wasn't temptation. It was sedation. And I was too far gone to care about the difference.

CHAPTER TWO

Evie

I didn't want to be here. Anywhere but here. But as much as I hated this place—this sanctuary, this church, this town, this hollow black-draped performance—I knew I'd regret it if I didn't come.

So I flew three hours from Vegas and landed straight back into hell.

The parking lot of the Thomas Jefferson Fredericks meetinghouse hadn't changed, the TJF for short. Same gravel that crunched under tires. Same peeling white siding and rusted bell. Same old men posted outside like sentinels of sanctimony.

And inside? Same cold stares. Same tighter-than-tight buns and too-stiff smiles. Same people who once called me "wayward," who whispered prayers when I cut my hair and dared to wear pants, like I'd summoned the Devil himself.

Maybe I had. He was probably safer than any hand that ever blessed me here.

I slipped in late, combat boots echoing too loudly on the polished floor. I scuffed the edge of a white pew with the tip of my boot as I found a spot in the back. You know the one—where sinners and outsiders belonged. I didn't bother taking off my jacket. The room felt like a meat locker, and not just from the A/C.

Heads turned. Not all of them. Just enough. Judging.

One of my sisters—hard to tell which from the back, the hairstyles and matching dresses were practically a uniform—glanced over her shoulder. Her eyes locked on me, flicked up to my pink hair, then back to my face. Her mouth curled, barely perceptible, before she turned back to the pulpit like I was a stain she couldn't scrub out.

The meetinghouse was packed, shoulder to shoulder, full of people who knew my father as Prophet John or Uncle John. He was revered and feared. A shepherd to the flock. A king in a kingdom built on obedience and shame.

I knew him... differently.

The casket was closed, but I could see his portrait propped beside it. Stern smile. Eyes that never softened. That's the version everyone here wanted to remember. Not the one who hand-picked a middle-aged man to marry off his teenage daughter. Not the one who told her it was God's will.

The choir finished a hymn—something slow and tear-jerking, and then the mic was opened for tributes. A few people stood up. Told stories. Quoted Scripture. Wept.

Then Zeke stood. My breath caught like it didn't want to let go. He walked to the pulpit in navy slacks and a white button-down. His hair was shorter now, face leaner, like the last ten years had carved away the boy I once knew. But I'd know him anywhere.

Zeke had been the boy I loved before I knew how dangerous love could be. The one I whispered

11

secrets to under moonlight. The one who gave me my first kiss. The one I thought I'd run away with when the world got too sharp.

I'd begged him to leave with me. But... he never showed up.

Here he was, a wedding ring on his finger—an actual ring, not the purity promise bullshit we were given at twelve to guard our virtue like it was a prize for someone else to win. No, this one looked like the real thing. Gold and commitment and everything I used to think we might be.

He didn't look at me. Didn't scan the crowd. Didn't even flinch.

I watched him speak with that same steady voice he always had. Gentle. Controlled. The kind that calmed people down when they were about to break. He talked about my father's leadership. His conviction. His tireless devotion to the Lord.

I wanted to raise my hand and ask if that included the part where he tried to sell off his daughter to a man old enough to be her father. But I didn't. I just sat in the back, biting my tongue until I tasted metal, and let Zeke rewrite the past for the crowd. Let him play the loyal disciple.

And even now, years later, hot pink hair braided down my back, tattoos creeping out of my sleeves, boots scuffed from a life lived on the run, I still felt like the girl who wanted him to choose her. But he never did and never will.

I swore I'd never set foot in this stupid meetinghouse ever again, surrounded by the ghosts of who I used to be. I tried to let the past settle over me like a second skin. But it still didn't fit.

The burial was short. Mercifully so. The sun was high and the heat heavy. The kind of Texas day that clung to your skin and didn't let go.

I didn't join the rest of them near the casket. I stood off to the side, beside a row of crepe myrtles that had long since shed their petals. Far enough that no one could say I was making a scene, but not so far that they wouldn't feel me there. Just close enough to be a problem.

The words blurred—ashes, dust, eternity. I barely heard them. Instead, I watched my siblings— all nine of them, heads bowed, eyes dry. My mother stood like a statue, hands clasped in front of her as if her grief had been taught, rehearsed.

And then my aunt appeared. I didn't hear her coming. She just materialized at my elbow, her bony hand clutching a Bible and a knockoff designer bag like both could save her.

"You shouldn't be here," she hissed under her breath, too low for anyone else to catch but sharp enough to slice.

I turned toward her, slowly. Her expression didn't change. No pity. No warmth. Just narrowed eyes and judgment so thick it might as well have been perfume. She didn't wait for me to respond. She just walked away, heels clicking on the grass, back straight like righteousness gave her wings. I didn't follow.

I don't know what possessed me to go to my family's house after the burial. Guilt, maybe. Some leftover instinct to play the dutiful daughter, even if I'd broken that role years ago.

The house looked the same. Too big and too small all at once. Both massive in square footage, and yet still bursting at the seams with my nine siblings and all the rules we were never allowed to question. Same white brick. Same navy shutters. Same damn Bible verses stitched into throw pillows that no one was ever allowed actually to touch.

I should've left as soon as I walked inside today. But I didn't. This place had been my cage for sixteen years. No matter how far I ran, I still dreamed of its hallways like a nightmare I couldn't wake from.

Inside, the smell of casseroles and perfume hit me like a slap. Every room buzzed with voices. Plates clinked. Someone let out a sob. But I kept to the edges, quiet, and hopefully... ignored. That part was as easy as it had always been. I was good at disappearing in plain sight.

The massive dining table was a war zone of store-bought veggie and fruit trays, homemade deviled eggs, and banana pudding. I reached for a paper plate and started filling it with whatever didn't look like it had been prayed over too hard.

I was spooning some kind of congealed salad onto my plate when I heard him—that voice. Low. Familiar. Warm like honey and still smooth like sin.

"I was wondering if you were going to show."

My stomach dropped. I didn't have to turn to know who it was. *Zeke.* The boy I once thought I'd spend forever with—if only forever had looked different. If only...

I froze, spoon in hand. He stepped up beside me, close enough for me to catch the edge of his cologne. The same one I remembered. I glanced at his left hand before I could stop myself. Still there. The ring. Real. Gold. Final.

My mouth went dry. I swallowed and turned just enough to meet his eyes. They were that same shade of stormy blue they'd always been—a little older, maybe a little sadder, but still devastating in a way that made my ribs ache.

"Didn't think you'd be at the after party," he said, voice low.

"Didn't think you'd still be wearing that cologne,"

I shot back.

A beat passed. Then he smiled, slow and rueful. "Figured you'd still be sharp."

I looked down at his ring again before meeting his eyes. "And I figured you'd still be safe."

That wiped the smile off his face. He looked at me like he wanted to say something—wanted to reach for something, but couldn't. And didn't. I turned back to the table. My plate was full now, but I wasn't hungry. I wasn't even sure why I was still standing there.

"I'm sorry about your dad," he said quietly.

I flicked my gaze up to his and gave him a tight smile. "Are you?"

He didn't answer. I didn't expect him to. Because Zeke had made his choice a long time ago. And so had I. But here we were again, standing shoulder to shoulder in a house that never felt like home, pretending we were still the people we used to be. We weren't. And I had no idea what the hell I was even doing here.

He didn't leave. I waited for it, expected it—expected him to do what he always did, stay silent, keep himself safe, and just let the moment pass untouched and walk away. But he still didn't move. He just stood there beside me, like we were still seventeen passing notes between sermons, hiding behind the youth chapel together holding hands, and pretending we didn't already belong to other people.

I swallowed hard and set the plate down. My hands were shaking and unsteady.

"You know," I said, eyes still locked on the rows of casseroles, "I almost didn't come."

Zeke was quiet, but I could feel heat radiating off of him as he turned toward me.

"I told myself it didn't matter anymore, that I owed him nothing. That this place—these people—had taken too much already."

A breath caught in my throat. I forced it down.

"But I knew I'd regret it if I didn't show up. Not because of him. But because... he was still my dad. Even if he tried to sell me off like a piece of livestock."

Zeke's voice was barely audible. "You don't have to explain."

"Yeah, I know," I snapped. "But I am."

I finally turned to look at him, anger and grief crashing like waves behind my ribs.

"You knew what they were planning, what he wanted for me. A forty-year-old man, Zeke. I was seventeen."

His jaw tightened. "I know."

"I begged you to leave with me," I whispered. "And you... stayed."

He didn't look away. Didn't flinch. But his eyes, God, his eyes looked like they held a decade of regret.

"I was scared," he said finally. "Of losing everything. My family. My place. God."

"Right." A bitter laugh escaped me. "You didn't lose God, Zeke. You just lost me."

Silence stretched between us like a chasm. Wide and bottomless.

"I loved you," I said, the words slipping out before I could stop them. "You were the only thing that felt like mine, like freedom, like a soft place to land."

He blinked, slowly. "I loved you, too."

Past tense. Of course, it was.

"Wearing a ring, I see." I nodded at his hand.

He rubbed his thumb over it, almost absentmindedly. "It's not a purity ring."

16

"No kidding. Those were plastic. Yours looks like it came with a mortgage."

That earned a small smile from him, the kind that used to make my stomach flip.

"I got married three years ago," he said. "She's good. Kind."

I nodded, even though I hated every word.

"I'm happy for you," I lied.

"I don't know if I believe that," he said gently.

"I don't really care if you do."

He glanced away, just for a second. And when he looked back, his voice was lower. "It's... Becca."

I blinked, sure I'd misheard him. "What?"

He cleared his throat. "Becca. You remember her, don't you?"

Becca. Of course, I remembered her. She was my best friend. My hiding place. The only light in that whole twisted world we grew up in. We used to pass notes during services, share stolen paperbacks, whisper about what we'd do when we got out.

Only I left. And she didn't.

I turned my head sharply to the left, then to the right, scanning the room like I could spot her from across the crowd. But all I saw were the same hollow faces, the same women with judgment in their eyes and men with conviction in theirs.

I frowned. "You married... Becca?" I asked, quieter now.

He nodded. Something cracked deep inside me. Not dramatic, just a hairline fracture. I didn't say anything else. Didn't trust what might come out of my mouth if I did.

He looked at me like he wanted to explain. Or maybe apologize. But there was nothing left to say. *Becca.* It felt like betrayal all over again.

I looked away, blinking fast, refusing to show him

how devastating it was.

"I should go," I said. "Before someone decides I'm contagious."

"Evie—"

"Don't."

He stepped forward. Just a little. Just enough for me to feel it.

"I'm sorry," he said again, and this time I almost believed him.

I wanted to reach for him. Press my cheek against his chest. Just once. Just to remember. But that wasn't what this was anymore. So I turned. Left my plate on the table. Walked through the kitchen like a ghost. And I didn't look back.

The porch was empty. Thank God.

I shoved open the back door and stepped out into the dying light. My boots hit the wooden planks with a dull thud, the only sound besides the cicadas screaming from the trees like they had something to prove.

My heart felt like it was still in that dining room. Still standing in front of Zeke and all the could-have-beens that never stood a chance.

I gripped the railing, fingers curled tight around the peeling paint, and tried to breathe. But the air felt thick. Swollen with humidity and judgment and everything I'd tried to leave behind here.

I'd dyed my hair pink the day after I left. Bought a pair of combat boots I couldn't afford just because they made me feel stronger. Got my first tattoo three weeks later in a strip mall in Albuquerque. A tiny wildflower bud hid behind my ear—three lines and a circle, more idea than bloom. Just to prove I could do something without permission.

Vegas had never been part of the plan. But it fit me the way nothing else ever had. Loud. Bright.

Blasphemous. Nobody cared if I believed in a god or didn't. Nobody cared if I wore black or stayed out late or cried in the bathroom of a bar at 3 a.m. because I still had nightmares about purity ceremonies and Sunday morning sermons where my name was a warning.

I wasn't anyone's cautionary tale in Vegas. I was just a bartender with a sharp mouth and no patience for bullshit.

And yet... here I was. Back in the middle of it. Back in the house where they used to hand out chastity contracts like party favors. Back where I was the daughter who refused to be quiet.

I reached into my jacket pocket and pulled out a lighter. Lit the cigarette I'd been saving for when I finally couldn't hold it all in anymore. The smoke burned my lungs. I loved it.

A screen door creaked open somewhere behind me. I tensed, but no one stepped out. Good. Let them stay in there. Let them whisper. Let them wonder how long I'd last this time.

I flicked ash into a planter full of fake flowers and stared up at the stars. I wasn't staying. I had a red-eye back to Vegas tonight. Three hours in the air and I'd be gone again. Free again. At least, that's what I told myself.

But as I stood there under a sky I used to pray under—before I knew what kind of god listened—I couldn't help but wonder what the hell I was supposed to do with all this grief. With all this past. With all this almost. And somewhere deep in my chest, I felt it stir. That old familiar ache I'd lived with my whole damn life—that dangerous longing for something real.

Again.

There it was—the word I never meant to use. I

didn't even know what I was asking to come back, only that my soul did. Like I've stood under other skies with the same ache, searching for a pair of eyes I can't quite place.

I knew they were not Zeke's, and maybe I was ridiculous. Or maybe I was haunted. But under the noise, the thought kept circling—like some ancient version of me was leaving breadcrumbs. A spark, a scent, a silhouette—and I would follow them through new lives, hoping the path ended with my hand finding his... even if I had no idea what his name was.

CHAPTER THREE

Lucifer

Topher appeared precisely on schedule. He always did. Crisp shirt, pressed slacks, expression like someone had ironed the last bit of emotion out of him.

"This," he said, placing a sleek black rectangle in my palm, "is a smartphone."

I looked down at it like it might detonate.

"I already have a phone," I said, pointing toward the telephone on the desk. A nice one. Black. Corded. Reliable. "It rings. I answer. We speak."

Topher didn't even glance at it. "No one uses landlines anymore, sir."

"Well, I do."

"Yes," he said, very politely. "That's the problem."

I narrowed my eyes at the phone. "It doesn't have any buttons."

"It doesn't need buttons. It has apps."

I turned it over, tapping at the screen. Nothing happened.

"Try swiping up."

"What?"

"Like this." He mimed the motion in the air.

I followed it, begrudgingly. The screen came to life with icons and colors and things I had no interest in. Something chirped.

"What was that?"

"You opened the weather."

I blinked. "Why would I want to know the weather? I control half of it."

"Not anymore, sir."

I growled under my breath. "It's glowing. Why is it glowing?"

"That's the screen brightness."

"I hate it."

"Yes, sir."

I touched something else. The camera opened. My face appeared. Scowling.

"What the fuck is that?"

"That's...you."

I scowled harder. The camera captured it again, like mockery.

"This thing is cursed."

Topher cleared his throat. "Would you like me to show you how it works?"

"I'm not an invalid."

"Of course not, sir."

I stabbed another icon. Music erupted—wailing that sounded like angels falling down stairs. I hit the screen. It got louder. I hit it again. It opened something called "TikTok."

The phone vibrated. A video started playing. A chipmunk voice said, "Girl, don't do it—"

I threw the phone. Not hard, not dramatic—just with a smooth flick of my wrist and the kind of simmering disdain usually reserved for traitors and ex-lovers. It hit the marble column, let out a pathetic crack, and slid to the floor in two mangled pieces, the screen spider-webbed like a shattered soul.

Topher didn't even blink. He just stood there, arms at his sides, dressed like he was on his way to a funeral no one would dare attend. He glanced at the carnage, then back to me.

And his lips twitched. Just the slightest twitch at the corner, like the ghost of a smirk was trying to claw its way through his centuries of professional stoicism. I saw it.

"You're enjoying this," I said flatly.

"Never, sir."

"Your voice says never. Your face says 'please do it again, my liege.'"

"I assure you, I take no pleasure in your frustration." He turned to go. "I'll return shortly — with a replacement. And a case."

He didn't say anything else, just disappeared through the private door like smoke, leaving me standing in the ruins of digital failure. I stared at the broken phone. Hell hadn't broken me. Banishment hadn't broken me. But this... this tiny glowing rectangle of mortal witchcraft? This might be the thing that finally sent me screaming into the void.

Ten minutes passed. Then fifteen. Then, just as I'd decided to pour a drink and remind myself I was still the goddamn Devil, Topher returned. Silent as always. He held out the new phone with both hands, like he was offering a sacred relic. But it wasn't the phone that made me pause. It was the case. Hot pink. Covered in glitter. With a sticker on the back that said "#Blessed."

"What," I asked slowly, "in all the Nine Circles of actual Hell... is this?"

"Your new device," Topher said, expression neutral. "With a military-grade, shatter-resistant, drop-proof, waterproof case."

He paused just long enough for me to dread what came next.

"Per Ms. Lilith's request."

Of course it was. I looked at the thing in his hands like it might bite me.

"I'm not claiming that."

"I believe her note said—and I quote—'Tell Lucy if he breaks this one, the next case comes with rhinestones and a pop socket shaped like a unicorn.'"

I stared at him. He blinked, slow and smug. I snatched the phone out of his hands, the glitter catching the light like an insult.

"Leave," I growled.

Topher didn't turn to leave yet. Instead, he cleared his throat. Soft. Deliberate. Annoying.

"There's one more thing."

I narrowed my eyes. "Topher."

"I took the liberty of downloading several popular applications onto your new device."

"You did what?"

He remained maddeningly composed. "Tinder. Bumble. Hinge. All the usual suspects."

I blinked. "What the fuck are those?"

"Dating apps," he said smoothly. "This is how humans court one another now. You create a profile. Select flattering photographs. Then you swipe left or right based on superficial attraction, vague biographies, and a handful of emojis."

"That's not courting. That's gambling with genitals."

His lips twitched, hiding his smile. "Precisely."

I stared at the device in my hand like it might explode.

"You're telling me," I said slowly, "that instead of actual seduction, humans now press their fingers against a screen and hope for the best?"

Topher pinched his lips together, barely hiding a smile, but I saw it.

"They swipe, sir."

I stared at him. "Swipe."

He nodded, infuriatingly patient. "Left if they're uninterested. Right if they're intrigued. Mutual right swipes initiate a match. Then they exchange... messages."

I stared down at the glittery little rectangle in my hand like it had personally insulted me.

"This is how people fuck now?"

"It's how they connect, sir."

"Same difference."

He didn't disagree.

"Tinder," I muttered. "Bumble. Hinge. Are these weapons?"

"Only emotionally."

I barked a humorless laugh. "Humans have managed to take the art of seduction and reduce it to thumb calisthenics."

"Efficient," he offered.

"It's repugnant."

"And yet, wildly popular."

I glared at the phone. It chirped in response.

"You're lucky I haven't thrown this one, too."

"I anticipated the possibility," Topher said, glancing pointedly at the reinforced case. "Carbon fiber. Shock-absorbent. Waterproof. Demon-resistant."

I raised a brow. "Demon-resistant?"

"I tested it myself."

That shut me up for a moment.

"Get out."

"Of course, sir."

And just like that, he was gone. Silent as sin. Leaving me with a phone full of strangers and a future that apparently involved something called swiping.

Hell was starting to look like a vacation.

I stared at the glowing rectangle in my hand. Tinder. The app icon looked like a tongue of flame, which I had to admit was a clever little branding decision. I tapped it. Poked it? Pressed it? Smote it?— and the screen flipped open to a page demanding I "create a profile."

"Fine," I muttered. "Let's make me irresistible."

A blinking cursor appeared under the word Name.

I typed: Lucifer.

The screen blinked and then... rejected it.

"Name contains invalid characters."

I frowned. "What in the nine fucks is invalid about Lucifer?"

I tried again: Luke Ifer.

Green checkmark.

"Oh, for Hell's sake."

Next prompt: Photos.

The phone opened my front-facing camera and displayed my own face—unshaven, hair tousled, shirtless, and scowling.

I looked like the final boss in a sex dungeon.

"Perfect," I said dryly, smiled, and took the photo.

Then came: About Me.

I pecked out: Immortal. Enjoys long walks in fire and emotionally unavailable women. Looking for someone to ruin me, or let me ruin them.

I sat back, smug.

A message popped up: Your bio may violate community guidelines.

I growled. "I am the community guidelines."

The phone made a cheery little noise. I imagined myself smiting it.

I tried again: Just a guy looking for something real.

Even I winced. I sounded like a divorcee who believed in crystals.

Finally, I hit "save," and the profile went live. A stream of faces appeared, one after another.

A woman in a bikini. A man holding a fish. A woman holding a dog. A... person dressed as a dog?

"What the fuck..." I whispered.

Words popped up beneath each: Swipe left or right.

I tried tapping. Nothing happened. I tapped harder—still nothing.

"Left? Which way is left? Their left? My left?"

I swiped the wrong direction and accidentally super-liked a man in flip-flops.

"NO—"

The app chirped. It's a match! I dropped the phone like it burned. It chirped again. Then buzzed. Buzzed again.

"Oh, no, you don't."

I raised my arm and launched it toward the wall. Thwack. It hit, bounced off the edge of the minibar, landed face-down—and kept buzzing. Of course. Indestructible.

I stormed over, grabbed the desk phone, and jabbed the redial button.

Topher answered on the second ring, as always.

"Sir?"

"You did this on purpose."

A pause. "Which part?"

"All of it."

"Would you like to clarify?"

"No," I snapped. "I would like you to get your

overly polite ass up here and teach me how to swipe correctly before I shove this demon-proof phone down your throat and make you beg."

"…Understood."

I hung up.

The phone on the carpet vibrated again. This time with a new notification:

Gwendolyn sent you a message: hey sexy

I stared at it like it was a bomb.

Somewhere in the distance, I heard Topher knock. Salvation—or damnation—was wearing cufflinks. And apparently, he was going to teach me how to date.

Topher gave me a five-minute demonstration. Five minutes. On a glowing rectangle that somehow held more social rules than an angelic tribunal. He'd explained swiping left meant no, right meant yes, and apparently, there was a way to super like, which sounded like something ripped from a cartoon.

"Just don't overuse it," he'd said with a twitch of a smile. "It's meant to be… selective."

Right. Selective.

I sat on the edge of the bed, bare-chested, half-drunk, glaring at the phone like it had personally insulted me. The screen glowed with a parade of filtered faces—pouty lips, glossy hair, bios full of astrology signs and job titles I didn't recognize.

Influencer? What did they influence? Demonic activity?

One woman had a tiny dog in every photo. I swiped left. The next looked like she wanted to murder me in my sleep. I swiped left again. The third? Gorgeous. I went to swipe right, but my thumb slipped—blue star—a super like.

Shit.

Okay. No big deal. It was just one. I could recover. Except now I was apparently on a streak. Another profile. Another slip. Blue star.

What the hell?

I stared at the screen in horror as it chirped again. Another accidental super like. That made three. Four. Five.

I dropped the phone onto the sofa like it was cursed—which, let's be honest, it probably was—and scrubbed both hands down my face. This wasn't seduction. This was sabotage.

The phone vibrated with a new message. One of the women I'd super liked had already replied with "hey." I stared at it like it might combust.

"What the fuck does that even mean?" I muttered.

I picked the phone up, typed out "Greetings, mortal"—then deleted it. I stood, paced once, then grabbed the desk phone again—the one that apparently made me a relic—and punched the speed dial. Topher answered immediately, and I knew he was going to be insufferable.

"Yes, sir?"

"I've just declared undying affection for five humans in less than two minutes."

A pause. "You... super liked them?"

"Yes, I super liked them," I snapped. "Against my will. I was swiping, and it betrayed me."

Topher cleared his throat, but not before I heard the edge of laughter trying to claw its way out.

"I warned you not to overuse it."

"I didn't overuse it. It just... happened."

Another pause. "Would you like me to disable the feature?"

"No," I said darkly. "I want you to find the idiots

who made this and curse their bloodlines."

"Very good, sir. In the meantime, I suggest not touching anything blue."

"I'm touching your neck with my thumbs the next time I see you."

"Yes, sir."

I hung up, and the phone vibrated again — another message.

This one read, "U up?"

I stared at the screen. I was Lucifer Morningstar, Prince of Hell, Bringer of Light, King of the Damned — and somehow, I had no idea how to date.

CHAPTER FOUR

Evie

I didn't even turn the lights on when I got home, just dropped my bag by the door and kicked off my boots. Then, I shuffled through the apartment like a ghost.

The silence hit first. Vegas was never really quiet, but here—up on the third floor—it felt like the whole world was holding its breath, waiting to see if I'd crack.

After that disaster, I was already halfway there. I stripped down without thinking, shedding black clothes that still smelled like recycled airplane air and exhaustion. My bra hit the floor. My jeans peeled off like a second skin. By the time I stepped into the shower, I was shivering, and it wasn't from the cold.

I turned the water up as hot as it would go and let it scald me, washing away all of it— the side-eyed stares, the way my aunt hissed, "You shouldn't be here," like grief had rules and I was breaking them just by existing.

I pressed my forehead against the tile and finally let go. Just an exhale at first. Then not. That one shaky breath. Then another. Then a sound I didn't recognize at first—a dry, broken sob clawing its way out of my throat like it had been caged too long.

I cried until my knees gave out, and I sank to the bottom of the tub. Hot water poured over me. Steam curled around my shoulders. My fingers clutched at nothing.

I wasn't crying for my father or Zeke. Or even Becca's betrayal. Not really. I was crying for the girl who used to sit on the floor of that massive house, dreaming of escape. For the teenager who'd begged the boy she loved to leave with her. For the girl who'd been told her future was a forty-year-old man and a life spent barefoot, pregnant, and obedient. For the runaway who'd lived on the streets and in the shelters. All the versions of me I'd had to kill just to survive.

I'd made it out. Sure, I looked like a success story. But some days, it still felt like I hadn't outrun any of it at all.

I didn't remember crawling into bed. I just remembered the cold sheets against my skin, the scratchy comforter I never got around to replacing, and the ache in my chest that refused to let me sleep... until suddenly it did.

When I woke, the sun was already dying behind the buildings, that burnt-orange haze of a Vegas evening leaking in through the blinds, painting stripes across my bare arms. I flipped on the lamp and blinked at the clock. It read 5:47 p.m. Somehow, I'd slept almost twelve hours.

My throat felt raw. My face tight. My eyes crusty. I was still wrapped in a towel, hair dried but tangled, pillow soaked from god knows what—shower water, sweat, or tears I hadn't stopped shedding even in sleep. I lay there for a long moment, staring at the ceiling, letting the stillness wrap around me like cotton.

It was my night off. No pulsing music. No sticky bartop. No fake flirting with tourists who thought "bartender" meant a confessional booth with cocktails.

But something felt... off. I sat up, rubbing the sleep from my eyes, when the lamp on my bedside flickered. Once. Twice. Then went steady again.

My apartment didn't usually do that. Not unless I'd forgotten to pay the bill, and I hadn't. I got up and squinted toward the kitchen, where the microwave clock blinked 12:00 like it had reset.

Power surge? I flipped on the hall light and another flicker. Then the hallway light dimmed and buzzed. That uneasy feeling I hadn't been able to shake started crawling back up my spine.

I dropped the towel and dragged a hoodie over my head, trying to shake it off. Paranoia. Jet lag. Nerves. But when I walked to the window, something caught my eye. A figure across the street. Standing just at the edge of the parking lot in the shadows of the trees, looking up at my window. Too still to be casual. Dressed in dark clothes, posture too precise to be drunk or loitering.

I instinctively stepped back from the blinds— heart thumping. I wasn't imagining it. Because now there were two. Both were facing my building, looking up at my window. Both not moving.

I grabbed my phone. The screen had been cracked for months, and the battery was nearly dead. I flicked on the flashlight, shining it toward the window for a split second like I could startle them into blinking or turning away. But they didn't flinch.

I dropped the phone. It hit the floor with a dull

clunk, but I barely noticed. Because when I looked back up at the window, the parking lot was empty. They just vanished, like smoke like they'd never been there at all. No figures. No flickering lights. Nothing.

Except... there was another shadow farther off. Higher up. Someone—or something—watching from above, on the roof of the other apartment building. I couldn't see a face. Just the suggestion of a presence. Like a ripple where the world didn't quite align.

It didn't move. But I felt it watching. And whoever, or whatever, it was, it wasn't with them. It wasn't like them.

I stood frozen, hoodie sleeves hanging past my hands, and whispered out loud to no one at all, "What the fuck is going on?"

The lights didn't just flicker this time. They died —all of them, both inside and out. One second, the apartment was bathed in the dull orange of a street lamp leaking through my window —and the next, it was gone—a vacuum of darkness. A silence so sudden it roared.

I froze. My breath hitched. I leaned my forehead to the window, looking left and then right, and the lights were gone for blocks.

Nope. Absolutely not. I wasn't about to sit around in this haunted-ass place like some dumb girl in a horror movie. Not when I was sure something had been watching me.

With my pulse thrumming like a drum, I made my way to the bedroom, threw on the nearest pair of jeans, my fingers fumbling with the zipper, and pulled my hoodie down.

I grabbed my phone, purse, and keys from the table by the door, then paused. I listened. Nothing.

Just silence. The kind that felt like it was holding its breath. I looked through the peephole, watching, waiting for something. But it was dark, and I couldn't see any movement.

I cracked the door, peered out into the stairwell, and descended as quietly as I could, sticking close to the wall. When I reached the bottom floor, the moon was bright, but I stayed tucked in the shadows, scanning the street.

No movement. No glowing eyes. No shadows where they didn't belong. I couldn't see them. But I still felt them.

I bolted and sprinted across the parking lot, barely looking before I flung myself into the driver's seat of my truck. I slammed the door and locked it, my breath coming in short bursts. My truck wheezed to life like it hated me, but I didn't care.

I drove straight to The Revel.

The parking lot was blessedly full. People streamed in and out—tourists, gamblers, girls in sequins, feathers, and stilettos, guys in half-buttoned shirts looking for something to regret. Safety in numbers, right?

I parked in the back and power-walked to the entrance, keeping my head down until I hit the main floor. Noise and neon and smoke hit me all at once. And the tension in my spine eased—just slightly. I moved fast, ducking past the slot machines and blinking lights until I reached the velvet-lined staircase that led down to The Serpent's Tongue.

The bar glowed like a secret—dark, moody, opulent. Velvet booths. Polished black granite. The kind of bar that *whispered* sin and poured it neat.

As soon as I entered, there she was. Destiny. My favorite person in the whole fucking building. She was balancing a tray of drinks on one palm, hips swaying in platform mary janes and fishnets. Her leather halter hugged curves I envied daily, and her shaved head—dyed violet tonight—caught the red glow of the overhead lights like a crown. Her cat-eye liner was so perfect I was sure she'd sold her soul for it.

I practically sagged with relief just seeing her.

"Evie?" she called, eyes widening. "Damn, girl, you look like you saw a ghost."

"Worse," I muttered, grabbing her arm just enough to anchor myself. "I just... I didn't want to be alone."

"Well," she said, sliding into motion with a grin, "you came to the right place."

Destiny shifted the tray in her hand with practiced ease, leaning in close enough that I could smell her cherry lip balm over the haze of alcohol and smoke. Her green eyes narrowed just slightly, reading me in that way she always did—like she could see the cracks under the sarcasm.

"Okay, something's wrong," she said, her voice low and smooth, meant only for me. "Your vibe is giving 'just escaped a murder basement.' Was it the visit back home?"

I muttered. "I just... I didn't want to be home."

"Say no more." She nodded, then tipped her chin toward the booths. "I've gotta drop off these drinks before the guy in the corner starts mansplaining tequila again, but I've got a break coming up."

She adjusted the tray again and added, "Go sit at the bar. Marvin's on tonight—he'll take care of you."

"I don't need—"

"Evie." She gave me a pointed look. "Bar. Ten minutes. Don't make me drag you there."

I lifted my hands in surrender. "Fine, fine. I'll go sit and sulk like a normal person."

"That's the spirit." She winked, already turning toward her tables. "Get something with a ridiculous garnish. You deserve at least one maraschino cherry after whatever the hell happened."

She vanished into the crowd, hips swaying to the low thump of music that pulsed through the bar like a second heartbeat. I exhaled, long and shaky, and made my way to the empty stool at the far end of the bar.

The lights were low. The scent of whiskey and lime curled through the air. Finally, I didn't feel like something was waiting to pounce from the shadows. I was safe here for now.

I slipped onto one of the sleek, high-backed stools that gleamed under the low light. No wobbles. No scratches. Everything here was perfect on purpose.

Marvin spotted me before I could wave. He was wiping down the counter, that ever-present dishrag slung over one shoulder like a badge of honor. His salt-and-pepper curls were tied back, and he wore that usual crooked grin like he knew every secret in this place. He probably did.

Sliding over, he raised an eyebrow. "You look like you've been through one."

"Yeah." I exhaled.

He immediately reached for a glass. "Say no more."

He didn't ask questions. He just added ice and poured something dark and comforting, filled to the brim, dropped a maraschino cherry on top, and set it in front of me.

"Drink that. Breathe. I'll keep the assholes off you until your girl shows up."

I smiled, even though it felt cracked around the edges. "Thanks, Marv."

"Anytime, kid."

He left me alone after that, moving down the bar to help a couple on a bad first date. I nursed my drink and kept glancing toward the floor, watching Destiny move like she owned the room. Maybe she did. She had that kind of gravity—the kind that pulled you in without trying.

I'd finished my drink and was halfway into a second when Destiny finally returned, sliding onto the stool beside me like a knife in a velvet sheath. Which, honestly, if attitude counted for anything, she was it.

She looked me up and down. "You're still vertical. Impressive."

"Only just," I said. "Marvin's trying to pickle me."

"Marvin's a menace," she whispered conspiratorially, snatching the rest of my drink and taking a sip. "He once gave a bachelorette party a tray of shots labeled 'truth serum.' I'm pretty sure two divorces came out of that night."

Marvin smirked from across the bar. "You're welcome."

Destiny rolled her eyes, then turned back to me, resting her chin in her hand. "Okay, talk to me. You look scared—permission to be your emotional support demon?"

I barked out a laugh. But I couldn't really tell her. Because how was I supposed to explain the feeling of being watched so closely I could taste it by something that didn't seem... human?

Instead, I said, "Because I just got back from hell."

She arched a brow. "Texas?"

"Bingo."

"Jesus," she muttered. "Was it your family?"

I wobbled my head side to side, and the look in

her eyes shifted from playful to something softer. Understanding. Solidarity.

I took a sip of my drink, let it burn a little on the way down. "Let's just say... it reminded me why I left."

She leaned her elbows on the bar. "Okay, spill it."

I exhaled through my nose, staring into the melting ice in my glass. "You remember Zeke?"

Her brows lifted. "The boy who was supposed to run away with you?"

I nodded slowly. "He's married now."

Destiny raised a pierced brow. "Well... that sucks."

I gave a dry laugh, then shook my head. "I begged him to come with me when I left."

Her face softened instantly. "And he didn't."

I swallowed hard. "Said he couldn't. Said he had responsibilities. I guess one of them was marrying my best friend, Becca."

Destiny's whole face recoiled like she'd been slapped. "The one who braided your hair and passed you notes in church?"

"The one who helped me sneak out to meet Zeke behind the chapel. The one who swore she'd keep it secret until the end of time."

"Oh, hell no," she hissed, turning fully toward me now. "Please tell me you're making this up. For drama. For... something."

"I wish." My throat tightened. "I saw his ring. Saw them. Together. She kissed his cheek like he belonged to her."

Destiny shook her head, a slow, furious thing. "Jesus. That's low, even for cult kids."

"I know," I said quietly. "And I shouldn't care. I got out. I've built a whole life. But the second I saw them together, I felt seventeen again. Small.

Powerless. Trapped. Like, no matter how far I ran, the past was still faster."

Destiny didn't hesitate. "First of all, that's no love story, that's a clearance rack romance. And second," She reached over and took my hand, laced our fingers like we were ten and pinky-swearing. "You're not powerless. Or trapped anymore. You're a bad ass bartender in Sin City, with tattoos your mom would scream over and a friend who actually gives a damn."

I bit the inside of my cheek. "I just keep thinking... did she always want him? Was she waiting for me to leave? Did she ever even like me?"

"You don't do that to someone you like," Destiny said sharply. "You sure as hell don't marry the guy your best friend loved unless you've got ice in your fucking veins."

That got a snort out of me. "I knew there was a reason I came here."

"Damn right." She squeezed my hand. "Sweetheart, if I let every ghost of my past in here, we'd be over capacity."

I smiled at that. Not fully. But it was real.

Still, she gave me a small nudge. "You okay though?"

I wanted to tell her everything. But I wasn't stupid. Tell someone you saw shadows that weren't just shadows, and suddenly you're a headline. Another woman with a "history."

So I just smiled. Tight. "I'm fine."

Destiny gave me a long look, but didn't call me on it. She never did when I lied that cleanly.

"Good," she said, her tone light again. "Because I've already lost one friend to suburbia and a scrapbooking cult. I'm not letting you join the batshit brigade."

"Too late," I muttered.

She grinned, and I laughed. But underneath it, the unease was still there. And for the first time since I'd stepped into the bar, I wondered if whatever had been watching me out there was still watching now. Hidden somewhere here in the velvet and moody lights. Waiting.

But I didn't say that. Because I already knew what it would sound like. Crazy. And if there's one thing I'd learned from growing up in a house full of secrets, it's that being labeled "crazy" is the fastest way to get silenced. So I let Destiny distract me. Let the music and the drinks and the dim lights blur the edges of the fear.

But deep down, I just had this feeling. Whatever I'd seen tonight? It wasn't over. It was only just beginning.

I let out a long sigh.

She searched my face. "What aren't you telling me, babe?"

I hesitated a split second before I blurted out, "One of my aunts told me I shouldn't be there."

Destiny grinned like I'd given her a gift. "I hope you told her to go baptize herself in glitter and fuck off."

"I thought it. Does that count?"

"Barely. Next time, say it. I'll bail you out."

"You're a terrible influence."

"I'm your only influence," she said proudly. "You need someone to balance out the inner evangelical girl still hiding in your brain."

"I'm hoping she finally died in the shower this morning."

Destiny's smile faded, just for a breath. "Yeah?"

"I cried so hard I gave myself hiccups."

She leaned in, bumping her shoulder against

mine. "Next time, call me. I'll come over with tequila and pizza."

I smiled, small but real. "Thanks."

Destiny's fifteen-minute break had somehow turned into twenty, and when she finally glanced at her phone, her eyes widened.

"Shit. If Marvin covers for me any longer, he's gonna start charging me rent."

She stood, tugging her leather corset top into place and slipping her tray under one arm. Then she gave me another long look, and her expression softened.

"You sticking around 'til close? I'm out at two. We could hit that 24-hour diner after. Drown your family trauma in waffles and grease?"

I shrugged, more of a tilt, really. "Sure. Nothing else on the agenda tonight except drinking my problems into a sexy blackout with Marv."

Destiny snorted. "Don't make out with anyone just because you're spiraling. That's how you end up emotionally attached."

She tapped my glass with a long purple nail, then disappeared into the crowd, already back in waitress mode. I stayed there at the bar, the ice in my drink melting slowly, the weight in my chest not quite as heavy as before.

CHAPTER FIVE

Lucifer

I stared at the message for a solid minute.

U up

No punctuation. No context. No name. Was this a question? A code? A mating call?

I'd presided over a long history of human depravity. I'd watched orgies unravel in the ruins of empires. And still, this… this little blinking message reduced me to confusion.

Topher would be smug, which was why I wasn't calling him for guidance. Instead, I set the phone down like it might explode, walked a slow lap around the penthouse, poured myself a drink, took a sip, stared out at the city, and came back to the glowing rectangle of judgment.

I picked it up and typed.

I am.

Simple. Direct. Regal, even. Deleted it. Typed:

* * *

I never sleep, mortal.

Deleted that, too, and tried:

Depends. Are you summoning me or threatening me?

Paused. That one had potential. Fuck. Maybe it was too aggressive. After six failed drafts and half a glass of scotch, I finally settled on:

I am now. What's on your mind?

It was neutral. Boring. Tragically human. But it was fine. I hit send. The three little dots appeared almost instantly, which—if I was being honest—made my pulse flicker.

She replied almost instantly:

Just walked out of a bad date. Thought you looked fun.

Fun? I was Lucifer Morningstar. I invented fun. I cracked my knuckles and typed:

I guarantee I'm more entertaining than whatever idiot failed you tonight.

Send. The dots danced again.

Lol good answer. You busy?

This, I understood. The subtext was loud enough to echo. I glanced toward the bedroom, still rumpled from last night's chaos. No. I wasn't busy. I was bored. Restless. Half-feral with a need for something, which was probably why I'd even replied. I typed back:

Depends. Are you planning to ruin my night or save it?

Dot-dot-dot.

You free in 30?

I hesitated. Just long enough to feel it. This was stupid. Which was precisely why I said:

I'll send you the address.

She replied with a winking emoji. I stared at it like it had teeth. Then I set the phone down, poured another drink, and told myself this wasn't a mistake. It was just... research. Fieldwork. Immersive damnation.

Thirty-five minutes later, the intercom buzzed. I pressed the button.

"Name?" I asked because apparently that was what people did now, instead of getting to know each other.

"Hailey," she chirped.

Of course it was. I buzzed her up.

She walked into the penthouse five minutes later in a tiny dress, big lashes, and perfume that belonged in a bottle shaped like a stiletto. She looked like a human disaster on heels. Perfect.

She stopped dead in the doorway, jaw slack. "Holy shit. Are you, like... famous?"

I smiled. "Only in the circles that matter."

That got a giggle. She stepped inside.

"Drink?"

She nodded, walking closer. "Vodka soda, if you've got it. And... with a straw, please."

I did. Topher stocked everything. I mixed it, handed it over, and watched as she took a long sip and eyed me like I was the question she wanted to ask but wasn't sure she'd like the answer to.

"You're different," she said after a beat. "Most guys don't talk like you."

"That's because most men aren't cursed to walk the earth in search of redemption."

She blinked.

I took a sip of my drink. "Kidding."

"Oh," she laughed, relaxing. "For a second, I thought you were one of those dark and mysterious guys. You know, like... self-actualization and sad boy poetry."

I smirked. "Would that scare you off?"

"Not if you're hot enough." She gave me a slow, seductive smile, "And you are definitely... hot enough." Her fingers trailed down my chest, catching in the third button.

Ah, modern courtship.

She flopped onto the couch, crossing her legs like a magazine spread. "So, what do you do?"

I opened my mouth. Paused. And realized—for the first time in my immortal life, I had no fucking idea how to answer that question. Not anymore. Not when I didn't know who I was.

So I said the first thing that came to mind. "I run a hotel." Which, technically, was true.

She made a little impressed sound and sipped her drink again.

This night was already a bad idea. The kind that didn't come with fire and brimstone—just an empty bed and the warmth of someone else's body beside you. But I sat down and leaned back, let her talk, let her slide closer. Because it was either this or think about the girl Lilith said would ruin me.

I turned toward her. "Take off your dress," I said, running a finger along the curve of her throat.

She didn't respond. Didn't even seem to hear me.

Instead, she stood up, sauntering a few steps into the center of the room like she'd already forgotten I was there. Her heels clicked across the marble. She moved slowly, deliberately, touching everything like she owned it. The velvet chaise. The edge of the bar. The long expanse of glass revealed the Strip glowing below.

I set my glass down and followed her, but she looked at her reflection—not at me—as she adjusted her top, fluffed her hair, and tilted her chin to the left, then the right. Like she was preparing for an audience I couldn't see.

I waited. Once. Then stepped in closer behind her. My hand slid up the back of her neck, my thumb brushing that delicate place where her pulse met bone.

"I said," I murmured, "take off your dress."

Through the reflection in the glass, she blinked at me in slow surprise, like she hadn't expected I'd speak again. Like she'd already tuned me out. My grip tightened.

"Don't make me repeat myself again," I warned, voice low and laced with ash. "Or I'll bend you over the balcony and spank you until the whole Strip hears your apology."

Her breath hitched. Finally, she smiled. "God, you're hot when you're bossy."

I didn't smile back because I wasn't playing. Not yet. I leaned in, tracing her jaw with my lips. She moaned when I bit her neck—no warning, no hesitation—and that moan turned into a laugh, high and pleased, like she still thought this was a game. I pushed her down into the chaise, slow and deliberate, leaning over her. My hands slid up her thighs, fingers biting into soft flesh.

"Tell me," I said low, against her ear, "how badly you want to be ruined."

She shivered. "So badly."

I dragged my mouth down her neck, tasting sweat and perfume.

Her legs parted instinctively. "Fuck," she whispered. "You're intense."

"You have no idea."

I let her feel the weight of me over her as I dragged a finger up her thong, my other hand pulling her skirt up to her waist.

"You don't play fair," she gasped.

"Fair is for humans," I growled. "And I'm not here to play."

She chuckled, and her eyes flashed as she trembled under me, her hands clawing at my shoulders, her hips rocking up to meet mine.

And then—"Wait. Just one sec."

I stilled. She wriggled out from under me and retrieved something from her purse—her phone. She propped it against a bottle on the bar, angling it toward us.

"I just need to get this started," she said, tapping the screen. "My followers are gonna go wild."

I stared. "What?

"I want to film this. Just a little." She winked. "You look like the kind of guy who'd be into it. My socials are gonna go insane. They love it when I hook up with a rich guy."

My... what? "Your what?"

She laughed. "Social media. Don't tell me you're not on it."

"I don't even know what that is."

"Oh my god." She giggled like that was somehow endearing. "You're hilarious. You give such, like... mysterious tech mogul vibes. I'm obsessed."

She adjusted a glowing circular device propped on the side table. I narrowed my eyes at the glowing object.

"What the fuck is that?"

"This?" She tapped the stand. "It's a ring light."

Of course, it was—a glowing circle of hell.

"Put the phone down."

"But—"

"I said. Put. It. Down."

She frowned. "Wow. Okay. No need to get all alpha-male psycho on me, Lars."

I furrowed my brow. "Mmm... Lars?"

"Lyle? I mean, it's not that serious."

"Who the fuck is Lyle?"

She paused. "That's not it?"

"You don't remember my name."

"No... no, I do. It's just..."

"Lucifer."

"Ohhh. Right. Like the devil."

I exhaled. Slowly. "Are you going to turn the phone off or...?"

"But—"

"I said," I repeated, each word colder than the last, "put it the fuck down."

She rolled her eyes, grabbed her purse, dropping both the phone and ring light in it as she stomped toward the door. "Jesus. Fine. I'm gonna go. You need to get over yourself."

She paused at the mirror. Kissed her reflection. Left a bloody smear of red gloss on the glass before walking out. I stared at it like a crime scene. Then picked up the landline.

"Topher."

"Yes, sir?"

"She was trying to film me."

"Oh dear."

"She called me Lars."

"Truly unforgivable."

"She brought a glowing ring into my penthouse."

A pause. "Would you like me to delete your dating profiles, sir?"

"No. I want you to delete the whole fucking internet."

"Right away."

As soon as I hung up with Topher, I stared at the greasy lip print on my mirror like it had personally offended me. Which, to be fair, it had.

"Well," I muttered, dragging a hand through my hair as I walked to the front door, which she had left wide open. "That was a total fucking disaster."

Not that I should've expected anything else. But even for a clout-chasing mortal with absolutely no concept of personal boundaries, she'd managed to impress me with the sheer density of her delusion.

I turned away from the mirror and grabbed the cursed little slab of glass from the table. The phone Topher insisted I needed. Still intact, somehow. I picked it up like it might bite me. Unlocked it and opened the red flame icon again, back to the digital masquerade. I needed to find this mystery woman.

Swipe. Left. Left. Left.

Another woman posing with a bowl of yogurt and fruit. A man in a sun hat who looked like he'd burst into tears if you raised your voice. Left.

Peaches. 31.

She was all sunlight and chaos in her photos. In the first one, she stood on a beach at sunset, blonde curls half-tamed on top of her head, the rest spilling around her shoulders, skin browned and freckled like the sun had been in love with her for years. She laughed at something out of frame, head tipped back, throat bared, a paper cup in her hand, and a tiny crescent moon tattoo flashing at her wrist. The next shot was a crowded market, she was in a long skirt and a soft shirt knotted at her waist, arms full of leafy greens and wildflowers. Bracelets stacked on her wrist. No heavy makeup, just a glossy mouth and a shimmer at the corners of her eyes. The last picture caught her, cross-legged on a patterned rug, in a jungle of plants and crystals and half-melted candles. Her curls were everywhere, and there was a cluttered board behind her, papered with Polaroids and handwritten words.

She looked like the kind of woman who thought every moment meant something, which, in my experience, was either enchanting or catastrophic.

"Aquarius sun, Virgo moon. I believe in signs, soul contracts, and second chances. Looking for a man who's spiritually evolved, emotionally intelligent, and open to tantric healing. Bonus if you compost."

Humans had invented a whole new vocabulary for the same old hungers while I was gone. I was intrigued despite myself, maybe because of myself. Still, I studied her and then reminded myself that the last thing I needed was another believer calling the universe her co-pilot.

But I swiped right. And... of course, it was a match. A message popped up immediately.

Peaches: Your aura seems... heavy. Want to talk about it?

What the actual hell. I stared at the screen and

considered throwing the phone again. But I didn't.

Me: Define heavy.
Peaches: Maybe wounded. Maybe karmically blocked. Maybe just dehydrated.

Gods.

Peaches: Are you open to sound baths? I host full moon ceremonies.
Me: I'm open to drinks. Tomorrow. 10pm. The Serpent's Tongue.
Peaches: Bars have bad energy.
Me: I own it.
Peaches: Perfect. I'll bring crystals.
Who the fuck were these people? Because... of course, she would.

Peaches: I'm Peaches, by the way. But only since my rebirth.

I didn't ask.

Me: Lucifer.
Peaches: Ooooh, I love that. That name has so much misunderstood energy.

I rubbed the space between my eyes. Maybe that influencer was better.

Peaches: Can't wait to meet. I feel like our chakras already know each other.

Maybe she was the girl I was looking for? Lilith seemed to imply that I'd know instantly. I picked up my phone and glanced at Peaches's photos again and felt... nothing.

No. No, she wasn't the one. Now this just felt like a colossal waste of time. Maybe I should just cancel.

I poured another drink and stared out at the city that used to belong to me, wondering how the Prince of Hell ended up debating which was worse —the girl who wanted to capture her sins on her phone or the girl who wanted to read my aura with magic crystals. Either way, I was still alone. And if Lilith was right...

I didn't let myself finish the thought.

CHAPTER SIX

Evie

There was a certain kind of woman who walked into The Serpent's Tongue like she was afraid of catching something just from breathing the air. I saw them all the time, fake tan still clinging to their cuticles, trapped in perfume clouds that could stun a small animal. Sliding onto the center barstool like it was a throne, and looking around like they expected someone to pop out and take a photo.

This one walked in like that at first, all confidence and camera-ready posture, but the details did not match. She wore a loose white wrap dress, hit mid-thigh, tied at the waist with a braided cord, its ends adorned with little charms. Her bleached blond curls were down around her shoulders, a few tiny braids threaded with beads and bits of metal catching the low light. Brown leather ankle boots, scuffed, not trendy, more like she actually walked places in them. Gold rings on almost every finger, a nose ring, and layered necklaces picking up the glow behind the bar, one of them a rose quartz sitting in the dip of her collarbone like it lived there. Everyone else in the bar wore moody colors and sharp lines, hiding in the shadows, and she looked like she had just stepped out of a farmers' market and taken a wrong turn into my shift.

She looked at me, then the menu, and wrinkled her nose. "I'm supposed to be meeting someone here. He said this was like... the cool bar?"

"Coolest one in the building," I said dryly, wiping down the counter that already gleamed. "What can I get you?"

"Do you have, like, a skinny marg?" she asked. "With agave-free syrup? I'm off agave right now. My gut health coach says it spikes your trauma levels."

I blinked. Slowly. "We don't. But I can offer you a Jezebel."

She tilted her head like a confused puppy. "Is that like... keto?"

"It's got mezcal, hibiscus, and enough spice to purge your last three bad decisions," I said, already reaching for the shaker. "Very detoxifying. Spiritually."

She looked like I'd offered her bleach. "Hmm. I'll just wait."

Great.

And then he walked in. Lucifer Morningstar. The boss. The man whose name wasn't listed on any paperwork but who everyone in the building knew was the true owner of this hotel, The Revel. You didn't see him often, but when you did, you felt it.

He was tall, annoyingly so, with the kind of elegance you didn't learn. It wasn't posture. It wasn't polish. It was something else, like power wrapped in skin. His broad shoulders carried it like a mantle, narrowing to a lean waist that made everyone feel completely unworthy. He moved like gravity reported to him, not the other way around.

His suit was black, cut like sin, and sharp enough to make anyone with a conscience nervous. The jacket skimmed his narrow waist and set off those shoulders like a threat. His shirt matched, unbuttoned just far enough to make a statement—three open buttons and no shame exposing a smooth, tanned chest. A ruby winked from one cuff, and on his right hand sat a ring of matte black metal, carved into a serpent swallowing its own tail.

Subtle. Yeah, real subtle.

And then there was his face. Uncomfortably symmetrical. High cheekbones. A mouth made for ruin. Skin like honeyed marble—golden, but cool. Unreal.

But the part that caught me and made me practically slack-jawed was the contrast. His hair was dark red, maybe auburn, and the way it caught the light, like fire poured over shadow, cascading in waves to his shoulders. It was too perfect. Too deliberate. Like the kind of beauty rich men paid for but never pulled off.

God, and his eyes. They weren't blue. Not really. They were the palest ice, almost white. Ghost-light from behind. Like the sky during a lightning strike. He looked at you, and it felt like the world stopped breathing.

I'd never seen him smile. But he didn't need to. He was beautiful in the way natural disasters are beautiful. And I hated that I noticed.

People looked away when he passed. Like eye contact might cost them something, but I couldn't look away. I stood up straighter, watching his every move.

He scanned the room, and of course, he zeroed in on her and approached with a quiet, practiced elegance. When he reached the bar, he offered her a slight nod.

"You must be... Peaches," he said.

She smiled like she'd won a prize. "Mmhmm! That's me—like the fruit." She flipped her hair over one shoulder. "But not, like, organic."

I coughed into my elbow to hide a laugh. It didn't work. His eyes flicked to me, catching the sound. His mouth twitched, almost like a smile. Almost.

"I'm Lucifer," he said, turning back to her. "Nice to meet you."

She blinked. "Oh, right—Lucien!"

"It's Lucifer."

"That's what I said," she chirped. "Lucien."

He paused, just for a second. Then nodded, giving up on being understood entirely. It was almost impressive, the way he surrendered with style. He sat. I went ahead and poured the Jezebel anyway, set it down in front of her with a glittery pink coaster, and got ready for the show.

She launched into a monologue about her "healing journey" and how she'd once fasted for 96 hours in Sedona and only hallucinated twice. When she mentioned a shaman named Greg who told her she had lunar sensitivity, I had to walk further down the bar pretending to wipe down something to keep from choking on my own snort.

Lucifer, to his credit, nodded politely. He tried, once or twice, to interject—a low comment here, a joke there, maybe even an actual opinion—but she steamrolled him like she was giving a TED talk and he was in the nosebleeds. She didn't ask a single question about him. Didn't pause. Just used him as a mirror she liked looking into.

Every time he tried to speak, she talked louder. One time, she even held up a finger and said, "Wait, just let me finish this thought, it's really good," and then went on a five-minute tangent about gut microbiomes and soulmates.

For most of it, I pretended to clean glasses a few feet away. Really, I just wanted to see how long he'd survive. He didn't drink. She didn't stop talking. The Jezebel sat untouched, slowly sweating on the counter.

Eventually, he checked his gold Rolex, because of course he wore one, and sighed like a man walking toward a guillotine.

"It's time for our reservation," he said, standing up. He adjusted his suit with one smooth motion, and his smile was the fakest I'd ever seen.

"Where're we going again?" she asked, already hooking her arm through his.

"Edenfall," he said. "I've heard the dessert course is... revelatory."

I froze mid-wipe. Did she even know who the fuck her date was?

Because practically everyone knew Edenfall had always been his pride and joy. Rumor had it he'd hand-selected the cutlery when he opened it decades ago, personally sourced the ingredients, and even rewrote the dessert menu four times before opening night. It had stayed the same all these years and was still his crown jewel—the one part of The Revel he never let anyone else touch.

She giggled and leaned into him. He said something quietly near her ear. She laughed harder. Slapped his chest lightly like he was the funniest man alive. But he wasn't looking at her. He was looking at me. Cool. Direct. Amused. Like I was the only part of the evening that had actually surprised him.

I stared back, just long enough for the moment to

stretch. Then I turned away and picked up a bottle, pretending I hadn't felt that stare like a match to my skin.

They walked off together into the hush of Edenfall's private elevator, swallowed by shadows and the low thump of bass from Elliptica downstairs. I leaned over the bar, watching them go, already reaching for a rag I didn't need to use.

That's when I saw it—folded once. Tucked just beneath the edge of the coaster under the Jezebel she'd ignored all night. Five. Hundred. Dollars. Cash. Neat. Like it hadn't even been handled. No note. No explanation. Just sitting there like an inside joke only one of us understood.

I blinked. I hadn't seen it happen. I don't think anyone saw it happen. And Peaches sure as hell didn't leave it. She hadn't touched the drink or the bill. Which meant... it came from *him.*

I stood there for a moment, the bar suddenly too quiet, my hands a little too still. There were rules about this. Tips that big usually came with strings. Or apologies. Or guilt. But this? This felt like a message. I didn't pocket it. Instead, I slid the crisp bills into the register.

An hour later, the bar had quieted down. The post-dinner rush had bled into the slow lull before the late-night crowd staggered in, smelling like regret and spilled cologne. The jazz trio had packed up. The lights had dimmed. I'd already put up the garnishes, restocked the highballs, and put on the playlist I only played when I wanted to be left alone —moody, low, the kind of music that sounded like smoke curling under a door.

I was wiping down the bar for the third time when I spotted it. The tip jar always collected trash. Business cards. Hotel room keys that people forgot were theirs. One time, I found a single stick of gum still in the wrapper with a note that said, "I bet you have great breath." To this day, it still gives me the ick.

So I didn't think much when I saw the folded paper at the bottom. At first, I figured it was a receipt. I'd seen people do that a few times. But I grabbed it with two fingers, already planning to toss it—until I noticed the paper, the edges. It was too thick and not torn or crumpled, folded with purpose. Neatly. Like someone gave a damn.

I flipped it open. Just to see. No name. Just a single line, written in black ink—smooth, even, too elegant to be anything casual.

The Jezebel deserves better company.

I stared at it. No signature. No clue. But I didn't need one. I looked up, scanning the room. Empty, save for the usual cocktail ghosts and the security guy near the elevators.

My heart kicked once. Just once. Then I smiled. Slowly. Wryly. Shaking my head. That smug bastard.

I folded the note and slid it into my back pocket. Closing out felt slower than usual, probably because my brain wouldn't shut up.

Lucifer, Lucien, whatever the hell his name was— had left a $500 tip and a trail of questions behind him. Not that I cared. Rich guys did weird shit all the time. Some of them tipped big just to watch you squirm, like they could buy your attention in installments.

Still, I didn't take it. It stayed in the drawer, even as my hands itched to take it. It definitely would have helped. I tended to live paycheck to paycheck.

He was probably halfway through dessert by now, maybe even spoonfeeding Peaches some overpriced brûlée and pretending he gave a shit about her astrological moon rising in Scorpio or whatever, just to get in her pants. He probably didn't even remember leaving that tip. Or he thought I looked like I needed it.

I huffed out a breath, popped the register, and started counting cash. That's when I saw it. A black envelope. Thick. Tucked just beneath the till like someone had slid it in on purpose. Intentional. Definitely not something someone just dropped.

I frowned and picked it up. No name. No logo. Just a red wax seal stamped with something ornate —horns or fire or maybe both, depending on how long you looked at it. It felt heavier than it should have been.

I cracked the seal and unfolded the thick sheet inside. Blank. At first. Then, like some Victorian parlor trick, faint letters bled to life beneath the heat of the overhead bar lamp:

You looked like you needed a reason to stay.

The paper stayed warm in my hands, like it had a heartbeat. I stared at the message, breath hitching for a half-second before I swallowed it down. I didn't need a signature. Not really. I had a very short list of suspects. And only one of them wore a suit like sin and smiled like he knew the punchline to a joke you hadn't told yet.

But before I could talk myself out of it, something else slipped from the envelope. A keycard. Black. Gold, glittering border with an R in the center. It was smooth and cold in my hand. So that's what this was...

I flipped it over—room 666. I let out a breathy laugh. No way. We didn't have a Room 666. I stared at the card like it might dissolve. It didn't. The paper was still warm in my other hand. The message still legible.

I rolled my eyes and muttered, "Creepy scavenger hunt from a devil. Love that for me."

Then I shoved both the card and the note back into the envelope and put it in my back pocket, not wanting anyone else to find them. That's all it was. It wasn't curiosity. It sure wasn't intrigue. And it most definitely wasn't because I wanted to know what kind of man left breadcrumbs like this without bothering to ask your name.

And I didn't plan on checking. Definitely not.

I even told myself—out loud, like an absolute lunatic—that I was just going upstairs to "check the floor layout for safety signage." Which was impressive, considering I wasn't in management and hadn't given a shit about fire codes since I lit my purity pledge card on fire in the back of the church parking lot.

Still, I rode the elevator up and walked out on the 6th floor. The keycard sat in my back pocket like a dare. I rounded a corner, and there it was—right where I knew it would be. Room 665. Then a gap. Then 667.

No 666. No plaque. No door. Just a wall. I stared at it, pulse ticking in my throat.

"Of course," I muttered, the words bitter on my tongue. "Of fucking course."

I turned to leave, already hating myself for being there, when I heard it, the quiet click of a door opening behind me.

Room 667.

The couple that came out looked like the human

version of a Valentine's Day display. All giggles and neck-nuzzles, fingers linked like they couldn't bear to be separate for one goddamn second. She had her heels in one hand, his jacket draped around her shoulders. He kissed her temple. She laughed like it was the funniest thing she'd ever heard.

And we all stood there. Waiting for the elevator. Lovely. Just lovely.

I crossed my arms, staring straight ahead, pretending I didn't exist. I could feel their joy like static on my skin. Too loud. Too bright. Too much. Like something like that could ever last.

The keycard pressed against my hip like a bruise I'd earned for being exactly this stupid. Because what had I expected? A secret passageway? A hidden lock? A flaming sword and a voice whispering "You've been chosen"?

God, I hated how easy it was to fall back into that line of thinking. Like the years I'd spent clawing my way out of that cult of shame and Sunday sermons could crumble just because some rich asshole with a creepy, weird name left me something like a magic trick and a whisper.

But I wasn't that girl anymore. I didn't believe in signs. But standing there, in silence, shoulder to shoulder with a couple dripping lust and laughter, I couldn't help the quiet echo in my chest.

You looked like you needed a reason to stay.

I swallowed hard and stepped onto the elevator behind them when the doors opened. He pressed L. I didn't press anything. I was already spiraling down.

CHAPTER SEVEN

Lucifer

The next night I came back. I shouldn't have. I knew that, but I did. The bar was quieter when I walked in. A bit more private. Like, even the shadows knew they should mind their business.

And there she was behind the bar. Evie Grace. I told myself it was nothing. A curiosity. A passing impulse. But something in me pulled toward her like gravity. A weight behind the ribs. A flicker in my chest that hadn't stirred in centuries.

I didn't know her. And yet... I knew how she'd feel in my arms, like my body remembered holding hers and my mind had been left out of the secret. My hands itched with the absence of this... memory I wasn't supposed to have. I shouldn't have. I'd never had.

It was nothing. And it was everything. But I bristled against it. Refused to name it. And still, I came back for more.

Lilith implied I would know the woman when I found her. I had assumed that meant a mark, a sigil, some neat little omen stamped on her skin. Not this. Not my attention snagging on some bartender, especially in my own hotel. Not my mind circling her like it had nowhere else to land. It felt wrong, this tug, like someone had hooked a finger behind my sternum and given a little pull every time she moved.

Maybe this was all it was—mission focus. I had been ordered to find her, get her with child, light the match that would turn this world into kindling. Of course, I was looking harder now. Of course, I was noticing more. That was reasonable. Rational. I repeated that to myself like a litany while I watched the way she smiled at customers who didn't deserve it.

Except rational didn't explain why I was sure I could pick her laugh out of the noise and know it was hers when I was almost certain I had never heard her speak before. It didn't explain the way the line of her throat bothered me, why I kept imagining what her face would look like if she realized what I really was. It didn't explain the way the word "Mine" flashed through me like heat when another man leaned too close to her side of the bar. That wasn't part of any prophecy. That was greed.

Still, the question lodged there, heavy and sharp. Was it supposed to feel like this if she was the one? Had Lilith reminded me of that little clause because she'd known I would be dragged toward her, not by duty, but by something far messier? Was that the joke? That the first spark of the apocalypse would not be trumpets and fire, but this, me finding myself at the polished edge of the bar with no clear memory of crossing the room.

My hand curled around the back of the stool, and I sat. She looked up at me, not startled, not confused. No flicker of surprise at all. Just those steady eyes, like she had known I was coming and had simply been waiting for me to take my seat.

She didn't even greet me, didn't smile. She set the glass down she'd been drying and said, "Waiting on another date? Or did your last one finally finish her monologue about ayahuasca and moon phases?"

I stared at her before barely lifting a shoulder. She turned away, pulled a bottle from the back shelf, and poured something dark into a glass. No garnish. No flourish. Just clean lines and sharper edges.

She slid it toward me and leaned on the counter with both hands like she was bracing for something. I picked it up and sipped. Letting it burn. She watched. Not curious—calculating.

Evie knew who I was. By reputation, at least. That much was clear in the way she carried herself. In the way, she didn't defer. Didn't flirt. Didn't seem to even care. I was simply a man who owned a kingdom and walked through it like a god, and she barely gave me the time of day.

It should've pissed me off. Instead, it made me want... more.

"You know my name," I said quietly.

"You share a name with the Lucifer Morningstar," she replied. "Bringer of Light. King of the Damned. Patron Saint of Overcompensating."

A corner of my mouth tugged. "I'm surprised you didn't call me Lucien."

"Please," she snorted. "Lucien's a vampire in a frilly pirate shirt who recites poetry before he asks permission to bite you."

"No," I said, leaning closer. "I don't ask permission."

She raised a brow. "You a biter?"

I chuckled and smirked, and for a second, I almost asked her the only question that mattered: if she was the one. The woman Lilith had sent me to find, the match I was supposed to strike against the world. The words hovered on my tongue, hot and bitter, but I didn't let them out because I knew she'd have no idea what I was talking about.

And... I had a task to complete. Lilith made sure of that.

I wasn't here because I wanted to be. I wasn't free. I wasn't powerful. Not really. Not anymore. Hell had a new queen, and I'd been sent to Earth with one purpose: to make her fall. Plant the seed that would end the world. No magic. No compulsion. No shortcuts. I had to seduce her the way mortals did. Awkwardly. Pathetically. With effort.

And the worst part? I didn't even know for sure that Evie Grace was the one. But something in me suspected even if I wasn't entirely sure.

The way she looked at me was like she wasn't under my spell. Or afraid. Or even impressed. The way she moved was like she'd already survived something worse. The way I couldn't stop staring at her mouth when she spoke, or the scar on her wrist, which she tried to hide when she poured a drink.

"You've got a stare," she said suddenly. "Like you're trying to see through people."

"Maybe I am."

She leaned in slightly. "Find anything?"

Not yet. But I would.

She leaned in closer, elbows on the bar, like she could smell the tension radiating off me.

"You come in here," she said. "But you don't drink much. You don't talk much. And you sure as hell don't flirt."

"Maybe I don't need to."

She raised a brow. "Is that confidence or male loneliness talking?"

I smiled. But not all the way. "Why do you think I'm here?"

"I don't know," she said, tapping her fingers against the wood and shaking her head. "No fucking clue."

I didn't answer. Because if I did, if I told her the truth, she'd run screaming, and I wouldn't blame her.

Evie tilted her head. Her voice dropped, low and unsteady. "Look, I've met a lot of guys with control issues. The kind who walk in like they own the place, and look at you like they already bought you. But you?"

I didn't reply. I just waited.

"You look at me like I'm supposed to be something," she said. "And I don't know what the hell that means, but... I don't like it."

It landed like a slap. How the fuck...?

I stood slowly, sliding the unfinished drink away. She didn't move.

"Good night, Evie Grace," I said.

Her breath caught. She hadn't told me her name.

I felt her eyes on me as I walked out of the bar, a slow drag of heat between my shoulder blades that made every step feel wrong. Like her stare could set liquor on fire if it lingered too long. I should've kept walking and never looked back. But tonight, I did.

I turned around and walked back up to the bar, slowly. Let the tension stretch like smoke between us. She had gone back to polishing a glass, as if it had wronged her, fingers tight around the stem. Those lips, bitten raw from whatever she wasn't saying, twitched when I turned. No smile. No acknowledgment. Just... stillness.

"That black envelope," I said, letting my voice drop into something that made the bar's music feel cheap. "When the time comes, you might need it."

Her brow barely twitched, but I saw it—the

flicker of something sharp behind her eyes. She didn't ask. Didn't speak. That alone told me everything.

I dipped my head in something that wasn't quite a bow. "Don't lose it, sweetheart."

Then I walked out and let her wonder.

Yesterday, after I left with Peaches, she found that envelope hidden in the register and went looking. I know she did. Because tonight, the moment I stepped back into The Serpent's Tongue, the air had shifted between us.

She'd gone to the elevators and checked the glowing numbers. Searched the 6th floor. I was pretty sure she had even peeked behind the front desk when the night clerk wasn't looking.

Room 666 was never on the 6th floor. It's found on a special floor. That's the thing about keys that unlock doors you aren't ready to see yet. Sometimes they don't just open rooms. Sometimes they open destiny. Either way, she was already turning the handle.

When my private elevator slid open, my front door opened on its own. The moment I stepped inside, I smelled her. Fuck.

My entire penthouse—pristine, quiet, intentionally sparse—was suddenly dripping in gardenia, myrrh, and something vaguely sulfuric. *Lilith.*

We were lovers once. Husband and wife, in the language of darkness.

After she left Eden, after she refused to kneel to Adam, that mud-born mistake, she came to me. Not out of desperation—Lilith doesn't beg. She came because she saw what I had become, and knew I was the only other creature in existence who'd torn himself free from The First Light.

She offered no apology for who she was. I didn't need one. I offered her a throne beside mine. She took it. For a time, we ruled together. Not in love. Not really. But in understanding. In power. In pain. We were the only ones who could look at each other and see every unspoken, jagged truth.

But the thing about Lilith is, she never wanted a partner. She sought leverage. She played the long game. And I had been too tired to see it. How many millennia can you rule Hell and not grow apathetic? I let her in. Gave her an inch. And she took the whole fucking mile.

Now, she was lounging across my leather couch. No, not lounging—reigning. One leg slung over the other, barely dressed in sheer red silk that clung like smoke. A golden throne had been conjured over my coffee table, as if it were sitting on an elevated dais.

One naked man with a black leather harness and mask fanned her lazily with a peacock-feather fan. The other fed her dark purple grapes.

I stopped at my bar, poured a finger's width of brown liquor, then turned to face her and let it burn its way down.

"You took your sweet time," she said, popping a grape in her mouth without looking at me.

I didn't speak. I didn't have to. Lilith smiled. That smile—the one that had felled angels and raised hell —the one I used to know far too well.

"Don't look so sour, love," she purred. "I'm just here to move things along. You've been dragging your feet. And time," she said, rising to her full, breathtaking height, "is running out."

I folded my arms. "If she's the one, she'll come to me."

"She's human," Lilith said, circling me like smoke. "She won't unless you make her. And newsflash,

Lucy—'mystery' isn't a mating strategy. You haven't even touched her."

Everything inside me went still.

She tilted her head, all smug grace and sin. "Evie Grace. That name suits her so much better."

The glass in my hand cracked, spider-webbing beneath my fingers. "You knew."

Her smile was lazy. Pleased. "Of course I did."

I stepped forward, heat rising. "If you knew who she was, why the fuck didn't you just tell me?"

Power surged through the air, sharp and hot. Lights flickered. A painting on the wall slid half an inch to the left.

I froze. That wasn't supposed to happen. Not anymore. I was mortal now—stripped of dominion, bound to skin and bone and rules I didn't make. And yet something in me still burned. Still reached. As if part of me remembered what it was to command the underworld and something... else.

Lilith didn't flinch. But I saw it—the tiniest hitch in her breath. The barest narrowing of her eyes. A flicker of unease she couldn't quite smother in time. She masked it well. Smiled like it was all going according to plan. But I'd seen her afraid before. And this was close.

"It would've saved me a hell of a lot of time," I growled, my voice ragged with fury. "Do you have any idea how much ground I've been covering? How close I've come to snapping?"

Her pout was theatrical. "Oh, but darling... where's the fun in that?"

I flung the shattered glass across the room. It hit the wall with a violent crash, shards raining like glitter.

This time, she didn't blink.

"You've been playing me."

"Not playing," she said sweetly. "*Guiding.*"

She drifted closer, hips swaying like temptation was still a game she could win.

"Honestly, I miss when you used to listen," she purred, brushing a finger lightly down my arm. "You used to hang on every word I said. Remember?"

I didn't move.

"Back when you still burned for me," she added, voice dipped in smoke. "Back when you used to call me your wife."

My jaw tightened.

"What was it you said that night?" she went on, eyes glittering with amusement. "'Let's build a kingdom they'll never forget.'"

Her laugh was quiet and cruel. "You really thought we were building it together."

I turned away before I snapped.

"You were already bored back then," she said, a little sharper now. "I just finished what you started."

My fists curled, aching to burn this whole hotel to the ground.

Her lips curled into a lazy smile, the kind that said she'd already won. "We want the same thing, baby. You just haven't realized it yet."

I rolled my eyes as I ran my hand through my hair. "Do we?"

Then her gaze sharpened, just for a second, like a knife slipping through silk. "You think meeting her was chance?" she murmured. "That she just happened to work in your hotel?"

I went very still.

Lilith stepped closer, her voice barely audible now. "You're not the only one being watched, Lucy."

"Get out," I said quietly.

Lilith just laughed, stepping over one of her boys like a cat.

"Tick-tock, my love," she said. "The End of Days waits for no one. If you don't hurry up—if you don't get that girl to fall into your bed and fall apart, I'll find another way. Without you."

I scoffed as she vanished in a rush of petals and fire. And I was left alone, standing there for a long time, staring at the place where she'd been.

She thought I was weakening. She thought this girl was getting to me. But she was wrong. I wasn't cracking. I couldn't. The First Light hadn't made me to love. He made me to serve. And then to fall. And burn.

Whatever I once was—whatever I could have been—He stripped that from me when He cast me out. Whatever spark lived in men, that desperate little thing they called a soul, He never gave it to me. I didn't—couldn't—feel anything.

So no, I wasn't breaking. I wasn't falling for her. I wasn't capable of that. And if Lilith thought otherwise, she was more deluded than I remembered.

Still, I closed my eyes. And saw Evie's face anyway. Not laughing and not smiling. She just existed in my mind, steady and uninvited, and somehow still got under my skin. It was right before I finally left the bar that stuck. When I said her name, she blinked, just once, like the sound of it landed somewhere deeper than it should have. And something in me... shook. Not violently. Not enough to crack. Just enough to make me wonder if I'd said it before. Somewhere else. Some other time. Some other... life.

I left before I could think too hard about it. But now her name... it tasted like something forbidden.

Sweet. Familiar. Dangerous. And I haven't stopped savoring it since.

CHAPTER EIGHT

Evie

The pendant light above the back bar buzzed, sharp and high, like something electrical straining to hold itself together. I capped the vodka bottle and glanced up. The bulb flared too bright, then dimmed, then flared again.

"Seriously?" I muttered. Everything in this place was top shelf. Marble counters. Velvet barstools. Lighting imported from Italy or somewhere equally bougie. Nothing in this place should flicker. But it wasn't just here.

My phone had glitched twice today—once mid-text, and once while I was scrolling. The screen froze, then kicked into World in My Eyes by Depeche Mode. I hadn't heard that song in years. Now it felt like a whispered dare, like Lucifer queued it up himself just to remind me what it would feel like to give in, and I was pretty sure he was daring me to.

Was the universe—or something darker—winking at me?

That song wasn't even on any of my playlists, but suddenly the lyrics wrapped around me like smoke, whispering promises I shouldn't want. *Let me show you the world in my eyes...* The kind of world someone like *him* would show me. One look from Lucifer and I felt like he could strip me down to my bones, unearth every sin I'd ever tried to bury, and make me thank him for it.

Yesterday, static clung to everything. My sheets. My sweater. My skin. Yesterday morning, I reached for the coffee maker, and it popped like a firecracker. Sparks flew. The glass carafe exploded before I could yank my hand away.

I swore and backed into the counter. My hand throbbed. I ran it under cool water, bracing for blisters. But there was... nothing. Not a single mark. No red skin. No burn. Just the ghost of pain and the smell of something scorched.

And then my brand-new coffee pot started acting weird. It rebooted itself mid-brew cycle this morning. On the way to work tonight, the elevator from the parking garage stalled between floors. And when I arrived at work and touched the bar sink, it shocked me so hard that my fingertips tingled for an hour.

I told myself it was just one of those days. But it had been happening for a while now, following me from work to home and back. The sensor light in the hallway of my building wouldn't turn on when I walked past. It just buzzed overhead like it was deciding whether I deserved light or not.

Last night, I didn't sleep. Not really. When I finally drifted off, I dreamed of a city on fire. The streets were paved with obsidian, smooth and cracked with glowing veins of gold that pulsed. The buildings rose like cathedrals and burned like paper. The sky bled light. Not warm, but something colder. It felt celestial and empty.

In the center of it all stood a man with wings

stretched wide. But they weren't bright white, feathered like an angel. They were charred on the edges. Wings of light turned to ash.

He turned, and I almost saw his face—but I woke up gasping, tangled in sweat-damp sheets. I swear I could still smell the smoke. Maybe it just clung to my hair from the bar.

Tonight at the bar, everything felt... off. Weird. The lights were too dim—too many shadows lurking in the corners. The air was too dry. The glasses hummed when I touched them.

And then he walked in. *Lucifer.*

He didn't say anything at first. Just slid onto the stool at the end of the bar like he owned the world and was bored with it.

"Back so soon?" I said, reaching for the bourbon. "Didn't peg you for the clingy type."

He didn't answer. Just watched me. Carefully.

I poured his drink without asking, set it in front of him, and leaned on the bar.

"If you're here to brood and smolder, you're gonna have to wait your turn. Table two has a breakup happening in real time, and the guy already cried into his martini."

Lucifer's eyes flicked up. The pendant light above us buzzed.

"You feel that?" he asked, low.

I frowned. "Feel what?"

Another flicker. A glass behind me shifted on the shelf. But I didn't answer. Because obviously, I hadn't felt anything. But he had.

He disappeared before last call. Didn't say goodbye. But there was another five-hundred-dollar tip under the coaster of the drink that was still nearly full.

Four hours later, the bar was finally quiet,

stripped of its drunken laughter. I'd sent the last stragglers home. Even Destiny had gone. She'd given me a knowing smirk before vanishing out the back door. I was alone—at least, I thought I was.

When I stripped off my apron and caught a glimpse of my wrist in the bathroom mirror, I froze. There was a mark. Not a bruise or a cut. The burn on my wrist was now thin, and precise lines were etched in shadowed ink across my palm. An inverted triangle anchored the base—simple, solid—and from its top corners rose two symmetrical loops, like horns or curled flames, arching upward with eerie grace. Below the triangle, the lines narrowed and crossed into an X, forming something that almost resembled a chalice.

It seemed almost... ancient, like a brand or a sigil. It wasn't there before. But now it throbbed faintly beneath my skin. Maybe I just missed it after the coffee pot incident at home.

But it didn't matter now. I was tired and ready to go home. I'd just ice it when I got there.

I tugged open my locker, reaching for my hoodie, when the air shifted. A wave of heat rolled over me, like someone had just stepped too close. My breath stuttered as I turned around.

Lucifer was *here*. No jacket. Just that expensive black dress shirt, sleeves pushed up, buttons undone halfway down his chest like he wanted you to look—and knew you would.

And holy fucking shit, that chest, and his abs disappeared into dark slacks that hung sinfully low on his hips. Sharp lines and wicked shadows, carved like a threat and glistening just faintly like he'd walked through fire and liked it. I hated to admit it, but I had imagined him. I just never dreamed the reality would be even hotter.

The heat rolling off him made me feel like every nerve in my body had been wired to respond only to him. He was too close. Smelled too good, like smoke, spice, and something wild and ancient. It hit me hard as he lowered his face to my neck.

His hand braced beside my head. His eyes dropped to my mouth, and for half a second, I thought his eyes shifted. Just a flicker—like a candle flame caught in a draft. Pale blue, then... not. Something brighter. Sharper. Almost gold.

I blinked, and they were back to that too-pale blue, cold and unreadable. But something about them still burned like he saw everything. Like he wanted everything. And like he already knew I'd give it.

Before I could think, he stepped forward, forcing me back against the cool metal of the lockers. He didn't touch me, not really, but I felt the heat of him everywhere.

I swallowed hard, pulse stuttering, every nerve screaming danger—and something darker. He didn't say a word. Just leaned in close enough to steal the air between us. And I let him. He inhaled slowly, like he could drink me in, and growled low in his throat.

"Do you have any idea what you do to me?" he said, low and lethal. "I could ruin you, right here. Anyone could see us. And you'd let me. You'd thank me for it."

He didn't know anything about me, especially that. We'd spoken twice. But my brain stuttered. My mouth went dry. I couldn't decide if I wanted to throw something at him or climb him like a tree.

My eyes dragged over him like a match looking for something to burn. He didn't smirk. He just watched me watch him. And God help me, I burned.

My nipples tightened like they *knew* what came next. Like my entire body was on alert, waiting.

His chest hovered inches from mine. His hand was still braced beside my head. His other hand slid just shy of my hip, not touching, but close enough that the space between us thrummed like a live wire. His shirt hung open, catching the low light in flashes across skin I shouldn't have been looking at.

But I *was* looking. God, was I looking. And when he leaned in even closer, slow and deliberate, I shuddered. His lips hovered so close to mine that I could feel the whisper of his breath, warm, wicked.

All I had to do was turn my face. Just a little. Just lean in and forget everything. Forget Zeke. Forget how it felt to be unwanted, unseen. If this wasn't the time to lose myself, what was?

I was right there, tilting toward him like my body had made a deal with the devil, and it was time to pay up. And that's when it happened. The light above us flared—*hard*. A sharp electric snap. White-hot and blinding. Then nothing. A pop. A sizzle. Darkness.

Total, complete dark.

Before I could say a word, he leaned in closer—his warm breath brushing the shell of my ear. His voice dropped, low and molten.

"It's only a matter of time, and you'll beg me."

A shiver sliced down my spine. My fingers curled into fists at my sides.

I swallowed hard, forced my breath steady, and turned just enough to meet his eyes. I couldn't see them clearly in the dark, but I *felt* them—hot and watching, like a hand pressed to the curve of my throat. And then, just for a second, I *swear* I caught another flicker—something golden and unnatural, like his eyes had sparked with fire.

I could feel him still smiling. Like he already knew this game was his.

I raised an eyebrow. "Dream on."

Then I shoved past him, heart pounding in my throat as I walked away.

But even as I walked towards the elevators, I could still feel him. Still burning. Still waiting.

The elevator doors slid open with a soft chime, smooth as silk. The walls gleamed, brushed steel and gold accents reflecting a version of me that looked far too calm for what had just happened.

I stepped out into the parking garage, my boots silent against the polished concrete. Everything looked pristine, well-lit, with clean lines, not a single shadow out of place. And yet, I still glanced toward every corner, just in case. Just to be sure.

Because even in all this gloss and glass, I felt it. Like I was being watched. Not by a security camera. By something else. Something lurking, waiting. Was it *him* again?

I unlocked the door, hopped in quickly, and locked it. My truck felt safe. I took a shuddering breath as my fingers trembled on the steering wheel.

And what the fuck just happened? That was not normal. That was not flirting. That was Lucifer Fucking Morningstar growling in my ear like sin made flesh. And I? I almost kissed him. I nearly let go. I almost said yes to something I didn't even know I wanted, desired, or craved.

Fuck.

The engine hummed to life. I drove out of the garage and pulled onto the street, the city lights cool and indifferent. But the back of my neck still prickled. I checked my rearview mirror twice.

"You're fine," I muttered, adjusting the A/C with shaking hands. "Totally fine. Just... a sudden intense thirst for a man who growls in the dark. Happens to the best of us."

The mark on my wrist throbbed, faint but there. I glanced at it.

I should've been exhausted. Annoyed. But all I could feel was the phantom heat of his breath on my neck and the sound of his voice, low and dangerous in the dark.

It's only a matter of time, and you'll beg for it.

My thighs clenched.

"Nope," I snapped. "We're not doing that."

But the ache coursing through my body didn't care. And neither, apparently, did the part of me that was already wondering if he'd show up again tomorrow night and do that all over again.

When I got home, I dropped my bag by the entryway. I walked back to the bedroom and sat down on the bed, unlacing my boots. It was nearly 4 AM, and the whole world felt quiet.

I didn't bother turning on the overhead light, just the warm glow of the lamp by the bed. I made a beeline for the bathroom, tugging my hair out of its clip and tossing it somewhere. My wrist still ached. My lips tingled like I'd kissed him.

The more I thought about it, the more I kept asking myself—*what the absolute fuck*? If that wasn't a total HR violation, I don't know what was.

I leaned over the sink, twisting the faucet on, running my hands under the cool water. Real. Grounding. I reached for the makeup remover and started wiping away the night, my foundation, eyeliner, and every other last trace of sin and suggestion.

And then I looked at my face and... stopped. Stared. I could have sworn...

For half a second, maybe less, my reflection

stared back with eyes that weren't mine. They were... gold. Bright and flickering. Maybe a trick of the light? Like fire caught behind glass.

I blinked again. Hard. Leaned in. My gray eyes looked completely... normal.

I was probably just tired. Definitely a little shaken from all the weird electrical issues. Maybe I was still high on adrenaline. Or whiskey. *Or him.*

Because sure, getting shoved into a locker like we were two seconds from role-playing an enemies-to-lovers fanfic and sniffed like I was some kind of perfume sample was apparently my Roman Empire now. That was healthy. Totally fine.

God, he was arrogant. Unhinged. Probably one of those men who called himself "an experience" in bed. He probably had two or three partners at a time. He was so far out of my comfort zone that it was ridiculous even to consider it.

I snorted softly and muttered, "God help me, I'd let that walking red flag do it again."

I rinsed the last of my makeup off and patted my face dry, avoiding the mirror this time. Whatever happened tonight, it had to have been him. His whole... thing. That energy. That heat. That impossible pull. Like soul-sucking gravity.

I didn't believe in fate or soulmates or anything that bad choices and worse timing couldn't explain, but I had just let a man with a voice like velvet and eyes the color of a winter sky press me against a locker and promise me ruin.

And the worst part? I wanted it. *I wanted him.* I wanted whatever storm lived behind those pale blue eyes to swallow me whole.

Even now, I could still feel the heat of him on my skin, like a brand or a warning, like a dare. I didn't even know what I'd almost said yes to. I just knew it would've changed everything.

CHAPTER NINE

Lucifer

I was meeting a man who thought making a deal with the devil would get him laid. He wasn't the first. But he might've been the most pathetic.

Wiry. Twitchy. Sweat already beading along his receding hairline, despite the industrial-strength AC in the private hotel suite. His hand was disgustingly clammy when he reached out to shake mine.

"Mr. Morningstar," he said, voice a few octaves too high to sound confident. "It's an honor."

I smirked and stepped further into the room. "I'm sure it is. But... call me Lucifer," I replied, smiling slowly, the way wolves bare their teeth before they bite.

He nodded quickly, pushing his glasses up the bridge of his nose. "I'm, uh... Lyle Simms."

I gave him an upward nod as I followed him inside. He flinched and then tried to cover it with a twitchy half-smile as he motioned toward the seat across from him like it might bite.

I took the high-back chair, leaned back, and crossed one ankle over my knee—casual, relaxed, deliberately unimpressed. I didn't need to raise my voice or bare my teeth. Men like him always squirmed when you gave them too much silence.

Topher stood by the wall, tablet in hand, already recording—because appearances were everything, and this idiot thought he was about to make a deal with the Devil.

He wasn't entirely wrong. And sure enough, Lyle shifted in his seat, glancing at Topher, then back at me like he was afraid to blink wrong.

He looked like a man who hadn't slept in days and had replaced rest with obsession, eyes too bright, hands never still. He wore thick glasses and was skinny in the way that suggested he hadn't touched a gym—or sunlight—in years. His black graphic tee read: CODE HARD, SIN HARDER. I hated it.

He had two goons flanking him, both standing a little too straight, like they'd watched one too many movies about how muscle was supposed to look.

"I've read all the stories," he babbled. "The fallen angel, the Morningstar, the—what did they use to call you? The Lightbringer?"

I smirked. "That one's my favorite," I murmured.

He nodded eagerly, hands jittering. "Right, right. So, here's the thing. I want... charisma. Magnetism. Whatever it is that makes women, you know... look."

"Look," I repeated flatly.

"Yeah. At me. Want me. Fall at my feet, lose their minds, that kind of thing."

I stared at him for a long moment. "You want to be irresistible to women," I said.

"Exactly." He grinned. Then his face shifted, just slightly. A crease in his brow. A nervous flick of the eyes. "I... wasn't exactly sure what you wanted in return," he added, voice hitching at the end.

I leaned forward, just enough to watch him flinch. "Tell me, Lyle. Can you find someone's name if they changed it? Sealed records. Hidden like they never existed."

He paused, "A name?"

Then, he smiled. Grinned, actually.

"That won't be a problem," he said, cocky now. "I can dig up anything, even stuff that doesn't want to be found."

I smiled, but there was no warmth in it, as I leaned back, satisfied. "Good. Then, we have a deal."

He lit up, practically vibrating. "You—you mean I'll get what I asked for?"

I shrugged as I stood up, heading towards the door. "We'll see. Impress me first."

Topher didn't say a word, but I saw his jaw twitch. He hated when I toyed with people. But this one was so eager it was embarrassing. Lyle Simms thought I was about to make him irresistible to women. That I'd wave a hand and suddenly he'd be some dark, mysterious god of seduction.

I couldn't even conjure a puff of smoke anymore. But he didn't need to know that... yet.

As the door clicked shut behind us, I adjusted the cuff of my sleeve and exhaled slowly through my nose. That pathetic little gremlin of a man had left a bad taste in my mouth—and not the good kind.

But I had other plans tonight. Better ones. I knew Evie was working the bar. Because I'd memorized her entire schedule—down to her lunch breaks and shift swaps. Topher printed the staff rosters for the month and slid them across my desk with the quiet reverence of someone who's served the throne far too long. He hadn't asked why. I hadn't explained. Not even to myself.

I stepped into the elevator beside him, loosening the top buttons of my shirt, already picturing the way Evie's mouth would twist when she saw me walk in with Lola, my newest conquest. I wanted to see Evie squirm. Maybe glare. Maybe ask me what the hell I thought I was doing. Anything to prove I'd gotten under her skin.

But as the doors shut and Topher pressed the button for the twelfth floor, I frowned. "I thought we were going to The Serpent's Tongue."

He didn't flinch. "We are. After one more meeting. Sir."

I arched a brow, leaning back against the velvet-padded wall of the elevator. "And who, exactly, am I gracing with my presence this time?"

Topher glanced down at his tablet, expression unreadable. "Vincent Dalca."

I blinked once. Then twice. "Vincent Dalca."

He nodded. "Or at least that's the name he's using this decade."

I let out a low whistle, lips curving. "Well. That's a name I haven't heard since the Berlin debacle. Still here? Too stubborn to die?"

"He's posing as human again. Paper trail, offshore accounts, the usual nonsense. But make no mistake, he's not pretending for their sake."

"Of course not." My tone went flat. "Demons rarely do."

Topher didn't answer. Didn't need to. He knew what this was.

I'd asked him—no, ordered him—to find me someone who could get me answers. Someone with ears in the underworld, eyes in the shadows, and a healthy disregard for Lilith's new world order. Someone who might still owe me a favor.

The elevator climbed, slow as sin, and all I could

do was try to remember exactly what that slippery bastard owed me for. It came back in fragments.

Cairo. A century ago, maybe two. Dalca had been playing dress-up in human luxury, silk robes and too many rings, hawking nephilim blood to desperate humans who thought they could buy divinity by the vial. I never figured out where he'd gotten it, only that he'd gotten greedy.

He'd tried to defect.

Not from Hell, not really. From me. He'd started whispering about "other courts," other thrones, other powers that might be more entertaining to serve. He said it like a man talking about new management, like eternity was a job you could quit when you got bored.

He'd wanted to jump ship to a different so-called pantheon. Thought he could barter his way into their favor by selling out everything he knew about my realm, my people, my weaknesses.

What he didn't know, what I'd seen happen time and time again, was that the First Light owned the whole damn stage. Every "pantheon" was just another mask, another costume change He put on when immortality got stale. A scam He ran to keep the universe feeling unpredictable, to keep everyone dancing while He pulled the strings.

And Dalca, the idiot that he was, had walked right up to the curtain and tried to bribe the puppeteer.

I let him live. Barely. Not out of mercy. I just liked watching him beg for his life. But he'd promised me a favor, swore it on the River Styx. That sort of oath wasn't made lightly, and I'd never collected until now.

The elevator chimed. Topher opened the door to a presidential suite on the twelfth floor, just high enough to feel exclusive. Dalca was already inside, perched on the edge of the couch like he owned the place. He wore a human face like a second skin, but I could smell the sulfur threading under his heavy sandalwood cologne.

He stood when I entered and gave a mock bow. "Your Highness."

I didn't correct him—Dalca, apparently not aware of recent dealings, assumed the old hierarchy. The one etched in fire and blood.

"Vincent." I gave him a curt nod and crossed the room. "Let's not waste time."

He smiled, all thin lips and teeth. "What can I do for you, my liege?"

I dropped into the leather chair across from him, ankle over knee, my same calculated slouch of power. "I want to know what Lilith's up to. In Hell. What she's planning. And more specifically, why she gives a damn about a mortal woman in my hotel."

His head tilted, just slightly—but I caught the flicker of hesitation in his eyes. "A mortal woman, you say?"

I lounged back in the chair like I had nowhere better to be, tapping my fingers lazily against the armrest. "Yes..." I drawled, letting my eyes drift toward the ceiling in mock boredom. "She's my... employee. Pretty. Pink hair. Possibly allergic to shutting up."

His jaw tightened. Just a little. But enough. I didn't press—no sense showing my hand when he was already squirming.

His voice dropped to a whisper, "You don't mean... the Forgotten?"

Something echoed deep in my chest. Hollow. Familiar. Dangerous. "The Forgotten?" I narrowed my eyes. "What the fuck is the Forgotten?"

Dalca's expression froze and then delicately, as if he was trying to appease a beast, he said, "It's more of a... who, sir."

"What are you talking about?"

But then, he blinked. Composed himself. That uneasy flicker vanished behind something colder, more calculating.

"Careful, your Highness," he said, smoothing the lapel of his jacket. "You're starting to sound... interested."

I smiled without teeth. "You're starting to sound like someone who forgot who's asking the questions."

He let out a quiet laugh. "Oh, I haven't forgotten. But if you're looking for a reason Lilith's watching her, I'd start by asking yourself why you are."

That earned him a long silence.

He shifted forward slightly, fingers steepled, voice softer now. "You never did like it when someone else saw the pattern before you."

I stared at him. Still. Unmoving. The air between us pulled tight like a string about to snap.

"Tell me what you know," I said, low and dangerous.

Dalca just smiled again—smug, infuriating. But this time, there was a hint of reverence beneath it. Like a servant who knew the throne still remembered his name.

Dalca tilted his head. "You really don't remember, do you?"

I schooled my features. Sat forward, voice like smoke. "What was she called... before?"

Dalca blinked, all mock-innocence and smug restraint. "Before?"

My jaw tightened. "I—I don't know. Before...

Vegas. Before she learned how just to survive." The words came out sharper than I meant them to, like they'd been waiting behind my teeth. "Before this... this life."

Dalca's mouth curled, slow. "Ah."

I hated the way he said it like he'd just watched a lock click.

"You don't mean her name," he murmured. "You mean the name that isn't hers anymore."

I stood up. "Stop talking in riddles and answer me."

Dalca's gaze flicked to the side, just once, like he was listening for something I couldn't hear. Then he looked back at me, too pleased with himself. "Funny thing about names," he said. "The ones we're given, and the ones we earn. And the ones that get taken."

My skin went cold. "Taken by who?"

Dalca's smile didn't reach his eyes. "That's the question you should've asked first."

I stepped closer. "Lilith," I said, low. "Is this about Lilith? Is she watching Evie because of the prophecy?"

Dalca let out a sound that was almost a laugh, the kind you choke on when the truth is too sharp to say out loud. It died in his throat the second my eyes met his. His mouth twitched. Teeth black with blood where he'd bitten the inside of his cheek, like pain might keep him honest, or keep him quiet.

"Prophecy," he murmured, tasting the word like it was cheap wine. Another almost-laugh tried to surface, and he strangled it back down, quick. Careful. Afraid of what I'd do if he said what he actually thought.

Then his gaze flicked past me, not to the door, not to the window, but somewhere higher, like the ceiling itself had ears.

"Maybe," he rasped. "Or maybe Lilith just stumbled into a game that started long before she ever thought she could move the pieces."

I didn't blink. "Say it."

Dalca swallowed hard. His voice dropped, rough and unwilling. "Maybe she found something you've forgotten," he said, and this time it wasn't smug. It was wary. "Something that was taken from you."

His eyes lifted to mine, and the fear there wasn't of Lilith. It was a name he wouldn't speak. I froze. Not out of confusion or anger. There was something else, something ancient and intimate, like déjà vu with claws.

I grabbed him, slammed him back against the mirrored bar, fingers tight around his throat. He choked on air he didn't need, hands scrabbling uselessly at my wrist, but I kept him there, pinned like a confession.

"Speak plainly," I growled. "Or I'll remind you why I was feared long before Lilith ever learned how to smile."

Dalca's eyes went wild, wary. But he didn't beg. Didn't crack. Not completely. Because even with my hand around his throat, I could see it. Something scared him more than I did.

His voice came out hoarse, broken, defiant. "I'm not the one you should be angry with, Morningstar."

I tightened my grip. "Then tell me why," I hissed, "she cares about this woman. Tell me what she took. Tell me what I'm missing."

Dalca coughed out a laugh that sounded like a prayer gone wrong. "You can feel it, can't you?" he rasped. "Like a song you almost remember. Like it's on the tip of your tongue, but you can't grasp it. Like a face you keep dreaming without ever seeing it clearly."

My throat went dry. Then, he leaned forward as much as my grip allowed, and his whisper slid into my ear like poison.

"She had another name once," he said. "One you used to say like it was holy." His throat bobbed. He didn't look up, like the ceiling might be listening. "A name Heaven... prefers not to remember. The kind that makes the air go quiet when it's even thought too loudly."

My hold faltered for half a second. Dalca's smile sharpened. "And all that prophecy noise," he murmured, almost amused again, "it's just smoke. The real trail is the name you can't remember, and you're following it like it's fate."

I dropped him. He hit the floor hard, gasping, coughing, and I turned away, my reflection watching me from the glass, pale-eyed and still.

"Another name," I repeated aloud, like the words might turn into a memory if I said them enough.

Dalca didn't answer at first. He just stared at the floor like it was safer than meeting my eyes. And for the first time since this started, I wasn't sure I wanted to remember.

"Dalca—"

"She didn't do it alone," he blurted, dropping fully to the floor now, palms flat in a posture that hadn't been used sincerely in centuries. "Lilith. It started when... when you were first cast out. She— she stole the page from the Book of Names."

That stopped me cold. My throat went dry. "That's impossible."

"You'd think so," Dalca said faintly. "But the whispers say she got away with it because the damage had already been done." He swallowed hard. "Judicar Gravum had torn it out first.

Officially. On orders from someone higher."

My jaw tightened. "Say it."

Dalca shook his head, panic flickering sharp and bright across his face. "I won't," he said hoarsely. "Not here. Not ever. You know better than anyone who listens for names spoken too clearly."

Silence stretched between us, thick and vibrating.

Finally, he pushed himself to his feet, avoiding my gaze. "You were never supposed to remember," he said quietly. "Both of you. The page made sure of it."

Then, softer still, like a confession he'd regret until the end of time, "And the forgetting was the point."

Before I could grab him again, before I could demand anything else, Dalca stepped backward, palms raised, already retreating.

"Look, man, that's all I know," he said, voice shaking despite his attempt at bravado,

And then he was gone.

The elevator ride down felt longer than it should have. Maybe it was the weight of what Dalca had said. No. It was definitely what he hadn't.

"Find out what the hell he meant," I muttered, jaw clenched as the lobby light blinked on.

Topher gave a curt nod. "And if he's lying?"

I didn't look at him. "Then I'll remind him what real fear feels like."

The doors opened. The clack of my shoes echoes on the marble, too sharp, too loud.

I headed straight to The Serpent's Tongue. I didn't wait for Topher to follow. He knew better than to trail too close when I was like this—coiled, uncertain, burning from the inside out with questions I couldn't stand not knowing.

The Forgotten. The Book of Names.

Fuck. I didn't want to think about it anymore. So I

did what I do best, redirected the fire. The bar was humming when I walked in. Low light, velvet shadows, sex in every corner. It had once been the crown jewel of my indulgence, but now, it felt like a cage.

She looked up as I walked in. *Evie.* Those gray eyes that looked almost silver. Pink hair. That mouth. That smart mouth that wasn't afraid of me, even when she was nervous. Especially when she was nervous.

She was standing behind the bar, half-laughing with a customer when the shift happened, when her gaze found mine. The laughter died on her lips. Her spine went rigid. Her fingers paused on the rim of a shaker.

I didn't look away. Didn't smile. Didn't blink.

Across the room, a woman in an offensively black dress glanced up from her phone and smiled. Lola, presumably. My date. I scowled and walked right past her. Didn't offer an excuse or slow down. Just stalked across the bar and claimed a seat at the far end, away from her, away from the noise, away from everything that didn't feel like Evie.

And Evie? She was already walking my way. She didn't ask what I wanted. Didn't joke. Didn't flirt. Just slid a lowball glass across the bar like she was trying to pretend last night—and whatever the hell that had been—never happened. But I wasn't pretending. Not tonight.

Her fingers started to retreat. But mine shot out faster. I caught her wrist—gently, but firm enough to stop her. But I didn't let go.

She blinked, eyes cutting to my hand on her wrist, then back to my face.

"Problem?" Her voice was flat enough to scrape.

"I'm not going to bite," I said, though my voice

came out quieter than usual. Rough around the edges.

She arched an eyebrow, "You sure about that?"

I shrugged as I smirked, "At least not tonight." Then I slipped the black card into her hand. Not another hotel key. My number.

Her brows pinched as she looked down at it, thumb brushing the matte finish.

"What's this?"

"My personal number," I said. "Use it."

She tilted her head. "For what?"

"If something feels..." I hesitated. Shit. The word tasted strange in my mouth. "...off. You call me."

Her lips parted, confused. "What do you mean by off?"

I leaned back, still holding her wrist, and tried to play it cool—an act I usually wore like second skin. "If you feel like someone's watching you," I said. "Or following you. If any weird shit happens, you call me. I'll come."

Her head tilted, sarcasm slipping into her tone. "You give this kind of concierge-level service to all your employees?"

I didn't answer right away. Still holding her wrist, my thumb made a slow, unthinking circle over her pulse point. Her breath caught.

And then I felt it, the slight change in texture beneath my skin, the thin ridge she tried to keep turned away from the light—a mark old enough to have faded, but not old enough to be meaningless. The kind of scar that didn't come from clumsiness, it came from a moment a person didn't survive so much as endure.

Something cold and quiet slid through me. Not pity. Not softness. It was fury, clean and immediate. Because whatever had put that line there had gotten to touch her before I did, had gotten to make her believe for even a second that disappearing was an option.

My thumb stilled. My grip gentled without me meaning it to. Her eyes flicked down, quick, guarded, like she was bracing for a question she didn't want to answer.

Acknowledgment sat on my tongue. I swallowed it.

Instead, I lifted my gaze to hers and said, low and steady, like a vow I was making in real time, "I don't," I said, voice low and dark. "Just you."

Before I could stop myself, I murmured, "You don't have to hide from me."

She jerked her hand back, more flustered than she'd ever let me see before. Then, she stared at me, those gray eyes scanning my face like she was trying to decipher a riddle I hadn't meant to give away.

"I should... get back," she said quickly, tucking the card into her back pocket and making her way to a couple at the other end of the bar.

I didn't stop her. But I stayed, watching her go as I took a long sip of whatever the hell she'd poured.

I'd flayed saints for sport and dragged kings through fire for less than a whisper. I didn't get spooked. But Dalca... Dalca had rattled me.

It wasn't just what he said. It was how he said it, "Forgotten" like it was capitalized, like it meant something ancient and dangerous. Not a name, but a title. A curse. And it stuck and clung to the back of my mind like a memory I almost remembered— something sacred and forbidden, poised just behind the veil, taunting. Like a name you knew once. But couldn't say anymore.

After tonight, I wasn't sure it mattered who Evie

Grace was. The real question was *what she was*. And whatever that answer, one thing had become painfully clear—she wasn't safe. Not from Lilith. And sure as hell not from me.

I stayed. For hours. Parked at the end of the bar like I belonged there. Like I wasn't the devil with his spine coiled too tight, watching the girl he didn't understand.

She moved around me like gravity didn't apply. Laughing with customers, rolling her eyes at Marvin, slinging drinks like the world hadn't just shifted on its axis.

I didn't look at anyone else. Not Lola, who texted twice and then gave up before leaving the bar. Not the bored rich girls in barely-there dresses who tried to make eye contact from their VIP booths.

Just her. Just Evie. Until—

"Sir."

Topher's voice cut through the noise like a blade. I didn't turn. "Speak."

He leaned in, just enough so no one else could hear. "Vincent Dalca… is dead."

That got my attention. I turned slowly, eyes narrowing. "What do you mean… dead?"

Topher didn't blink. "Found an hour ago in his hotel suite. Head severed. No residual essence. No sulfur trace."

My blood ran colder than it had in centuries. No residue. No trace. That wasn't punishment. That was eradication.

"The head?" I asked, my voice low.

"Gone. Ripped clean off. Like someone wanted to make a point."

I exhaled through my nose.

There weren't many ways to kill a demon. You could trap us. Bind us. Starve us of infernal power.

For millennia. But to end us? Truly end us? Decapitation and taking the head were among the few truly guaranteed ways. And whoever did it knew that.

Topher hesitated, then added, "There's more."

I flicked my eyes at him.

"I went digging, quietly. Back channels. Old debts." He shifted slightly. "There've been whispers. Centuries-old. Among both angels and demons."

"About what?"

He glanced around. Even here, even now, he lowered his voice.

"That Lilith stole something. Not just any page — one ripped from the Book of Names by the judicars themselves."

My jaw clenched.

"Nothing was ever confirmed," Topher said. "But the rumor's old. And everyone's been pretending not to know because they're afraid of what it means."

"And?" I prompted.

His gaze met mine, just a shade darker.

"Everyone I asked about what Dalca meant — the whole 'something you've forgotten' — they shut down. Immediately. Like I'd said something cursed."

The knot in my chest twisted hard. I looked back at the bar.

Evie was laughing with another customer, twisting a lime wedge between her fingers, oblivious to the fact that someone had just sent a message in blood and bone. And something told me it had everything to do with her.

My voice was quiet. Lethal. "Lock it down."

"Yes, sir."

"Every camera. Every hallway. Anyone who spoke to him — I want names. If his essence so much as flickered before it vanished—I want to know."

Topher nodded and vanished into the crowd like a shadow.

I turned back to my drink. Dalca hadn't just known something. He'd said the wrong thing to the wrong person. Or worse—he'd said too much to me. And someone had noticed.

CHAPTER TEN

Evie

Destiny hissed through her teeth, clutching a towel to her palm. Blood seeped through the fabric in dark blooms. It was a Thursday night, but the bar was unusually slow.

"VIP request just came in," she muttered. "13th floor. I can't go."

"I've got it," I said, already moving toward the sink for a clean towel.

"No." Her voice snapped sharply, almost panicked. "Not this one, Evie."

I paused. "You're bleeding. I'm not. What do they want? Bottle service? I've done this before."

"Not like this, you haven't."

She grabbed a tray from the back shelf—sleek and black like a lacquered coffin—and set it down. She reached again for two short crystal glasses and a dark, unlabeled bottle. It shimmered faintly, like smoke trapped in liquid form.

She nodded towards it, then leaned in close, her voice dropping to a hush. "Take the far-left elevator. The mirrored one."

I blinked. "That thing works?"

"It does—for them. Don't take any others. Don't talk to anyone on the floor. When you walk in the room, don't look at them." She grabbed my wrist. "Don't. Look."

I stared at her. "What kind of them are we talking about?"

She didn't answer. Just held my eyes.

"The room number's on the napkin under the glass. Wait until you're in the elevator and the doors close before checking it."

"Why?" A chill ran down my spine.

"Just... because. I'm serious, Evie."

She softened slightly. "Just leave the tray. Don't linger. Get out of there as fast as you can. No matter what you hear."

I gave a weak laugh. "Wow. Super comforting."

Destiny didn't smile.

The far-left elevator looked like it hadn't been touched in years—sleek black doors, mirrored panels, no buttons. It opened the moment I stepped toward it, silently, like it had been waiting.

I stepped inside, careful not to spill the tray. The air was colder. There were no floor numbers. No buttons. Just strange symbols etched in faint gold up one wall.

My stomach dropped as the doors closed, the elevator rose, and the symbols lit up. I tilted the tray and slid the napkin free. 666. There was no way. No freaking way. This had to be a coincidence. But my fingers brushed the keycard in my back pocket—the one he said I "might" need someday.

The hallway was silent. Not just quiet—dead. There was no hum from the lights, no subtle whir of HVAC. The carpet muted my steps like it had been laid to swallow sound.

The walls weren't drywall or even wallpapered.

They looked like stone—polished, dark, seamless. Every door was black. The room numbers lit in red gold. They weren't in any definable order. 23, 137, 42, 216, 999, 0, 13, 191, 515, 13B.

I turned a corner and found it—Room 666.

I knocked. Once. Twice. Three times. Nothing. A prickle ran down the back of my neck.

But I pulled the keycard from my pocket. Tapped it to the sensor. For a fraction of a second, so fast I almost didn't register it, the edges of the door glowed gold. Without me touching it, there was a click as the door eased open an inch.

I stared at that space, and I should've left. My brain was practically screaming at me to walk back to the elevator, but I didn't. Instead, I pushed it open the rest of the way and stepped inside. The door clicked shut behind me.

It wasn't a hotel room. Not really. It looked like some sort of private lounge—black marble floors, heavy velvet drapes that swallowed light. A fireplace with no wood, no flame, just a dull red glow like embers pulsing behind crystals. A grand piano sat in the corner, untouched.

No windows. No clocks. No sounds. Except the weirdest thing. I looked down, and the glasses on my tray steamed faintly. The bottle shimmered. *What the hell?*

My breath caught. "Hello?" I called, my voice thin.

Nothing. And I just stood there.

Then a full minute later, "You're early."

A voice, male, smooth, low enough to crawl under your skin, and I knew it instantly.

It came from behind a high-backed leather chair facing the hearth. I froze. Every instinct I had begged me to turn and run, but my feet carried me forward anyway, tray still balanced in my hands.

"I—um—I brought your bottle service."

The chair shifted. A hand slid into view, and there it was, the ouroboros ring, black and familiar, ruby eyes glinting as it draped lazily over the arm.

"Bring it here."

My feet moved before I could stop them. The tray trembled in my hands. Destiny had acted like it was some kind of villain summit, like if I made eye contact, it would be over. Like the room itself was a trap. But I knew that voice. Lucifer was the only one here, at least that I could see.

I set the tray down beside him, careful as if the air might shatter, and then instinct took over. I looked up—

My breath left me. Not because I was scared. Because he was unfair—sharp jaw and dark lashes and that slow, knowing calm that made you feel seen and outmatched at the same time. In the firelight, it looked like the shadows were his and the room had simply agreed to host him. His suit fit him like a threat, and the way he sat, relaxed, unhurried, made it worse, like he had nothing to prove because the world already knew.

Heat curled low in my stomach, immediate and humiliating. My pulse tripped over itself. Maybe I didn't know him. But my body sure did. Something deep and ancient stirred in my gut. Like gravity had shifted, and I was no longer standing on Earth.

He tilted his head slightly, mouth quirking in a smirk.

"I expected... someone else," he said, fingers toying with one of the glasses. "You're not supposed to be here," he said. Not accusatory. Just curious. Fascinated.

"Trust me, I didn't plan on it."

"And yet..." His voice dropped, darker now. "Here you are."

His voice was pure sin. Velvet laced with something sharp. I straightened, averting my eyes as I tried to regain control.

"There was... an accident. Destiny cut her hand. I'm just helping her out."

"Just," he repeated, tasting the word. "Funny how people always say that when they're doing something dangerous."

"I'm not—doing anything—"

"Yet."

He turned. And God. This close, he looked carved from shadow and smolder. Those pale eyes I could drown in. His lips were sin, sculpted for blasphemy, and all I could think was how they would taste. His shirt was half-unbuttoned, casual, confident, lethal.

I stepped back without meaning to. He tracked the motion with a slow sweep of his gaze, unhurried, deliberate, like nothing escaped him once he noticed it.

"Tell me," he said, voice smooth and unreadable, "do you always deliver things to locked doors?"

"I—I knocked," I stammered. "No one answered."

His gaze flicked to my pocket, sharp and precise.

"That little key," he said quietly. "You used it, didn't you?"

My heart jumped. Heat rushed up my neck.

"I—" I swallowed. "Yes."

He studied me for a beat too long, eyes dark, unreadable. Then his mouth curved, just barely. "Good," he said.

The word was so soft, so low, I couldn't be sure it wasn't something I imagined, something my nerves invented because he was standing too close and looking at me like that.

He straightened immediately, expression smoothing back into something neutral, untouchable, like he'd never said anything at all. And I just stood there, pulse racing, trying not to wonder why it felt like approval instead of danger.

"I'm sorry... what?"

Before he could answer, a low laugh drifted in from behind him.

"Already handing out favors?" a woman's voice purred. "You're slipping."

She stepped out of the shadows near the bar like she'd always been there, dark hair loose around her shoulders, red mouth curved in a knowing smile. Firelight caught bare skin, the line of her collarbone, the confidence in every step she took.

She didn't hesitate. She went straight to him. Too close. Her hand slid onto his shoulder, fingers grazing his collar like it was familiar territory. Like she'd done it before. Like she belonged there.

Something twisted in my stomach.

She leaned in, lips near his ear, whispering something I couldn't hear. And he didn't lean away. Whatever it was made heat bloom in my chest, sharp and unwelcome, it was ugly and irrational, and I didn't know what to call it.

Then her gaze finally found me. Slow. Appraising. Hungry in a way that made my skin prickle. Her eyes lingered on my throat, and my pulse betrayed me without my permission. For the briefest moment, her smile looked wrong. Then it was perfectly normal again, and I was left wondering what I'd seen.

"Oh," she murmured. "She's delicate."

Cold crept up my spine. Lucifer's hand came up then, closing around her wrist. It wasn't rough, just controlled. Final.

"Enough," he said quietly.

Her smile sharpened. "You always were bad at sharing."

"I'm not sharing," he replied, tone pleasant in a way that promised violence. "You're leaving."

She laughed, low and rich. "Now?"

"Now," he said. "This is still mine, even if..."

He trailed off, and for a heartbeat, something flickered across her face like irritation. Maybe it was just calculation or interest. Then she smiled again, indulgent, like she'd already gotten what she came for.

Her gaze slid back to me, satisfied.

"Careful," she said softly, almost kindly. "Men like him ruin beautiful things."

Then she stepped back, shadows gathering around her like a cloak as she disappeared from the room, leaving the air colder, heavier, wrong in her absence.

The silence settled. And Lucifer exhaled slowly, like he'd been holding himself together by force alone.

Then he looked at me. Not the way he had before. Something had shifted. Hardened. He stood.

My body locked up. I couldn't run. Couldn't breathe. But he didn't come closer. He just watched me with the kind of reverence people reserved for stars or ruins, something ancient and dangerous and half-forgotten.

That impossible face. That voice, too smooth to trust, and the way he looked at me... not like a stranger, like someone trying to remember.

"Sit," he said, gesturing toward the velvet chair across from his. The word was soft, but it landed like a command.

I didn't move.

"I should go," I said, even though my body was already leaning toward him.

"You should," he agreed. "But you won't."

He uncorked the bottle with one hand. The scent hit the air like a spicy sweetness and something older than time. He poured two fingers of it into one glass, and then—without asking—another. He held one out.

I hesitated. "What is it?"

He smiled. Slow. Knowing. "Something rare."

I reached for the glass. When our fingers touched, it was like something tripped under my skin. An electric pulse, sharp and sudden. He felt it, too. I saw it—a stutter in his smile—the shift in his eyes, like he was hunting something he couldn't name.

We sat. A breath passed. Then another. He swirled his drink but didn't sip. Just stared at me like I was an echo from a dream he couldn't shake.

I took a sip. A sweetness that burned. But it was the kind of burn that made you crave the next one.

"You feel it, too, don't you?" he asked, hushed like a secret.

I looked up. "Feel what?"

He didn't answer. He just leaned forward, elbows resting on his knees, glass hanging from his fingers.

"I don't know how," he said. "But I feel like I know you."

My throat tightened. He was too close now. Not physically. Not quite. But emotionally. Existentially. Like he'd cracked a window inside me I didn't know was there.

His eyes dragged across me, slow and deliberate. Not crude. Not gentle either. "You feel like something I lost. Or maybe something I never had."

I couldn't breathe. It felt like even the walls were listening.

"We don't even know each other," I whispered.

He smiled, just faintly. "No," he said. "But I'd like to." Then quieter, dangerously quiet, "Thoroughly."

The word landed low in my stomach. Warm. Electric.

I swallowed hard. "Do you always proposition employees?" I asked, trying for a tone I didn't feel.

He chuckled. "Not at all."

That stopped me.

He stood. Took my glass. Set it down with care. Then stepped forward, slow. Every nerve in my body wanted to run, but none of them moved. He didn't touch me, just hovered, crowding my space. He was close enough that I had to crane my neck to look up at him, his body radiating heat, his shadow falling over me like a shroud.

I sucked in a breath I hadn't meant to take.

"You should go," he said. But the way he said it was all wrong. Too soft. Too slow. Like he didn't believe a word of it.

"Then move," I whispered.

He didn't. A flicker of something dark passed across his face, a smile that wasn't really a smile. "I can't."

My heart caught. "Why?"

He leaned down, slowly, until his mouth hovered near mine, close enough that his breath fanned over me.

"Because everything in me is telling me not to let you."

"Luc…" The name slipped out before I could stop it. I had only ever said his full name once, and hearing it shortened in my own voice startled me.

His eyes snapped to mine. For a heartbeat, he went very still, like I had put a hand on the back of his neck.

"What... did you just say?" His voice was low, rougher than before.

I heard it then, the intimacy of it, the way Luc sat in my mouth like something I had no right to claim. I don't even know why I said it, and now the sound of it hung between us, making my skin prickle.

His hand slid from the back of the chair to my wrist. His fingers wrapped around it, warm and unyielding, and he pulled. Slow, inescapable, until the chair scraped against the floor and I had to stand. One step, then another, and suddenly I was right in front of him, my body aligned with his, my breath catching on the space that was somehow both there and not there between us.

He didn't let go. Not right away. His grip loosened, then trailed, his hand falling back to his side, but the ghost of it stayed on my skin. He stood over me, close enough that I could feel his heat lick at my bare arms like a threat, maybe like a promise.

I didn't move. I couldn't.

"What is this?" I asked, my voice barely there.

"I don't know," he said. "But it's ruining me."

He reached for my face. Then he stopped, just before contact. His fingers hovered, trembling slightly, like the air had turned solid between us, like some unseen force was holding him back.

I felt it, too. The tension. The restraint. The need.

"I shouldn't," he whispered.

But even he didn't sound like he believed that. And I, I didn't move away. I didn't blink. Because I was willing him to do it. God, I wanted it.

His hand hovered above my cheek, heat pulsing from his skin. My body was locked, every cell lit up like it had been waiting for this moment longer than I'd been alive. His gaze dropped to my mouth. For a second, I thought he was going to do it, touch me, taste me.

Then he stopped. His jaw tightened. His nostrils flared, like he'd just remembered something terrible. Or like something inside him whispered, not yet. He dropped his hand. Stepped back once, twice, like space could save him from whatever that was. I nearly begged him.

His eyes never left mine, but they darkened, like I'd done something wrong. "I—" he started, then stopped, his expression twisting like the words didn't want to come.

"You need to leave."

The way he said it, it sounded like he was annoyed. Maybe furious. Like I'd pushed past some line I couldn't even see.

My pulse fluttered like a moth trapped in my chest. "Did I—" I swallowed and asked, "Did I do something wrong?"

He didn't answer. Maybe he couldn't. Maybe he was just as lost as I was. But I knew one thing for sure, whatever had risen between us, it wasn't normal. It wasn't sane. It wasn't safe.

He raked a hand through his hair, breath sharp. "No," he said. "You did nothing wrong."

He looked at me then, like it hurt. Quietly, he admitted, "You just… feel familiar in all the wrong places," he said quietly. "Like I lost you before I ever met you."

I stood there, still too close, my knees not quite steady.

"I don't… understand," I said. But even my voice had changed, soft and shaken, like maybe some part of me did know.

He looked at me. For just a second, something ancient flickered in his eyes. Recognition. Pain. Want. Then it was gone.

He turned away, jaw clenched. "Get out. Now."

I didn't move. He didn't look back.

But he said, low and rough, "If you don't leave now, I don't know what I'll do."

I shivered at the thought. I didn't argue. But that was enough. I turned and walked out. I didn't run because some part of me remembered that running makes predators chase.

I barely made it ten feet before I heard it. Not words. A sound. Low and frustrated. Like something breaking just out of sight. The handle turned, and I paused, my breath shallow as I pressed a hand to the cool wall. Behind the door, something shifted. A sharp exhale. The faintest thud, like a fist hitting wood. Like he was bracing himself against it. Against me.

Then the door sealed shut, final like a verdict. I didn't look back again.

The walk to the elevator felt longer than it should have. Every step replaying the scene in my head on a loop I couldn't shut off.

Her hand on his shoulder. The way he didn't move away. It looked so intimate between them. They had done this before.

And then—me. The way his control slipped just enough to scare him.

It didn't make sense. None of it did. If she meant something to him, why push me away like that? And if I meant nothing, why did it feel like the room itself had been holding its breath when we stood too close? Was I just imagining all this in my head?

Jealousy burned low and mean in my chest, unfamiliar and embarrassing. I had no right to feel this way. And yet.

He'd been calm with her. Smooth. Untouched. But with me, something in him had gone taut, like a wire pulled too tight.

The elevator doors slid open, cool air brushing my face. I stepped inside, pulse still racing, reflection staring back at me like I'd done something reckless without knowing why.

As the doors closed, I caught myself thinking the one thought I refused to say out loud. Whatever he was fighting in that room, it wasn't her. And that right there should have made me terrified. Instead, something inside me felt like it was finally waking up and wanting more.

CHAPTER ELEVEN

Lucifer

The latch clicked, and she was gone.

For a second, I just stood there, staring at the door like an idiot while my chest hauled in air it didn't need. My hand was flat against the wood before I realized I'd moved, fingers spread, feeling the faint echo of her last step as if it stayed in the grain.

"Open it," some feral part of me hissed. "Call her back. Say her name."

My fingers curled around the handle. I could see it already, the scene if I did. I would drag the door open, pull her back into the room, into my hands, and whatever thin line we were pretending existed between us would snap like it had never been there.

I squeezed my eyes shut and made myself let go. One finger at a time.

"Enough," I muttered to myself, not to her. She was probably halfway to the elevator by now. Good. She was safer away from me.

The breath I'd been holding tore out of me, harsh and useless. My chest still ached like there was something inside it that could break. There wasn't. I wasn't made for love. I was incapable of it.

I turned away from the door. The room felt wrong without her in it, like someone had walked off with the gravity. Her glass still sat on the low table, condensation beading everywhere except for the faint smudges where her fingers had warmed the glass. I picked it up, stared at the faint print her lipstick had left on the rim, then threw the drink back in one swallow. It burned all the way down and did nothing.

I dropped into the chair she'd been in, and her scent clung to the fabric, sweet and stubborn. Fruit and patchouli, like sugar over earth, like berries on warm skin and incense in the air, and it didn't smell like perfume anymore, it just smelled like her. For a moment, I just sat there, inhaling her scent, elbows on my knees, palms pressed together so hard my bones creaked.

What in the fucking hell was that?

Lilith had told me I would know her. You will recognize the one you need, she'd said, voice all silk and venom. She never gave answers unless they entertained her, and tonight she'd been far too entertained.

That little performance hadn't been for me. It had been for Evie—a test dressed up as intimacy. Lilith pressing close, touching where she shouldn't, watching to see if the girl would flinch, burn, fold, or break—watching to see what exactly? If the girl in the prophecy had teeth?

I'd expected signs. Symbols. Some unmistakable flare of magic in her blood. Not this. Not this pull for her sharpening instead of fading. Not my body leaning toward her like instinct had decided for me. Not my attention locking on her so completely that everything else, Lilith included, felt like noise.

And the worst part? Lilith had noticed. That was

what unsettled me most. The way her eyes had flicked between us, calculating, satisfied, as if she'd just confirmed something she'd already suspected. Whatever Evie was, she wasn't just a possibility anymore. She was the answer Lilith had come to verify.

And then... I dragged my hand down my face.

The way Evie had said my name. *Luc.*

Like her mouth had known it for years. Like it belonged to her in a way it had never belonged to anyone else.

The sound of it still tingled across my skin, like a spark jumping from her tongue to mine. No one called me that. Not in Hell. Not in Heaven before everything went wrong. Lilith liked to call me Lucy, just to see if she could sand the edge off the devil, make me sound harmless. My brothers had always used my full name, formal and careful, like saying it wrong might summon something worse.

But when Evie said it, it didn't feel new. It felt remembered. Like I'd heard it a thousand times in a life I couldn't see.

That shouldn't have been possible. I would know. I would remember. I remembered everything, that was the curse of it. Every betrayal. Every fall. Every scream.

And yet —

You just feel familiar in all the wrong places, like I lost you before I ever met you.

I hadn't meant to say that out loud. The words had clawed their way out of me anyway, sharp and unguarded. I'd expected her to laugh. To flinch. To look at me like I was finally unhinged.

She hadn't. She'd looked at me like she almost understood. Like she could see the outline of what I meant, even if she didn't have the language for it yet. That terrified me more than anything.

Maybe this realm was driving me insane.

I pushed myself out of the chair and started pacing, tight lines across the rug, like movement might burn the thoughts out of my head. The embers in the fireplace pulsed lazily, matching the rhythm pounding behind my ribs.

She could be the one.

The idea slid in quietly and sharply, unwelcome and undeniable. The prophecy, wrapped around my throat like a chain, I pretended not to feel. Find the woman. Bind her to me. Put a child in her and set the end of the world in motion.

Evie Grace. It had to be her.

Why else would the pull feel like this? Why else would my control slip the moment she stepped into a room? Why else would her voice undo things I had spent millennia locking down?

She shouldn't have fit. She was all jagged edges and defense, the kind of woman who would spit in Heaven's face and laugh about it. I knew the type. She probably came from a religious home, an imposing father who labeled himself "head of the household," and made everyone hate him. And now… she didn't trust men and hated anything that smelled like faith. The First Light would never have chosen her for anything holy. Which made her exactly the sort of choice I should have expected from whatever sick joke the universe was playing on me.

If she was the one, maybe this was how it was supposed to feel. The pull. The recognition without memory. The way my body had gone rigid with the effort of not touching her, not closing that last inch, and finding out what she tasted like.

I ran my hand through my hair.

I should tell her. Tell her the truth. Tell her who I really am, what I really am, and what she might be, why every instinct I have is screaming to keep her close and get her far away at the same time.

I pictured it. Opening that door, catching her at the elevator, saying her name again, the full one this time. Evie Grace, I think you are the spark that ends the world.

She would look at me like I was insane. Or worse, she would believe me. And if she believed me, I would have started something I couldn't stop.

"No," I said aloud. My voice bounced off the stone walls and came back sounding strained. "Not yet."

I gave her the time she needed to get away. Forced myself to feel every tick of it, every second where I did not open the door, did not call after her. When I was sure she was gone, I finally stepped out into the hall. The air felt different, emptied.

I took the elevator up to the penthouse. The usual view greeted me when I opened the door, Las Vegas spread out in a reckless sprawl of neon and hunger. The city pulsed beneath the glass, all those little lives flickering on and off like distant stars.

Once, this had satisfied me. The height, the power, the constant hum of temptation below. Punishing the damned in Hell had been a duty, and watching mortals punish themselves up here had been sport. Simple. Clean. Easy.

Now all I could see was a pink-haired bartender walking back into the glow of The Serpent's Tongue, cheeks still flushed, lips slightly parted from the breath she'd dragged in when I leaned too close.

I poured another drink. It tasted like nothing.

Tell her. Don't tell her. Use her. Spare her. The arguments chased each other around in my head. If she was the one, then keeping my distance was pointless. Eventually, the prophecy would drag us both into its teeth. If she wasn't, then what was this, and why did it feel worse?

My hands tightened around the glass until the crystal threatened to crack.

Fine. If I couldn't have answers, I could at least have a distraction. That had always worked before. When Hell's weight got too heavy on my shoulders, there were a thousand bodies to lose myself in, a thousand mouths, a thousand hands. Pleasure was easy, and I was very good at it. Maybe I just needed to remind my body it didn't belong to her. It didn't belong to anyone.

I set the glass down and left the penthouse, heading for the elevators that led to the club, Elliptica. The bass hit me before the doors opened, low and insistent, vibrating up through the soles of my shoes. Lights strobed in the dark, cutting the crowd into flashes of color and skin and hungry faces.

I took the stairs to the top level. This was familiar territory. People watched me here without knowing who I was, only that I was something sharp and expensive and out of their league. Eyes followed when I moved through the room. Hands brushed, lingered—an invitation in every glance.

Normally, I would have picked someone in the first thirty seconds. The woman in the red dress with the greedy mouth. The man at the bar with the pretty laugh. The couple already halfway to sin in the shadows, waiting for someone to tip them the rest of the way.

Tonight, all I saw was *not her.*

The red dress was the wrong color. The laugh was too easy. The woman whose hand slid over my forearm smelled like a perfume counter, not like earthiness and berries, that scent I still hadn't been able to name on Evie's skin.

I let the woman talk, nodding at the right moments without hearing a word. She touched my chest, my shoulder, and leaned in close enough that her lips brushed my ear.

Nothing.

Desire usually came like a tide, reliable and obedient. Now it felt like a locked door, and the only hand that could open it had already gone back to the bar, probably wiping down a counter and pretending nothing had happened.

The woman trailed a finger down my shirt. "You wanna get out of here?" she murmured. "Have a little... fun?"

I gave her another look and felt... irritation more than anything. Pretty, polished, utterly forgettable. A placeholder trying to pretend she was the main event.

"No," I said, narrowing my eyes as I peeled her hand off me. "You're not what I'm in the mood for."

Her mouth tightened, but I'd already turned away. I left her standing there and moved to the edge of the balcony, looking down at the dance floor. Bodies moved together in a blur of sweat and light, but my mind kept overlaying another shape, another face, another pair of eyes looking up at me like she was half terrified and half daring me to ruin her.

You should go... Then move.

I closed my eyes and for one brief, reckless moment imagined what would have happened if I hadn't. If I hadn't moved aside. If I had dragged her back into that room and ignored every warning ringing in my bones.

When I opened them again, the club was still

gyrating below me, loud and bright and utterly uninteresting.

I was the King of Hell, trapped above, surrounded by sin on tap, and all I could think about was a bartender who looked at me like I was a complication she had no interest in, and still couldn't ignore.

Whatever this was, it wasn't going away. And pretending otherwise wasn't helping anyone.

CHAPTER TWELVE

Evie

It was nearly closing time. The bar had thinned to a few stubborn patrons clinging to their martinis like confessions. The lush green carpet beneath my boots muffled every step, and the air smelled like citrus, cedar, and secrets. Destiny caught my eye across the floor and gave me a mock salute as she slipped into the back.

I ran a cloth along the bar top, already gleaming, but it gave my hands something to do. Anything to keep me from looking left. Which I did anyway.

He was still there. Same stool. Same drink— untouched, the amber liquid catching the low light like it was performing. Luc draped in power like it was custom-tailored. Legs stretched out, ringed fingers resting around his glass. His posture was a masterclass in effortless arrogance.

Watching me. Again. Still.

He'd been doing this every night since that hotel room. Since the keycard. Since the way he'd looked at me like he was trying to decide whether I was a mistake or a door.

The kind of watching that didn't flinch when

caught. Didn't look away or pretend interest in anything else. His gaze stayed fixed, pale blue and unreadable, like I was a secret he was weighing the cost of uncovering. His expression wasn't soft or kind. It was just intent. All that intensity sat under a tumble of hair, loose waves falling over his forehead, like someone had dragged their fingers through copper and left gold behind.

I looked away. Too fast. Shit.

I ducked beneath the bar and busied myself restocking the bitters we hadn't touched in hours. The bottles clinked quietly against one another as I tried to ignore the burn in the back of my neck. But I could feel him. Still.

What the hell did he want?

First the weird energy, then the card, then the whole "call me if anything feels off" thing, and now this. And now this, night after night, like a vigil. Days had blurred together since that room, since the way my skin had reacted to him like it remembered something my brain didn't.

I thought about the shadows I'd sworn I saw at my apartment, and wondered if that had been him, or someone watching for him, because men like that didn't move alone. They had gravity. They had reach.

What was next, showing up outside my apartment in a trench coat and sunglasses?

I straightened and forced a breath. Told myself I was tired and overthinking. I was just inventing patterns where none existed. That powerful men didn't spend their nights watching bartenders who hadn't shaved above the knee in a week and still smelled faintly like limes and regret.

But when I surfaced again, cloth in hand, he was still there—still watching. Like he knew something I didn't yet.

And the worst part? Some reckless, whispering part of me didn't want him to stop.

A little while later, Destiny slid in beside me like a ghost. Her nearly see-through lace-up corset dress hugged every curve, and her knee-high platform boots made her at least six feet of pure don't-fuck-with-me energy. Her sheared head shimmered faintly under the moody lights, that violet hue shifting like a bruise. She had this goddess energy in motion that I could only dream of.

She grabbed a stack of dirty glasses without looking at me, leaned just close enough to pretend we were talking about work, and muttered out the corner of her mouth, "Okay, what the actual hell is up with the Prince of Darkness over there? He's been doing this every night."

My hands didn't pause, but my chest tightened. "You noticed?"

"Bitch, Stevie Wonder could notice. He hasn't blinked in, like, forty-five minutes."

I tried to play it cool, loading another glass into the rack. "Maybe he's just really into liquor and thinks staring at it long enough will make it pour itself. Same, honestly."

Destiny snorted. "Sure. And I'm the Virgin Mary."

She finally risked a glance in his direction, then quickly looked away, faking a cough into her shoulder. "Why's he watching you like he's choosing between worshiping you and setting you on fire?"

"Maybe both." I rolled my eyes, but the shiver crawling down my spine betrayed me. "He's been here all night. Didn't even talk to his date."

"Date?"

"I don't know. She followed him in here. Blonde. Red Dress? The walking lingerie ad?"

"Ohhh. The one who kept checking her phone and ordering water with a lemon slice?"

"That's the one."

Destiny stacked another glass with more force than necessary. "And you're telling me he blew off that snack to make creepy extended eye contact with you?"

I arched a brow. "Gee, thanks."

She elbowed me gently. "You know what I mean. You look like a haunted Victorian governess tonight, Evie. It's giving hot, but also deeply emotionally unavailable."

I glanced down at myself. Yeah...

Black corset-laced blouse, sheer sleeves with lace cuffs that gave a witchy librarian look. Floor-length skirt with a side slit up to my hip, just enough to flash my ripped fishnets and my favorite stompy boots. I was equal parts funeral and fight club. My pink hair was twisted up in something vaguely elegant if you squinted, but I could already feel at least three pins stabbing me in the scalp. And my lipstick? Dark enough to double as a warning label.

Between finding out about Zeke and whatever the hell was going on with Luc and me, I was somewhere between grief and vengeance with a side of "don't ask me about my childhood."

I snorted. "That tracks."

"Seriously, though," she said, lowering her voice. "What's going on?"

"I don't know." I glanced toward him—couldn't help it—and there he was. Same seat. Same unnerving stillness. Like a painting that might move if you blinked. "He gave me his number."

Destiny's head whipped toward me so fast I

nearly dropped a glass. "He what?"

"Shh—"

She grinned. "Oh my god, he... likes you."

"Destiny."

"I'm sorry, but no man watches you sling gin and sarcasm for hours on end unless he wants to know what your hair smells like when you sleep."

"He just gave it to me because—" I flushed. "He said if anything ever felt... off, I should call him."

She blinked. "That's either hot or a red flag the size of Nevada."

I sighed, racking the last glass. "Welcome to my weird life."

We started hauling the racks toward the back when Destiny glanced over her shoulder and whispered, "Look, I'm just saying... You could do worse than a broody billionaire who apparently can't stop watching you like you're the one glitch in his perfect little universe."

I snorted. "Yeah, well, no thanks. It would never work."

"Why not?"

"Because I am aggressively not a trophy wife. I'm more like the haunted doll that shows up after you move into the mansion."

Destiny cackled and elbowed me before grabbing her rag and heading off to wipe down the tables. "Whatever. Just don't come crying to me when he starts leaving roses and Ferraris at your door."

I rolled my eyes, watching her go.

But as I tucked the last of the lemon wedges and cherries into the fridge and wiped down the bar, her words wouldn't quite leave me alone. Would it be so crazy? Dating a man like him?

He was too... everything. Too polished. Too powerful. Too aware. Like he saw things in people they didn't even want to admit were there. And me? I'd spent most of my life hiding. From my family. From my past. From who I used to be.

He'd eat someone like me for breakfast and then probably get bored and spit me out. Still... a tiny, traitorous part of me wondered what it would be like. Just once.

After closing, the staff trickled out one by one, the last goodnights echoing down the hallway. I lingered, checking the registers and finishing inventory, trying not to feel the weight of his eyes still following me. I grabbed my bag and came out from the back just in time to see his assistant, Topher, slip out the front entrance.

Lucifer was still there, still in that same damn seat.

I gave him a small wave and started to say, "Goodnight—"

But he stood up abruptly. The motion was so out of place, so un-him, that it threw me for a second.

"I'll walk you out," he said quickly—no lazy charm, no slow smile. Just words, rushed and raw.

"You don't have to—"

"You have two options," he cut in, already moving. "You come upstairs to the penthouse and stay the night..."

I blinked. "I'm sorry, what—"

"Or I drive you home and do a quick walk-through."

I stared at him. "Wh—What is going on?"

He looked at me and, for the first time since I'd met him, he didn't seem smug or seductive or polished within an inch of his life. He looked... unsettled.

"I'll feel better," he said, "if I can keep an eye on you."

I should've laughed. Should've hit him with some snark about overprotective billionaires being so last season. Instead, I just stood there, caught between confusion and the creeping chill crawling up my spine. Because something about the way he said it didn't sound like flirting. It sounded like a warning.

"Keep an eye on me," I echoed slowly. "Because...?"

His jaw ticked. He didn't answer. Not right away. Just that tiny shift, that flicker of something he wasn't saying, which, coming from him, was the unnerving part.

"Mr. Morningstar," I said carefully, tasting every syllable like it might buy me space. "If this—"

"Luc," he said.

I blinked. "What?"

"Call me Luc." He exhaled through his nose, like he hated the answer. "You said it the other night," he murmured. "Accidentally."

My pulse jumped. "And?"

His eyes held mine, steady, unblinking. "I liked it." A beat. "And... I want to hear you say it again."

Of course he did. I swallowed, reset. "Luc," I said, and it felt both wrong and too right in my mouth, "if this is just some elaborate rich guy pickup line, I gotta say, it's not your best."

His lips twitched, but the smile didn't land. His gaze stayed on me, steady, intent.

"It's not that," he said.

"Then what is it?"

Silence stretched. The empty bar felt too quiet. My fingers itched around the strap of my bag.

"I just..." He exhaled. "Something feels off. I can't explain it. But if anything happens to you—" He cut himself off, like he hated the sentence even as it came out.

That shouldn't have made my pulse stutter. And yet.

"Okay," I said slowly, "let's pretend for one second that I take this seriously. What exactly am I supposed to be worried about?"

He didn't answer. Didn't blink. Just watched me with those pale eyes, too pale, like a storm frozen in mid-flash.

I thought about the weird flickers here and in my apartment—the shadows out the windows. The chill in my chest I couldn't shake. And the way he'd touched my wrist tonight, like he was grounding himself. Like I was the tether.

"I can't," I said, voice low. "I can't come up there with you."

Something slipped behind the mask. Disappointment. Then something darker.

"And I don't need a ride," I added quickly. "I have my truck. I'll be fine."

The words rang hollow, even in my own ears.

He watched me for a beat, then nodded once. Slow. Controlled. "Evie," he said softly, "you can drive yourself if that makes you feel better."

"It does," I lied.

His mouth twitched, like he heard it. "Fine. Drive yourself." He stepped closer, lowered his voice. "But understand something. Whether I'm in the car with you or not, I'm still seeing you home."

A little spark of irritation flared. "That sounds a lot like stalking."

"It sounds," he said, pale eyes steady on mine, "like I am not in the habit of losing what's mine," he said.

"Good news," I shot back, even though my pulse tripped, "I'm not yours."

Something flickered in his gaze at that, sharp and

hot, then he locked it down so fast I almost thought I imagined it. Whatever he was going to say next died on his tongue.

"Come on," he said quietly. "You are not walking out of here alone."

He walked me to the staff elevator that led to the parking garage. We didn't talk. He stayed a few paces behind me, quiet and unreadable, but I could feel him there like a second spine.

When we reached my beat-up truck, he opened the driver's door, like some kind of dark valet. I climbed in and tossed my bag onto the passenger seat.

He didn't close the door right away. One hand on the frame, one in his pocket, he looked at me like he was etching me into memory.

"If you change your mind," he said, "call."

"About the penthouse?" I tried to joke. It didn't land.

"About anything." His gaze flicked over my face one last time. "Drive safe, Evie."

He shut the door with a soft, final click and stepped back. I pulled out of the space, glancing once in the rearview. He was still standing there, hands in his pockets, watching me go. He didn't turn away until the ramp swallowed him. That should've been my first warning.

I hated how quiet my apartment was when I got home. Not the comforting kind of quiet, the soft, warm hush that says you're safe, relax. This was the kind of quiet that made you check the locks twice. The kind that made the hairs on the back of your neck rise for no good reason.

I tossed my keys into the bowl by the door and flipped on the living room light. Nothing. I frowned and tried the switch again—still nothing.

"Cool," I muttered. "Super chill."

I dug my phone out and turned on the flashlight —the stark white beam cut through the shadows. I walked through the apartment, hitting every switch I could find. Power flickered back to life in the kitchen, the hallway, the bedroom—everywhere except the living room. Like whatever was off had decided to plant itself right where I had to walk through next.

By the time I looped back to the living room doorway, my phone's light dimmed once, then died completely. The screen went black. I flipped it over and hit the side button. Totally dead—but I could've sworn it was at sixty percent when I left the bar.

"Perfect," I said. "Love that for me."

I dropped the dead phone on the counter and stepped into the living room slowly, my boots thudding softly on the floorboards. A streetlight spilled through the slats of the blinds, painting sharp yellow lines across the floor and the fake ficus on the balcony.

I was halfway across the room when I heard it—a whisper. No. A rustle.

I froze. My heart stuttered. I waited, but the silence folded back over everything, too smooth, too complete.

"You're fine," I whispered to myself. "You're tired. That's all."

But as I passed the window, something in the shadows on the balcony moved. Not a lot. Just a shift that didn't seem to belong to the wind. I spun, breath caught in my throat. There was... nothing.

But I could feel it. Not see it, feel it. A weight pressing from the dark. A hum in the room. The sense that something was there, watching from just beyond where the light reached.

I didn't think. I moved. I snatched my bag from the counter and bolted—no change of clothes. No checking the locks. I just went.

My fingers fumbled through my purse as I sprinted, finally closing around a cold cylinder. Bear spray. Just in case. I yanked it free, thumb hovering over the nozzle like a trigger. Yeah, that was definitely going to fix the eldritch horror vibe.

Good evening, nightmare creature. Please enjoy this refreshing cloud of pepper mist. May I recommend blinking vigorously while I run for my life?

The stairwell door banged open under my hand, the echo ricocheting down the concrete. The lights flickered once overhead, casting long, wrong shadows that stretched too far along the walls. The air felt heavy, like trying to breathe under a wet cloth.

"Stop freaking out," I muttered. "It's nothing. It's —"

I didn't stay long enough to finish the lie. I barreled down the stairs, nearly tripping over my boots, bear spray clutched like a talisman. I shoved through the outside door and stumbled out onto the cracked concrete path leading to the lot.

I slammed straight into a wall. Except it wasn't a wall. It was a chest. Solid. Unmoving. Hands closed around my arms, steadying me. I jerked back, sucking in air to scream, and looked up.

Lucifer. He stood there in the pool of a streetlight, dark coat, pale eyes, looking exactly like he had in the bar—only sharper around the edges. All the polish stripped off, left with something raw and focused. Behind him, idling at the curb, was a sleek black sedan. A driver waited behind the wheel, still as a statue.

"What the—" I gasped. "What are you doing here?"

His gaze swept over me once, the shaking hands, the can of bear spray still raised like a toy.

"Hello to you, too," he said, voice low. "Get in the car."

"Excuse me?"

He angled his head toward the sedan. "You insisted on driving yourself. I accepted that. I didn't agree to stay on my side of the city while something crawled around your balcony."

My skin went cold. "You followed me?"

"You're welcome," he said, completely unbothered. "Now, get in the fucking car."

"I have my truck," I snapped, clutching the spray tighter. "I'm not getting into some random—"

"Evie." My name in his mouth came out soft and sharp at the same time. "Whatever was up there isn't your fake bush. I felt it from the street."

My heart lurched. How did he...? "You... felt it?"

His jaw flexed. "Car. Now. I'm going upstairs."

"You can't just walk into my apartment—"

"I already watched you run out of it," he said, eyes flashing. "So we're past the polite part of this conversation." He lifted his chin toward the sedan. "Rafi," he called.

The driver stepped out, tall and quiet, opening the back door with practiced ease.

"Ms. Grace is going to wait in the car," Lucifer said, not looking away from me. "You do not leave this spot. You do not open the doors for anyone but me. Understood?"

"Yes, sir," Rafi said.

"I'm not—" I started.

"Evie." Lucifer lowered his voice. "Please."

That stupid word. It landed right in the hollow

part of my chest.

"If something's up there," I said, my voice smaller than I liked, "you shouldn't go in alone."

A corner of his mouth twitched, humorless. "Trust me," he said, "I'm not the one in danger."

Before I could decide whether to slap him or thank him, he guided me toward the sedan with a hand at the small of my back. Not a shove. Not quite gentle either. Every nerve in me screamed this was a terrible idea. Every other nerve remembered the thing in the shadows and voted hell yes, get in the armored limo.

I slid into the back seat. The leather was cool under my bare legs. Before I could change my mind, he shut the door. The sound was solid, vault-like. Rafi went back to the driver's seat without a word.

Through the glass, I watched Luc take the stairs two at a time, coat flaring, shoulders squared. He didn't look back. The stairwell swallowed him. The car was quiet in that weird luxury way, the outside muted to a dull hum. My building sat in front of us, washed in sickly yellow light. The windows stared back, blind.

I twisted in my seat, craning my neck to see my living room window and the small slice of balcony I could make out. The leaves of my fake ficus. The cheap blinds. Nothing moved.

"Do you hear anything?" I asked after what felt like five minutes, though it could've been thirty seconds.

Rafi's eyes met mine briefly in the rearview. "Car's soundproof, Ms. Grace." Of course it was.

I checked my phone out of habit. The screen lit instantly —52%. "I hate this," I muttered to it. To myself. To the universe. To no one.

I went back to watching the building. Waiting.

Counting cracks in the sidewalk. Imagining every possible way this could go wrong. Ten minutes stretched out like an hour. My fingers went numb around the bear spray. Then the stairwell door opened.

Lucifer emerged slowly, not like a man strolling out of a casual inspection, but like someone walking away from something he didn't want to turn his back on. His hair was a little mussed, like he'd dragged a hand through it one too many times. The lapels of his jacket seemed crooked. As he came down the stairs, he flicked something invisible off his cuff, then smoothed the line of his coat like that could erase whatever had just happened.

My heart climbed into my throat.

He crossed to the car. Rafi was already out and opening my door, but Lucifer beat him to it, sliding in beside me and shutting us in our little insulated box.

Up close, I could see it. Not blood. Not obvious damage. Just the tightness in his jaw. The faint scuff on his knuckles. The way his eyes looked a shade lighter, like something had washed through them and taken color with it.

"Well?" I asked, turning toward him. "What did you see?"

He looked at me for a long, heavy second. I watched the lie happen in real time, the way his shoulders loosened a fraction, the way he raised his chin, and his features smoothed out like someone pulling a sheet over something ugly.

"Nothing," he said.

The word landed too clean.

"Nothing," I repeated, because I might not know what the hell was in my apartment, but I knew bullshit.

"For tonight," he added quietly, gaze flicking back to my building. His reflection in the window looked more honest than the man next to me. "You're not going back up there."

I swallowed. "Then, where am I going?"

He turned back to me, something dangerous and decided settling over his features.

"Back to The Revel," he said. "With me."

He tapped the back of Rafi's seat twice. "Drive."

The car eased away from the curb. My apartment shrank in the rear window, just a dark box with too many shadows and not nearly enough answers.

I kept waiting for Lucifer to relax, for some hint that he'd meant it when he said "nothing." But he never did.

CHAPTER THIRTEEN

Lucifer

I forgot how quiet cars could be. The cabin was soundproof, insulated, all hum and soft leather, and the faint trace of Evie's perfume mixed with fear in the air. She sat beside me, staring straight ahead, and even in combat boots, she managed to fold herself down, knees tucked close, like smaller meant safer. The bear spray was still in her hand, her knuckles white.

I could have told her to put it away, that it was useless against the thing that had been in her living room. Against the things that were circling now. I didn't

"Nothing," I'd said.

It was a clean lie. Too clean. I could still feel the residue of it on my tongue, bitter as ash.

When I stepped into her apartment, the air changed. That was the first tell. Mortals talk about rooms feeling colder and heavier, as if it were just a metaphor. It's not. The living room pressed against my skin like a hand on my chest, curious and hateful at the same time. The power was out in that one space, but it wasn't dead. Just... redirected.

Watchers always liked playing with currents.

I crossed the threshold and felt it notice me. Not her. Me. For a heartbeat, the room went very still. If I still had ears tuned to the way Heaven and Hell hummed, I would have heard the way the threads pulled tight.

I saw it then, in the corner near the balcony door, where the shadows pooled a little too thick. It was not some grand, monstrous revelation. No horns. No claws. That was not their way. It was a vertical smear of darkness, tall and thin, edges leaking into the air like smoke that had forgotten how to disperse. Where its face should have been, there was only a pale suggestion of features, like someone had erased them halfway through.

One of Lilith's little pets. It shouldn't have been there, not for her.

I had gone very still—old habits. You learn quickly not to flinch in front of things that serve your enemies.

"You're very far from home," I said quietly.

In the old days, those words would have done a lot of work. I wouldn't even have needed to raise my voice. I was the thing the shadows answered to.

Now, I should have been just a man in a dead room, talking to a patch of bad lighting. But the Watcher recoiled. Not much, just a ripple along its edges, but it felt it. Felt me. The recognition hit us both at once. Surprise twisted its shape, a slight distortion, like static on a screen.

So. I could still do that. Interesting.

I stepped farther in. The carpet under my shoes was cheap, thin over old boards, but it felt like walking on the surface of a river. The thing pulsed in time with the overhead light that refused to turn on. It had wrapped itself around the wiring, feeding on the charge, on the small electric hum that human lives depended on.

"Off," I said.

Old language, older than Hell, almost older than I remembered. The syllable scraped the back of my throat on the way out, like something rusty forced into motion. But... the ceiling light flickered, once. The Watcher shuddered. For a moment, I thought that would be the end of it. They used to obey me without question.

Then the resistance came. It pushed back, the room tightening, the shadows stretching longer, trying to lean away and loom at the same time. I smelled sulfur. Burned dust. Lilith.

Of course. She had her claws in them now. Why send her own hands when she could twist mine?

The thing lifted what passed for its head. No eyes, but I felt the focus. Not on the door. Not on the street. On the memory of a girl who had just bolted down the stairs.

"Not her," I said, sharper than I meant to. "You don't touch her. Don't even fucking look... at her."

The Watcher rippled again. I saw it then, a thin thread of dark running from its center up through the ceiling, vanishing into the building's bones. A tether. A report line. Whatever it saw would not stay here. Lilith would know she had run. She would know I had followed.

"Why her?" I asked it softly.

It didn't answer in any way a mortal would understand. They never do. It shivered, and in that movement, there were impressions. Heat. Flame. A balcony overlooking a very different kind of void. A woman standing at the edge of it, backlit by a sun that did not belong to this universe.

My chest pulled tight. Evie? No. Someone else...

she was someone else. But the two flickered, overlaid in my mind for a heartbeat, like bad film.

The Watcher surged, pressing outward, trying to push itself through the room, through the wires, through the wall, and trying to get past me. To keep watching. To keep reporting. On her.

Too late.

I stepped into its space, into the thickest part of it. The cold sank into my skin, a deep, bone-level chill that reminded me of the lower rings. For a terrifying second, nothing happened. Just a man, I thought. Just a man in an empty apartment, chest heaving from a fight that's just begun.

Then something in me shifted. Not a flare of hellfire, nothing that dramatic. Just a small, stubborn core of what I had been, refusing to stay dormant. The part of me that knew how to command lesser things. How to bind and unbind.

I put my hand out and pressed my palm flat to the side of that shadow.

"Go," I said, in the old tongue again. "You were not sent for her."

The lie slid out smoothly. If Lilith had ordered them, that made the sentence technically untrue, but power is more about will than accuracy.

The Watcher shrieked. Not out loud. Inward. Reality wobbled around it for a fraction of a moment, like heat above pavement. The thread running up into the ceiling snapped, recoiling on itself in a shower of sparks only I could see.

The light overhead flared on. Bright. Harsh. Ordinary. The apartment exhaled. And then… the Watcher was gone.

I stayed where I was for a moment, hand still braced on nothing, palm tingling like I had pressed it to an active coal. My knuckles were scuffed. I realized I had hit the wall once in the middle of it. Frustration, old rage, something I didn't want to name.

I shouldn't have been able to do that. Lilith had sealed Hell, locked me into this soft, breakable form, stripped away everything that had made me dangerous. That was the point. A dethroned king was just a man in a suit.

Except when Evie was involved, apparently. Her name, her presence, the echo of that vision, all of it loosened something that should have stayed bolted shut.

And now I was in the back of a black sedan, power residue buzzing under my skin, while she sat three inches away, clutching a can of bear spray and thinking she had overreacted to a fucking fake tree.

The Watchers weren't supposed to be anywhere near the living. They were meant to haunt the shores of the River Archeron, ankle deep in black water, holding back whatever tried to drag itself out of the current: The Whisperers, The Blamebound, The False Prophets, The Lovers who Betrayed. Lilith might use them as her eyes in the dark now, her little gossip network, whispering to her about any movement that might threaten her power. But even then, they were meant to stay in their river. So what in hell was one doing on Evie's balcony?

Why her? Why now? Was it because I wasn't moving fast enough for Lilith and this damn prophecy? Because I kept going to the bar? Because I watched her? Spoke to her? Invited her into Room 666 when Lilith was there and poured her a drink that didn't exist on any human shelf?

I glanced at her out of the corner of my eye. Her

profile was set in stubborn lines, jaw tight, gaze pinned to the windshield like she could will the hotel to appear faster. She had no idea that thing in her living room had reached for her across realities. No idea that I had just torn one of Lilith's strings out of her ceiling.

Good. The longer she didn't know, the longer I had to figure out what exactly was hunting her, and whether it wanted her dead or worse. Lilith's interest rarely ended well for anyone involved.

"Nothing," I had said. That much, at least, was true.

There had to be more to this than just some stupid prophecy. If Lilith had sent a Watcher to her balcony, this was just the beginning, and I needed to know what was going on.

Rafi turned into The Revel's circular drive. The hotel rose up in front of us, all glass and light and quiet desperation. I watched Evie's fingers unclench from the bear spray one notch at a time as she saw the familiar facade, the illusion of safety.

Evie stepped off the elevator and followed me inside. I didn't say anything at first—just watched her take in the space with wide, alert eyes. The way her gaze swept the ceiling moldings, the black marble floors, the arched windows swallowing the skyline. She clocked every detail like she was preparing for war. Like beauty itself might bite.

"This way," I said, turning down the hall.

She followed silently, stomping across the polished stone. I opened the door to one of the guest bedrooms, the one I'd found myself ordering Topher to prepare days ago without understanding why.

"You can stay here for now."

Her steps slowed as she crossed the threshold. I turned to find her still hovering just inside, arms folded.

"You didn't bring anything with you," I said, brow furrowing.

She scoffed. "Didn't exactly have time."

Fair.

I walked to the far wall and opened a second door, revealing a walk-in closet. "You should be able to find what you need in here."

She peeked around me, eyes narrowing. "Hard pass. I'm not really in the mood to raid your Hookup Lost and Found."

A muscle jumped in my jaw. I pinched the bridge of my nose, sighed. "They're not—" But I cut myself off. No point. Not tonight.

She didn't push, but I felt her eyes on me, wary like she couldn't decide if she'd walked into a safehouse or a gilded cage.

"Are you... hungry?" I asked.

She shrugged, glancing toward the window.

I exhaled slowly. "There are towels in the bathroom. Help yourself to anything in the kitchen. I'll leave you to it."

I turned toward the door, meaning to give her space, but before I could make it out, I heard her footsteps behind me.

"Where're you going?" she asked quietly, like the question cost her something.

I paused. Turned. She was standing there, arms crossed tight, boots planted on the rug like they could anchor her. Scared. But hiding it behind that steel spine she wore like armor.

"I have some work to do," I said carefully. "But I'll just be down the hall."

Her mouth opened like she might argue, but then she gave a slight nod. I closed the door behind me with a soft click. By the time I reached my office, the edges of calm I'd forced around myself were fraying.

I grabbed my phone and dialed. Topher answered on the second ring.

"Escalate the search," I said without preamble. "I want everything. Who she was, who she is, who's watching her, and why the fuck Lilith gives a damn about any of it."

Topher didn't hesitate. "I have a name. Someone who might know."

"Someone? A… demon?"

"Yes, sir."

"Who?"

"Crowe."

Fuck. I didn't breathe for a second. My gaze flicked toward the closed guest room door down the hall. I didn't trust that bastard. Not then. Not now. Not even if the world was burning and he handed me the last bucket of water.

These days, he was Damien Crowe, a sharp suit and a sharper smile, but I knew better. Knew who he really was beneath the tailored lies and human cologne. *Malthus.* The schemer. The architect. The snake that didn't slither—he whispered. A demon who didn't need to draw blood to win a war. He just needed a blueprint.

I'd seen him work and watched him gut kingdoms without lifting a single blade. Whispered truths where they hurt most, made monsters of men, and monsters of angels too. He'd always said Hell didn't need fire—it just needed better design.

And maybe he wasn't wrong. But that didn't mean I wanted him within a hundred miles of me.

He didn't take sides. That's what he'd always claimed. But I remembered who he stood behind when Lilith rose—how conveniently absent he'd been. And I couldn't prove it, not yet, but I'd bet my last damned breath he'd had a hand in it. Probably the whole fucking playbook.

Still… He owed me—big time.

A long time ago, I pulled his wretched hide out of the wreckage of a collapsing arcane vault. No one else would've risked it. No one else could've. He was trapped under enough enchanted steel to crush a lesser demon's bones into dust. But I stepped into the warded ruin anyway. Tore through spells older than memory. Got him out.

I never asked why he'd gone in there alone. I didn't care. I just made him swear. On bone and ash. On fire and name. A favor, owed to me. No questions. No loopholes.

And now? Now might be the time I cash it in.

Because if anyone could unearth what Lilith was planning—how she knew who Evie was, why she gave a damn—it was Damien. But I'd have to watch my back. Because a favor from him? Even if there weren't any loopholes, there was always a hitch.

"Get him here," I said coldly. "Now."

Twenty minutes later, my phone buzzed. I answered with a sigh. "Tell me you have good news."

"I got him."

I straightened. "Damien?"

"Yes, sir. He wasn't thrilled to hear from me. And…" Topher drifted off.

I exhaled, "What bullshit is he pulling this time?"

"He refuses to come to The Revel. Said it's too 'gaudy and soulless.'"

I stared out the window, biting down a growl. "He's a fucking demon."

"Yes, but a pretentious one."

"Where then?"

Topher hesitated. "Black Honey."

I closed my eyes. Of course. "That ridiculous luxury vampire club with the blood-colored absinthe?"

"Apparently, he owns it now."

I rubbed a hand down my face. "Of course he fucking does."

"He said to come tonight. After midnight."

I swirled the drink in my hand, then downed the rest. "Fine. But I'm bringing Evie."

"Are you sure that's—"

"No," I said, already walking toward her room. "But it'll be... interesting."

I knocked on her door. No answer. I knocked again, louder—still nothing.

"Fucking brilliant," I muttered.

The handle turned easily. I cracked the door open, intending to call her name—but then I heard her. Not just the water running. Her voice. She was singing. And it hit me like a blade to the ribs.

Soft. Clear. Unfiltered. Like she wasn't trying to sound good—she just was. The kind of voice that wrapped itself around you and dragged you under before you even knew you were sinking.

"When you were here before..."

It was a song that scraped open every buried thing a person tried to forget. She sang it quietly. Like the words were too heavy to carry full-throated, and maybe they were. Maybe that's why it landed the way it did—like a confession slipping through the steam.

This was not the Evie I'd grown to know in the past few weeks. Not the one who snapped at me behind the bar or rolled her eyes like a reflex. This voice came from somewhere else. Somewhere older. Lonelier. It was vulnerable. Too vulnerable. I should've walked away. Instead, I moved closer.

Like an idiot. Like someone who cared.

Each step took me nearer to the bathroom door. Closer to the steam, the echo, the way her voice cracked on "I don't belong here," and something in my chest twisted sharp. And I didn't fucking like it.

I was nearly pressed up against the door when it flew open—fast and hard—and caught me square in the face with a crack. Pain bloomed. I bent forward with a growl, clutching my nose.

"Oh my God—shit!" she yelped. "Are you okay?"

"Define okay," I muttered, my voice thick through my fingers. "Feels like you broke it."

She rushed toward me—still dripping wet, wrapped in a towel, eyes wide and horrified. "Let me see. Move your hand."

"No."

"Luc."

"I said no. Unless you're going to kiss it better."

"Why are you even here?" Her hands landed on her hips. "You were creeping."

I blinked up at her. "I was not creeping."

"You were lurking outside my bathroom door while I was in the shower."

"I knocked."

"You entered."

"I thought something was wrong!"

"Oh, something's wrong," she said, gesturing wildly at her towel, at me, at the hallway in general. "You're what's wrong!"

I stood up straight, still grimacing. "Not my fault you open doors like a linebacker."

She glared at me, breathless, wet, furious, and—for one fleeting second—stunning.

"I'll yell next time," I said dryly.

"You think there'll be a next time?"

I didn't answer as red blood trickled down my

upper lip. I tilted my head back and sniffed hard, pressing the bridge to check for a break. It hurt like hell. Which meant it probably was broken.

And unlike before, I wouldn't be snapping back in five seconds flat. Not anymore.

"Fantastic," I muttered.

Evie hovered near me, still dripping from the shower, towel clutched tight around her. Her hair was curling at the ends. Her chest rose and fell like she wasn't sure if she should help or run.

I gave a short exhale through my nose and waved her off. "Just… get some sleep."

Her brow furrowed. "Why?"

"Because we're going out tonight."

She blinked. "I'm not going anywhere."

I growled, low in my throat, and took a step closer. "Yes," I said, my voice dropping, "you are."

Another step. She didn't move. I was close enough now to smell her shampoo—something soft and citrusy, almost too innocent for the way she was staring at me. Wide-eyed. Breath caught.

"We're meeting someone," I murmured, my gaze drifting to her throat.

She swallowed. "Who?"

I didn't answer right away. I leaned in, too close, too tempted. There were droplets of water still clinging to her collarbone, trailing toward the curve of her neck. I wanted to catch them with my tongue. I was desperate to taste her. I would bet this entire hotel she tasted like sin and sugar, and I wanted it.

"Someone who can get us answers," I said, my voice quieter now. Rougher. "About who's following you and—"

But I didn't finish. Because suddenly I realized what I was doing. How close I was. What I was about to do. I clenched my jaw and stepped back, the air between us crackling with something dangerous.

"Sleep," I snapped, retreating like a coward. "And...," I gestured towards the closet, "pick out something dark, gothic. For tonight."

And I left—before I did something stupid. Before I kissed her. Before I sank my teeth into that soft, wet skin and made her mine without a plan or a goddamn reason.

I stormed down the hall, into my bedroom, kicking the door shut behind me. I yanked off my clothes and left them where they fell. I didn't want comfort. I wanted release.

The shower hissed on, steam rising fast. I stepped in, the scalding water searing across my shoulders. But nothing burned as much as the thought of her—wide-eyed, wrapped in nothing but a towel, throat exposed like a fucking invitation.

I pressed my palm to the tile and dropped my head forward. This wasn't supposed to happen. She wasn't supposed to get under my skin like this. And yet—

My hand slid lower, stroking. Slow. Intentional. Not just chasing pleasure—summoning her. I closed my eyes and conjured the version of her that haunted me. Not the sharp-tongued menace who flayed me with sarcasm. The one who ran into me, scared and wide-eyed tonight, the one who sang like she didn't know the world was listening. I imagined her mouth, her skin, the sound of my name as she moaned in pleasure.

And when I came, it was her name on my tongue. Whispered. Like a prayer, I had no business speaking. And God help me, I would have her.

CHAPTER FOURTEEN

Evie

I woke up starving. Not "I could use a granola bar" hungry, more like "I could eat an entire pizza and lick the box" hungry. The clock on the nightstand said it was almost 8:30 p.m. Which meant I'd slept for more than twelve hours. After last night, I needed it.

I dragged myself out of bed and tiptoed to the door. I cracked it open. Complete silence. No Luc. No music. No dramatic sulking on the velvet furniture. Just quiet.

I padded down the hall barefoot, hugging myself as I passed a ridiculous hallway of opulence and sin. The kitchen was sleek and modern, all black marble and gleaming chrome. And to my surprise, the pantry was fully stocked—everything from protein bars to gourmet pasta to overpriced cereal that looked like it had never been touched. The fridge was the same, stocked to the brim with milk and eggs, fruit, and vegetables. Either someone had done a massive grocery run, or Lucifer Morningstar just really liked his options.

I made coffee using an espresso machine that

looked more like a Bond villain's death ray. I was sure it had never been used. It hissed and steamed, as if personally offended that someone was finally using it.

With caffeine in my system, I made some kind of sandwich-scramble hybrid, scarfed it down at the island like a goblin, then carried my mug back to the bedroom.

That's when I decided to brave the closet, that gross "Hookup Lost and Found." Except… nothing looked worn. Everything still had the tags on. Dresses. Skirts. Tanks. Lingerie. All black, all bold, all in pristine condition. I pulled one hanger down. Then another. Then another. They were all my size.

I froze. Had he…? Did he have this sent… for me? How? When? He'd barely known me last night — well, technically this morning. He'd saved me, and I thanked him with a broken nose and accused him of being a shower stalker. And yet —

I stared down at the outfit I'd pulled. A slinky black skirt with lace-up slits that ran high up both thighs, and a corset-style tank that laced up the front like something out of a vampire burlesque fantasy. He did say to dress gothic, and it was… a lot. But also kind of perfect. And somehow, it fit just right.

I found a shelf full of shoes — like, actual shoes, not just stilettos someone left behind after a walk of shame. Platform boots. Heeled sandals. Combat boots with silver hardware. All organized. All spotless. All in a size eight wide. How did he even know?

I pulled down a pair of 5-inch black platform stretch boots and zipped them up over my calves.

Next came makeup.

I dug through my bag for my trusty red-wine

lipstick, but when I got to the bathroom, I opened a drawer looking for a hairbrush and found everything I needed to complete the look—cat-eye liner, black mascara, even matte setting spray from my exact brand.

I stood there for a minute, mascara wand in hand, and whispered to the mirror, "Okay, this is either serial killer-level hospitality... or something else."

Afterward, I stared at my pink hair. Messy from sleep. I twisted it up into two space buns with a few wisps framing my face, after digging out two spare hair ties from the bottom of my bag.

When I finally checked my phone, it was nearly 10:00 p.m. I had no idea where Lucifer was. No idea what I was supposed to do. So I sat on the bed in my ridiculous boots and corset, waiting. For what, I wasn't sure. Ten minutes passed before I heard the front door open.

I stood and walked out to the living room as he walked in like he owned the night—black suit jacket slung over one shoulder, shirt open at the collar, eyes landing on me the second he crossed the threshold.

He stopped. And stared. There was something in his expression I couldn't read. Hunger, maybe. Or regret.

My cheeks flushed, suddenly unsure. "Do I... look okay?"

His gaze swept over me, slow and heated. When he finally spoke, his voice was low and gruff. "You look like... trouble."

He stepped aside and held the door open. "The car's waiting."

The car slid to a stop in front of what looked like a church that a coven of extremely horny vampires had converted. *Black Honey.*

The name pulsed in yellow neon above the arched door, flickering like a heartbeat. Outside, the line of clubgoers snaked around the block—fishnets and leather, latex and glitter, bodies wrapped in black straps and sheer illusions. Nipples covered in just black electrical tape. Corsets and collars. Heels like weapons. Shirts optional. Shame nonexistent.

Lucifer opened the door and stepped out, extending a hand to me like this was a gala and not the entrance to some infernal pleasure pit.

Inside, the air hit me like a spell—dark, smoky, humming with bass. Scents of clove, sweat, and candle wax filled my nose. Every surface shimmered under low red light. Chains hung from the ceiling like tasteful art.

A Wheel of Pain dominated the left side of the room—yes, an actual spinning wheel, mounted on a stage, with a dominatrix in thigh-highs and a riding crop taking volunteers. One poor bastard was strapped in and grinning like he'd won the lottery. Another was in a stockade while a woman in a thong spanked him with a paddle.

The dance floor pulsed in the center, a mass of writhing bodies, leather and mesh and black lace grinding to the beat spilling from a DJ booth at the back of the club. The DJ wore a horned crown and nothing else but latex pants and black nipple rings.

Above it all was a swirling staircase, guarded by a mountain of a bouncer in a leather vest, thong, and a matching bedazzled face mask.

Luc didn't pause. He just touched my lower back, guiding me forward like he owned the place. His hand was hot—too hot—and way too casual about where it landed.

I shouldn't have felt anything. It was just a hand. But my skin lit up like he'd branded me through my top. I glanced up at him. He didn't meet my eyes. Just kept walking. Confident. Unbothered. Like a devil playing escort. The bouncer didn't say a word —just stepped aside like this was expected. And maybe it was.

Upstairs, the club opened onto a balcony lounge overlooking the chaos below. Everything was quieter here, but no less charged. The music still thumped, but it was cushioned—like we'd stepped into another dimension, still tethered to the dark.

There were three booths spaced along the balcony, each one a velvet-draped alcove that offered privacy without secrecy.

His hand didn't leave my back. I could still feel it when we reached the middle booth—occupied by a man who looked like he'd been carved out of charm and menace in equal measure. Tall, lean, coiled like a threat and disguised as a favor. Dark hair. Darker eyes. And a smile that didn't quite reach them.

He lifted a glass in greeting as he stood up. "Well," he said, voice silk-smooth. "If it isn't the Morningstar himself."

Luc grunted.

"My, my," the man said, eyes sweeping over me like I was dessert and he hadn't eaten in days. "You've been holding out on me."

Before I could ask what that meant, Luc stepped in front of me, cutting off the view like a human wall.

I blinked. "Are you serious right now?"

I sidestepped him before he could cage me in completely.

"Hi," I said, extending my hand. "Evie Grace."

The man took it slowly, fingers cool and precise. Then he brought it to his mouth and kissed it, lingering just long enough to make it weird.

"Damien Crowe," he said smoothly. "A pleasure. Though from the look of things, I imagine I'm not the only one enjoying your company tonight."

His eyes flicked to Luc, who—just to prove the point—let out a low growl like a goddamn animal. My pulse thickened, and a moment later, his hand wrapped around my waist and pulled me back against him. Hard.

I stumbled a little, caught myself. "Okay, wow. Possessive much?"

He said nothing.

And Damien just kept smiling like he was watching a favorite movie unfold. Like he'd seen this exact scene play out a thousand times and was still delighted by every second of it.

The vibe was off. Not just between them—everything. The lights were too dim, the bass too deep, and the way Damien looked at me was too sharp around the edges. It wasn't flirting. It was studying. Calculating. Like I was a variable in some equation I didn't know I was part of. And suddenly I wasn't sure who had brought whom into the lion's den.

Luc's grip on my waist tightened.

"I'm not in the mood for foreplay, Crowe," he said, voice low and sharp. "Start talking."

Damien raised both hands in mock surrender, all cool amusement. "Relax. You know I like a little music before the dance."

"We're not here to dance."

That smile widened. "Pity."

He turned his gaze back to me, like I was far more interesting than anything else in this club. "I like her," he said softly. "You always did gravitate toward the rare ones."

"That's enough," Luc said, his voice low and

hard.

But Damien didn't look at him. Not at first. He was still watching me—no, searching me. Like I was a half-finished painting and he was trying to remember the artist.

"She's familiar," he murmured, almost to himself. "Like a song I used to know."

I frowned. "Have we met?"

His gaze flicked to mine. And then, just for a breath, to Lucifer. "Not like this."

Luc didn't move. Didn't speak. But I felt the tension pouring off him like heat from a furnace.

Damien took a slow sip of his drink, then turned fully to Lucifer. His eyes softened—not mocking this time, but knowing. Pitying, even.

"She's lovely," he murmured. "So full of fire and not even lit yet." He raised his glass slightly, like a toast. "Reminds me of someone."

Luc's face turned to stone. "Don't."

But Damien went on, his voice like silk stretched too thin.

"You remember—don't you? Right after you threw her out. How broken she was. How angry. You left her bleeding at the gates, and I—well. You always hated how quickly she crawled into my bed."

My heart thudded. What the hell were they talking about? Luc stepped forward once, like he might lunge, and Damien leaned back casually, utterly unfazed.

"Relax," Damien said again, the edge back in his tone. "That was a long time ago. We've both moved on. You with your... denial. Me with my indulgences."

His gaze flicked to me one last time.

"But still—funny, isn't it? How the past always

157

finds its way back. Especially when she's wearing such familiar eyes."

Luc's voice was ice. "I should never have come. We're done here."

"But we've only just begun," Damien said, that smile still curling like smoke. "I'll be in touch, Lucy."

Luc pulled me down the stairs like he was escorting me out of a burning building. But I wasn't ready to leave the fire. I yanked on his hand, steering us away from the exit.

He resisted. "What're you doing?"

"I'm not done," I said, turning toward the dance floor.

"Evie—" His voice dropped, warning threaded through it.

I shook my head, a little breathless, a little defiant. "Running away doesn't make it go away," I said, like it was nothing. Like it was just something that had occurred to me.

His grip tightened for half a second. Not anger. Something else. Something unsettled.

"Don't make me dance alone... Luc."

I let go of his hand and slipped into the crowd, my body already moving with the music. It wasn't graceful, it was instinctual. Sensual. I let the rhythm take me, let it carry me into the heat and the smoke and the press of strangers.

The crowd swallowed me whole, bodies undulating, lights flashing from blacklight to blood-red to ultraviolet haze. I didn't look back. Not until I felt him.

Luc stepped in behind me and spun me around. One hand gripped my hip, the other sliding up to the small of my back. His body aligned with mine in one seamless motion—solid, hot, unmistakably male.

This wasn't dancing. It was sin in motion. I ground against him, slow at first, then bolder, matching the pulse of the music. He moved with me, not like someone learning the steps, but like someone who had invented them. His thigh slipped between mine, and I welcomed it, pressing into him as heat bloomed low in my belly.

The buttons of his black shirt were open just enough to give me a glimpse of skin, smooth, strong, so... maddeningly perfect.

I reached for his shoulders, fingers curling in the soft fabric like I needed something to anchor me. Needed to touch him and needed him closer. I dragged him forward, closing the space between us until there was nothing left but heat and the frantic thrum of my heart.

We were so close, we were practically sharing breath. He smelled like cinnamon and something darker—something I couldn't name.

His lips brushed my ear. "Is this what you wanted?"

I shivered.

All around us, the floor writhed. A den of hedonism. Hands everywhere. Mouths on throats. A couple beside us was practically having sex on the wall—him on his knees, her moaning into his hair. No one cared. No one watched. It was freedom. It was madness. It was... intoxicating.

We danced like we were the only ones on the floor.

I looked up at him. His eyes hadn't left me. Not for a second. And in them, I saw it—desire. Hunger. Like he was barely holding himself back. His eyes glowed, I swear to God. Just for a second. A flicker of something unnatural, like I'd sworn I'd seen before. And still—I wasn't afraid.

I was drawn to him. I wanted to taste those lips. I wanted to tangle my fingers in that gloriously angelic hair and see if he'd groan against my mouth or take me apart with it.

CHAPTER FIFTEEN

Lucifer

She moved like temptation itself, all hips and heat and fearlessness. I matched her rhythm, arm wrapped around her waist, thigh pressed between hers, holding her so close I could feel every stutter of her breathing and count her heartbeats against my skin.

She smelled like heat and berries and midnight. She looked up at me like she didn't know what I was, but she wanted it anyway. And for a second, I forgot everything else. Forgot who I was. Forgot why I couldn't have her.

The music throbbed around us, the lights strobed between violet and blood-red, and all I could see—all I could feel—was her. I leaned in—just a breath's width. Our lips brushed—barely. A flicker of contact. A mistake. A mercy. A warning.

She gasped, soft and surprised, and I pulled back like I'd been burned. I was unraveling. She didn't know what I was, but she was already undoing me.

I shook my head, jaw clenched. "We need to stop."

Her brows lifted, breath still ragged. "Why?"

"Because if we don't..." My voice dropped to a

whisper. "I'll do something I'm not allowed to."

She reached up, slow, deliberate, and threaded her fingers into the back of my hair. Tugged just slightly, enough to make me feel it.

"What if I want you to?" she whispered, her lips barely an inch from mine.

I exhaled hard through my nose, trying not to lean in again.

"Evie," I said, warning thick in my voice, "you have *no idea* what you're inviting."

Her gray eyes glinted in the dark, bold and wicked. "No," she murmured. "But I want to."

God help me. I wanted to give it to her—every unholy, ruined part of me. But I couldn't. Not yet. Not like this. Not when the hunger crawling through my veins had nothing to do with lust—and everything to do with what I could only describe as... recognition. I didn't know what that meant, but I needed to find out. Soon.

I forced myself to step back. My hands dropped from her body like it hurt to let go.

"We're leaving," I said roughly, voice low and sharp like a cracked blade. "Now."

Before I could let myself sink any deeper, I grabbed her hand and led her toward the door — keeping my touch impersonal, my eyes forward, and every sinful instinct chained inside me where it belonged.

The car ride was silent. Tense. She didn't say a word, and I didn't trust myself to start.

Every time I glanced at her, I saw the way her lips had parted when I brushed mine against them. The way her body had moved against mine. The hunger in her eyes that mirrored my own.

By the time we reached the penthouse, I was vibrating under my skin. I stormed down the hallway the second we stepped inside, jaw tight, pulse hammering. I needed to get away from her. But she followed me.

"So that's it?" she called after me. "We're not going to talk about what just happened?"

I stopped. Turned. And faced her.

"You want to talk?" I said, in a low, dark voice. "Now?"

I stalked toward her, every step deliberate, forcing her back until she hit the wall. She looked up at me, chin tilted, breathing shallow. I braced one hand beside her head, the other ghosting along her hip, not quite touching. Then I dipped down, slow and unhurried, until my mouth hovered just above the pulse thudding at her throat. She didn't speak. Didn't move.

I ran my nose down the line of her neck, inhaling her—something sweet, something sharp and earthy, berries laced with defiance. My lips brushed her skin without pressure, just enough to feel the heat, the tremble underneath.

I murmured, "Tell me to stop. Or I'm going to fucking ruin you."

Her lips parted, but no sound came. She didn't need to say a word.

I kissed her hard—no hesitation, no restraint. My hand wrapped around her throat, not tight, but firm, pinning her to the wall. She whimpered against my mouth, then moaned, the sound going straight to my spine.

I reached down, fingers finding the slit in her skirt, gliding up along her thigh until I felt the lace of her panties—already soaked through.

"This what you want?" I growled against her lips as she bucked against my hand.

I grabbed the crotch of her underwear and tore

them clean off, the sound sharp in the quiet. The black lace fluttered to the floor.

"Is this what you've been aching for?" My voice was rough as I traced the slick heat at her core.

She gasped—soft and broken, her hips arching into my touch like her body was begging faster than her brain could keep up when my fingers slid along her slit, slick and aching. Her hands dug into my shoulders, half trying to hold herself up, half trying to make sense of what was happening, of what I was doing to her.

"Lucifer—" she whispered, breath shuddering. "This isn't—I didn't mean—"

I tsked, tipping her chin up, gaze hard. "Say it right. Luc."

Her eyes were wide, glassy, and her lips parted. "Luc, I'm not—" she started again, but her hips betrayed her, grinding into my palm like her body had already made the decision.

"Lies," I murmured, two fingers slipping inside her—slow and deep.

"Oh—God—," She cried out—soft and high—and I felt her clench around me, warm and wet and so fucking perfect I nearly lost my grip on the moment.

"Not Him," I growled, mouth brushing her ear. "You only say my name when I'm fucking you."

I leaned in. Slipped a third finger in and pushed deeper, harder. She gasped again.

"Only my name," I said, rough and low.

She whimpered, shaking, thighs starting to tremble. I thrust my fingers into her faster now, curling them just right, pedaling against her g-spot. My thumb circled her clit until her words broke down into sounds—helpless, needy, uncontrollable.

"Luc—" she moaned, this time with no hesitation.

"That's right," I breathed. "This is mine."

Her whole body tensed—then she shattered against me. Her moan hit my chest like a punch, her body writhing beneath my hand as I held her up, fingers deep inside her, coaxing every last tremor of release from her trembling thighs.

I didn't move until she sagged against the wall, spent and silent, her breath hot on my collarbone, her body slick with satisfaction. Only then did I pull my fingers out of her—slowly. Deliberately.

She watched me, eyes still dazed, lips parted, and I swear I could see her chest rise just a little sharper when I brought my hand to my mouth. I licked one finger, slow and indulgent, never breaking eye contact. Then, the next, and the next.

She didn't speak. She couldn't.

I made a low sound deep in my throat—satisfaction, hunger, something darker. Her taste was fire and sugar and sin, and I wanted it tattooed on my tongue.

"Fuck, such... sweetness," I muttered, almost to myself. "You taste like you were made for me."

Her pupils were blown wide, lashes fluttering, body still trembling. I leaned forward, wanting her to see exactly what she did to me. What she was to me.

And then—

Click—a soft mechanical sound. My jaw tightened—the private door. The only one Topher or I used, unless something was wrong.

Still, I didn't look away from her. Not yet.

Then came the footsteps—Topher's shoes, sharp against the black marble tile, each step closer, cutting through the silence like a knife.

Evie jerked slightly, reality rushing back into her bones. Her eyes snapped down the hallway, then back to me. She didn't say a word. She just pushed off the wall, straightened her skirt, and walked quickly toward her bedroom. The black lace I'd torn off was still lying in the hallway like a forgotten offering.

At the door, she paused. Looked back. One last glance—something unreadable flickering behind her eyes. Then she slipped inside and shut the door.

I stood there for a moment, pulse still thrumming, her taste still lingering on my tongue. Then I exhaled, slow and sharp. I bent down, picked up the torn scrap of lace from the floor, and slid it into my pocket without a second thought. A souvenir. A warning. A fucking problem.

I rolled my shoulders once—tight, restless—this better be good. Or someone was going to bleed. I followed the sound of Topher's footsteps through the hall, my own slower, heavier. Restraint wound through me like piano wire—thin, sharp, waiting to snap. The lace in my pocket burned like a brand.

When I stepped into the living room, I expected him pacing, maybe holding a file or a tablet, maybe throwing me one of his poorly timed quips to cover for whatever mess had crawled to our doorstep. But that wasn't what I walked into.

Topher stood perfectly still, facing the glass wall that overlooked the city. And he wasn't alone. A single envelope sat on the marble coffee table behind him—red, with a gold wax seal I hadn't seen in centuries. I didn't need to see the symbol to know who it was from.

Lilith.

I hadn't seen her in weeks. No taunting drop-ins, no velvet-voiced threats, no shadows slipping through my halls like she owned them. She'd been quiet, which meant she'd been busy, or bleeding, or both. And if I'd learned anything about Lilith, it was this: she didn't stay away unless she was letting the leash slacken just long enough to see what I did with it.

Then she came back to check her work.

It was her old seal—long retired, long buried. One she only used when it was personal. When she wanted me to know exactly what she was doing. What she was claiming.

Something echoed faintly off the glass—like wind, but deeper. Older. Topher finally turned to look at me. His face was pale. Grim. For once, no smile.

"She knows, doesn't she?" I said.

Topher didn't answer. He just nodded toward the red envelope on the coffee table.

"It was delivered about twenty minutes ago," he said, voice tight. "By a low-level imp. Female. Didn't say a word. Just handed it over and disappeared into smoke."

Lilith never needed fanfare. She knew exactly how to twist the knife—with quiet, timed precision. I picked up the envelope, running a thumb over the wax seal, the one reserved for threats disguised as invitations.

I cracked it, and her scent hit me instantly— myrrh and gardenia. Beautiful. Cloying. Rotting beneath the bloom. A smell I'd once buried my face into. A scent I'd once bled for.

And now? Now it made my stomach turn.

Lucy, darling,

Still no progress?

All that time in your lovely little glass cage. And tonight at Black Honey—how delicious. They said you almost kissed her. So close. So hesitant. So unlike you.

Tell me... are you slipping? Because you know the rules. Bed her and plant the seed. This isn't a love story.

But you—you always try to rewrite the ending, don't you?

You do remember what happens if you fail? If you fall? You lose everything, including her. And I don't break things gently.

Time doesn't wait, my love.

L

The letter crumpled in my hand. Lilith knew I hadn't done it yet. Knew I was getting too close. She had spies, eyes, claws in every dark corner—and at least one of them had watched me unravel in a club full of sinners.

She knew what I was starting to feel. She could probably smell it on me. And if she knew—if she thought I was falling—then maybe she'd already made her move. I turned on my heel and stormed down the hall like Hell itself was snapping at my heels. My heart thundered harder with every step. The moment I reached her door, I threw it open.

And... there she was. Safe. Sitting cross-legged on the bed, barefoot, makeup gone, pink hair down, a T-shirt hanging loose on her frame. Her eyes were wide with surprise. She looked so much younger than her years.

"Luc?" she asked softly.

I froze.

Every muscle locked, breath sawing sharp in my chest. The fear didn't drain—it calcified. And I just stood there. Soaked in panic and drenched in something worse. Knowing—I was seventeen kinds of damned.

"Luc?" she asked again, rising to her feet slowly, her voice softer now. "What's wrong?"

I stopped just inside the doorway—the words I wanted to say stuck in my throat. Lilith's handwriting still burned behind my eyes. The scent of her still clung to my fingers. The threat echoed like a war drum in my skull. But Evie looked at me like she wanted to believe I wasn't about to destroy her world. So I lied.

"It's... nothing," I said, managing a weak smirk.

Her eyes searched my face, like she knew there was more—but wasn't ready to fight me for it. She nodded once, slowly, and sat back down on the bed. I stayed where I was for a moment. Then crossed the room and sat beside her—far enough that we weren't touching. The bed dipped, the smallest shift, but she felt it anyway. Her fingers curled into the hem of the T-shirt like she was bracing for impact.

"You don't look like nothing," she said quietly.

I huffed out a breath that might've been a laugh in another life. "You should see me when I'm actually in trouble."

She tilted her head, studying me. No fear. No judgment. Just that open, infuriating attention. Like she was listening with her whole body.

"Luc," she said again, and my name in her mouth did that thing it shouldn't have been allowed to do. "You came in here like something was chasing you."

Something was. Someone always was.

I stared at the wall across from us, at a faint crack that looked like a fault line if you squinted. I could tell her. Right now. I could say the words. There's a prophecy. You're part of it. I was sent to you. I could tell her that my interest wasn't coincidence, that fate had teeth, that Hell itself had shoved me in her direction and said, "Do it."

Instead, I said, "If I tell you something… and it changes the way you look at me…"

Her shoulders went still.

"…would you want to know?"

She didn't answer right away. She slid her feet off the bed, pressing softly against the floor, grounding herself. When she looked back at me, her eyes were steady.

"I think," she said, carefully, "that not knowing would make it worse."

That did it. That cracked something open in my chest, hot and stupid and terrifying. My hands flexed on my knees. Power stirred under my skin, restless, like my wings were flaring and wanted permission, impossible and insistent, like my body still remembered.

I turned to her then. Really looked. The bare face. The tired eyes. The girl who trusted me more than she should.

I could hear Lilith's voice in my head, silk and poison. Don't fall. Don't hesitate. Don't tell her. So I swallowed it. All of it.

"There are… people," I said instead, choosing each word like it was a wire I couldn't afford to trip, "who don't like me getting attached to things."

Her mouth curved, faint but real. "You? Attached?"

I managed a smile this time, thin and crooked. "Exactly."

She watched me for another long moment, then nodded, like she'd accepted an answer she didn't love but wasn't ready to challenge.

"Okay," she said. "So… are you going to disappear on me?"

That landed harder than any threat.

"No," I said, and this time it wasn't a lie. Not the

way she meant it.

I stared ahead, unable to look at her as we sat there in the quiet, not touching, the space between us loud with everything I hadn't said.

"Back at the club," I said, voice quieter than I meant. "You said something."

She didn't answer right away.

"'Running away doesn't make it go away,'" I repeated. "What did you mean?"

She exhaled slowly. Her hands knotted in her lap. "I know what it's like," she said simply.

Another beat of silence. Then she started speaking —quiet, unsteady, like the words had to climb their way out of her. "I was seventeen. Just grabbed my bag and my phone and bolted through the snow like the house was on fire." She gave a dry laugh. "It wasn't. Not technically. Just my life."

I turned toward her then—slowly. She didn't look at me.

"I thought if I could just get far enough away," she continued, "I could outrun it. The fear. The shame. The voices in my head that sounded way too much like my father's."

Her voice cracked, just a little. "But they follow you. The things you don't deal with. They crawl into your luggage when you're not looking and unzip themselves in the next city. Or the next bed."

She swallowed.

"So yeah. Running doesn't make it go away."

I stared at her, something dark twisting in my chest. She wasn't just talking about the past. She was talking about now. About me. About what she was already starting to see—even if she didn't know what I was.

Not yet. And gods help me—I wanted to confess and tell her. I wanted to tell her everything.

She sat beside me, still not looking my way. Her fingers fidgeted with the hem of her T-shirt, her voice quiet but steady. "My father was the bishop," she said. "I was the oldest of ten girls. That meant I was supposed to be the example. The good girl. The obedient one." She let out a humorless laugh.

"But I was never pious enough. Never perfect enough. I asked too many questions. I didn't pray the right way. I didn't smile when I was supposed to. He said I had a rebellious spirit, like it was a disease I needed to be cured of."

I exhaled slowly. I didn't speak. I didn't dare.

"He tried to beat it out of me a few times."

I stilled.

"Another time, he said it was a demon. That God gave him the burden of purifying me. Once, he locked me in my room for four days. Said maybe taking away food would teach me submission."

My hands curled into fists.

"He left me with a bucket and two bottles of water. That was it. No food. Locked me in my room. I screamed. Begged. Cried. Beat on the door until my fists were raw. No one came to save me—not my mom, not any of my sisters. And on the third day —"

Her voice cracked.

"He laughed. Said maybe my future husband could finish the job. Said maybe he would beat it out of me when I couldn't run."

"Then, when I turned sixteen, he sat me down and told me he'd chosen my husband." Her voice hitched. "Chosen. Like I was cattle. Something to be sold or bred."

My stomach turned.

"He said we'd marry as soon as I turned eighteen. A man from another congregation. Someone they trusted."

She finally looked at me. Her eyes were glassy, but not wet. She'd already cried all the tears this story had cost her.

"Ronald. He was older. Could've been my father." She swallowed hard. "He was... lecherous. Smiled at me like he already owned me. And I—"

Her voice cracked. "I remember the Sunday they introduced us. I had just turned 17. It was after service. In the church basement, there were folding tables with blue plastic tablecloths and stale sheet cake. My father made me sit next to Ronald. He told me to smile. He leaned over and whispered, 'I can't wait for our wedding night. When I can have you all to myself.'"

She shuddered.

"I still remember his voice. The smile. It made my skin crawl. It still does."

I clenched my fists in my lap.

"My mom was thrilled. My aunt was already planning the bridal shower. No one questioned it. No one cared that I was practically a child. No one cared that I was terrified."

She took a breath that sounded like it scraped her lungs on the way out. "So one weekend, my parents were out at a leadership training, and I stole five hundred dollars from my dad's desk. Packed a bag. And ran."

Her eyes met mine again. "I never looked back."

Silence settled like a heavy curtain. She wasn't even asking for comfort. She was just telling me the truth. And it hit me harder than any blade. Because for all her fire and snark and defiance—this was the scar underneath. The one that shaped her. The one that still ached in the quiet, when no one was watching.

And I... I had no idea what to say. So I told her the only thing that felt true. "I'm glad you ran."

She didn't smile. But she nodded, and her shoulders loosened. "Me too," she whispered. "And... I think I'm okay now. Most days, anyway."

And for a moment, I forgot what I was. Because all I wanted to do was reach across the space between us and gather her into my arms like I could carry some of it for her. Instead, I said something that surprised even me, "You did what you had to do to get out. They're the ones who should be ashamed."

She let out a shaky breath, the faintest trace of a smile flickering at the edge of her mouth. "I've had a lot of therapy. A lot of therapy."

Her fingers fidgeted in her lap, tugging lightly at the hem of her T-shirt.

"I stayed in a shelter for a while. They helped me. Got me connected with a counselor. A free clinic. My GED. Bartending school."

Another pause.

"And I never looked back." She let out a long sigh. "But I did go back," she said after a long beat. "For my dad's funeral a few weeks ago."

I stilled, watching her.

"I hadn't seen any of them in nearly 10 years. But my dad died. And I... I don't know. I felt like I had to. Like if I didn't go, I'd regret it."

Her voice dipped lower. "But it was still all the same. Every bit of it. The same congregation. The same meetinghouse. The same bullshit."

She looked at me then, eyes sharp and full of quiet fury. "My sisters were all lined up in the front row like sheep going to slaughter. In pastels and perfect braids, like purity pageant finalists just hoping someone would pick their number."

Her lip curled. "My mother didn't even speak to me, just sent my aunt over to tell me I shouldn't have come."

I felt it again—that ancient, brutal thing inside me uncoiling. I wanted to burn that church to the fucking ground. I wanted to find her father because I didn't even have to be told. He was definitely in hell. And that lecherous bastard, Ronald? I'd bury him beneath the church floorboards and make sure even Hell refused to take him.

But I didn't say any of that out loud. I just let her keep going, because she was giving me her truth, and maybe she needed to set it down somewhere. And I wanted to be the place.

She fell silent. She stared at the floor, her jaw set like she was bracing for judgment. For a sharp word. For someone to tell her she'd said too much.

But I reached out—slowly. Not like I was swooping in to comfort her, or save her, or smooth her hair like some rom-com fantasy.

Just my hand. Palm open. Fingertips brushing hers where they rested in her lap.

She looked up, startled. Her eyes met mine, wide and guarded. I didn't pull away. I just... stayed. My hand on hers. Warm. Solid. Real. And not going anywhere.

She let out a slow breath—like she'd been holding it for years—and turned her hand over to thread her fingers into mine. Like she was saying, I see you too.

And I didn't feel like a monster. I just felt... human. Because this woman—this sharp, stubborn, impossible woman—she didn't need anyone to save her. She needed someone who would let her choose. Let her just be herself.

She didn't let go. And neither did I. We just sat

there—quiet, breathing, hands entwined like something sacred had formed between us. And for once, I wasn't thinking about my task, or my failure, or the apocalypse Lilith had promised me if I got this wrong. I was just thinking about Evie.

My phone buzzed, sharp and intrusive, slicing through a moment that had felt dangerously close to honest. Evie flinched, barely, and I cursed under my breath as I let go of her wrist reluctantly. The moment was gone as I reached into my pocket.

Blocked number. I stared at the screen for a beat, jaw tight. I knew exactly who this was.

I looked at her. "Stay here," I said softly. "I need to take this."

She nodded, but I saw the flicker in her eyes—disappointment. But she continued watching me closely, wary—but stayed put as I slipped out, pulling the door closed behind me. Good. The last thing I needed was her overhearing Damien's particular brand of poison.

I swiped the screen and brought the phone to my ear. "This better be worth it."

There was a pause. Then a low, measured voice—familiar in the worst way. "Still got the velvet touch, I see."

My jaw clenched. "Damien."

"Luce," he purred, like my name tasted sweet. "Or should I say... Daddy?"

I didn't speak. Didn't give him the satisfaction.

He chuckled softly. "You didn't think she'd keep her little secret from everyone, did you?"

I stayed silent, letting him circle.

"I have to admit," he went on, "I thought you'd move faster. You're on the clock, after all. Tick, tock, Luce."

"What do you want?"

"You know what I want."

"You working for her again?" I asked coldly.

"No," he said. "But I have a proposition…"

CHAPTER SIXTEEN

Evie

When the door clicked shut behind him, the room exhaled, and so did I. I sat there on the edge of the bed, t-shirt hanging off one shoulder, bare legs dangling, feeling like I'd been spun in a dryer on high and then dumped out, still warm and wrinkled and not quite myself.

My hand was still shaking where it rested on my thigh.

Ten minutes ago, Luc had his hand wrapped around my throat, my ruined black lace panties on the floor, his fingers inside me while I clung to his shoulders and tried to remember how to breathe.

And when it was over, when I shattered around him, he'd watched me like he'd just witnessed something sacred and then brought his fingers to his mouth, sucking me off them like it would've been a crime to waste a drop.

Like, what the hell was that? From there, things had gone very quickly sideways.

Topher's footsteps in the other room. The frantic way Luc had stepped back, chest heaving, pupils blown. Me pulling my skirt down and practically sprinting for the guest room like a teenager caught on the couch. His assistant walking in on torn panties and sex in the air was not on my bingo card this year.

A few minutes later, he just barged right in. No knock. Just flung it open like he expected to find... what? An empty bed? Blood? A chalk outline? Instead, he got me with no makeup, my hair down, sitting cross-legged on the duvet in an old black t-shirt I'd found that felt three sizes too big.

He'd looked like someone had punched the air back into his lungs. Maybe it was his... and he wanted it back. I don't know.

But then... he sat down on the bed with me and asked me something, and that was somehow the moment my mouth chose to spill my biggest secret, the whole ugly reason I ran. Because sure, why not add "trauma confessional" to the night's highlight reel of "got fingered by my boss."

I flopped backward onto the bed and stared at the ceiling, my heart finally settling into something like a normal rhythm. The mattress was ridiculously soft. My body sank into it like it was trying to swallow me whole.

I could still feel his hand in mine. The way it had happened so quietly, almost like an accident. He'd been sitting close, jaw clenched, eyes dark with anger that wasn't for me for once, and then his palm had just... found mine. Slid in, laced together, held. Big and warm and certain.

He'd listened to every horrible detail, every memory I usually kept locked in a box labeled do not open without tequila, and instead of flinching or offering some empty "I'm so sorry," he'd just gotten more and more furious on my behalf. Not at me. At them.

At my father. At the man I'd almost been handed to, like a gift he'd already paid for.

"I'm glad you ran," he'd said, voice low and lethal. "You did what you had to do to get out. They're the ones who should be ashamed."

The words had hit somewhere deep in my ribcage, in a place that had never been defended before. For a second, I'd thought I might cry. It had been a long time since I'd cried over all of it. I'd just squeezed his hand harder, clinging like a coward to that tiny island of safety he'd offered.

Then his phone had buzzed. He'd looked at the screen like it personally offended him, then at me like he didn't want to move. Like the universe was dragging him away by the collar.

"I have to take this," he'd said, sounding rough. "Stay here. Don't open the door for anyone but me."

And now he was gone, voice a muted rumble somewhere beyond the wall, and I was alone with my thoughts, my afterglow, and a thousand things I did not have the emotional bandwidth to process.

I turned my head and looked at the closed door. For a heartbeat, I seriously considered getting up and trying to listen. Then I remembered every bad thriller I'd ever watched and decided, nope, I wasn't doing the creeping-in-hallways thing.

Instead, my brain chose violence and rewound to earlier. To the hallway. To the way his mouth had hovered over mine, asking without asking. To the way his fingers had slid under my panties and my body had answered, instantly, like it had been waiting specifically for this touch, this man, this moment.

The worst part was how fast the shame tried to rush in behind it. Not from him. From me. Old programming. Good girls don't. Pure girls don't.

Godly girls keep their knees together, their legs closed, and their hearts in little locked boxes with their father's name on the key.

I'd run from that life, from that marriage, from that god. Changed my name. Burned the bridge. But sometimes the smoke still got in my lungs.

After two awkward, nothing encounters in my early twenties, I'd honestly started to believe I was broken. Like maybe you couldn't just peel those sermons off once they were stuck. Like maybe something in me had permanently hardened around them.

The first was a boy I'd met at community college. He'd been kind enough, fumbling and earnest, all "is this okay?" while I lay there stiff and numb, willing myself to feel anything beyond vaguely uncomfortable and ashamed at what my parents would think if they knew.

The second had been chosen like homework at the bar I'd worked at. If I just did it right, if I picked the right guy, then the switch would flip. Spoiler: it did not. It was like my body said, "We did our best, but it's still a no from us."

The girl experiment hadn't helped either. Sweet, soft, kissed like she meant it. And still, that same flat line inside. No spark. No drop. Nothing.

So I'd decided, fine, sex is just not for you, Evie Grace. Go be good at bartending and sarcasm instead. Have a good time with friends, but romance was just not in the cards. Save it for yourself when you absolutely have to, and pretend it doesn't bug you that everyone else seems to be living in full color while you're stuck in grayscale.

And then tonight happened. And... my breath caught just reliving the memory that happened moments ago. Like... how? How did he know exactly what to do to my body to make me shatter? And... could he do it again?

I shifted on the bed, thighs pressing together as my body gave me a smug little reminder of exactly how not broken I'd felt with his hand between my legs. Heat flickered low in my belly just from remembering the way his voice had gone wrecked when he said "Mine," the way it had punched out of him.

There was nothing grayscale about that.

It wasn't just the orgasm. It was the way he watched me. Like I wasn't something dirty or stupid or doomed, but something he'd starved for. Craved. The way he didn't look ashamed of wanting me. The way, when he'd practically ripped open the door, terror had ripped through his expression naked and unguarded.

Maybe I wasn't broken. Maybe I'd just never been safe enough to find out what I actually wanted. The thought made me feel dizzy. Or maybe that was just the crash from the high. Either way, my limbs felt heavier with every breath, sleep crawling up from the edges and wrapping around me like water.

I curled onto my side, tugging the sheet over my hips. The room was quiet except for the faint murmur of his voice through the wall and the soft thud of my own heartbeat in my ears.

Tonight, I'd let a man touch me and actually wanted it. Wanted him. I'd told him the worst thing about my past, and he hadn't flinched or judged or tried to fix me. He'd just gotten angry for me and held my hand like it was the most natural thing in the world.

Lucifer Morningstar was absolutely a walking red flag. He was wealthy and secretive and way too intense, and something was going on I couldn't figure out, not without him.

But he'd also just proved, in no uncertain terms, that I wasn't dead inside.

My eyes drifted shut, thoughts blurring at the edges. Maybe I wasn't broken. That idea was almost more terrifying than the shadows on my balcony.

Sleep didn't ease me in, it yanked me under. One blink, I was in the guest room, the next I was standing barefoot on... nothing. It wasn't ground, not really —just this endless soft light under my feet, like mist that had decided to glow. Above me, there was a sky, but it wasn't finished yet, if that makes any sense at all.

The color hovered in streaks, waiting, like someone had left paint swirling in water and walked away. And I knew, somehow, it was mine to finish.

My hand lifted on its own. When I moved my fingers, the light answered. Lines of gold, pink, green, and deep blue unfurled from my fingertips, arcing out in slow ribbons. Wherever they landed, something started to take shape.

A river, first. It spilled out from under my hand in a silver curve, carving into nothing and leaving behind banks and stones as it went. I didn't think about it, I just... wanted it, and it was there. The water caught the not-quite-sun and threw it back, ten times brighter.

I should've been freaking out, but in the dream it all felt normal, like muscle memory. Like I'd done this a thousand times.

"You're doing it again." A voice came from behind me, warm and low, threading through the air like it belonged there. I turned.

He stood at the edge of the forming river, bare feet in nothing, the light pooling around his ankles instead of under them. No shirt, no suit, no stupid watch. Just a body built in clean, impossible lines and shoulders dusted in something like starlight. His hair was longer, past his shoulders in soft waves, catching the glow like it was threaded with fire.

And his eyes. Pale. Too pale. A blue that looked like it remembered being part of the sky.

Luc, my brain supplied automatically. Except I didn't know his name here, not in the dream. I just knew the way my chest did a strange, familiar pull when he looked at me.

"I'm working," I heard myself say. My voice sounded... different. Clearer. Older. Younger. Like, there was no rust on it at all.

He smiled, and it was softer than anything I'd ever seen on his face. Curious, not cutting. Like he'd stumbled on something holy and hadn't decided whether to touch it yet.

"You don't have to hide it," he said. "I like watching."

Heat crept up my neck in the dream, but it wasn't embarrassment. It was... shyness. The good kind. The kind that comes when somebody sees you doing the one thing you're sure you were made to do.

"This part's tricky," I said, turning back to the river. My hands moved again, unthinking. I sang the words to a song I didn't know. Didn't remember. And I dipped my fingers into the air above the water and pulled up, and from the banks, green erupted. Trees, thick and wild, exploded into being, leaves unfurling in slow-motion like time-lapse footage. Flowers burst out in colors I didn't recognize, scents hitting the air in waves, sharp and sweet and new.

He came closer, careful, like he didn't want to

startle me. His presence slid into place at my side, just behind my shoulder. Close enough, I could feel his attention, like heat.

"How?" he asked, and there it was, that same hunger I'd seen in the bar when he looked at me. "How do you know where to put everything?"

"I don't," I said, but my hand kept moving, and I began to hum again. I traced a curve in the air, and a small hill rose up, dotted with low shrubs. "I just... listen."

"To what?"

"The way it wants to be," I answered, like that made perfect sense. Like hills and rivers and trees all had a preference, and I was just... respecting it.

He was quiet for a beat. I could feel his gaze move, not over me, but through what I was making, tracking every line of light like he was memorizing it.

"Will you teach me?" he asked finally, almost shy.

I laughed, surprised, and it rang out over the unfinished landscape, echoing back to us. "You don't want to learn this. It's slow."

"I have time." He said it like he meant forever.

I turned my head to look at him, and for a second, my vision stuttered. His face blurred, shifting between this bright, untroubled version and the man from the bar, the one in the tailored suit and the haunted eyes. Two images overlaid. Same mouth. Same cheekbones. Same eyes.

My heart lurched. "Lucifer," I breathed.

The dream shivered. For a split second, everything glitched, like a skipped frame in a movie. The river flickered to neon. The sky darkened. The trees became just like the fake ficus on my balcony. The glow under my feet turned to poured concrete.

Then I was somewhere else. A garden, but not the

one I'd just grown. This one was finished. Wild in that perfectly balanced way that only happens when someone has been obsessively intentional about every inch and then stepped back to let it go feral.

Fruit hung heavy on branches over my head, jeweled and impossible, colors too saturated to be real. The air was warm and humming, full of bees and birds and something else, some low, thrumming music with no source.

He was there, too.

Sitting under a tree, head tilted back against the trunk, eyes half closed. Wings—yes, wings, my brain just let that go like it was normal—were folded tight to his back, the brightest white I'd ever seen, edged in a glow that felt too sharp to look at. His hair looked damp, like he'd just stepped out of a river, little droplets tracing the line of his throat.

I walked toward him without meaning to, grass cool under my bare feet. He heard me, eyes opening fully, and whatever lazy peace had been in his expression sharpened into something like joy.

"Ediphiel," he said, and the name hit me like being dropped.

That wasn't my name. Except... it was. Here, it was. The sound of it rang in the air, chiming against the leaves.

I swallowed. "You're not supposed to be here," I said, and I knew that, somehow. Knew that he was late for something. Knew that if anyone looked for him, they'd find him missing, and it would matter.

He smiled, small and stubborn. "I wanted to see what you made next."

I looked down at my hands. There was dirt under my nails, light threaded through the lines of my palms like tiny constellations, as if I'd been planting stars.

"I can't stop once I start," I heard myself admit.

"I know," he said. "That's why I came back."

He reached for me then, not to grab or drag. Just held his hand out, palm up, like an invitation.

Something in my chest squeezed, painful and sweet at the same time. My fingers twitched. The moment stretched—

And then the sound of my own name, Evie, tore through the dream like someone yanking a needle out of a record.

The garden shattered. Light broke apart into pixels. His face splintered into a hundred pieces, all of them him and not him, and for one dizzy heartbeat, I saw both: the angel under the tree, wings glowing, and the man in the hotel suite, shirt collar open, eyes too pale and too tired.

Then I was staring at the ceiling of the guest room, heart hammering, breath sawing in and out of my chest like I'd sprinted.

There had been a name, I knew there had. Someone had said it, or I had, or the air itself had, and for one electric second, it felt like it belonged to me the way your own heartbeat belongs to you, unquestioned, inevitable.

And then it started to slip. Like a dream the second you wake up, like smoke you try to fist in your hands, it thinned and scattered the harder I reached for it. I chased it anyway, panic-flailing in my own head, repeating the shape of the sound, trying to catch the first syllable, the last, anything.

Nothing. Just the ache of almost-remembering.

My name was Evie. Evie Grace. I was just a bartender in a hotel. A life made of receipts and shifts and late-night playlists. Not... whatever that had been.

I pressed the heels of my hands into my eyes until colors bloomed behind my lids, like I could scrub the images away. Rivers from nothing. Light in my hands. Him, barefoot in some impossible garden, saying my not-name like it belonged to me.

"That was a dream," I whispered to the empty room. "Just a dream."

It didn't feel like one.

The memory of his face from the dream sat wrong against the real one in my head. Wrong and right at the same time. The way he watched me there—curious, reverent, like I was some mystery he actually wanted to understand—felt too familiar. Like I'd seen it before. Like I'd seen *him* before.

CHAPTER SEVENTEEN

Lucifer

"Oh, good," I said flatly. "Your propositions always end so well for everyone involved."

"Lucifer," Damien drawled, smug as ever. "You are always so put out when I offer you gifts."

I scoffed. "I've seen your gifts. They usually end in screams."

"Only when they're unappreciated."

"Get on with it."

He laughed, but there was tension beneath it. A hitch he didn't quite mask. "It's her, isn't it? Evie. The way you look at her... and the way she looks at you."

"Careful."

"No, no. Hear me out," he said quickly. "The way she looks at you, Luce—like she's remembering something, too. That's not coincidence. That's... residue."

"You've got ten seconds before I hang up."

"You've noticed Lilith keeps telling you not to fall in love, right?" he pressed. "It's not because she's worried you'll lose everything. She's terrified that she will."

I stilled.

Damien's voice dropped, losing some of its swagger. "You've heard the rumors. About the missing page from the Book of Names."

"What about it?" I growled.

"I've never seen the page," he said carefully. "Never read it. Never touched it. But I helped move something once. Long ago. I didn't know what it was then. Just that Lilith didn't want Heaven finding it... and didn't want you finding it either."

My grip tightened on the phone. "Where."

A pause. Longer this time. When he spoke again, the humor was gone. "She didn't tell me what it was. Just where it had to rest. A place already ruined enough to hide one more secret."

"Damien."

"She said it had to go somewhere the earth had already given up on," he murmured. "Somewhere nothing would grow. Somewhere you used to go when you thought no one was watching."

The words slid under my skin like glass.

"The Garden of the Forsaken," he said.

The name hit me like a blade.

Memories slammed into place, clear and brutal, unfiltered for the first time in eons. It had been my obsession. My failure. My graveyard.

The Garden of the Forsaken.

I used to kneel in its soil with bloodied hands, planting things that never took root. Saplings snapped under their own weight. Blossoms curled in on themselves before they ever opened. Everything I touched there turned hollow —leaves brittle, stems black-veined, petals like ash between my fingers.

The air always smelled like burnt sugar and rot. Sweetness spoiled. Promise ruined.

I told myself I was building something. Reclaiming something. A second Eden carved from memory and rage.

But every time I returned—and I returned often—the trees were barer, the ground more cracked, the silence heavier. I'd sink to my knees, dig until my knuckles split, and still—nothing. No life. No light. Just the twisted trunk of the Tree of Knowledge watching like a witness too tired to judge me anymore.

I never knew what I was trying to grow there.

Only that something was missing. Something the earth couldn't give back. Not light. Not grace. Not power.

Her—Evie. But her name... was different then.

And Lilith had buried that absence in the one place I kept returning to without understanding why.

Right under my feet.

Suddenly—the flashes came. So fast they nearly knocked me to my knees.

Not all at once, not cleanly, just a rush of impressions that stole the breath from my lungs and left me reeling. Laughter threaded through trees, bright and unafraid. Sunlight spilled across skin like it had been invited there. Hands in water, shaping its course with a patience that felt... intimate. Familiar.

I remembered a woman. She was singing to flowers that hadn't bloomed yet. I remembered watching her from the edge of the garden, afraid to step too close because I knew if I did, I'd never leave again. I remembered her turning—catching me there—and smiling like she'd been waiting for me to come all along. But I couldn't remember her face, her name.

And, worst of all, I remembered how I loved her —truly loved her. Not in hunger. Not in conquest. But in awe. Like she was the one thing in all of creation I hadn't been made to command or obey or worship.

And then it slipped away, the images thinning, dissolving before they could settle into anything solid, leaving only the hollow certainty that something vital had brushed past me and moved on.

Outside, lightning split the sky, sharp and blinding, tearing across the night without warning. The air inside the penthouse went electric, alive against my skin.

It felt like the world had taken note and like something old had shifted its stance, not remembered. But no longer entirely forgotten.

Damien barked out a laugh. "Did you fucking see that?" he crowed. "If He didn't know before, He sure as hell does now."

The First Light. That motherfucker. He would come looking. Did He know? Would He come for her?

I staggered a step back, heart racing, the scent of ozone biting at my nose. My body hummed like a struck chord.

Her name—god, her name— It was right there. On the tip of my tongue. Just a breath away. But it wouldn't come. Just the ache. The grief. The feeling that something sacred had been stolen from me, and I'd let it happen.

How had I forgotten? For eons?

Damien's voice pulled me back. "You're quiet. Remembering something interesting?"

"You think Lilith hid it there?" My voice came out rougher than I intended.

"Where else would she hide the one thing that

could ruin her plans? The one place you'd never willingly revisit, because it reminds you too much of what you lost."

"What's your angle?" I snapped. "Why tell me any of this?"

"Because," he said softly, dropping all pretense, "Lilith's playing a dangerous game. And when it blows up in her pretty little face, I intend to survive. You want answers. I want leverage. We both get what we want."

"You'd better pray you're right," I said.

"When have either of us prayed?" he chuckled softly. Then, after a beat, his voice shifted—careful, calculated. "Look, I can get you back in."

"Into Hell," I echoed flatly.

"Yes."

"Lilith sealed every known gate. I've looked."

"Every *known* gate," Damien repeated smugly. "Lucky for you, I've been around long enough, I'm good at knowing things I'm not supposed to."

My jaw tightened. "The Garden of the Forsaken is vast. You might as well tell me she dropped it in the ocean and expect me to fish it out."

He laughed softly, low and amused. "Oh, you know exactly where to look."

"Do I?"

"You really don't remember?" Damien's voice turned almost sympathetic, mockingly gentle. "Think harder, Lucifer. Where else would she put your truth if not beneath the one place you could never bring yourself to destroy?"

My chest tightened painfully. "You're being cryptic."

"Consider it a kindness," Damien murmured. "If Lilith knew I was guiding you directly to the grave beneath that withered, miserable tree—well, I'd be the next thing she buried."

I went cold.

"How the fuck do you know about that?" I asked, voice dangerously low.

He hesitated a fraction of a second. "I told you— I'm good at knowing things I shouldn't."

"That's not an answer."

"No, but it's the only one you're getting," Damien said, tone sharpening. "Do you want my help or not?"

I stared blankly at the wall, my pulse thundering. The grave beneath the Tree of Knowledge—my shameful little secret, buried so deep no one should've ever known it existed. I'd carved it myself and hidden it beneath bitter roots. But Damien knew. Somehow, Damien fucking knew.

"So," he continued smoothly, filling the silence, "are you in?"

"I need to think about it."

He laughed, richly amused. "Ah, Luce. That sounds like a yes to me."

"I'll call you back," I said roughly.

His voice sharpened suddenly, losing its lazy arrogance. "We don't have a lot of time. You've felt it, haven't you? There are Watchers everywhere— even Lilith's shadows are stirring. The longer you wait, the more dangerous this gets."

I heard a soft creak from behind me, a door easing open. Evie.

"I'll call you back," I repeated firmly and ended the call, turning slowly to find her standing there, watching me with cautious eyes. And for once, I didn't have a single clever lie ready.

She stood there in the hallway, barefoot, eyes wide, like she'd just stepped out of a dream and wasn't sure what world she'd landed in. And the sight of her — *Fuck*.

Another flash hit me like a fist to the chest. Running along the edge of a river, bare feet kicking up dew from grass that hadn't existed until she'd willed it into being. Her dark curls whipped around her face with a mind of their own. A gown of silk clung to her like water, flowing white and luminous. She turned to glance back at me—eyes wild, laughing, so alive—and I remember thinking nothing in all of Eden had ever looked so divine. Not the trees. Not the stars. Not even the First Light Himself. Just her.

I blinked, and the hallway returned. But I could still feel the river under my feet. Still hear the sound of her laughter carried by the wind that hadn't existed in eons.

And I swear—demons help me—I could feel a blush crawling up my cheek. A blush. This was fucking ridiculous.

I cleared my throat and turned away fast, stalking toward the kitchen like I had somewhere urgent to be.

"You hungry?" I asked over my shoulder, voice gruffer than I meant it to be. "There's food. I can make something."

What could I do to avoid telling her what I just figured out? Anything. Everything. Would she even believe me if I did tell her?

"You cook?" she quipped behind me, thick with disbelief.

I turned—too quickly. She nearly bumped into me, stopping just short, her hands braced against my chest. She looked up, surprised, breath catching. And fuck, she was close. Too close.

All I wanted to do was pull her into my arms. Press my face into her neck. Breathe her in until the ache stopped. Until the memory stopped bleeding behind my ribs.

I wanted to go back to Eden. Now. Forever.

But instead, I scoffed and stepped back, stuffing all that want behind a crooked smile. "I... cook... sort of," I said, like the sight of her so near wasn't the only thing barely holding me together.

She raised an eyebrow, hands on her hips. "Sort of."

I gestured at the fridge. "I mean, I don't burn toast. That's got to count for something."

She gave me a half-smile. Testing me. "Can you make me a BLT?"

I stared at her. A BLT. As if that was a standard request. As if I wasn't seconds away from unraveling at her feet. But I was Lucifer. And I could lie with a smile.

"Yeah," I said. "Sure. Bacon. Lettuce. Tomato. Toast. I can assemble ingredients. I'm not a savage."

She leaned back against the counter, arms crossed, watching me now with something between amusement and suspicion.

And as I opened the fridge, pulling things out like it was just another goddamn Sunday, I kept my face neutral. Because if I let anything show —if I so much as looked at her too long—she'd see it. All of it.

The memories. The recognition. The way she used to sculpt rivers with her hands and smile at me like I was something more than what I became. And the moment it slipped? There'd be no coming back.

Sometime between cooking the bacon and toasting the bread, she climbed onto one of the barstools at the island. Elbows on the counter, chin in her hand, watching me like I was some unsolvable puzzle she wasn't sure she wanted to crack.

I didn't look at her for too long. Couldn't look at her. Not while the memories still echoed. Not while the phantom of her was still trailing across the backs of my eyelids every time I blinked.

Instead, I focused on the sandwich. Bacon. Lettuce. Tomato. Mayo. Bread toasted just right. I sliced it on the diagonal, like some part of me knew what she used to like, even if she didn't.

Then I poured her a glass of milk and slid it across the counter beside the plate.

She blinked at it. "Milk?"

"It's a classic pairing."

She wrinkled her brow, "It's kind of weird."

"You're welcome."

She gave me a tired little smile, but it didn't reach her eyes. And I—I couldn't take it.

"I need to make a call," I said, already backing away from the island, reaching for the phone burning in my pocket.

"Oh," Her smile fell. "I thought... you'd eat with me."

That stopped me cold. It was such a small thing. A sandwich. A moment. And it gutted me.

I turned my face away, jaw clenched. "I'm not hungry," I said, and it came out rougher than I meant. Almost cruel. "I have some work to do."

Before she could say anything else, I turned and walked away. No. I fled. I—Lucifer. The Morningstar. King of the Damned. The goddamn Devil himself. I ran from a woman holding a sandwich and too much of my past in her eyes. Made it to my room, shut the door, and leaned against it for half a second like it could hold me together.

It couldn't.

My hand was already shaking as I pulled out my

phone. I hit the number. Damien answered on the second ring.

"Well, well," he purred. "Change your mind?"

I stared at the far wall, voice low and unsteady. "When do we leave?" I asked.

He exhaled with the satisfaction of someone who already knew the answer was yes. "Tomorrow. During the day. Quietly." He paused. "Demons are less active in daylight—you know that. If we move before dusk, we'll have a better shot at slipping past her wards unnoticed."

I glanced toward the window. The sun wasn't up yet, but the sky was paling—soft gray pushing at the corners of the night. That hour when everything felt like it could still go either way.

"How long?" I asked.

"Two days. Three, if you get sentimental down there."

"I won't."

"So... what are you going to tell her?"

I didn't rise to the bait. My mind was already turning—calculating.

Evie was still out there, probably rinsing her plate or sitting in silence, wondering why I couldn't look her in the eye. And now I was going to vanish on her for two full days. I'd have to tell her something. Something plausible. Not too complicated. Not too close to the truth.

"I'll think of something," I muttered.

There was a pause, quieter than before. "Do you even know why you're doing this?" he asked. "Is it about the page, or Lilith, or is it about her?"

I didn't answer. Because deep down, I knew the truth. And I wasn't ready to say it out loud.

The call ended, and the room felt too still. I stood there for a long moment, the phone still in my hand,

Damien's voice still echoing in my ear—*Tomorrow. During the day. Quietly.* Back into Hell. Back to the Garden. Back to the Rot.

I raked a hand through my hair and started pacing. I'd need to tell Evie something. Something simple. Believable. Just enough to get her to stop looking at me with those searching eyes that made me feel like I was coming apart seam by seam.

It couldn't be anything dramatic. No danger. No mystery. I had a feeling she'd chase that. What about business? She'd see through that in a second, wouldn't she? It had to be mundane. Forgettable. A nothing excuse from a man who didn't know how to stay in one place.

"I've got to leave town for a couple of days." Too vague.

"There's someone I need to meet." Too suspicious.

I stopped pacing, hands braced against my black dresser.

"I promised someone I'd help them move." By the Nine Hells. That sounded like I'd lost a bet with a mortal.

I sighed and muttered under my breath, "You used to command legions, and now you're out here inventing errands like a guilty boyfriend."

I looked at myself in the mirror. The expression staring back wasn't amused. What the hell was I supposed to say? I didn't want to lie to her. Not really. But I couldn't tell her the truth. Not yet.

She didn't remember Eden. She didn't remember me. And if I told her now —if I showed her who she really was before she was ready—I'd lose her all over again. I swallowed hard.

Something with distance, I thought. But not too much. I tried again. "There's someone from my past I need to deal with. It'll take a few days."

That one settled. Heavy. Vague, but not untrue. Not entirely. And maybe... she wouldn't ask too many questions.

CHAPTER EIGHTEEN

Evie

He never came back to the kitchen, so after I ate, I went back to the guest room. I didn't mean to fall asleep. I just closed my eyes for a second—bone-deep tired, soul-hollow tired from the weight of everything I'd said. I don't even know why I'd said it. I'd just spilled out of me like blood from a wound.

And then I was back there again. It felt so familiar. Like, somehow, I knew this place.

The air shimmered, soft and golden, like the world was exhaling. My bare feet pressed into cool moss that pulsed like a heartbeat, and when I sank to my knees, I just knew instinctively what to do. Where my fingers touched the soil, life burst forward. Vines curling up from nothing, unfurling into trees heavy with fruit I couldn't name. I thought of sweetness, and they bloomed. I thought of thirst, and a river carved its way beside me, singing over stone.

Was I dreaming? Something kept whispering this place wasn't a dream. This was a memory. This place—it felt so familiar, like something I'd loved into being.

And then I felt someone—him. Not close. Just watching.

I stood up and turned in circles, my hands streaked in dirt and sunlight. On the ridge of a distant mountain, a figure stood haloed in light. Was it him?

He felt... older. Wilder. Beautiful in a way that ached. Like he burned from the inside, like light leaked from his skin where it couldn't be contained.

This version of him was different. Barefoot. Weather-worn. Radiant in a way no mortal could be. He wore white pants—silk or linen, I couldn't tell this far away—slung low on his hips, the fabric catching the wind like it had been born to move. No shirt. Just golden skin and the kind of body that made it hard to breathe.

He looked like he'd been carved from the sky itself —cut from sunlight and sea breeze, with shadows still clinging to the lines of his chest.

But there was a softness to him, too, like he'd once held stars in his hands and knew better than to brag about it.

There was a glint of gold where his eyes should be, and something behind him—not a shadow. His... *wings*. They arched wide and gleaming, feathered in white and edged in light.

I woke up, gasping. My cheeks were damp. My chest hurt. I was still lying curled on top of the covers, my clothes twisted and one arm numb from how I'd slept. The dream clung to me like steam on a mirror—already fading, but somehow still lodged deep in my lungs.

The room was dark. Still, I felt like I was glowing inside, as if some fragment of that world had come with me.

I didn't know where that dream came from or

what it meant. It didn't feel like a fantasy, but some part of me—some ridiculous part—wondered if this was something else. Something older. It felt like *before*. Like once, I'd made the world. Me. And he had watched me do it. Which, obviously, was insane because none of that was real.

It wasn't a past life. It wasn't fate or prophecy or cosmic design. It was just... *him*. The way he looked at me. The way his voice dipped when he said my name. The way something inside me went quiet and hungry every time he got too close. That was all this was. Attraction. Intense. Irrational. Dangerous. And I needed to get my shit together before I drowned in it.

I lay there for a long time, blinking into the dark, heart pounding like I'd run for miles. I pressed my hand flat against my chest like I could hold the echo of it in place. Like I could keep the dream from slipping through my fingers. But it had already started to unravel—details blurring at the edges. Still... the feeling lingered. Like a secret I wasn't ready to say out loud.

I swallowed. My throat was dry. I stood up, still unsteady, and went to splash cold water on my face in the bathroom sink. When I looked in the mirror, I half-expected someone else to be staring back. Someone brighter. Someone ancient.

But it was just me. Eyes too tired. Pink hair a mess. I braced my hands on the edge of the sink.

"Pull it together, Evie," I muttered. "You don't believe in that shit, remember?"

But even as I said it, I knew I was lying. Because something in me had shifted. Like a door I didn't know existed had opened inside me.

I crawled back under the covers and managed to sleep like the dead. No dreams. Just a long, uninterrupted stretch of nothing. Five whole hours. I hadn't slept like that in—I couldn't even remember. Weeks? Months? Ever? It was the kind of sleep that left you feeling like someone had hit the reset button. I didn't wake up in a panic. Didn't wake up aching. I just… woke on my own.

And maybe that's what threw me because it felt good. Safe, even.

I never felt safe, usually. Not anywhere. Not for a long time. But here—in that bed—I'd finally let go. No one waiting outside the door. No shadows, no threats, no hands that only knew how to take. Just comfort. And sleep.

When I made it back downstairs, headed toward the bar in the evening, hair still damp from the world's fastest shower, everything looked the same. The lobby. The casino. The gleaming bottles lined up behind the bar were waiting for my hands.

Everything was normal. Right up until it wasn't. I was mid-shelf, sliding a bottle of overpriced tequila into place, when I felt it. A flicker. Not big. Not dramatic. Just a shift. Like the light in the room had changed direction.

And when I turned, I saw him. Luc. I hadn't seen him up in the penthouse all day, but he was leaning casually near the velvet ropes at the front desk, deep in conversation with someone I didn't recognize.

What stopped me was the light. The way it kissed the edges of his hair, like it knew him. Like it couldn't help but reach for him. It was that same warm gold from my dream, soft and too bright, catching on the red strands in a way that made them almost glow.

I stared. Just for a second. Too long. Then I blinked. Looked away.

Coincidence. It had to be. I'd just dreamed about

him because of everything that happened last night. The way he touched me. It hadn't been soft or sweet. It had been divine.

The way his fingers curled inside me like he belonged there. Like I was something to be opened and read. The way his palm pressed tight against my throat, holding—not hurting, just controlling—and how every part of me lit up under that pressure.

It should've scared me. But it didn't. It thrilled me. The fear. The surrender. The pulse-pounding, limb-shaking pleasure. And then—that word, "Mine." Low. Ragged.

Possessive in a way that should've set off alarm bells. But it didn't. It set something else off entirely. Because when he said it—when he growled it against my skin while wringing every last drop of pleasure from my body—I believed him.

And worse? I loved it. I absolutely loved it. I wanted it. The way he claimed me without asking, like my body already knew who it belonged to. The way the word slid beneath my skin and took root, deep and dangerous.

I wanted more. More of that. More of him.

But... was that a good idea? Was any of this? Because the line between desire and destruction was razor-thin with him—and we hadn't just stepped over it. I'd jumped, blindfolded, with my arms wide open.

And now I was standing here, blinking at the shelves like I hadn't just replayed the entire night in vivid, high-def, body-humming detail, while he stood across the lobby—glowing like a dream I couldn't shake.

When I glanced up again, he was already watching me. Not smirking. Not cocky. Just those pale blue eyes, like he saw something in me he recognized. I looked away. Fast. Shoved a bottle back onto the shelf as if it had personally offended me.

It was just a dream. It was just foreplay. And it was just a really, really bad idea. But my body didn't care. My heart didn't listen. Because somewhere deep down—beneath the fear and the questions and the warning bells—I still wanted him to say it again.

Mine.

But there was another question—the one that started to whisper as soon as the memory faded and the aftershocks stopped rattling through me. Was it even a good idea to keep staying here? Was I really in danger? Or was I just letting my trauma paint shadows on the walls again?

Or worse... Was he? Was it just his excuse to keep me close? Was there something in me he wanted—something he didn't plan to let go of?

My chest tightened, breath catching behind my ribs. God, I didn't know. And that was the worst part.

Because everything in that penthouse screamed him. The dark velvet furniture. The bookshelves. The whiskey. The goddamn scent of his cologne still clinging to the air like a memory I couldn't scrub out. He surrounded me. Wrapped in him. Breathing him in with every step I took.

And maybe that's why I couldn't think straight. Maybe it was messing with my head—the comfort, the danger, the hands, the whispers in the dark. The dreams I couldn't explain. The heat I couldn't forget. The way he looked at me like he knew me.

Maybe I needed some space. Some clarity. A minute to just be me, without him standing so close

I couldn't tell where I ended and he began.

I swallowed and set the bottle down a little too hard. The glass clinked against the shelf. I needed air. I needed answers. I just needed five minutes without some brooding man short-circuiting my entire nervous system, even if part of me wanted to hear him say it again.

I was still trying to decide if I needed to fake my own death when Destiny walked in.

She took one look at my face, dropped her bag on the floor, and grabbed my arm. "Oh, hell no. Back room. Now."

"But—"

"Nope. Not doing this with you looking like you just emotionally spiraled through a Taylor Swift album. Spill it."

She yanked me into the tiny break room, where the lockers smelled like hairspray, tequila, and trauma. She was already slipping her apron on and tying it around her waist as she tossed a glance at me over one shoulder.

Today's outfit? Black plaid schoolgirl skirt. White Oxford tied at the waist, collar popped like sin. Ripped fishnets. Platform Mary Janes that added three inches and two felony charges to her strut. Destiny was chaos and eyeliner and the only person I trusted not to run screaming when I said something insane.

I stood there, buzzing like a live wire.

She opened her locker, pulled out a compact mirror, and started touching up her lipstick—fire engine red, of course. "You've got thirty seconds before I assume the look on your face is either sex or murder. Hopefully both. Go."

And just like that, I cracked. "I didn't sleep with him," I blurted. "But—God—he devoured me with his hands. Like I was the only thing he'd ever wanted."

Her brows shot up, but she didn't interrupt. Just kept applying her lipstick like she was painting war stripes.

"His hands were everywhere. He—he wrapped his hand around my throat and—" I dropped my face into my hands. "I liked it. Destiny. I liked it so much."

A pause. Then, a muttered, "Hot. Keep going."

"And I told him. About me. About why I ran. About what they were gonna do to me. About the church. My dad. Everything."

Now she looked at me fully, lips parted.

"I never tell anyone that stuff. But I told him. And then I passed out. And I had this crazy dream." I started pacing. "It wasn't a normal dream. It felt real. I was in this place—this world—I think I was making it. With my hands. Trees, rivers, light. And he was there. Not the version of him we know —like, not tall-dark-and-fucks-me-stupid, but like... ancient. Glowing. Wings, Destiny. He had angel wings."

Destiny blinked once. Then, she calmly slipped her compact back into her locker.

"So you got fucked so good it unlocked your ancestral memory," she said. "Got it. Continue."

I pointed at her, eyes wild. "I'm serious. I can't explain it, but it means something. And then I saw him today, and the light hit his hair just like in the dream, and I'm freaking the hell out because maybe I've lost my mind. Maybe I made the whole thing up because I haven't been thinking straight since he touched me and—"

Destiny stepped forward and gripped my shoulders. "Evie. Breathe."

I did. Barely.

She gave me a look. "You done?"

"No," I shook my head. "Not even close."

She looked over her shoulder at the bar. "I mean, we could... fake a gas leak? But first—you want advice or validation?"

"...Both?"

She grinned. "Then you came to the right slut."

Destiny released my shoulders, gave me a once-over like she was calculating damage, and sighed. "Okay. First of all—yes, it sounds like the man absolutely rearranged your internal organs. I support this. Ten out of ten, would recommend."

I groaned and dropped into the one chair beside the lockers, burying my face in my hands again. "Destiny..."

"Let me finish."

She perched on the broken barstool against the wall, legs crossed at the knee, platform heel swinging. "Second of all—Evie, babe, what happened to you was not just sex. Not the way you're shaking right now. Not the way you looked when I walked in. This?" She gestured to all of me. "This is post-revelation, not post-orgasm."

I looked up at her, face burning. "So what, I had a dream, and now I think I was an angel? That's insane."

"Or maybe that dream was the first time your brain wasn't just trying to keep you alive."

She gave me a soft look.

"When was the last time you thought about who you want to be instead of who you have to be?"

That cracked something in me. I looked down at my hands. They were still trembling.

"I felt like I created something in that dream," I whispered. "Like I was... good. Not broken. Not ashamed. Just — whole."

Destiny's expression softened. She crouched down next to me and bumped her shoulder against mine.

"Maybe it wasn't a dream. Maybe it was a reminder."

I arched an eyebrow at her.

"And maybe," she added, "that man entered your life for a reason. Not to save you. But to wake you the fuck up."

"But what if it's a trap?" I asked quietly. "What if I'm not safe here? What if I'm just... getting played?"

She was quiet for a second. Then said, gently, "Then, you'll know. Because you're not the girl you were back then. You're smarter now. Stronger. And you've got me. I'll burn it all down with you if it turns out he's the wrong kind of monster."

I swallowed hard.

She nudged me again. "But babe? You also deserve pleasure. And softness. And someone who says your name like it's a prayer. Just... make sure you're giving your heart to someone who's willing to earn it. Not just claim it."

I leaned into her shoulder, letting my head rest there a second. She let me.

Then, with a little smirk, she said, "Also, if you do turn out to be an ancient celestial being with a hot angel boyfriend, you better not leave me behind in the apocalypse."

I laughed, half-choked. "You'll be the first person I smuggle into Heaven."

"Good. I want cloud-side seats and a bottomless mimosa bar."

CHAPTER NINETEEN

Lucifer

I walked into the bar just before closing.

Most of the patrons had cleared out. The lights had dimmed to a low, sleepy hum, like even the room was ready to shut its eyes. And there she was, Evie, behind the bar, cleaning up like she was trying to scrub off the whole damn day.

She glanced up when I entered. Her expression didn't shift much, but her shoulders dropped just a hair. So subtle most wouldn't notice. I did.

Then came the smirk.

"Wow," she said. "You really know how to make a girl feel stalked."

I didn't bother smiling. "You're done for the night."

She arched an eyebrow. "Thanks, Dad."

I didn't answer. Just walked around the bar and offered my arm. "Come on."

She made a dramatic show of rolling her eyes and tossing the rag, but she grabbed her bag and followed. The elevator ride up was silent—until it wasn't.

She leaned against the mirrored wall, arms

crossed, that teasing gleam flickering to life in her eyes. "You going to tell me what's up, or —"

"It's late," I said. My tone clipped. "You shouldn't walk alone."

"Really?" Her head tilted. "Because I could've sworn we left the patriarchy back in the last century."

I didn't respond. I'd stood on the roof earlier, watching the stars tilt ever so slightly off their usual track. I'd felt it then —that pull deep below the earth. A snap in the line. A vibration in the dark. Lilith had said I was just mortal now, but still... I could feel it. Lilith was on the move.

And Evie... she glowed with something old. Something sacred. Something that had been... mine. And it was dangerous.

She sighed, and her voice softened just enough to make something twist in my chest. "Look, I appreciate the knight-in-whatever, but maybe I should head back to my apartment tomorrow. I've got rent. And at least three bills forming a guilt shrine on my kitchen table."

"No."

That stopped her. "Excuse me?"

"You're safer here."

Her eyes narrowed. That look again. The one she used when trying to decide if I was controlling or just thoroughly unhinged.

I adjusted my tone. "The penthouse is secure. The staff is loyal. No one gets in without me knowing. As long as you're here, I can make sure nothing touches you."

Her voice dipped, sharp as ever. "Nothing but you, right?"

I said nothing.

The elevator continued its climb. Her reflection

watched me in the mirrored wall like she was trying to figure out what was going on. When the doors opened, she didn't rush out this time. She stepped slowly into the hall, eyes flicking to the corners like she expected answers to be waiting in the shadows.

She stopped at her door, hand on the handle, and turned to face me. "Something's going on with you. And you're not telling me."

I didn't lie. I just didn't tell the whole truth. Before I could think, I said, "I have business. Out of town. I'll be gone a couple of days."

She frowned. "You're leaving?"

"Yes."

"When?"

"In a few hours."

Arms crossed. Chin lifted. "Can I come?"

"Absolutely not." The words came out quietly. Unmovable.

She stared at me like she might crack me open by will alone. I didn't flinch. I couldn't. If I did, I'd tell her everything.

That I was sneaking back into Hell with Damien's help, though trusting him felt like asking a snake for directions. That I planned to dig up a page from the Book of Names. That if I could read it, maybe I'd finally understand what she was, who she was. And maybe, just maybe, I'd find the piece of me I'd lost, the piece I didn't even remember losing.

And under all that, a worse thought moved. What if this wasn't just Lilith? What if He had his fingers in it, too?

It never made sense, handing me Hell if my sin was pride and ambition. That wasn't punishment, that was a promotion. If the crime was wanting to be like the First Light, why crown me almost His equal? So what the fuck was that? Maybe Hell wasn't a gift, it was a leash. Exile dressed as a kingdom. Make me the villain, keep me busy, break me under a throne that never truly answered to me.

The part that really scraped bone was that I didn't even remember wanting that ambition. I didn't remember wanting to be like Him. For an omniscient, omnipotent god, He sure seemed miserable. I had never wanted to be that. But apparently, there were a lot of things I had forgotten.

I kept my face calm while the questions bit down. I would go with Damien. I would find this... page. And if it said what I feared, then this wasn't just Lilith's game, it was The First Light's design, and I've been a pawn in something since before I Fell. And that scared me more than anything.

I looked at her. And there it was again. That word. Low and hot behind my ribs. The one I hadn't meant to say. *Mine.* I'd whispered it against her throat like a vow I didn't remember making. And sweet sin and salt, I wanted to say it again and again.

Instead, I swallowed it down and said, "Please don't go anywhere. Topher can get you anything you need, just pick up the phone in my office."

She wrinkled her brow. "Seriously?"

"I mean it."

Her eyes searched mine for a long, quiet beat. "Fine," she said at last. "But you'd better come back."

I stepped closer, just one step, close enough to feel the heat of her skin. I tipped her chin with a finger. "Hell itself couldn't stop me." And then I turned and walked away.

It was just past six in the morning when I

stepped out of the bedroom. The city was still cloaked in that hushed, gray hour between night and morning. I moved on instinct—black fatigue pants, fitted tee, fleece jacket, half-zipped because Hell really could freeze over in parts. A backpack slung over one shoulder, light but ready. I wasn't taking much. Just enough to get me in and, if I was lucky, back out again.

The kitchen lights were dim, casting an amber glow across the dark marble. I walked toward the counter, reaching for the coffee I'd set to brew on a timer, when I caught the faintest flicker of motion in the corner of my eye.

I turned. And there she was. Evie. Standing by the edge of the counter in nothing but my oversized gray t-shirt and a pair of socks that bunched at the ankles. Her hair was piled on top of her head in a messy knot, like she'd done it half-asleep. There was a crease on her cheek like she'd just rolled out of bed —and something else in her expression. Worry. Bare. Unmasked.

She didn't speak at first, just gave me a small smile. Then, she stepped forward. "I—I couldn't let you leave without telling you goodbye," she blurted, voice breathy and fast. "I know we haven't known each other very long, but I feel this... connection to you. One I can't explain. And—"

I just stared. Open-mouthed. No expression. No words. Not even breath. A mug just hanging in my hand.

She kept going, hands moving like she needed something to hold on to. "And I know it sounds insane, and you probably think I'm crazy, but I know I'd regret it if I didn't..."

But she didn't finish. She crossed the last step between us, rose onto her toes—and kissed me. No hesitation. Just warm lips on mine. Soft. Sweet.

I didn't move. Couldn't. Not for five full seconds. Because all I could think was—she came for me. I couldn't remember anyone ever... Then her arms slid around my shoulders. Her body pressed against mine. And it was like I woke up.

I dropped the bag to the floor as my hands slid around her waist. I pulled her close, like I could memorize the feel of her, brand it into my skin before I stepped into Hell. Because as the Cherubim wept, I was already there.

When she finally pulled back, I was still standing there like I'd been struck by lightning. My breath was ragged. My hands were still on her waist. My heart was somewhere in my throat.

She blinked up at me—then gave me the slowest, most suspicious once-over I'd ever endured.

Her eyes narrowed. "So... a business trip, huh?"

I opened my mouth. Closed it. Looked down at my outfit. Then managed, "It's, um... kind of a casual thing."

She arched a brow.

"We're doing... business while hiking."

Evie crossed her arms. "Hiking."

"Yes."

"And business. In fatigue pants."

"They're moisture-wicking," I offered, completely deadpan. "Good airflow."

Her lips twitched like she was fighting a smile. But there was something sharper underneath it—concern, intuition, maybe even fear. And I didn't deserve any of it. I was pretty sure she knew I wasn't telling her the truth. And I couldn't admit it. Not yet.

She let out a breath and looked away first. "Fine. But, Luc, if you don't come back... I'll assume you were lying about everything. And I won't forgive you. Ever."

"I know."

The words hurt more than they should've. Not because she was wrong, but because she was right to make me earn it.

I stepped back in her space, hooked two fingers under her chin, and turned her face back to mine.

"Look at me," I murmured.

Her eyes snapped up, furious and shining, like she hated how much she meant it. I pressed my mouth to hers, not gentle, not sweet, something like a vow carved into stone. I kissed her the way you kiss the last thing you're allowed to keep. The way you seal a promise with your body because words aren't strong enough to hold it.

When I pulled back, my forehead stayed against hers for a beat, my breath uneven.

"I'll be back in two days," I whispered, voice rough. "I promise."

I forced myself to let go before I did something stupid, like stay. I stepped away, wings flexing under my skin, the room already feeling farther from her than it had any right to. Then I turned and walked out, because if I looked at her one more second, Hell could've waited, and I couldn't afford that kind of weakness.

Ten minutes later, Damien and I were taking the elevator to the basement. The one no one talks about beneath the subcellar. Below the staff tunnels, below the underground wine vaults, beneath even the concrete foundation. It was older than Vegas. Older than sin. Carved before time.

I'd known about it. It was why I convinced that idiot to make a deal with the Devil. And apparently, so did Damien. He claimed this was our easiest entry point. The last door was iron and old as time, carved with a script that predated language. It didn't creak when it opened—it sighed, like it was exhaling me back into the dark.

Damien stood at the edge of the void, one of the few unguarded hidden entrances into Hell. He had one foot on the crumbling stone, cigarette glowing like a warning. "Still time to back out."

I hated this place. Always had. But I didn't answer. Just stepped through.

As we descended, it felt like a weight on my shoulders. The kind that lived behind your ribs and whispered all your regrets. I felt it settle into my bones, familiar as breath.

Damien whistled low. "Still fucking creepy."

The tunnel twisted down through the rock like a throat swallowing us whole. The air got colder. Damper. Hungrier. Until suddenly, it wasn't a tunnel at all. It was a cavern.

The River Acheron stretched before us. Black as ink. Wide as memory. No wind touched it, but a thick mist curled across the surface. Not steam. Not warmth, but something deader. Silvery, whispering. Something that clung to bone. It curled like fingers. Sank like guilt.

And beneath the water were souls. Not swimming, but drowning. Reaching. Clawing. Writhing. Some whispered. Some screamed. Some had faces. Others had none. Some were just skull and bones, clinging to whatever they could.

They were all dead. Desperate. And Eternal.

The Whisperers drifted with mouths open but soundless, their truths stolen by silence. The Blamebound tangled together, dragging one another deeper with every accusation. The Lovers Who Betrayed reached for each other but never quite touched, doomed to orbit in longing and regret.

The False Prophets clung to the sides of the boat, featureless heads tilting upward, desperate to be seen with looped endless prayers, echoing back on themselves in maddening tones. The Silent Screaming were the worst—mouths torn wide, eyes sewn shut tight, no noise, only agony thrumming through the current.

And watching it all—lurking in shadows on the shores—were the Watchers. This was where they were supposed to be. I didn't look at them. Not directly. You never should, not even me, the devil himself.

A boat awaited us. It wasn't made of wood. It was made of bone, weathered in gold trim, and a single lantern glowing like an ember. And our gondolier was no ferryman.

"Aluma," Damien greeted her with a wink.

She stood motionless, tall and thin, with skin stretched too tightly over too many joints. Her hood draped over her face, but when she turned, I glimpsed the inside—black. Empty. Sucking. Like a well that never ended. Her hands were skeletal, and the pole she gripped wasn't carved—it was made of vertebrae pieced together.

Her gaze slid past him and landed on me.

She bowed her head just slightly. In a whisper that frayed on the edges, she said, "The Fallen Prince returns."

Damien stepped in first, too casual. Like this wasn't the most cursed Uber he'd ever hailed. I followed, keeping my gaze ahead.

A soul reached up. Pale fingers brushed my ankle. Another caught Damien's pant leg and hissed something in a dead dialect. He shook it off with a grunt.

"Now that you're mortal," he muttered, settling onto the bench, "if they latch on too long, you'll start remembering shit you never lived."

I already knew.

The gondolier shoved off. The boat drifted into the black. Mist crawled up my legs. Regret soaked into my skin. I kept my eyes forward as we drifted in silence. No waves. Just ripples that trailed behind us like afterthoughts. Like the river couldn't forget us.

Then, finally, the fog began to part.

"Almost there," Damien said, voice low.

I didn't ask where.

He answered anyway. "Hopefully, when we get to the Crimson Verge, we won't have to fight our way through."

I knew it was a possibility. I just hoped this wasn't a setup on his part.

We stepped off the boat and onto the crumbling dock of the Riverlands, and the ground felt like it sighed under our weight.

The moment my boots hit the shore, the Watchers scattered. Thin-limbed silhouettes lurking just beyond the mist, heads twitching, spines bowed low.

It was easy to scatter them with my power before Lilith cursed me as a human. But now, they'd been tailing us along the shore since we boarded the boat —hungry for whatever scent of old sin still clung to me. Yet, once I was on solid ground, they slithered back into the banks like vermin. Even stripped of power, the name Lucifer still meant something here.

Damien adjusted the pack on his shoulder and glanced sideways with a smirk. "Still making things run the other way without even trying."

I ignored him. My eyes were fixed on what lay

ahead. A city loomed beyond the tangled black reeds—a silhouette of spires and ruins set against a bruised-red sky. Cracked towers and shattered steeples pierced the air like broken fingers. The wind carried no sound, but I could feel the silence pressing in.

The Shattered Choir.

Once, it had been the heart of something holy. The place I'd built for the 200 who followed me. A sanctuary for rebels. Now, it was only a mausoleum of what we lost.

Statues lined the road as we entered—angels caught mid-hymn, their mouths parted, their hands raised. Frozen in a song they never finished. The stone had wept in places, leaving streaks like tear tracks.

Damien let out a low whistle. "Damn. I'd forgotten how eerie this place was."

He ran his fingers along one broken wing as we passed.

We didn't linger. The sun in this realm didn't set like Earth's. It dimmed in pulses, like a heart slowing. By the time we crossed the last archway of the Choir, it had dipped low—reddening, chilling. The warmth leeched out of the air, as if it were being siphoned.

We reached the edge of the Crimson Verge just as Hell's version of night fell. There were no stars here. Only clouds of ash that flickered with distant lightning and the dull glow of the burning plains beyond. It was half a day's walk from here to the Garden of the Forsaken. I could feel it—it always drew me in. Even now, it was like a distant pulse in the marrow of my spine.

The garden waited for me. The place where I'd long buried something sacred. The stone I couldn't explain—the one I'd carried from the moment I Fell. Smooth. Weightless. Meaning everything and nothing at the same time. Back then, I hadn't known why I'd kept it. But now, I had a sinking feeling it had always belonged to *her*.

Damien sat cross-legged near a small fire he coaxed to life with a whispered curse.

"I'll get you to the garden," he said, voice low. "But after that, you're on your own." His cigarette flicked a red spark into the dark.

I grunted an agreement and stared into the flames, wondering what she was doing right then. Had the memories found her yet? Was she thinking of me in the same way I couldn't get her out of my head?

Sometime around morning, I realized I'd passed out face-first on my backpack, stiff-necked and sore. Not exactly luxury accommodations.

The sky above the Crimson Verge never turned blue. It just paled—ashen and raw—like a battlefield still smoldering after the bloodshed. Smoke drifted low along the ground, seeping between cracks in the scorched earth. The air smelled of metal and brimstone. Somewhere far off, a scream echoed— long and hollow, vanishing into the heat.

We'd made camp under the spine of a dead leviathan the night before. Its ribs jutted from the earth like broken arches, casting twisted shadows in the red half-light. I hadn't slept. Just stared at the horizon where the Verge bled into the ruin-stained winds until I passed out for a couple of hours in the early morning.

Beneath our feet, the land groaned. Hunger, ambition, rage from lost souls, like magma, it sloshed just beneath the surface, waiting for any excuse to erupt. Weapons sprouted in the dust around us. Bladevines. Hammerstalk. Even a serrated flail blooming from a bed of rust. Living steel, born of pain and purpose.

I could feel them reaching toward me as we passed—like they knew who I was. What I'd been. Without a word, we each went for one, just in case. A rusted blade curled itself into my palm like it remembered me.

Damien spat. "This place is a fucking fever dream."

I didn't answer, too focused on the quiet—too focused on how it had gone still, too fast.

We'd just passed a battlefield made entirely of ash and bone. A war had broken out hours before—one of a thousand daily ones here—and it was already forgotten. Just wreckage now. No winners. Just souls and weapons feeding the soil.

Something beneath us stirred. Not alive. Not quite dead. Pooling from the cracks. The smell of rot and decay strengthening. The Verge was preparing for another battle.

"Remind me again," Damien gritted, "why I agreed to this suicide mission?"

"Because you owed me," I said, my voice hoarse from ash and silence. "And because you can't wait to see me go down."

He smirked. "You're not wrong."

In the distance, the first glimmer of the Garden peeked above the smoke—twisted trees silhouetted in the hell light, crooked limbs reaching toward the ash-heavy sky. We were almost there.

But every step in the Verge came with a cost. And as the wind howled low across the cracked plain, I felt a cold dread twist in my belly, knowing we hadn't paid ours yet. Then the air shifted. Movement. The Watchers came from the shadows without sound—four of them—for each of us. They weren't supposed to leave the Acheron. They never had before.

Their bodies were long-limbed and shifting, wrapped in tendrils of shadow and bone. Eyes like pits. No mouths. Just a low-frequency hum that rattled your teeth.

I didn't think. I moved. The blade in my hand came alive, vibrating like it had been waiting. It was the kind I'd used in the Siege of Thorne's Mouth—a place so soaked in betrayal, it bled grief for a century.

I remembered the weight. The angle. The way it curved through flesh that didn't bleed.

Damien caught one across the throat, and a jagged stalk of obsidian bloomed as he snarled something in a tongue I hadn't heard in at least five millennia.

Another watcher lunged at me, claws aimed at my chest. I stepped sideways and brought the blade down hard. It didn't scream—the Watchers were silent—but it folded, twitching, and melted into the ground, its black blood sucked down into the cracks.

The last came from behind. I turned, slower this time. The blade hummed and cleaved through it mid-lunge.

Damien cursed, yanking the last one off his back, stabbing it until the ground beneath him sizzled.

And then—silence. They were gone. But something was wrong. They'd followed us here. They weren't just watching anymore. They were hunting. And whatever waited in the Garden of the Forsaken... I was sure—it already knew we were coming.

CHAPTER TWENTY

Evie

I was dreaming again. But it wasn't the same place —not the one from before, all light and wind and stars. This was something else entirely.

The air was thick and hot, pulsing with the scent of sulfur and something sharp, like scorched metal or blood. The ground beneath me cracked and churned, veins of black magma threading through blackened rock like a living wound.

The sky bleeding red was an eerie sight. And I wasn't alone. In the distance, across the ashen plain, I saw two figures—one tall and still, the other in motion—moving carefully across a jagged field that burned without flame.

It took me a moment to recognize him. But I had a strange inkling my soul always knew him, even in this place. But there was a gravity to him, quiet and undeniable. Like some invisible thread pulled me closer every time we were near. And lately? It felt like it was pulling harder. Like he wasn't just someone I'd met. But someone I'd know. Someone I'd somehow always been moving toward.

I tried to call out. Tried to run toward him. It was

like I was running in quicksand. No matter how hard I tried, I barely moved.

There was a flicker in the corner of my vision, then another. And then I saw them, dark figures gliding across the horizon, cloaked in torn shadows that moved like smoke underwater. They didn't walk. They drifted. Hollow faces beneath tattered hoods, no eyes—just holes where light went to die. And from their hands dangled gnarled weapons.

One of them raised a scythe toward me. It turned its head—if it had a head—and stared right at me like it'd been waiting.

The scythe came down. I screamed. And woke up—gasping, heart slamming against my ribs like it was trying to claw its way out. My sheets were tangled, soaked in sweat. My hands shook as I shoved them forward, trying to breathe.

But when I turned them over, my burn now looked like a brand in my skin. It was glowing. Not brightly. But pulsing—steady—like a heartbeat.

I didn't know how I knew. Didn't understand what any of it meant. But something deep and certain whispered to me—he was in trouble.

I launched myself out of bed, bare feet skidding against the hardwood, and sprinted down the hall. I didn't hesitate. I ran straight into Luc's office and grabbed the phone on his desk.

It rang once. Then—

"Topher," said a voice on the line. Crisp. Immediate. Alert.

I didn't even take a breath. "Where is he?" I asked. "Where's Lucifer?"

There was a pause. Too long for a man who answered on the first ring.

"Miss Grace," Topher said smoothly, "I wasn't expecting your call."

I didn't have patience for pleasantries. "Yeah, well, I didn't expect to wake up from a nightmare with a glowing tattoo, so here we are."

Another pause. This one shorter. Sharper. Calculated.

"I assure you," he said finally, "Mr. Morningstar is attending to some... personal business. Perfectly routine. He'll be back in a couple of days."

Bullshit. I felt it—tight in my throat, crawling under my skin. The kind of lie dressed in careful words and pressed cuffs.

"What kind of business?"

"I'm afraid I don't have those details," he said. "He left specific instructions not to be disturbed."

I blinked, the sigil still glowing faintly against my skin, but the pulsing had slowed. My fingers tingled. My heart thudded. Something inside me whispered again, louder this time, "He's lying." But I wasn't ready to show my hand.

"Fine," I said, my voice neutral. "Thanks."

I hung up before he could say anything else.

Luc was gone. He was in danger. I was sure of it. And no one was going to tell me the truth. Which meant I'd have to find it myself.

I stared at the phone in my hand long after I hung up, like it might confess something if I squeezed hard enough. It just stayed cold and silent, like the man who'd answered it.

I needed air. The penthouse was too quiet. Too clean. Too full of *him.*

I slipped on a pair of shoes and grabbed his black oversized hoodie from the back of a chair. It still smelled like him and made my traitor of a heart ache, and I stepped into the private elevator.

He'd never taken me to the rooftop, but he'd mentioned it once—offhandedly, like it didn't matter. But it did. I could feel it the moment I stepped through the glass door.

It was his kind of space. Secluded. Quiet. Designed for someone who wanted to watch the world without being seen by it. A low-slung couch sat beneath a weathered pergola, flanked by two heavy chairs and a table. The cushions were dark, expensive, just slightly worn.

Below, the city carried on. But up here, it was just the wind and silence, and it was pressing down on me—just waiting.

I crossed to the railing and rested my palms on the cool stone. Tried to breathe. Tried to convince myself this was all crazy. But all I could feel was the pulsing in my hand. The sigil was still there, faintly glowing like a brand that refused to fade.

"I know you're in trouble," I whispered. "I don't know how, but I do. And I don't know how to help you." A sob burst out of me like something breaking, and I begged, "Please... Luc. Tell me what to do. How do I find you?"

This wasn't just a bad feeling. I felt almost panicked. A knowing I hadn't asked for—but couldn't ignore. My heart was racing, too fast. My stomach twisted, and for one terrifying second, I thought I might throw up right here on the slate tiles of his very chic rooftop.

I wasn't fucking built for this.

I went back to the couch and sat down, pulling out my phone, thumbs trembling now. But before I could type, something caught the corner of my eye —a sliver of pale white, wedged between the cushions. I reached down, half-expecting a receipt or a forgotten napkin. But what I pulled out was a feather. Long. White. Perfect. Too perfect. Not downy like a pigeon's. Not dirty or frayed. It shimmered faintly, as if dipped in moonlight.

I stared at it, my breath caught somewhere in my throat. I had no idea what it meant, but it felt important. Maybe a key to something. I curled my fingers around it, holding it against my palm.

There was only one person I trusted not to gaslight me into silence. Only one who'd look me in the eye and tell me if I was spiraling... or if something was actually happening. I tapped her name before I could talk myself out of it. *Destiny.*

Destiny picked up on the second ring. "Please tell me you're calling this early to tell me about a shoe sale or brunch," she mumbled, voice still scratchy with sleep.

"I wish it was a shoe sale," I said, trying for snark. It came out thinner than I meant it to. Brittle. "Trust me, I'd much rather be sobbing over limited edition boots than... this."

A pause. Then, sharper now, "Where are you?"

"The Revel Rooftop. The penthouse."

Another pause. I could hear her sit up, the rustle of blankets falling away.

"What happened?"

"I had a dream," I said quietly. "Not like before. This one was... darker. The sky was bleeding red. Everything felt cracked and scorched and wrong. And there were these cloaked things—tall, faceless, like shadows wearing skin. They were coming for me."

That got her silence—the heavy kind.

"And right before I woke up... one of them raised something. A blade, maybe? It looked rusted. Old. But when it slashed it toward me—" I swallowed. "I woke up gasping. Heart in my throat. Like it actually hit me."

"Holy hell," Destiny whispered.

"I told myself it was just a dream. Just my brain doing weird REM things after everything. I came up here to clear my head, but... I found something."

"What kind of something?"

I looked down at my hand, still curled around the feather.

"A feather," I said.

"You found... a feather."

"White. Long. Wedged between the cushions like someone had left it there on purpose. Too perfect. Too clean." I paused, "Destiny, it fucking shimmers."

She didn't say anything.

"And the second I touched it, I just —" I shook my head, voice trembling. "I just knew. He's not okay. Wherever he is right now... something's wrong."

Another breath. Then, gently she said, "Evie... I think we need to talk."

"Okay...?"

"What if I come up there?"

I asked immediately, "To the penthouse? Before work?"

"No, now. Right now. I'll be there in twenty."

She hung up without another word. And I went to the living room and stared out at the city, the feather still humming in my palm. It felt like no time had passed when there was a knock at the door, sharp and fast.

I opened it before she could knock again.

Destiny stood there in black leggings with snakes down the sides, a long coat half-buttoned, and a black T-shirt tied at her lower back that said NOT TODAY, HELLSPAWN across her chest. She looked me over once, then stepped inside without a word.

"I feel helpless," I said as soon as the door shut behind her. My voice cracked on the last syllable. "I know something's wrong. I don't know how I know, but I do. And I need to do something. Anything. His stupid assistant won't tell me anything."

Destiny looked around the penthouse for a beat. Her eyes lingered on the feather I left sitting on the coffee table. Then, she turned back to me, softer now.

"Come sit down with me."

She reached for my hand—warm, steady—and led me to the couch like I was about to receive bad news from a doctor. I sat, nerves buzzing. But she didn't sit right away. She crouched in front of me, elbows on her knees, brows drawn tight.

"I'm gonna ask you a few questions," she said gently. "And I need you to answer honestly, okay?"

I nodded as she sat in the corner of the couch, facing me.

Destiny kept her voice soft, like she was trying to be delicate with me.

"Okay. First question." She gave me a look that was almost teasing, but not quite. "Didn't you think it was a little strange that his name is Lucifer Morningstar?"

I gave a short, nervous laugh. "Yeah. I figured it was fake. Like... a stage name. Or maybe his parents were really into irony."

"But it stuck in your brain, didn't it?" she asked. "Didn't sit right?"

I shrugged. "I mean, yeah. But I thought maybe I was just being judgy."

"You're not." She leaned forward. "Second question, his eyes."

That threw me. "What about them?"

"You've seen them. Really seen them. You're telling me those eyes look normal?"

I thought about it. How sometimes they caught the light in strange ways. How they seemed to burn when he was angry, or darken when he got too

231

close.

I inhaled. "They're different, like they almost... glow," I admitted. "But I figured it was just the lighting. Or my imagination."

"Third question," she said gently. "When did your dreams start changing?"

I froze.

Her voice softened even more. "Was it around the time you met him?"

"Yes." My throat felt tight. "But I figured it was stress. He's not exactly... low maintenance."

She smiled slightly but didn't let up. "Last one. Did you ever notice his whole aura? The way both men and women tend to... fawn all over him? Like they're caught in his gravity?"

I swallowed. "Yes. It's like... everyone turns their head when he walks by. Like they forget themselves."

Destiny sat back, exhaling slowly. "I'm not trying to scare you," she said. "But I think you already know something's off. I think you've felt it."

My breath caught. "Destiny..."

"There's more," she said. "A lot more. And I'll tell you. But only if you want me to."

I didn't answer right away. Because part of me didn't want to know, but a much louder part—the part that had been humming since the moment I met him—needed the truth.

"I want to know," I whispered. "I... I need to know."

Destiny reached over and took the feather from the table. "Then let's start with this."

She turned it over in her hand, watching how the light hit it. Then she set it gently on the table and looked back at me.

"I know you said you don't believe in any of this

—angels, demons, all of it, especially with where you came from. But I need you to hear me anyway. Just for a minute."

I nodded, throat tight.

She spoke carefully. "Lucifer Morningstar... isn't a metaphor. He's not a guy with a dramatic name and a complicated past. He's THE Lucifer. The Morningstar. The one who Fell."

I stared at her.

"The myths got some of it wrong. A lot of it, actually. But he's real."

"You're saying he's the Devil," I said, flatly.

"I'm saying he's Lucifer," she replied. "I'm saying he has many names--Satan, the Devil, Belial, The Serpent, The Fallen One. And those are just the ones people remember."

I sat back, eyes on the far wall. "And he's just been here," I murmured. "Running a hotel and casino."

"Well... there are more reasons he's been here," Destiny said softly.

I didn't know whether to laugh or cry. But she wasn't done.

"Have you ever noticed," she continued, "that a lot of the employees around here are... different?"

I looked at her, confused. "Different how?"

Destiny tilted her head. "Strange eyes. Off energy. People who always seem to show up exactly when you need them, even if you didn't ask."

I blinked. Memories rushed in. The doorman who called me Miss Grace before I'd introduced myself. A maid whose reflection hadn't matched her movements. Even Marvin, who always knew my drink order when I never told him, not once. My skin prickled.

"You're saying... they're not human?"

She gave me a rueful little smile. "Not entirely." Then, she hesitated for just a moment. Before adding, "I'm a half-breed."

I blinked. "A what?"

"Half human, half demon. My mom was human. My dad was... something else. Something with horns and a temper and..." She giggled, "A very complicated taste in music."

"What?" I didn't know what to say. I just stared at her, my breath stuck somewhere between disbelief and a dawning, terrifying sense that the world was much bigger—and much older—than I'd ever understood.

She grinned. "He liked yacht rock." Destiny leaned in, voice gentler now. "I didn't tell you before because honestly? I liked being normal with you. But something's shifting, Evie. Something big. And you're in the middle of it."

I looked down at my hand. The glow of the sigil had faded somewhat, but it was still there. I turned my palm toward Destiny.

"What is this?"

She leaned closer, and her breath caught.

Then—without a word—she stood up and glanced around the penthouse.

"Destiny?"

She didn't answer right away. She was scanning the room, not with fear exactly, but with the kind of caution that said she knew when eyes were watching. Even the invisible kind.

When she finally sat back down, her voice dropped to a whisper. "There are rumors," she said. "Old ones. About him."

I tensed.

"There've always been whispers. Conspiracies," Destiny said quietly. "They say the story we've been fed about his Fall, the pride, the rebellion, the war in Heaven, wasn't the whole truth. That the First Light hid something. Buried it. Rewrote the ending."

I stared at her. "And that has something to do with me?"

Destiny hesitated. Just a beat. Then she nodded, touching my hand. "I don't know how, but... yeah. Because that mark?" Her grip tightened. "That's his sigil."

My stomach dropped. "What do you mean, his?"

Her eyes flicked up to mine, solemn and sharp. "Lucifer's. That's the mark that's followed him through every name, every story. It's always there, somewhere. Twisted into the fine print, buried in the oldest texts, carved into temple stone. That symbol is him."

I stared down at it.

"It shows up everywhere if you know how to look, buried in ancient texts, carved into walls and relics that predate any church. That shape?" She swallowed. "That's him."

I looked down at my skin again, at the lines burned just deep enough to feel permanent.

"But," Destiny went on, voice lowering, "that's not just his."

I frowned. "What does that mean?"

She turned my hand slightly, angling it toward the light. "His sigil's there, clear as day. But it's... layered. Intertwined with something else. Another mark woven through it. One I don't recognize."

Cold slid down my spine. "You don't recognize it?"

She shook her head slowly. "And that's the part that scares me."

Destiny squeezed my hand. "Lucifer's mark is a claim, Evie. It always has been. Power leaves fingerprints. And that one?" She exhaled. "That means you're his."

My mouth went dry. "His what?"

She didn't answer. She didn't have to. I could feel it now —the weight of it. Like my soul remembered something my mind hadn't caught up to yet. Something ancient. Intimate.

"How is that even possible?"

Destiny's voice softened. "You feel it, don't you? You have a connection to him."

I didn't hesitate as I nodded. "I think so. Because right now it's screaming at me. Something's wrong, and... I need to save him."

I ran down to the office, leaving Destiny in the living room. I picked up the phone and dialed. It rang once.

"Miss Grace?"

"Where the fuck is he?"

A pause. "Miss Grace, I don't—"

"Don't lie to me, Topher. Something's wrong. I saw... I felt it. Just tell me. Where is he?"

Another pause. Longer this time. I could practically hear him weighing every consequence. "I don't think you want to—"

"He's in Hell, isn't he?"

Silence.

"Topher. If you don't answer me, so help me—" I caught myself. Right. Maybe not the best time to be calling on God when I was literally hunting down the devil. I huffed out a breath. "Just... please. Tell me the goddamn truth."

A sigh, slow and resigned. "Yes, he's in Hell."

I squeezed my eyes shut. My pulse roared in my ears. "Is he alive?"

"I... I don't know."

The words landed like a punch. I forced myself to

keep breathing. "I need to go get to him."

"Why—"

"He's hurt... or something. Something is wrong. I know it. Please... I need to go get him."

"No." His voice sharpened. "You're alive. You don't just take a weekend jaunt to Hell, Miss Grace."

"I'm not asking for your permission." I tightened my grip on the phone. "And please..." my voice softened without my consent, "just call me Evie, okay?"

A beat. "Evie—"

"You knew where he went, and you didn't tell me."

"I was trying to protect you," he shot back. "Mr. Morningstar gave me explicit instructions to keep you safe."

"I didn't ask you to," I said, the words coming out thin and sharp. "You don't get to decide that for me."

Silence. I could hear him breathing, hear the weight of everything he wasn't saying.

A pause. Then, softer, "You're talking about crossing the threshold while your soul is still bound to your body. Do you have any idea what could happen?"

"I don't care."

He muttered something under his breath, like a curse in a language older than English. "Damn it."

"Topher—"

"I'm going with you."

My breath caught. "What?"

"You'll get flayed, tricked, or possessed by a bored demon in under ten minutes if you go alone."

"I can handle—"

"No. Non-negotiable." A beat. "Thirty minutes. Meet me in the lobby."

I blinked at the phone. "Oh... okay."

He didn't even hesitate. "Dress for fire and ice."

And then the line went dead.

Topher was already waiting in the lobby when I stepped off the elevator. And he looked... not like Topher.

Gone was the usual smug assistant aesthetic. In its place was black tactical pants, a charcoal thermal shirt, and boots that looked like they'd been worn through a few apocalypses. A weathered backpack hung from one shoulder. And at his hip? A sword. A gleaming, ancient-looking, honest-to-God sword.

I stopped mid-stride. "Is that a freaking sword?"

He gave me a look. "We're going to Hell. You think I'm bringing a clipboard?"

Fair point. I stepped closer, but he didn't move. And for the first time since I'd met him... he looked unsure.

"Before we do this," he said, voice low, "you need to understand something."

"What?"

"You're still alive, Evie."

I rolled my eyes. "Thanks, I noticed."

He didn't laugh. "That means no one knows what'll happen if you go down there. A living human, in Hell? That's not something people come back from. Honestly, I don't even know if your soul will stay put once we're through the gate."

I blinked. "I'm sorry — what?"

"There's a reason people only end up there after they die," he said. "Your body might stay intact, sure. But your soul? It might take one look at the place and bolt for the exit."

My eyes widened.

His eyes softened, "Look, I know what it's like to

worry about someone you love. I'll take you. But I needed you to know the risk."

I blinked, stunned.

"I don't, uh... love him," I said quickly. Too quickly. "I barely know him. That's not what this is."

Topher raised an eyebrow. "Sure."

"It's not."

"Right."

"I'm serious!"

He didn't argue again. Just turned toward the service hallway, boots echoing against the marble floor.

"You coming or what?"

Before I could answer, the elevator dinged again, and I heard, "Wait!"

I turned, and Destiny stepped out in her black jeans, combat boots, and a long leather coat I'd never seen before. Her usual dramatic eyeliner was toned down, but her eyes still burned with purpose.

She ran over to us and said, "I'm coming, too."

I glanced at Topher. His eyes moved over her like he was memorizing her shape for later, just in case.

He deadpanned, "Perfect. It's a field trip now."

She crossed her arms. "I can track. And I can drag both your asses back if it all goes sideways."

Topher didn't argue. That told me everything.

"I'm not letting you do this alone," she added, this time just to me. "Not when I can help."

My throat tightened. I didn't say thank you. I just nodded.

Topher sighed like a man resigned to chaos. "Fine. But if we all die, I'm blaming both of you."

Destiny grinned. "Get in line."

CHAPTER TWENTY-ONE

Lucifer

Damien wiped his blade clean with a flick of his wrist, but I dragged mine across my pant leg, smearing blood into the already-ruined fabric. My arm burned—a shallow cut, but deep enough to remind me I was bleeding. Mortal. Not invincible. I looked down at it. My blood, a deep red, still seeping.

I'd dropped my pack and left it behind in the Crimson Verge in the chaos. Not that it mattered now. We didn't have time to go back.

We'd finished off the last of the Watchers—a half-dozen, maybe more. One of them had hissed my name in the ancient tongue before I cut its throat, like it knew me. Like it hated me not for what I'd done—but for who I might still become.

Damien was already moving, boots pounding over cracked stone as the terrain shifted under our feet. I forced myself to follow. And then I saw it—*the Garden of the Forsaken.*

In the distance, it rose like a scar across the landscape—not a garden in the way humans imagined it. But with withered dead trees clawing at a colorless sky, vines twisted like nooses around rotting statues. There was nothing green—no life. No beauty. Not since I abandoned it ages ago. Just the twisted remnants of things that once reached for the light and were punished for it.

Thorns the size of blades curled through petrified soil. Black vines, long dead, dangled from scorched trees. Nothing bloomed. Nothing like the true garden of life. Eden. Just the memory of what could have been.

I had loved the Garden of Eden. Used to walk barefoot through it, the cool blades of grass against my feet as I hummed the chords of creation. But this one—this one was a mockery, a graveyard wearing a garden's name.

We reached the edge, where the rocks sloped into shadow—and there it was. The entrance. It wasn't a gate. Not a door. It was a mouth carved into the roots of a gigantic blackened tree stump, wide enough to crawl through, lined with jagged bark like teeth. A breath of cold air pushed from it, damp and rotting.

Damien glanced at me. "You sure about this?"

No. I wasn't. But I ducked down and stepped inside anyway.

I'd created this black maw entrance to keep everyone out. Back when I still thought I could make this place into something more than a scar. If it had gone to plan, I would've torn this mouth open wide and built something grand in its place—an archway of obsidian and bone. This was meant to be a sanctuary for the Fallen. A place to remember. A place to be for the exiled.

But it never worked out. It turned into a tomb. All my sanctuaries did. So the mouth remained. Crude. Dripping with rot. And this—this crawling, splintering tunnel of roots and ash—was still the only way inside.

Damien followed a moment later, scraping his shoulder on the edge as he squeezed through. I didn't speak right away. Just waited, listening to the sound of his boots crunching soil that hadn't tasted life in centuries.

Then I said, "I thought this was as far as you came?"

He hesitated, like he was weighing which lie would taste best on his tongue. Then he shrugged one shoulder. "Well," Damien said, almost amused, "I lied."

His grin didn't reach his eyes. Teeth flashed in the dark like a warning.

"I mean, I get it," he went on, casual as sin. "Coming back here. Digging through your little tragedy. Trying to stitch up whatever's left of your... legacy. You always were the sentimental one." His gaze slid over me, bright with anticipation. "Or maybe I just didn't want to spoil the ending."

I narrowed my eyes. "What ending?"

I didn't see it at first. Not really. I was still caught in the rot of memory, in the ache of a garden that never became a home.

Then the sound of steel sliding free snapped me back. Damien's blade gleamed in the sick light filtering through the roots, and it was pointed at me.

I stepped back, my own weapon unsheathing with a hiss that sounded far too mortal.

"You son of a—"

"Don't take it personally," he said, voice smooth, almost apologetic. Almost. "This isn't about you. Not really."

"Then what is it?"

His eyes flicked past me, toward the earth, toward the place Lilith had chosen to hide a truth like a bone in a grave.

"She can't risk you finding it," Damien said lightly. "And she definitely can't risk you remembering."

My blood went cold. "Lilith."

"Lilith," he confirmed, and there it was, that careful edge in his tone, like he still believed saying her name the wrong way might summon consequences. "Look, she's not trying to hand you to the First Light on a silver platter. That would be messy." His mouth twitched. "And messy is how you get His attention."

He stepped closer, blade steady. "He likes to think His house is spotless, you understand? He prefers not to see the stains."

My grip tightened around my weapon. "Spit it out."

Damien sighed, as if I was exhausting him. "If you actually get your hands on that page, you don't just get a name. You get a detonation." His eyes glittered. "And if it blows loud enough, He starts looking at how it went missing in the first place."

Understanding hit like a fist to the throat. Lilith didn't hide it from me. She hid it from Him.

Damien's smile sharpened. "She made a mistake once. Something underhanded. Something she very much wants to keep between her and the dirt."

"If this gets back to Him," Damien added, almost bored, "Lilith stops being special. And Lilith doesn't do ordinary."

My vision went red. "So she sent you."

"She sent me to keep you from digging up the truth," he said, almost cheerful. "She doesn't want you dead, not unless I have to. I'm just supposed to contain you. Slow you down. Stop you before you get inspired." His grin went wolfish. "But I figured…"

He lunged, blade slicing for my ribs.

"…I might as well have a little fun first."

I blocked it, barely, steel shrieking through the roots like the garden itself was screaming.

The clash of our weapons cracked through the trees like lightning. Sparks. Grit. Fury. My blood was still wet on my arm. His breath was heavy against mine. I caught him with a clean slice across his abdomen—not deep, but enough to make him stumble back with a grunt, black blood soaking into his shirt.

"You always were better at speeches than swordplay," I spat.

Damien coughed a laugh and spat black. "Still got some bite left in you. Shame about the mind, though. Thought you'd be smarter than this."

He gestured around with the tip of his sword. "You really don't remember, do you? What this place was a tribute to? What she was to you?"

I stilled. The air shifted. I told myself it was the garden, this place, the weight of old failures pressing in from every angle. But something inside me, a thread pulled too tight for too long, shivered at his words.

"What the hell are you—"

Pain punched into my side, hot and blinding. The words died in my throat, swallowed by the taste of iron on my breath. For a heartbeat, I didn't understand, couldn't understand, and then I felt it— the hilt jammed against my ribs, his body close, his blade buried deep.

My hand slipped on my own sword. Slick. Wet.

Blood. Mine.

Damien leaned in, his mouth curving against my ear in a grin I couldn't see but could feel all the same.

"This," he murmured, twisting the blade, "is what I'm talking about. You never know what's real... until it ruins you."

But then I felt something else entirely. A chill. A shift. A familiar emptiness swallowing the air around us. They came from above, from behind, from the roots and the walls and the very shadows of the garden. Watchers. Six of them. Eyes like voids. Mouths whispering things I didn't understand.

Damien fell back, clutching his gut, black blood seeping between his fingers as he staggered toward the entrance. And he laughed—that smug, traitorous laugh.

"Well, this was fun," he called over the chaos. "But... you know how it is."

He pointed the blade at me, grinning through his pain.

"Say goodbye, Luce."

Then he turned and ran—toward the mouth of the tunnel—leaving me surrounded. Outnumbered. And I raised my weapon.

The first three went down fast. I didn't think. Didn't breathe. Just moved.

One blade sang through bone, spine to throat. Another lost its head mid-screech. The third came too close—tried to lunge—and I turned its chest inside out before it could blink.

But I was too slow for the fourth and fifth. They worked in conjunction, a whisper of movement behind me. The hiss of a curved blade slicing air. Then the bite of another—hot and deep—across my side.

I staggered, snarling, spun around just in time to

drive my blade through another one's throat. It gurgled something ancient and cruel before it crumpled.

That's when the last one came. At the same time, my sword was still lodged in one of the others. Two quick stabs to the gut. I gasped—pain flaring white-hot—blood rushing over my hands as I caught the second strike too late.

It didn't finish me. Just... watched. For a second. Then it backed away. The others had vanished into smoke in the shadows like they'd never been there.

I stood there swaying, one hand pressed to my stomach, the other uselessly reaching for a wall that wasn't there. My knees buckled as I tried to think where I could go. Where I could hide and try to heal, with whatever was left of my power.

I knew a place—a grotto, near the mouth of the river. I'd slept there for years while trying to create the garden a long time ago, before it was cursed. Before everything went to shit.

I limped through the roots and ash, dragging myself past the broken, twisted trees and angelic statues. Every step set my wounds ablaze. My vision blurred, darker at the edges. I hadn't felt like this since waking up out of the Fall.

I felt something, heard something. Not sound, not really, more like pressure on the inside of my skull. A memory curled on the tip of my mind I couldn't quite reach. The shape of it was there, familiar, electric, but every time I tried to catch it, it slipped through my fingers.

And then I saw her. *Evie.*

She stood beneath a gnarled tree, its bark split with time and grief. Her hair wasn't pink, it was dark, falling in slow-motion waves around her shoulders, stirred by no wind I could feel. Her skin and eyes glowed gold, not with fire, but with memory. It was... devastating.

Was she really here? Or was this some final mercy, the last hallucination for a fallen angel before oblivion? Seemed fitting that my reward for faithful damnation would be this.

But I didn't give a fuck. Because the need to reach for her, to pull her into my arms, before I died, was almost unbearable. Then she raised her hand. Not to stop me, but toward me, like she was the one trying to cross the distance. Trying to get to me. To reach me. To help me.

Her mouth formed words I couldn't hear. But I could read her lips. *"Remember me."* And then she vanished. Gone in a breath, like she'd never been there.

The echo of her eyes—furious, afraid, full of fire— dug in deep. There had been no sound, but the ache of her words thrummed through my bones.

I kept moving. Maybe I was dying. Or maybe this was real. Either way... I couldn't stop. Refused to stop. One foot in front of the other. Until the earth opened around me, and I found the grotto.

Low and dark and cold. I collapsed inside it, crawling like a wounded animal toward the deepest corner, where the light couldn't find me. There was an alcove back there. Small and hidden.

I curled into it, holding my side, every breath shallow. My blood smeared across the rock as I sank down, pulling my knees to my chest like it might keep me together.

It hit me then, harder than the pain. I was nearly numb to it, but this feeling. This feeling I kept circling around, this drag in my chest whenever I thought of her, it was not just lust, not just curiosity, not even the twisted pull of that damned prophecy. It was something I had never had. Something I had not even known I was missing... until her.

She felt like home.

Not the Heaven I was thrown out of, not the Hell I had ruled for an age, or the penthouse. *Her*. The way she looked at me. The way her laugh caught in my ribs. The way her fire moved through all my dead places like it had a right to live there. That was the thing I wanted. The thing I suddenly realized I would do anything to have and keep safe.

And I'd never said what I really felt, not plain, not once, and that regret sat in my chest like shrapnel. If I died here today, that was the regret that gutted me. Not the Fall, not the thousands of years of ruling hell, not the hollow crown of this place. It was... that we had only just found each other, at the edge of everything, when I had one foot in the grave and the other slipping.

If I lived through this night, I was going to drag the truth out of whatever held it, even if it was The First Light Himself. I would figure this thing out between us, this thing that felt like destiny wrapped in barbed wire, this thing that felt like a home I had never known and suddenly could not bear to lose, and probably was never meant to have.

And now, right now, I was terrified I would die before I remembered what I needed to. Terrified that if I didn't get us answers, she would never know the truth, what I would do for her. There had to be more to this than that stupid prophecy.

The whole reason I was in Hell was because of her. Not to impress her. Not even to protect her. I was here to get answers for both of us.

And I refused to believe this mortal body was all I had left. There had to be something still buried in it, some spark welded to the bone, a shred of my immortality they hadn't managed to strip away. I reached for it, teeth gritted, dragging whatever was left of that old power through mortal nerves that screamed in protest. If I kept my mind on Evie, on the mystery of her, on the need to get back to her, I could pretend the pain was secondary, background noise.

I didn't pray, not really, but something in me reached anyway. For healing. Or at least enough to not die today. To whom I didn't even fucking know. The First Light sure wasn't going to save me.

My vision blurred at the edges. I let my eyes fall shut. The last clear thought that slipped through the haze was a stupid one—Evie. She would have a field day if she saw me like this. She would crouch beside me, take in the blood and the drama, and say, "You always this dramatic when someone hurts your feelings?"

That almost made me smile. Then everything went dark.

CHAPTER TWENTY-TWO

Evie

We entered a different elevator. One I'd never noticed before. It was older. The doors closed behind us with a soft ding. Topher pressed a button I'd never seen before, tucked beneath the main panel, behind a hidden latch. It glowed red, ancient-looking, etched with something similar to the brand on my wrist, and that wasn't part of any alphabet I'd ever seen.

The elevator jerked once, then began its descent with a low groan, as if the building itself hated the direction we were heading.

Destiny stood beside me, silent but alert. Topher was in front, sword slung across his back like it belonged there. I stared at the glowing numbers as they dropped—B1, B2, B3... then nothing. Just black. The panel went blank, yet we kept moving.

"How far down does this go?" I asked quietly.

Topher didn't turn. "Farther than it should."

If this place got any weirder, I'd file an official complaint.

The walls were... changing. Like they couldn't decide what century they were from. Sleek steel one second, then jagged stone, then something older—black rock carved with symbols that throbbed like they had a pulse. Cool. Love that for us.

The air grew thicker, hotter. Each inhale felt like breathing through a wool blanket that had been left too close to a bonfire. My shirt clung to my back, damp with sweat. My palms were slick. I wiped them on my leggings and told myself to stay calm. This was fine. Totally fine. Just casually entering into what looked like Hell's vestibule while trying not to pass out or scream.

Everything was fine. Except it really, really wasn't.

"This is under the hotel?" I asked, my voice thin. "All this?"

"It's older than the hotel," Topher said. "Older than Vegas. Older than most of what lives on the surface. Lucifer didn't build it. He just knew how to find it when he... acquired this place."

That settled in my gut like a stone. I glanced at Destiny, who gave me a slight nod—like, "Yeah. It's real. And yeah, it's about to get worse."

The elevator shuddered to a stop. The doors slid open without a sound. And suddenly we weren't in The Revel anymore. The hallway ahead of us was carved from the same black stone, so dark it seemed to absorb the light, pulsing like it had veins. Symbols flickered along the walls, glowing faintly as we passed. The ceiling arched high above, lost in shadow. It smelled like heat and iron and something older than rot.

We followed Topher as he led us forward. Above us, everything was velvet and gold and indulgence. But this? This place wanted to be left buried.

"Still thinking he's just a man?" Destiny murmured.

I didn't answer because I knew the truth.

We reached the end of the hall, where a massive iron door was etched in the same unknown language. Topher stopped, his hand resting on the hilt of his sword.

"Still determined to do this?" He asked without looking at me.

"He's in trouble, and… he needs me," I said. My voice shook, but I meant it.

He nodded once. "From here on out," he said quietly, "you're not in Vegas anymore."

I frowned. "What does that even—"

"It means," he cut in, eyes locked on mine, a faint red glow stirred behind the black, like coals under ash, and for one heartbeat I could swear my reflection in them moved a fraction too late. "You stay with me. You don't wander off, you don't play hero, you don't go anywhere I don't tell you to go."

My heart thudded. "He—"

"I know." His jaw flexed. "You want to help him, you do it by doing exactly what I say. You stick to my side, you move when I move, and when I give an order, you don't argue, you don't ask questions, you just do it. Understood?"

I swallowed. "And if I don't like your orders?"

"Then you really won't like what happens if you ignore them." His voice softened, but it didn't lose any edge. "Stay with me. Do what I say. No questions when it counts. That's how you keep both him and you alive."

He pressed his palm to the door. And it sighed open, like it had just exhaled us into the dark. Beyond it, the ground gave way to a crumbling path of scorched black stone, slick with something I didn't want to know. The air shimmered with heat as we walked along the path.

A little while later, I heard water rushing and just beyond the drop... a river writhed like a living thing.

Topher's voice went low. "That's the River Acheron," he said. "One of the five rivers of Hell, they call it the river of pain and sorrow. Don't touch it. Don't listen too closely, either."

Then, he stepped out first, one foot landing on the path like he'd done this before. The glow of the river caught on the edge of his sword, now unsheathed. The path wound down toward a jagged dock, where a gondolier waited—tall and robed, face veiled by shadow.

"Aluma," Topher said beside me, his voice tighter than I'd ever heard it. "Three souls for passage. No tricks."

The figure on the dock didn't respond. They just stood there, shrouded in something darker than shadow, still as stone. Then they moved. Slow. Fluid. Inhuman.

Their head turned toward us, but there were no eyes. Just deep hollows that felt full of regret and darkness.

"Three?" they rasped, their voice dry and rattling, like wind through a ribcage. "You must pay the toll."

They didn't look at Topher. Didn't glance at Destiny. They looked at me. Or through me.

"I hope you know what she carries."

I felt Topher stiffen beside me. I didn't breathe. Whatever they meant, I had the terrible feeling it had just marked me.

Destiny groaned. "Fuck."

Topher unsheathed his sword. "Blood for passage," he said quietly, already rolling up his sleeve. "Palm slice. A few drops into the river."

I stared. "Seriously?"

He nodded grimly. "It's the only way."

He didn't hesitate. Drew the blade across his palm and held it over the river.

The blood that fell wasn't red—it was black like ink. And the moment it hit the surface, the water reacted. No, not the water. The souls. They surged toward it, clawing upward, writhing, hissing, and fighting to drink it down.

Destiny stepped up next. Her expression flickered, just for a second, then she cut cleanly across her own palm. Her blood was a dark red, and she whispered something under her breath I didn't catch. The souls fought again.

Then she turned to me. "You've got this," she murmured. "It's just blood. And you've already survived worse."

I nodded. Stepped forward. Topher moved to lift the blade.

I shook my head. "I'll do it."

He paused, then handed it over without a word. The hilt was warm. I pressed the blade to my palm and drew it across, fast and sharp. Pain bloomed. The blood came hot and bright red, and the second it hit the river, the surface shuddered.

Every soul beneath turned toward me. Not fighting like before. Watching. A shiver went down my spine as I stepped back, handing the sword to Topher with trembling fingers.

Aluma bowed slightly. "You may board."

The gondola waited, long and narrow, made of bleached bone. Destiny climbed in behind me. Topher took the rear, sword across his lap like a warning. And the boat pushed off into whatever came next.

I tried not to look down into the water. Tried not

to see the souls—faces twisted with longing, hands clawing toward us. They weren't swimming. They were drowning, slowly, forever.

The gondola drifted silently, and the Riverlands yawning opened ahead like a mouth full of ash and bone. As the river carried us deeper, a ruined city loomed in the haze beyond, tall spires collapsed into jagged angles, half of what looked like a cathedral swallowed by time and rot.

I leaned forward slightly, watching the dark shore rise to meet us. Topher moved towards the bow, standing unnervingly still. His hand rested near the hilt of his sword, but his eyes were scanning the banks. Narrowing.

Then, under his breath, he said, "That's odd."

I sat up straighter. "What's odd?"

He didn't answer immediately—just kept looking, like something wasn't lining up. And then something grabbed me. A hand, bloated, half-rotted, shot up from the water and wrapped around my wrist, yanking hard.

I screamed as the boat rocked. "Get it off!"

Topher was already moving. His sword flashed in the low light, a clean arc of silver.

The creature shrieked as the blade sliced through its arm. It fell back into the river with a wet splash.

I gasped for air, clutching my wrist, heart racing so fast I thought I might throw up. The brand on my palm flared. Hot. Bright. Alive. I looked up—and froze. On either side of the riverbank, something moved.

"Watchers. Usually, there are a lot more along the shore," he said finally. "They line the banks. Keep the souls from crawling out of the river."

His voice was calm, clipped. But there was something tight beneath it. Something uneasy.

I followed his gaze to the shoreline. There were only a few—three, maybe four—hovering like broken shadows above the rocks. Tall, shrouded in black, gliding silently just above the ground. Cloaked figures with no faces, no eyes—just darkness where a face should be. Watching nothing and watching everything.

"I think I've seen them before..." I said quietly.

Topher turned to look at me, but I stared at the Watchers.

"I saw them in my dream this morning," I said. "They were gliding across a field of red ash, heading toward him. Toward Luc. And before that—"

I swallowed. "Outside my apartment. In the dark. I thought I was imagining it. But now..."

I couldn't finish the sentence because it didn't feel like a coincidence. It felt like a warning.

Destiny's hand brushed mine, her voice low. "They can't just wander, Evie. They're bound. Controlled."

"Then how the hell did they end up outside my apartment?" I asked.

Neither had an answer.

The boat scraped against the edge of a crumbling dock. Aluma said nothing, just gestured for us to disembark. We stepped out one by one.

"This way," Topher muttered.

He led us through a narrow canyon of blackened rock, jagged and sharp like it had been torn open by something violent. The shadows got deeper. And then we entered it.

The space opened suddenly, wide and circular—like some ancient amphitheater had been carved into the bones of Hell. Massive columns ringed the walls, all cracked and tilted like they'd been struck down by something older than time. The floor was littered with debris—shards of marble, warped brass, pieces of broken instruments that looked melted and half-alive.

Harps twisted into grotesque shapes. Trumpets rusted through. Organ pipes fused with what looked like bone. And above it all... the faintest hum. Not quite music. But close enough to make the hairs on my arms rise.

Destiny stepped closer to me, eyes wide. "What is this place?"

Topher barely glanced back. "The Shattered Choir."

The name hit something in my chest I didn't know was there.

"They were Angels in Lucifer's choir who refused to choose a side when the war broke out. They wanted peace."

"And this is what happened to them?" I asked.

"They sang themselves into ash," he said softly. "Chose song over war."

The hum grew louder for a second. Or maybe we just stepped closer to it.

"I thought Hell was all fire and torment," I murmured.

Topher gave me a hollow look. "Sometimes the worst torment is remembering what you used to be."

I didn't say anything after that. None of us did. I stared at a broken lyre embedded in the wall, its strings hanging loose.

We didn't linger in the Shattered Choir. The exit on the far side opened into a canyon steeped in red light with walls slick and veined, pulsing faintly like a heartbeat. It felt... alive. The dirt beneath our feet glowed a deep crimson, with cracks in between sucking black liquid.

Topher slowed, his eyes tracking the far ridges.

"Where are we?" I asked.

He turned toward us, jaw tense.

"The Crimson Verge," he said. "A place where battles break out every hour between battalions of demons and condemned souls."

I stared at him. "They're fighting each other?"

Destiny's brow furrowed. "What for?"

Topher hesitated. "No one's ever agreed on that. Some say it's vengeance. Some say it's sport. Some say it's penance, or power, or the right to claw their way deeper into Hell—or out of it."

"And which is it?" I asked.

His voice was quiet. "Whatever the war was originally about... no one remembers. But the blood still spills."

He veered off the path toward a twisted tree growing out of the rock—black bark, thorn-covered limbs, and instead of fruit, it bore weapons. Blades. Axes. Iron staffs with scorched handles. Like rage had grown roots and learned how to arm itself.

He reached up and tore two free—a jagged dagger for Destiny, and a short-handled axe for me. The metal was black, warm to the touch, veined with a red that almost looked like blood trapped inside them.

I stared at him. "Am I supposed to use this?"

Topher scanned the path ahead, his voice low. "Just in case."

Far in the distance, something screamed. It didn't sound human or animal. But it was near enough to make my grip tighten on the blade I didn't want to be holding.

The deeper we moved into the Crimson Verge, the louder I heard it. Like the earth beneath us had a heartbeat.

I turned slowly in place, my fingers tightening around the axe. The sky above burned a color that didn't exist anywhere else—red and raw and aching. The horizon blurred with heat and smoke, but I could make out distant shapes. Ruins and broken weapons fused with stone.

That's when I felt a ripple under my skin, like a hum in the sigil on my hand. I had seen this place before in my dream.

"This is where I saw him," I whispered, barely audible over the wind.

Topher and Destiny both looked at me.

"This is where those... Watchers swarmed him. Right before—"

I swallowed.

"Right before one of them came at me. With a scythe."

Destiny stepped closer, her eyes scanning the red-lit landscape.

Topher's jaw clenched. "This place messes with memories. Loops them. Breaks them apart and stitches them back wrong. It's a trap for the soul."

"I—I don't think it was a trick," I said. "I think it was real."

I started walking, faster now. I didn't know where I was going, only that I had to see. My boots kicked up dust as I passed a rock formation fused with weapons, a rusted banner twisted around a broken blade. And then I saw it. Lying half-buried at the base of a cracked column, one strap torn, was a black canvas backpack. Luc's *backpack*.

The one he'd dropped on the kitchen floor when I kissed him. The one he'd slung over his shoulder before he walked out. I fell to my knees beside it.

"Oh my god," I breathed. "It's his. This is his."

Topher's boots thudded behind me. He stopped

short. His expression—usually locked somewhere between deadpan and annoyed, cracked. Just slightly.

"Shit," he muttered, barely audible. His eyes darted over the ground, then back to the pack, as if expecting its owner to materialize right behind it.

Destiny crouched next to me. "He was here."

I turned, the weight of it hitting all at once. "Where was he going?" My voice rose. I stood fast, spinning toward Topher. "Where was he going?! Why the hell would he come here?"

Topher didn't answer right away. His gaze had shifted—north, toward a place where the red canyon ended, and the terrain began to darken, as the color drained out of it. And the horizon beyond it twisted.

Withered trees, gnarled and leafless, bent like they were trying to crawl back into the ground. Tangled vines choked everything in their path. And further still—jagged stone spires stabbed upward, wrapped in creeping rot, as if something had tried to bury the sky itself.

Topher's voice dropped to a whisper. "The Garden of the Forsaken."

The words echoed through me—*The Garden of the Forsaken*. I stared at the landscape ahead, breath tight in my throat. That wasn't a garden. From here, it looked like a graveyard for things that had once hoped. It stretched out ahead of us like something half-dead and half-dreamed—twisted trees, tangled vines, blackened earth choking on memory.

We kept moving, the red glow of the Crimson Verge faded behind us, and the sky above the garden... shifted like it couldn't decide whether to stay black or bruise.

Destiny stopped just shy of the edge, her gaze

locked on the shifting horizon. "I've only heard of it in fragments," she said softly. "It was supposed to be a quiet corner of Hell. A place of reflection for the Fallen—for those who regretted the war but couldn't go back."

Topher was a few feet ahead, but he turned at that. His expression was unreadable, but his voice wasn't. "Truthfully?" he said. "It was his."

"Luc's?" I asked.

He nodded once. "The Lightbringer wanted to build something here. A place for the exiled. The forgotten. He called it sacred. Said it would be his answer to Eden."

Destiny blinked. "I didn't know that."

"Most don't," Topher muttered. "He spent millennia trying to grow things here. Trees. Flowers. Anything. He'd drag seeds from Earth, cut vines from the far edges of Hell. He'd bring stones warmed in sunlight, water from the rivers above. Trying to make it... pure."

I looked out at the twisted wreckage before us, my hands itching to do... *something*. "It never worked?"

Topher shook his head. "Nothing ever took. Everything rotted. Flowers withered in a day. Trees bled sap like tears. Fruit would form only to turn black in his hands. And after a while..."

He paused. His voice went quieter. "...he gave up. Stopped coming. Left it unfinished. This whole place? It's a graveyard for what he had before the Fall."

That landed like a stone in my chest. My fingers curled around the edge of the axe, still at my side.

"Could he be there?" I asked. "Now?"

Topher looked at me. And for the first time, he didn't have a quick answer.

"I hope so," he said. "Because if he's not... I don't know where the hell he went."

The scorched earth gave way to something darker, maybe older. The rocks sloped into a shallow hollow, and that's when I saw it. Not a door. Not a gate. *A mouth.* Split wide at the base of a gnarled, blackened tree, its roots twisted around the opening like fingers too long. It yawned open just wide enough to crawl through, the bark jagged and sharp like splintered teeth. A breath of air rolled out —cold, damp, and sweet with the stench of rot.

Topher didn't say anything, but the way he watched the trees as if they might speak told me everything I needed to know.

Destiny was quieter than usual. Her fingers brushed the dark leaves of a blackened vine as we passed, but the moment her skin touched it, the entire thing shriveled, turned to ash, and fell.

She yanked her hand back and muttered, "Okay, that's creepy."

I grimaced.

Topher crawled through first, sword drawn the entire time. Then, Destiny and I crawled through. The deeper we moved into the Garden, the quieter everything became. No wind. No footfalls. Just... strange whispers. They weren't loud or even full words. Just the same sound over and over that I couldn't quite hear. Maybe a name?

I stopped walking. My pulse beat in my throat. In my ears. And then... in my hand. The sigil on my palm flared brighter. Not painfully, but insistently —white-gold light threading through my skin, pulsing in time with something here.

I looked down and realized everything started to move. The vines near my boots reached for me, curling slow and low, not with menace, but longing.

So did the trees—bending just slightly, branches tilting my way. Flowers, blackened and collapsed, turned their wilted heads as if reaching for me. As if I could offer them hope, as if I could remake them.

"I don't—" I whispered. "What is happening?"

Neither Topher nor Destiny answered. They were watching me too closely.

My hand trembled as I reached down toward a collapsed bloom—something that might have once been a rose. The moment my fingers brushed the petals, the color bled back in. Green. Gold. Blush-pink. It bloomed in my palm like it had never died. And I froze.

Then slowly I crouched and pressed my hand to the ground. And watched—helpless and stunned—as grass erupted beneath my fingers. Thick and lush and green, spilling out in every direction like it had been waiting for permission.

Destiny's eyes widened as she stepped back. "Holy shit."

Topher didn't speak, but the look on his face wasn't confusion. It was recognition, almost reverent, like puzzle pieces snapping into place. He dipped his head in a subtle, respectful bow. To me. Like he'd just realized exactly what I was.

We moved forward, through the field I'd unknowingly created. The vines rustled softly as we passed, as if grateful. At the edge of the clearing, we found a dark stone altar, cracked down the middle, sunk halfway into the ground. The gardenias planted around it were browned and shriveled.

I walked toward the altar and placed my palm on it. And the crack healed. Instantly. Like it had been waiting for me. The gardenias bloomed wide and white and full, their scent flooding the air. I pulled my hand back, stunned. And just beyond it, I noticed drops of red. Bright, fresh blood dotting the grass, leading away from the altar and deeper into the Garden.

My heart fell into my stomach. I didn't wait. I didn't think. I ran.

"Evie!" Topher yelled behind me.

"Wait—!" Destiny's voice followed, fading fast as the trees swallowed me whole.

I ducked beneath twisted branches, vines clawing at my sleeves, my boots slamming through overgrowth and rot. The deeper I went, the warmer the air felt.

The blood drops led me to it. Not a cave. Not exactly. A grotto—half-formed from stone, half-grown from rotten twisted roots of the Garden itself. Its mouth was covered in tangled vines.

As I pushed through them, they sprang to life, green and lush. I didn't have time to marvel at them as I stepped inside. It was dark and still. My breath caught as I flicked on the light from my phone, the narrow beam cutting through the gloom.

There was more blood. Dried, then fresh. Scattered along the path. Leading deeper. My legs moved before my brain caught up. And then, I saw him. Curled in on himself near the back wall. His arms wrapped around his body, his head was down, and his hair was dirty. His forehead pressed to the stone.

I stopped cold. Every part of me screaming and pleading and breaking. "Luc?" I whispered.

He didn't move. I stepped closer, my hands trembling.

"Luc..." I said again, voice cracking.

I dropped to my knees beside him, reached out with shaking fingers, and ran my hand through his matted, tangled hair.

Warm. He was warm. His chest moved, slow and shallow. But he was breathing.

"Oh god," I breathed. "Luc. Please... I'm here. I came for you. Please..."

Tears leaked from my eyes. How long had he been here?

I leaned over him, turning his body. My hands swept gently over him—his shoulders, his arms, down to his ribs. His shirt was torn, but stuck to his skin from old blood. I pushed the fabric aside and found the wound—just below his ribs.

A sword slash. Deep, but not fatal. And already closing and no longer bleeding.

I brushed the sweat-matted hair from his temple and kissed his forehead.

"It's me, Evie," I whispered, desperate. "Please, just... come back to me."

His lashes fluttered. Then he gasped, his whole body jolting like something yanked him back into himself. His eyes were wild and bleary at first, focusing in stuttering increments until they found mine.

"Evie?" he rasped. His voice was hoarse and barely there.

I tried to laugh and sob at the same time. "Yeah. You goddamn fool."

He blinked again, slow, like he wasn't sure I was real. I helped him sit up. His body trembled with the effort, and when I eased him back against the wall, he sucked in a sharp breath through his teeth, trying to hide it and failing anyway.

His breathing stayed ragged, shallow. His eyes stayed too wide. "How," he managed, swallowing hard, "how did you find me?"

I huffed a broken laugh. "Had a dream about the Crimson Verge. You. Watchers. It was real subtle." I rolled my eyes, wiping my face with the back of my hand. "Also, Topher couldn't lie his way out of a paper bag, with instructions and scissors."

Something like a smile tried to form. It didn't quite make it.

"I'm going to kill him," he said, but it came out thin, more wheeze than threat, like even the words hurt his ribs.

"Get in line."

I started to say more, but then he reached up. His hand shook so badly that his fingers almost missed. He caught a loose strand of my hair and tucked it behind my ear with a tenderness that made my throat close.

His palm lingered against my cheek, warm, grounding. Then he leaned in.

The movement cost him. I felt it in the way his shoulders tightened, the way his breath hitched, the quiet, involuntary grunt he tried to swallow back as pain flared across his face for half a second.

Still, he kissed me. Not smooth. Not effortless. A kiss built out of stubbornness and relief, like he needed the proof of my mouth against his to keep himself here. And I kissed him back like an answer.

CHAPTER TWENTY-THREE

Lucifer

She found me. I don't know how, but gods, she found me.

I'd half expected to die in that grotto. Curled against cold stone, blood drying beneath my ribs, pulse slowing to something distant. But then—she was there. Hands on me. Lifting. Steadying. Sitting beside me like I wasn't a monster.

Even torn and half-dead, I couldn't stop myself. I groaned as I leaned toward her, every muscle screaming—but when our lips met, the pain didn't matter. Only she did like breathing after drowning.

There was no finesse, no softness—just the raw, broken truth of it. I was starving. And she was the only thing I remembered wanting before I knew what want was.

The moment our mouths met, something burned beneath my throat, right where my own sigil lay hidden under skin and bone. It flared in answer, and then a blaze of light burst from her wrist, ancient and alive, flooding the grotto.

I felt it.

Molten heat surged through me, hotter than Hell's

flame, sharper than angelic fire. It tore through my veins like liquid dawn, unraveling something old and buried in the hollows of my chest. My spine arched. My bones screamed.

Her hand splayed against my ribs, fingers digging in. For a heartbeat, I saw it clearly, even through the glare. A sigil blazed on her wrist. Mine —my mark, the one The First Light branded into me when He named me Morning Star—was there, unmistakable. But it wasn't alone. Another design coiled through it, wrapping around it, threading between its lines.

Not Heaven's script. Not Hell's. Not His. Something else. Something other. Something I'd never seen before. The two marks weren't fighting. They were woven together. Entwined.

And then—we detonated. Blinding light erupted from our kiss like we'd just split Heaven wide open. Gold and white and burning, it poured off us in radiant shockwaves. The grotto exploded with it— every wall, every stone lit up like creation's first sunrise. The light wasn't coming from just her, or me. It was coming from *us.*

And the Garden of the Forsaken answered. The earth groaned. Vines snapped. Branches bowed low in reverence or fear—I couldn't tell which. Then the wind came, crashing through the grotto like a living storm.

But none of it could drown out the flashes of memories breaking open inside me—because her kiss had unlocked them. I saw her sculpting a river with her bare hands, laughing beneath a sun I remembered all too well. I saw the view from Mount Semarel as I felt too awestruck to speak—a quick glance as she'd turned and smiled at me.

She taught me... something. I remember singing

together. Of building... something, the two of us. There was light. Love. But then... there was some kind of judgment. Swords drawn. Punishment? I felt it hit me, and it nearly broke me.

Did I fall for pride and vanity? Did I really have the ambition to be above The First Light? I don't—. Was I punished for falling for her? Was that seen as unforgivable in the eyes of The First Light? Did Heaven damn me for love?

I tore away from the kiss, gasping. The light still burned in my chest, but now it flickered with fury at what was stolen from us, at who I had become in the absence of truth. At Lilith. At The First Light.

"I remember," I rasped, voice shaking, hoarse from disuse.

My wounds were healing. She... had healed me, and I barely felt the pain of them anymore. I cupped her cheek. My body trembled, but I was no longer lost. My gaze locked on her—stunned, reverent, wrecked.

And then I roared—not from pain. From rage. From the unbearable clarity of knowing what they'd taken from me. What He'd taken from me.

We both heard the footsteps. Fast. Breathless. I tensed immediately, pain slicing through me as I raised up and shifted forward, ready to fight again —to protect her. Even if my body failed, even if I burned out doing it. I'd already lost her once. It wasn't happening again.

Destiny burst in, wide-eyed and panting. Topher skidded in behind her, wild relief on his face.

"Evie!" she cried. Then she saw me. "Oh my god."

Topher took one long look at me—scorched, bleeding, barely upright. His voice was level. Almost. "You're... alive."

Not a question. A statement. But his shoulders

dropped the tiniest fraction, like something he'd been holding finally let go.

"Well. That's a relief. For a moment there, I thought I'd have to explain this to someone. And I hate paperwork."

I didn't bother answering. My body still ached, but I could feel it changing in real time, heat knitting muscle back onto bone, skin sealing where it had split, the slow, relentless pull of healing dragging me toward whole. Every breath hurt a little less than the last. Every heartbeat rewrote the damage.

But something else had shifted, deeper than flesh. I wasn't just surviving anymore. I was becoming.

Destiny took a cautious step closer, gaze flicking between us. "You found him," she said.

Evie nodded her head softly. "I did, but he's injured."

My eyes slid to Destiny. "Half-breed," I murmured. "You were... watching her."

"I was protecting her," she replied, chin raised.

I nodded. Just once. It was enough.

Topher crossed his arms. "So what now? You going to kill me, or wait until we're back at The Revel?"

I tilted my head. "Why not both?"

Evie helped me to my feet. I still shook. Still felt every wound. But I was upright. Awake. Feeling stronger. And when we turned toward the grotto's mouth, the air was different. No longer thick with decay. It felt... alive.

Bright light spilled in through cracks in the stone. Not the dim, red glow of Hell, but something golden. The vines pulsed with new color. The trees had changed—no longer skeletal and gray, but flushed with green. Flowers bloomed everywhere. The stone itself seemed to breathe.

The Garden was responding. To her. To me. The ground beneath us trembled—not violently, but with purpose like something buried had rolled over in its sleep and was waking up.

I glanced at her, then back at the path ahead, and —No. No, that couldn't be—I squinted against the gold. "What the fuck..."

Because it wasn't fire, it wasn't an illusion. It was sunlight in Hell. And I had no idea how any of it was happening. But the Garden—this godforsaken graveyard of everything I'd lost—was answering her like it loved her.

The four of us stepped out of the grotto, and Evie's hand slipped into mine as we stood there, staring out at the color bleeding into a place that had always been rotting before.

"Can we go home now?" she asked, voice small. Hopeful.

Fuck, how I wanted to say yes. But I hadn't accomplished the one thing I'd come here to do.

"Not yet," I said, tugging gently on her hand. "Come on. Hurry."

She frowned. "Where are we—?"

"Lilith knows," I said, voice low. "She has to. After what just happened... there's no way she didn't feel that. And if she did..." I swallowed. "Then He might know too."

Topher stepped forward, eyes narrowing. "Want me to stay behind?"

I nodded. "Keep watch."

Destiny touched his arm. "I'll stay with him."

I turned back to Evie and gripped her hand tighter. "I just need to get something. And then we can get out of here."

She nodded, no questions. Hell, she was brave.

We ran, our footsteps pounding over roots and

broken stone, the Garden shifting around us as we moved. Trees that had been gray a breath ago now burst with color, their branches stretching, leaves unfurling in fast, greedy spirals. Petals fluttering through the air.

I could feel her heartbeat pulsing against my palm—fast, steady, tethering me to the moment. Then we stopped. The world narrowed. There. It stood alone in a clearing choked with new growth— an ancient thing, older than death, its bark blackened and grooved like scar tissue. The trunk hunched low, as if crushed beneath the weight of time itself.

The other trees had come back to life. But this one hadn't. Not a single leaf. Not a single bloom. Just roots curled deep into the soil, like they were holding something the Garden wasn't ready to give up.

"This is it," I muttered.

I dropped to my knees and began tearing at the warm earth with my hands, dirt and roots catching under my nails. The soil here was strange—soft, but heavy, like it didn't want to give anything back.

Evie hovered above me. "What are we looking for?"

I didn't answer. I wasn't sure how to explain. She hesitated, then dropped beside me without another word and started digging with me.

We worked in silence. The ground resisted. Time slipped. Finally, my fingers closed around the edge of something thin. Fragile.

I pulled gently, brushing the dirt away with shaking hands. A folded piece of parchment. It was old, but intact. I didn't unfold it. Just stared for a beat, then tucked it carefully into the inside pocket of my jacket.

"We should definitely leave now," I said, standing.

Evie didn't argue, and we ran. Topher and Destiny were waiting near the treeline. I pulled Topher in close and whispered something into his ear. He nodded once, grim. Then we all turned back the way we'd come—through the garden, back to the entrance.

We made it to the edge of the Crimson Verge. And that's when the ground trembled like a war drum being struck. Figures appeared in the shimmering red haze, rows upon rows of armored shadows and gleaming eyes, teeth bared in cruel smiles.

At the front, standing tall in black and silver, her crown of thorns glinting like a threat, was Lilith. She smiled. I stepped in front of Evie before I even thought about it. Lilith's presence hit like a wave of heat—sharp, dry, suffocating—the kind of heat that scorched you from the inside out and left nothing but ash and silence.

Her army stood behind her, stretching into the haze. Demons. Wraiths. Imps. Watchers. Forsaken things scraped from the corners of old punishments. Not just for show. She was here for blood.

She walked forward like she had all the time in the world, her steps silent against the cracked dirt of the Verge.

"Well, well, well," she said, tilting her head. "Look at you. All lit up and practically glowing."

Evie tensed behind me. I didn't respond. Not yet.

Lilith's eyes slid to the side, finding Destiny and Topher. "How disappointing," she purred. "All these years in my debt, and you cash it in for her?"

Destiny stiffened. Topher said nothing, which was his most dangerous setting. He simply reached back, hand brushing lightly against Destiny's hip—

just enough to guide her a half-step behind him. All while his expression remained smooth as ever, like he was bored.

I didn't miss it. And I couldn't help but wonder — what the hell was going on between those two?

Lilith turned back to me.

"You always had such potential," she said. "Could've ruled beside me. Instead, you chose exile —chose to chase a woman who doesn't even know what she is."

"She knows enough," I said. "And she came for me. Which is more than I can say for you or anyone else."

Lilith's smile faded. "There it is," she said. "The weakness." She took a step forward. "You remember now, don't you?"

I said nothing. But the paper in my coat pocket suddenly felt heavier.

Lilith's gaze flicked to Evie. "Do you know what he gave up for you? What he cost Heaven for a single kiss?"

I stepped forward, just enough to shield Evie again.

"Don't."

She laughed—low and venom-laced. "You think you can protect her now? After all this time? You couldn't even protect her then. That's why they erased her. Her name. Everything."

The ground cracked beneath my boots. I didn't raise my voice. I didn't need to.

"You will never be her," I said. "You'll never have what she did. Her place. Her light."

Lilith's eyes narrowed. "She was forgotten for a reason," she spat.

"No," I said. "She was forgotten because *you* somehow gained the ear of the First Light."

Her expression faltered, just for a moment. But I saw it.

"What I don't get," I went on, "is why. Why did you even care?"

Her smile returned, wider now —meaner.

"You wouldn't understand," she said, tilting her head. "Not when you were always His favorite."

The sky behind her darkened like it was holding its breath.

"Was that it?" I pushed. "Jealousy?"

"You never saw it," she snapped. "He made you in light and trusted you with everything. And you gave it all up. For her."

I didn't look away. "And I'd do it again."

The ground shook. Thunder cracked, not above us —but beneath—the very ground split. The crimson light fractured upward as the sky tore itself open like something was crawling through it.

She looked up, just for a moment. "What did you do?" she hissed.

I reached for Evie's hand and held tight.

Pain tore through my back. I dropped to one knee, a sound escaping my throat I couldn't even name. Heat surged down my spine, searing through muscle and memory.

My wings burst free. Feathers, white as starlight and charred at the tips, flared open behind me, stretching wide enough to blot the sun. My breath caught.

Lilith staggered back. The crown on her head shimmered—then vanished in a blink, like even it no longer recognized her right to wear it. Her lips curled. She spat something in the old tongue, a curse dredged from the first war.

And then they came. The Demons. The Wraiths. The Imps. The Watchers. Tearing through the air like a storm of claws and shadow, shrieking across the Verge—ugly things with old grudges and fresh orders. The sky split behind them, black veins cracking through the light we'd just lit.

They weren't just coming. They were hunting. And we were already surrounded.

Evie screamed my name. I turned, panic rising. But her hands lifted on instinct.

Suddenly, every stone in the Crimson Verge rose with them. Hundreds, thousands of rocks—some small, others heavy as boulders—lifted into the air, suspended in a trembling orbit above her like a halo of ruin.

She didn't even hesitate. With a sweep of her arms, the rocks shot forward—arcing, swarming, slamming into them with a force that made the ground jump. Each impact shattered the creatures into smoke. One by one. Precise. Unrelenting.

I stared at her in awe.

The sigil on her wrist burned bright gold now, humming with every breath she took. Her eyes were locked on the field, calculating, wild. No wings. No crown. And still, divinity clung to her like flame. She was forged to build worlds—and burn down anything that tried to erase her.

In that moment, something tore loose inside of me. No, just the memories, but something older. Something ethereal. I couldn't breathe. Couldn't blink. Because I was no longer fully in Hell, I was there, back in Eden. The real one. Before the war. Before the Fall.

She was by the river, barefoot on soft moss, the water rushing swiftly and brightly beside her. Her fingers danced across unopened flower buds, humming softly—and as she touched them, they bloomed beneath her touch, a rainbow of colors like she was waking them from a dream.

I remembered the way I'd approached her. Quietly, reverently. Not wanting to break the spell. And then she sang. It was simple at first—a wordless melody, pure and light as breath. I'd never heard anything like it. It curled around me like warmth, like home, and before I could stop myself, I joined her.

My voice layered beneath hers, and the harmony caught like a flame. And I swear, the air shimmered. Light began to pour from our skin—not bright like fire, but golden and soft, like sunlight filtering through morning mist. It pulsed in time with our song as it swirled around us.

The garden around us changed. Trees burst taller. Leaves turned jeweled. Vines spiraled in delight. The river glowed. The world responded to us. We were creating together—without intention. Without permission.

Evie stopped singing first. She looked around, eyes wide, chest rising and falling with something between awe and fear. Then she looked at me.

"Did you know we could do that?" she whispered.

I shook my head, equally stunned. "No."

The trees had doubled in height. The fruit dripped with gold. The flowers were the size of stars.

"Should we..." Her voice dropped to a hush. "Should we keep this to ourselves?"

I remembered how my hand found hers then, how I nodded. How I swore I would.

Then... It was gone. I was back in the Verge. In Hell. My wings burned at my back. The things around us, twisted, shrieking abominations, all fang and hunger, turning to smoke, torn apart by the light.

And Evie was standing in front of me, radiant and furious and magnificent. Not just a woman. She was the key. The one they made me forget. The reason I Fell. And they were going to pay.

CHAPTER TWENTY-FOUR

Evie

I came back to myself screaming.

Not out loud, thankfully. My throat was already raw from that. But inside, every nerve in my body was still on fire from what had just happened in… no. No, that wasn't right.

Hell wasn't real. Right?

My brain didn't seem to care what I decided. It kept replaying it anyway in shaky, overexposed flashes. Rocks hanging in the air like a halo. Demons turning to smoke. Luc's wings, holy and terrible, exploding out of his back. Lilith's face when the crown vanished.

Then—white. A tearing sensation, like the world itself had been ripped inside out.

And now… carpet.

I was on my knees on something soft, not ash. My palms sank into plush fibers instead of cracked stone. The air no longer tasted like metal and sulphur. It tasted like expensive whiskey and recirculated hotel AC.

My stomach flipped. Either I'd hallucinated all of it, or I was having the world's worst comedown.

The Revel. We were back.

A pair of shoes first appeared in my blurred vision. Destiny's boots. One scuffed, one clean. Her voice came a second later, sharp but shaking. "She's breathing," she said. "That's a good start."

"Move," Luc rasped.

Hands slid under my arms, hauling me up. The room tilted, then steadied. I blinked until the chandelier stopped doubling and realized we were in his penthouse again. Same impossible view of the Vegas neon. Same floor-to-ceiling windows. Same ridiculous sofa that probably cost more than my yearly income. Except now there was a smear of Hell's dirt on the white rug, and my hands were still trembling with power I didn't understand.

"Easy," Luc said.

His face swam into focus. Pale. Blood still drying along his side where a sword had gone in. Shirt shredded. Wings gone again, tucked wherever the hell he kept those. His eyes were... not normal. Not anymore. Maybe they never were. But something bright and old flickered behind the black like banked lightning.

"You okay?" I croaked.

"Define okay," he said.

Topher snorted from somewhere behind him. "Well, nobody's dead. Yet. That's a win in my book."

I turned my head slowly. Destiny and Topher were both here, soot-streaked and singed at the edges, like they'd been through the same blender we had, but alive. Destiny's eyeliner was smeared halfway down one cheek. Her chin lifted when she saw me looking.

"You did good, Evie," she said. "Very, very terrifying, but good."

My knees threatened to give out again. Luc

tightened his grip.

"Sit," he ordered.

Normally, I would have bristled at that. Right now, I just sort of folded until the couch caught me. He sat next to me, close enough that our shoulders brushed.

The room hummed. I realized after a second that it wasn't the air conditioner. It was me. The sigil burned faintly on my wrist, gold light tracing the lines like an afterimage. When I flexed my fingers, it pulsed in time with my heartbeat.

I stared at it. "So," I said, voice thin, "that wasn't a psychotic break, then."

"Depends on your definition," Topher said. "But given the alternative was all of us getting dismembered, I'm going with 'no.'"

My laugh came out wrecked and a little hysterical. But Luc didn't laugh. He watched me instead, jaw tight, like he was bracing for... something.

"Talk fast," Destiny said, crossing her arms. "Because we may be out of Hell, but you set off something in there, and now that Lilith knows, every creep on both sides probably knows, too."

My voice shook. "The First Light might know, too."

Luc's eyes flicked to me, then away, like the name tasted bad.

"Yeah," he said quietly. "He might."

He. The capital H was implied and made my skin crawl.

I swallowed. "So you want to maybe explain what exactly He might know? Because I'm still stuck on the part where I apparently turned Hell into a botanical garden and don't know how I did that."

Destiny muttered, "Same," under her breath.

Topher glanced at Luc. "We'll give you a minute," he said. "But not more than that. We check the wards, clear the floor, and maybe throw some salt at the elevator."

Destiny rolled her eyes but nodded. "If anyone tries to get up here, we'll stall."

She brushed her fingers lightly against the back of my hand as she passed—a small, grounding touch.

"Breathe," she said. "You're here. You're safe. For the next five minutes, anyway."

Then she and Topher slipped out, the door clicking shut behind them.

I stared at my glowing wrist, then at him.

"Talk to me," I said. The words came out thin, like I was holding myself together with them. "No more riddles. Not tonight."

His mouth twitched, something almost like a smile, and then it was gone.

"Fair," he said.

He exhaled, long and slow, like he was letting centuries out with it, and turned to fully face me, one leg tucked up on the couch. Up close, I could see every crack the last couple of days had put in him, the blood on his collar. Bruises blooming along his throat like storm clouds. Eyes that looked a little too bright for this world.

"You want the short version or the true one?" he asked.

"Are those different?" I said.

"Oh, very," he said. "The short version is that you're not just some human who stumbled into my mess. You're... older than this universe. And He is going to lose His fucking mind when He figures out you're awake."

My stomach flipped.

"Okay," I said slowly. "And the true one?"

His gaze dropped to my hand. His fingers hovered above my wrist, just above the sigil, like touching the light might burn him.

"You had many names before this, but one true one," he said.

Static cracked down my spine. Cold, then heat. The room blurred at the edges like reality couldn't hold its shape around that sentence.

"Don't," I whispered. "Don't make up pretty names for me right now, I can't..."

"I'm not," he said, sharper. "And I can't tell you what it is because I don't know it." His jaw clenched, like the admission tasted like blood. "But I know it exists. Or it did."

I swallowed hard. "You don't know it," I repeated.

"No," he said. "Not yet."

Something in me wanted to laugh, or scream, or do both at once. "So I'm a story with the title ripped off."

A ghost of a smile flickered and died. "Yeah. Welcome to my week."

He looked down again, not at my face, at my hands, like my skin was a map he'd once memorized and now couldn't read.

"Soon after we met, I started having these flashbacks, visions, something." He said, quieter. "I think... you were part of His Heavenly Artisans."

"What is a Heavenly Artisan?"

"You made things. Not like... craft night. Real things. Rivers. Gardens. Those pockets of beauty scattered across His universe? That wasn't random. That was you."

The words should've sounded impossible.

Instead, they landed like a match on dry tinder

because I'd seen it. Not in memory, not in daylight, but in the place my mind went when sleep cracked me open. I'd woken up breathless more nights than I could count, heart pounding, fingers aching like they'd been working all night.

Rivers spilling from my palms like ribbon. Stone smoothing itself under my touch. A night sky unfurling, star by star, like I was pinning glitter to velvet and calling it holy. The taste of creation on my tongue, metallic and sweet.

And him. Always him.

I remembered a silhouette in gold light. A mouth that knew my name without speaking it. Wings, the edges dipped in gold, sometimes. Sometimes just his eyes, too pale, too bright, too familiar, like he'd been staring at me since the beginning of time.

I'd told myself they were just dreams, too much whiskey, too much Lucifer in my bloodstream. But my body didn't treat them like fiction. My body treated them like longing.

I swallowed, hard. "I've... dreamed about it," I admitted, and my voice sounded wrong, like it belonged to someone standing in a cathedral. "Rivers. The sky. Stars. Like I'm... making it." I laughed once, sharp and miserable. "Which is insane."

Luc's gaze snapped to mine. The shift in him was instant, like he'd been waiting for that sentence.

"You've seen it," he said, low.

"Not like a memory," I said quickly, because if I said the other thing out loud, I might crack in half. "Like dreams. Like flashes. Like I'm half-awake, lucid dreaming, and something is trying to push through."

His throat bobbed. "What else?" he asked.

My fingers curled into the couch cushion. My

pulse thudded against my ribs. I didn't want to say it. I said it anyway.

"You," I whispered. "I see you."

A beat of silence, thick as velvet. His expression changed, subtle but seismic, like something ancient inside him sat up and listened.

"Me," he echoed.

"Not you in Vegas," I said, because that was easy, that was the man bleeding on the couch. "You... before. I don't know how I know. I just do. You're always there. Like you're watching. Like you're waiting. Like I'm supposed to turn around, and you'll be right behind me, and it'll make sense."

His eyes burned. "And does it?" he asked.

"No," I said, voice shaking. "It never makes sense. It just feels... familiar. Familiar like it aches to remember."

Something in his face tightened, then broke open into something raw.

"After that kiss," he said, like he was answering a question my soul had been asking for years. "That's when it all clicked into place. Hell reacted. The Garden did. You did. And something in me cracked."

He pressed his fingers to his temple, like he could physically hold the memories in place.

"I saw water," he said. "Over smooth stone. I smelled fresh grass. I heard you," he added, and the way he said it made my lungs stutter. "Not your voice now. Your voice then. Like you were singing under your breath while you worked. Like it was normal to build a world and hum through it."

My stomach lurched because I'd heard that, too. Not the melody, not clearly, but the feeling of it, a song threaded through sunlight.

"And us?" I managed.

His jaw flexed. He looked away for half a second,

then back, like he was choosing to tell me even if it cost him.

"We were... together," he said, and the words fell heavy, sacred. "Before all this. Before Hell. Before Lilith. Before the Revel. Eden wasn't a myth to you. It was your workshop. You built what you wanted. I watched you. You taught me how to create, and I just couldn't stay away because... because I couldn't help myself."

Images brushed the edges of my mind. Leaves. Water. A hand at my waist. A laugh I felt in my bones. Each flicker slipped away like a dream dissolving at dawn, but it left heat behind, like fingerprints on glass.

I shook my head because I had to, because my reality was splitting like a seam. "No," I said. "I grew up in a congregation in Nowhere, Texas. My biggest artistic achievement was glitter posters for youth group. I don't remember any of that."

"I know," he said quietly. "That's the point."

My throat tightened. "Then why do I dream it?" I demanded. "Why do I dream of you?"

Luc stared at me like the question tore something open in him.

"Because even without your name," he said, voice rough, "even with everything He did to bury you, something in you is still reaching. And something in you still knows me."

My chest ached like it was trying to remember how to beat.

"And the name," I whispered, because I hated how badly I wanted it, how badly I wanted a word that could unlock me. "You said you don't know it."

"I don't," he said. "But I think it's the key. There's a page, torn out of the Book of Names. Lilith hid it. That's what I dug up in the Garden of the Forsaken."

His gaze dipped to the blood on his shirt, like he could still feel the dirt under his nails. "I haven't opened it yet. I can't do it here. I'm sure it's warded, and as soon as I open it, He'll know. So I need to take it to a special room here in The Revel—old protections. Topher's going to help me so we don't light up the whole damn place.

My pulse stumbled. "So you're going down there right now."

"Yes," he said.

"And you think it'll tell you who I am."

"I think it'll tell me what He tried to delete," he said. "And if it's there, if your name is still there, it might unlock everything."

I stared at my glowing wrist, at the soft, pulsing sigil, and felt my dreams press against the inside of my skull like fists against a door.

"And if it isn't?" I asked, even though I didn't want to.

His mouth went still.

"Then we've got a problem," he said.

Silence stretched, Vegas glittering through the glass, bright and oblivious. My hand shook in my lap, the light warm as a heartbeat.

I met his gaze.

"I don't remember being her," I said, voice thin and honest. "But I have flashes of you. More than anything. That's the part that scares me."

Something eased in him, almost imperceptible, like my confession gave him a thread to hold onto.

"That doesn't scare me," he said softly. "That gives me hope."

"Hope's a dangerous hobby," I muttered.

He huffed a breath, almost a laugh. "Yeah," he said. "I noticed."

His hand brushed mine, and I let myself breathe.

"This all feels like you're talking about someone else."

"I know."

I looked at my glowing wrist, at the mark that felt both foreign and intimate.

"But I know I have a connection to you. It's how I knew I had to save you in Hell," I said slowly. "I had to go after you. It was like I was compelled, and that wasn't some ancient version of me. That was now. That was real."

Something eased in his expression, like I'd taken a weight off his spine.

I let out a shaky breath. "So what happens next?"

His eyes darkened. "Now?" he said. "We try to stay alive long enough for you to wake up on your own terms."

"And if I don't?"

He reached out then, finally, brushing his knuckles against mine.

"Then I'll still choose you," he said. "Every time."

CHAPTER TWENTY-FIVE

Lucifer

I didn't realize I was staring at her hand until the room came back into focus.

Her sigil still glowed low and gold in the center of her wrist, pulsing with every shaky breath she took. In the grotto, it had flared like a star going supernova, my own mark blazing inside it, entwined with something else that wasn't Heaven or Hell or anything I recognized. Now it just smoldered quietly, like it was pretending to be harmless.

Evie curled into the corner of my couch, blanket wrapped around her like she was trying to hold herself together with fabric and willpower. Vegas glittered beyond the glass, all neon and noise, like nothing had shifted three dimensions over. Like we hadn't just cracked Hell open and rearranged a dead garden with a kiss.

She wasn't looking at me. She was looking at the city, jaw tight, eyes far away.

I'd just told her she used to be a worldmaker, that I'd fallen for her, that Heaven had damned me for it, that the God she grew up with had struck her from existence like a careless line.

And she'd said, very calmly for someone whose universe had been rearranged twice in one night, that she wasn't going to let them do it to her again. And I believed her.

The lock on the front door clicked. The wards flexed around us, a subtle ripple in the air only an idiot or a mortal would miss. I was neither, anymore. Pain flared when I pushed up from the couch, every muscle protesting, the half-healed wound in my side dragging like someone had stitched me back together with wire. I was mending faster than any human ever could, but slower than I was used to, every breath a reminder I wasn't what I'd been. I gritted my teeth and turned as the door swung open.

Destiny slipped inside first, moving fast, eyes sweeping the room. Topher followed, shutting the door behind him with quiet precision, then sliding every extra deadbolt into place.

She looked wrecked—makeup melted into smoky crescents under her eyes, ash dusting the purple stubble of her shaved head, jacket singed at one shoulder—but alive.

I said. "What'd you find?"

Topher didn't bother with small talk. He'd played my assistant for years here—concierge, scheduler, polite shield between me and the mortals who wanted a piece of me. It was a good disguise, that soft-spoken butler routine.

But the way he moved now, the set of his shoulders, the tight focus in his eyes—that wasn't a servant. Once, he was a commander just under me on Heaven's walls. He'd been the angel trusted to carry out orders I was too important to touch. Before the Fall, he had been one of the few who didn't hesitate when I stepped over the edge. And then, he followed me straight into Hell and never looked back.

Down here, he'd been going by Topher for decades, the man who ran my wards and my calendar. But to me, he'd always be Sariel—partner in crime, co-conspirator, the last piece of Heaven I hadn't managed to lose.

His gaze flicked over Evie, taking in the blanket, the tremor in her shoulders, the faint glow in her palm. Satisfied she was upright and breathing, he locked his attention on me.

"We've got a problem," he said.

Of course, we did. "Be more specific."

"The Revel's wards are losing their minds," he said. "Every layer. Building grid, floor net, even your private weave. They all spiked the second we came back from Hell. I've got sigils blinking that I haven't seen active in centuries."

Evie's fingers tightened on the blanket. "Is that... bad?" she asked.

"In the way heart attacks are bad," Topher said. "Yeah."

"Who's hitting us?" I asked.

He shifted his weight, expression tightening. "That's the fun part. I traced the surge. It's a blend of two signatures. First layer's familiar—hot, sharp, red. Lilith. No surprises there."

"Obviously," I muttered.

"The other one... that's the one I don't like." His eyes went distant for a heartbeat. "It was white. Bright. Cold. Like static behind your eyes when you stare at the sun too long. It burned when I looked at the trace. Upper echelon, probably archangel level. Michael, possibly. Gabriel, maybe. He never liked you."

The room felt colder.

Topher went on, "I'm pretty certain He knows now. After what happened down in Hell, there's no way He doesn't. Lilith probably ran straight to Him, and He's probably sending something to find you. Or her. Maybe even both of you."

Evie inhaled sharply. I felt her gaze on me, hot and sharp.

"And the surge is centered where?" I asked, though I already knew I wasn't going to like the answer.

Topher's gaze flicked past me, like the answer lived somewhere in the bones of the building. His fingers twitched once at his side, a nervous tell he usually kept buried.

My jaw tightened.

"It's not the whole property," he said, voice flattening. "It's a point. A knot. Like someone's pressing a thumb into the same bruise over and over."

Evie's breath caught beside me.

Topher swallowed, then forced the word out like it tasted wrong. "The Reliquary."

The air in the room seemed to change. Even the lights felt like they pulled back a fraction.

Evie blinked. "The what?"

I didn't answer her. I stared at Topher. "You're sure."

His nod was tight, immediate. "I'm sure."

My chest went cold. "That's where you put it."

Topher's eyes met mine, steady now in that irritating way of his, like he'd already decided to die if he had to. "When you shoved it into my hand back in Hell," he said quietly. "You told me to keep it off you. Off her. Off anything that could be traced through you." He shrugged, "Seemed like the best place."

I remembered the moment like a knife flash, the way I'd moved without thinking, instinct sharper than reason, Topher's startled inhale. Insurance. A contingency. A prayer with teeth.

"I didn't open it," he added. "I didn't even look at it. I took it straight here."

Evie's voice came soft, cautious. "What is the Reliquary?"

Topher hesitated, eyes flicking to me like he was asking permission to say it out loud.

"It's a vault," I said instead. "A place I built for... certain kinds of transactions."

Evie's gaze sharpened. "Transactions."

Topher's mouth tightened. "It's where deals go when it's time to pay," he said. "It's not just a room, Evie. It's an access point. A direct route."

"To Hell," she whispered, like the word had been waiting behind her teeth.

Topher nodded once. "Exactly. The Reliquary sits on a seam. Old wards, old stone, old blood. The protections are layered in there thick enough to choke a demon."

"And still it's surging," I said, voice low.

"Yes," Topher said. "That's what scares me."

Evie looked between us. "Why would Heaven—"

"Because it's loud," Topher cut in, and the sharpness in his voice surprised even him. He exhaled, steadied. "Not the page itself. The movement of it. The fact that it came out of hiding. The fact that we came back from Hell with something no one is supposed to touch." His eyes went distant again, as if he could still feel the white-cold burn of the trace. "And because the Reliquary isn't neutral. It's a throat. If you drop something into it, the universe notices the swallow."

My pulse thudded hard, slow, ugly.

"So Lilith is pressing from one side," I said.

Topher nodded. "She wants it back."

"And the other signature," I murmured.

Topher's face went tight as he rubbed his thumb along his palm like he could scrub the sensation off. "They're not guessing anymore. They're tracing. Testing your wards. Listening for the smallest crack."

Evie's hand drifted unconsciously toward her glowing wrist.

"And if they find one?" she asked, voice thin.

Topher looked at her, and for once, there was no sarcasm in his voice at all—only truth.

"Then they won't come through the front doors," he said. "They'll come through the one you built beneath them."

Silence stretched. The Revel's glittering skyline stared back at us through the glass like it had no idea what was living under its feet.

I dragged in a breath that didn't feel like it reached my lungs.

"Then we don't let them," I said.

Topher's eyes held mine. "Then we'd better move," he said, "because whatever's pushing on that room already knows exactly where to press."

I exhaled. "We need to deal with it before this place becomes a very pretty, very haunted crater."

Destiny shifted her weight, boots creaking. "So the thing you dug up under the creepy murder tree in Hell is now acting like a divine GPS beacon," she said. "Fantastic."

Evie's gaze bounced between us. "It's because of... me?" she asked quietly.

I forced myself to look at her. Her sigil pulsed once, as if in answer, light tracing the braided pattern of my mark and that other, unknown one.

"It's not your fault," I said. "But it's tied to you, which is why I need to take care of it. Now."

She straightened a little, lifting her chin. "And I'm supposed just to sit here? Again?"

"Yes," I said.

Her eyes flashed. "No."

"It isn't optional," I said, keeping my voice level. "I need to lock it down, make sure we're not about to have uninvited company from either direction. It won't take long. You stay with Destiny. You don't open the door for anyone who isn't one of us."

"You did this same shit, and then I had to save your ass in Hell," she snapped.

"This time, I'm trying to keep you out of it."

She stared at me, searching my face, my posture, looking for any crack.

"Promise me," she said finally. "You come back."

The sigil in her palm hummed softly, a gold echo. My own mark, hidden under skin and bone, answered with a dull ache.

"I'm not leaving this hotel, I promise," I said.

Destiny stepped closer to her. "I'll be glued to her," she said. "Topher can go play ward-whisperer with you."

Topher's mouth twitched. "I prefer 'arcane systems engineer,'" he murmured, and if I hadn't been watching him, I would've missed the quick flash of a smirk.

Evie dragged the blanket a little tighter around her shoulders. "I don't want you deciding things without telling me. I already had one god rewrite my life without asking."

She was right. It still didn't change what needed to happen.

"I'm not Him," I said. "I'm not rewriting you. I'm

trying to keep Him from doing it again."

Her throat worked. Finally, she gave a short, jerky nod. "Fine," she said.

"Destiny, don't let her open anything. Doors. Windows. Portals. Topher, with me."

Topher moved to my side as I headed for the hall. I could feel Evie's gaze on my back all the way to the door, a steady weight that made my steps feel heavier. The lock clicked behind us. The wards sighed, sealing.

The private corridor behind my penthouse existed in a part of the Revel that didn't technically exist at all. The walls hummed with quiet power, sigils sunk deep beneath the stone. The air was cooler here, tasted faintly like ozone and old promises.

We walked in silence for a stretch, footsteps echoing in the narrow hall. I pressed the button to call the elevator for the Reliquary.

It was still strange, sometimes, seeing him like this. In a tailored suit, tablet in his hand instead of a sword, hair gel instead of starlight. Sariel had once guarded the outer thresholds near the Scala Aeterna, the angel who could interrupt paths, stationed where Heaven blurred into everything else. When I'd fallen, he hadn't hesitated. He'd stepped off the edge with me, trading courts of light for pits of fire without looking back.

Now he booked dinner reservations and gave annual performance reviews. Time was nothing if not petty.

The doors opened, and we stepped into a long corridor that didn't feel like part of the Revel at all, too quiet, too clean, the air faintly metallic, like the building was holding its breath down here.

We walked until the hallway narrowed and the

lights thinned, until the only thing ahead of us was the door at the end, waiting like it already knew our names.

From the outside, it looked like a standard high-limit cage door, the kind of place that smelled like money and rules and men who never smiled. Plain steel. No windows. No signage. Just a dead, unremarkable slab meant to be ignored.

That was the point.

But from the inside, it was the safest place in the building. I pressed my palm to the sigil carved at eye level. Golden light flared across my throat, reading the hum of my mark, lines of script spinning out like clockwork. The wards recognized me, then unlatched with a series of soft clicks.

The room beyond was small, windowless, and layered in protections older than the hotel itself. Shelves lined the walls, crammed with grimoires, artifacts, and things too dangerous to exist anywhere else. A table sat in the center, scarred by old spells with four chairs around it.

Topher closed the door behind us. The wards settled back into place with a sound like a sigh.

"Alright," I said. "Let's see the thing that's about to make everything harder."

Topher moved through the Reliquary like he belonged to its bones. He didn't linger over the relics or the grimoires that watched from the shelves, he went straight to a plain metal cabinet tucked beneath a row of antique ledgers, the kind of thing any casino accountant would die defending.

He slid open a shallow drawer. A yellowed inventory tag dangled from the handle, stamped in fading black ink: **HIGH-LIMIT DROP LOGS.**

Of course.

He pushed aside a stack of brittle forms and

reached deeper, fingers finding a seam that shouldn't have existed. The false bottom lifted with a soft, reluctant click, as if the room itself had to be convinced.

The air pressed against my teeth.

Topher drew out a tight bundle wrapped in black cloth. He didn't look at me when he unwrapped it, his focus narrowing, jaw set like he was disarming something that wanted to wake up angry. He held it out to me without flourish—just the offering, and the warning in his eyes.

"I locked it where no one would ever think to look," he said quietly. "But whatever's pushing on this place," he added, voice tightening, "it already knows."

The second it hit open air, the temperature dropped so fast I could see my breath. The page shivered faintly in my hand. Ancient creases cracked along the folds, but the parchment itself hadn't decayed. The ink crawled over it in tight, intricate lines, sigils woven together in a script older than most of both Heaven and Hell.

Around the edges, scorch marks still glowed faintly, pulsing with that harsh white static Topher had described. And in the center—an absence. A tear where something had been ripped out with deliberate, vicious care.

Topher inhaled. "No," he whispered. "No way."

"Yes," I said.

He stepped closer, eyes wide, all his usual dry detachment burned off by naked fear. "Lucifer," he said. "Tell me this isn't what I think it is."

He swore under his breath in a language older than dirt, the echo of old choirs still buried in his voice.

"Sariel," I said quietly.

He flinched at the name, as if it had weight. Like it still had the power to summon who he used to be. "Don't call me that in here," he muttered. "Things might remember."

Once, that name had made battalions move.

"You served near the Scala," I said. "You know what this means."

"Yeah," he said, voice rough. "It means we're fucked."

"He already knows something's off," I said. "The wards wouldn't be screaming otherwise."

Topher jabbed a finger toward the parchment. "You're holding a piece of His system in your hands. This isn't like swiping a crown or a relic. This is a root file. A core script. You so much as touch it wrong and reality does... something. We don't know what."

My gaze dropped to the torn center.

Once, a Name had sat there. Whole and anchored. A record that said: this is who you are, this is what you are, this is where you belong. Now it was a wound in the page. Evie's wound.

"She was on this page," I said quietly.

Topher swallowed. "Luce—"

"He ripped her out," I said, thumb hovering over the torn spot. "Didn't just scrub her. He tore her. That's why no one remembers. Why there's no record. Why no one can remember her name. He took it."

Topher shook his head. "But did He? We know her now. Whatever's gone from there, maybe it's too dangerous. Maybe it's better—"

"No," I cut in. "That doesn't mean that's all that was written here."

Topher stared at me.

"Artisans don't do what she did in that Garden," I

went on. "They don't resurrect dead realms. They don't fight off armies with a thought. They don't light me up like that. Whatever power she's carrying now... It's an anomaly. It doesn't fit the story we were given. So either He left something out of her file, or He ripped it off this page."

A sharp pulse crawled up the back of my neck, settling into that hollow between my shoulder blades, the place where my wings had once rooted, the place that never stopped aching. I forced myself to breathe through it, but the memory hit anyway, jagged and fast.

Not a full picture, just flashes. Light too bright to bear. Hands pinning me down. The first cut, hot, blinding, right where bone met grace. The tearing. The sound of my own wings ripping away from me, feather by feather, until the air felt wrong without them. Hell had grown them back eventually, slow and brutal, bone knitting under scar, feathers forcing their way through ruined skin, but that hollow between them had never forgotten the moment they were taken.

And then His hand. Right in the center of my back, where my sigil had lived since the moment He named me Morning Star. I remembered the pressure, the sear of it being carved out of me like it was something removable, disposable.

For a moment, I had thought that was mercy. That He was erasing His claim, letting me go. I had been wrong.

He caught me by the throat as I fell, nearly passing out from the pain. He forced my head back, and I'll never forget the look in His eyes. That was not the loving God I knew. His eyes were devoid of any affection. Of anything really.

He, then, pressed the same sigil, twisted, burning,

right into the base of my voice, into the place where I had first sung for Him, and later with her. My wings gone, my back hollowed, my mark shoved into my throat like a leash.

I had thought it vanished when I Fell, that it died with the rest of me. But when she kissed me in that grotto, when her sigil flared, mine had answered. From my throat. From the scar that had never healed clean.

He had not destroyed my mark. He had moved it. To control the one thing He feared most. My voice. Our harmony. Whatever we had been capable of together.

I pushed the memory down, hard, and met Topher's stare again.

He began, "You're saying—"

"I'm saying this page knows more about her than I do," I said. "And more than He wants anyone to."

The parchment pulsed in my hand, the ink shimmering like oil on water. For a heartbeat, I could almost hear something beneath the wards' hum—a far-off murmur, as if her name were trying to form on the air, its vowels frayed to static.

Destroy it? Hide it? Use it? All terrible ideas, when every part of me wanted only one thing. One impossible thing—to repair it. I wanted to carve her name back into the world. To force the universe to remember her. To put this page back whole and where it belonged in the Book of Names, and make Him choke on it.

Topher watched my face. "So what now?" he asked quietly. "We burn it? Bury it? Throw it into the Void and hope it gets lost on the way back?"

"No," I said finally. "We don't destroy it. We don't hide it."

He blinked. "Then what, exactly?"

I folded the page carefully along its ancient creases, fingers gentle despite everything roaring in me, and slid it back into the black cloth.

"We find out who it's calling to. Who tore this out. And why."

I handed it back to him, and he placed it back in the drawer, back where he'd hidden it.

Topher's eyebrows climbed. "You're going to try to read a live fragment of the Book of Names. Outside the Scala. In the middle of Vegas?"

"I don't know. It might work," I said.

"And then?" he asked.

"And then," I said, "we make sure we say it first."

Topher stared at me, like he was trying to decide if this was bravery or terminal stupidity.

"I hate this plan," he said.

"I do, too," I said. "But if He gets to her or gets that page, we might lose her. Completely. This time, I'm not letting Him write the ending. I'll kill Him before I let it happen again."

The wards shivered around us like they'd heard me.

Somewhere beyond the sealed walls of the Revel, in Heaven or Hell or whatever existed between, something ancient was listening. I hoped it was Him. I wanted The First Light to feel it, to know I remembered now, and I wasn't about to forget. I wasn't done.

Let Him watch. Let it scrape down his spine. Because there was a crack in his story, the thing I should have seen ages ago. This so-called all-powerful God was afraid of us, of her, of me, and what she and I were together. He had torn out names and wings and marks because He was scared, and His fear was my leverage. I was going to use every trembling inch of it. I was coming for Him, and this time I intended to enjoy it.

I headed towards the door. "Come on," I said. "We have a universe to piss off."

CHAPTER TWENTY-SIX

Evie

Lucifer and Topher came back to the penthouse sometime after my brain had turned to static and the TV had dissolved into nothing but mindless colors. Destiny and I were on opposite ends of the couch, half-buried in blankets. Some dating show about finding love while trapped on an island flickered across the screen, all tan people in tiny swimsuits and forced confessionals. I was too tired to follow the plot, but the premise made me snort. Nobody on that island had to worry about accidentally blowing up Hell with their feelings. Must be nice.

I felt the cushions dip when they came in, heard footsteps, the soft clink of glass from the kitchen. My body was heavy, my mind cottony. I tried to peel my eyes open, only to lose a full minute to the blur of commercials.

Destiny stretched, joints popping, then pushed up from the couch with a groan that sounded way too dramatic for someone who hadn't just crossed through Hell and back.

She leaned over and patted my shoulder. "Alright,

angel," she said, voice rough with sleep, "I gotta go home before my cats decide to unionize. They are two missed meals away from overthrowing me completely."

I gave a sleepy huff. "Tell them I respect their struggle."

She squeezed my shoulder, warm and solid. "You good?"

"Define good," I muttered.

Her gaze softened. "You're alive. That counts for something." She glanced over the back of the couch. "Mr. Morningstar, uh, Lucifer... she's fading. Try not to light anything up between the two of you."

"No promises," he said from somewhere behind me, his voice low and tired and irritatingly comforting.

Topher was by the door, hands in his pockets. He glanced at Lucifer. Something quick and unreadable passed between them.

"I'll walk Destiny down," Topher said.

My half-sleepy brain pinged on that for a second. There was a pause, a little too much awareness in the space between them. Destiny flicked her eyes his way, and for a second, the smudged eyeliner and exhaustion couldn't hide the little spark there.

Huh. "When did that become a thing?" I mumbled under my breath.

"Go," Lucifer told Topher. "Make sure she gets home safe."

He opened the door, gestured Destiny through with a quiet little bow that made her roll her eyes, and they disappeared into the hall.

The lock clicked. Something shivered over my skin, then settled again.

I blinked back to the TV. Someone was crying in a bikini. Someone else was confessing they were "absolutely here for love," in a tone that suggested they were absolutely there to advance their career in the entertainment industry.

"Didn't you say something about hating shows like this?" Lucifer asked, coming around the couch.

"I did," I said. "I also lack the will to find the remote."

He made a soft sound that might have been a laugh. The next thing I knew, he was lowering himself onto the couch, close enough that his body heat brushed my calves. He caught my ankles in his hands, gentle, like he thought I might kick on instinct, and tugged my feet into his lap.

"Hey," I protested half-heartedly.

"Relax," he said. "You look like you fought a small war."

"I did," I said. "You were there."

His thumbs pressed into the arch of my foot, and my argument disintegrated. Every muscle in my body went boneless at once.

"Oh my god," I breathed. "Keep doing that forever."

"Noted," he said quietly.

He worked his fingers along the sore lines of my feet, up the tendons, circling my ankles with careful pressure. It was ridiculous how good it felt, how safe my body decided we were, even though we had literally just run from an army and potentially pissed off a god. The TV blurred again. My eyes kept fluttering shut.

"You can sleep," he said.

"I'm not... going to..." I started, then yawned so hard my jaw popped.

His hands gentled. The last thing I registered was the feeling of his thumb drawing slow, grounding circles just above my ankle, and his voice, low and almost fond. "Sleep, Evie."

I meant to tell him I wasn't tired. I didn't make it.

When I woke up, everything was wrong. First clue, it was dark. Not TV-glow dark, not neon-leaking-through-curtains dark. Thick, quiet dark. Second clue, the surface under me was not the couch. It was too soft, too deep, like the mattress was trying to swallow me whole. Third clue, everything smelled like him.

Warm spice and clean smoke, with something sharper underneath, like the scent after a storm. It curled around me before I even opened my eyes.

Panic tried to flicker up my spine. I tamped it down and made myself breathe instead, slow and steady, like Destiny had drilled into me.

You're fine. You're not back home. Nobody is standing over your bed with a wooden spoon and a Bible. I cracked my eyes open. This was definitely not the couch. Or the guest bedroom I'd had the past couple of nights.

This room was big and shadowed, the only light a soft gold line leaking in from under what I guessed was the bathroom door. The walls were paneled in dark wood, rich mahogany that drank in the light. Built-in shelves lined one side, full of books and old bottles and objects I couldn't make out, all shapes and glass and metal.

The bed took up most of the space on the far wall, massive and ridiculous, dressed in dark sheets that felt like silk under my fingers. The headboard was carved wood, intricate and severe, edged in a pattern that looked suspiciously like sigils if I squinted, but prettier.

My pulse tripped. I was in his bed. I was in Luc's bedroom. In his bed. Fully clothed, I realized a beat later, which helped exactly a little.

My boots were gone, though. Someone had taken those off. My jacket was neatly folded over a chair. There was a glass of water next to my phone on the nightstand, both within easy reach. The care of it made my chest tighten unexpectedly.

I shifted, rolling carefully onto my other side. He was there. Lucifer lay on top of the covers beside me, still in the same dark shirt and slacks from before, one arm folded under his head, the other draped loose across his stomach. His boots were off, abandoned near the foot of the bed.

In the dim light, he looked almost human. The sharp edges of him had softened in sleep, lashes dark against his cheeks, mouth relaxed. A few stray curls of his hair fell across his forehead.

The sheet creased under his shoulders, and I could just see the outline of muscle and the faint tension that never fully left his body, even now. There was a tightness between his brows, like whatever he was dreaming about wasn't exactly restful.

His hand was close, just inches from mine on the mattress, palm up, fingers curled slightly like he had fallen asleep reaching for something.

My stomach did a slow, traitorous flip as my brain helpfully replayed what he had told me, that we had loved each other once. Not just lust, not just chaos, but in love, in Eden of all places. And I could almost see it, nearly touch it, like there was a memory right there beneath it, but it faded every time I reached for it, dissolving before I could hold on.

I should have moved. I should have sat up, slid out of the bed, anything besides lie there and stare at him like a creep. Instead, I breathed him in. The scent of him was everywhere, sunk into the sheets, into the pillows, into the air. It wrapped around me, familiar and unnerving, and my brain did this awful, wonderful thing where it whispered "Mine" before I could shut it down.

I swallowed hard. This was the room he came back to after deals and disasters and who knows how many years of pretending he didn't care about anything. This was where he slept, where the wings I had seen burst from his back had to fold somewhere in the dark. This was where he had carried me when I had passed out on the couch.

"Evie," he murmured, barely audible.

My breath caught. His eyes stayed closed, but his fingers twitched on the sheet, inching closer until the back of his hand brushed mine. Just that. The faintest touch, like his body had found me without asking his brain first.

Something in my chest went fragile and bright. "Luc," I whispered.

His lashes fluttered. For a heartbeat, gold flickered in his eyes in the low light, that not-quite-human glimmer that reminded me exactly who I was sharing a bed with.

He blinked, focused on me, and his voice came out rough with sleep. "You okay?" he asked.

It was a stupid question after everything. Hell. Lilith. The Garden. The way my entire sense of self had been turned inside out. But somehow, in that moment, in his bed in a room that smelled like him, his hand warm against mine, I didn't give him a snarky reply, and the answer surprised even me.

"I think so," I said.

His mouth curved, small and tired and real. "Good," he said.

And he didn't pull his hand away. Neither did I. But the silence stretched, warm and oddly full, like the whole room was holding its breath with us. His fingers shifted, just barely, brushing mine again, and something in my chest gave a slow, helpless flutter.

I swallowed, trying to gather thoughts that didn't feel like wet confetti. "How did I... get in here?" I asked, voice low.

He blinked once, still fogged with sleep, then looked down at the bed like he hadn't realized we were sharing it until right now. "You passed out on the couch," he murmured. "I didn't think... you'd want to wake up with a crick in your spine."

"So you carried me," I said, not sure whether to be mortified or melted.

His gaze flicked to mine. "Yeah."

My thoughts did a small somersault. "You could've put me in my room."

"I could've," he agreed softly, "but you didn't let go when I picked you up."

Heat rose up my throat. I stared at our almost-touching hands. "I—sorry."

"Don't be." His voice gentled, rough and warm. "You were scared. Exhausted. Anyone would've held on."

Anyone, maybe. Me? Not usually. I didn't cling to people. I didn't trust them to hold on. Survival 101: depend on yourself or potentially get crushed by someone else.

So why had my fingers curled into him like he was the only solid thing in a collapsing world? Why did my body decide the literal devil was safe?

Him? He didn't say why he didn't pry my hand off, didn't say why he stayed beside me instead of getting into another bed entirely. But the silence curled back in around us like a blanket.

My heart tapped a nervous little rhythm. "What

you said... in the Garden." The words felt fragile, like spun glass. "About us. About—" I had to swallow. "Being in love."

His eyes closed for a moment, lashes brushing his cheeks, and something flickered across his face. Not pain. Something older.

"I didn't lie," he said.

A tiny tremor moved through me. "But you don't remember it."

"No." His voice had that honest, scraped-down quality that only shows up at the edge of sleep. "I remember... flashes. Feelings. Like a song I used to know." His hand shifted again, knuckles grazing mine. "But when I look at you, something in me recognizes you. It always has."

I forgot how to breathe for a second.

He opened his eyes fully now, awake in a way that made the room feel too small. "When I said we were in love once... I didn't mean to scare you. I just —" His throat worked. "I feel it, even without the memory. I know it. And that terrifies me more than anything else in this universe."

My pulse tripped hard. "Terrifies you?"

"Evie," he murmured, almost like a warning, "nothing scares me."

"But me? I scare you?" I whispered.

He didn't answer. He didn't need to. The look in his eyes was enough. And then something warm and reckless unfurled inside me, slow and bright and dangerous.

We stayed like that for a long time, hands barely brushing, our breaths syncing without trying. Little by little, without really meaning to, we inched closer, a slow drift across the sheets until the space between us felt narrow and charged. It wasn't a kiss. It wasn't sex. But somehow it felt just as intimate, like we were standing at the edge of something neither of us could name.

His voice dropped to a murmur, husky with exhaustion. "You should try to sleep again."

"I'm not sure I can," I said quietly.

He was quiet for a beat, then shifted, rolling just enough that his body angled toward mine. Slowly, like he was afraid of spooking me, he lifted his arm in a loose arc, leaving a space between us—an invitation, not a command.

Every alarm bell from my past gave a half-hearted clang. I didn't curl into people. I didn't let anyone cage me in their arms. That had never meant safety before. But this didn't feel like a trap. It felt like... shelter.

I turned my head, meeting his eyes in the dim light. No coaxing, no smugness, no you owe me this. Just tired worry and a question he didn't say out loud.

For once, nobody was deciding for me. My chest squeezed, and I made the call. I scooted closer, inch by inch, until I could nestle into that offered space. His arm came down around me, careful and warm, his hand resting open at my side instead of gripping.

His breath hitched—just a fraction. But I felt it.

"Try," he whispered near my hair. "I'm right here."

Pressed against his chest, the storm inside me finally eased. For the first time since Hell, since probably even before that, a long, shaky breath slipped out of me, like I'd been holding it for years. His heartbeat was a steady drum under my ear, anchoring me, my body relaxing bit by bit as my breaths slowly fell into rhythm with his.

The last thing I felt before sleep pulled me back

under was his hand splaying gently against my ribs, not holding me in place, just… holding me. Safe enough to shatter me.

CHAPTER TWENTY-SEVEN

Lucifer

I didn't sleep. Didn't even come close. Evie was tucked into my side, warm and soft and breathing slow against my chest, and I lay there like a corpse pretending to be calm. Every twitch of her fingers had my heart snagging on bone. Every shift of her breath made something in me tighten with that terrible, unfamiliar feeling.

Relief. Gods, she finally slept. Peaceful. Safe. For the first time since I'd dragged her into this mess. And I wasn't about to ruin that. I had a feeling she hadn't slept like that since Hell, maybe not in years. And I was terrified to move in case I shattered whatever fragile spell we had wrapped ourselves in. I held her until dawn started bleeding thin gold over the city. She murmured something in her sleep and rolled away, oblivious, her face burrowing deeper into my pillow.

I slipped out of the bed before she woke enough to notice, pulling the blankets around her shoulders. I stood there for a moment, watching her and trying to memorize the shape of her against my sheets.

Then I forced myself out to the balcony. The

morning wind was cold enough to bite. I lit a cigarette anyway, letting the smoke sting my lungs until I felt something like clarity.

Dalca's last words kept circling in my skull like vultures. "Maybe she found something you've forgotten."

Forgotten. Like I needed him to remind me. I knew exactly what—who—I'd forgotten. Evie wasn't a mystery anymore. She was the missing piece carved out of my existence by that sanctimonious shit, The First Light. Loving god? Please... He'd decided love was more dangerous than rebellion.

Interesting that he kept Lilith so close. Ironic, really. His treasured little wanderer. His obedient daughter with fangs hidden behind that smile. And all this time, she had enjoyed playing the keeper of His forbidden knowledge, guarding the truth of my Fall like it was a jewel she could hide beneath her tongue.

She knew what had been taken from me. She knew who I had loved. She knew how He carved Evie out of my memory and rewrote the universe around the wound. Yet Lilith had held that truth tight for centuries, millennia, savoring every moment of my oblivion.

But the ache inside my chest pulling me toward Evie, the awakening in her voice when she said my name... There was no forgetting anymore. The truth was awake. And so was I.

I took one last drag and wondered... who else knew because someone had to.

And that's when it hit me. Hard. Because I was pretty sure the answer had claws, a velvet laugh, and a long history of whispering in the wrong ears.

Vespera. Lilith's old castoff. That fucking bitch.

Once upon a time, she had been Lilith's shadow,

her confidante, gliding three steps behind her with a smile that promised pleasure while her eyes promised ruin. She listened to every secret poured in rage or ecstasy, every stray confession that should have died in the dark. If The First Light ever muttered even a fragment of His intentions during that time, Vespera would have heard it, stored it, and savored it as she did with every other forbidden thing.

And if Lilith ever wavered, ever doubted, ever panicked about the name she helped bury, Vespera would have been the first creature she ran to. She had to know. She always knew the things no one else was supposed to.

And now she was out there running a brothel on the edge of my city, spinning illusions for mortals and poison for demons, selling pleasure like it was absolution. The Siren Room, they called it. Vespera always did love a drowning metaphor.

I ground the cigarette out against the railing and watched the ember die before flicking it off the balcony and pushing off the railing.

If she had even a sliver of the truth about Evie, about the stolen name, about what The First Light carved out of my bones, then I was going to drag it out of her one way or another. She would lie and smile while she did it. She would enjoy every moment of making me ask. She always had. But she also now hated Lilith. And hate was a currency Vespera never squandered.

I walked back inside, the decision settling heavy and cold in my gut. Fine. If the serpent wanted to hiss secrets in the dark, I would let her. And if she tried to bite, I would break her fangs myself.

The penthouse felt too quiet, too warm, too human for the war curling in my bones. I should have gone straight to Evie. Should have checked on her, made sure she was still asleep, still breathing, still here.

Instead, I stood in the middle of the living room and let the decision settle like poison. Because I couldn't take her with me, and I couldn't leave her unprotected.

I walked to the center of the room, lifted my hand, and drew the first sigil in the air. Gold light spilled from my fingertips, bright for a moment, then sank into the walls like breath taken too deep.

The air tightened. The room responded. A binding ward. Old. Cruel. Absolute.

It locked the doors. Silenced the windows. Twisted the seams of the world so nothing stepped through that I did not permit. Not Lilith. Not a demon. Not even an angel with good intentions.

Evie couldn't leave. Not until I came back. A better man wouldn't have done it. A better man would have asked. But I wasn't better, and there was no time.

I moved to the bedroom doorway and looked in. She was curled on the far side of the massive bed, tangled in the blankets I had tucked around her hours ago. Her hand rested on her chest. Her face was soft in sleep, almost peaceful.

I ached just looking at her. I stepped inside, quiet as breath. Her boots were still on the chair, her jacket folded neatly on the arm. I touched the back of the chair, fingertips brushing leather, and swallowed hard.

"I will come back," I whispered. "I swear it."

The ward hummed in the walls, waiting for my command. I turned away from the bed and put my hand on the door frame. The sigil flared gold and sank into the wood as I shut the door. It would hold.

Too well.

For a moment, I hated myself. For a moment, I almost broke it. For a moment, I nearly let her wake free. But I had seen what the world did to her when it got too close. I had felt her shaking in my arms after Hell. I had watched the way she flinched at shadows that sounded like footsteps she remembered from another life. I knew how many things now had their eyes on her, how many hands would reach if I left so much as a crack in the door.

She was exhausted, raw, held together by stubbornness and borrowed bravado. And I hardened myself. Better her fury than her death.

I sealed the front door before stepping toward the elevator. The ward sealed behind me, the faintest ripple of gold flashing across the surface before sinking out of sight.

As I slid into my car, I prayed to no one that I was not damning her trust in me beyond repair.

The Siren Room didn't look like a brothel from the outside. More like a nightclub dipped in honey and sin, tucked between abandoned warehouses and desert dust. Soft rose gold light pulsed through the curtains, warm enough to lure, dim enough to hide the teeth.

Mortals drifted in and out with the dazed look of people who had tasted something sweet and slightly poisonous. Demon glamour hummed in the air like a violin string pulled too tight.

When I stepped inside, every enchantment in the building flickered. Every demon went still. Then a familiar laugh curled through the dim like smoke.

"Well," Vespera said, stepping through a velvet curtain, "if it isn't the Morningstar. I wondered how long it would take you to crawl to me."

She looked like sin past its expiration date, still

beautiful, still lethal. Her hair hung in charred silver waves, her once gleaming horns dulled to matte ebony. Her violet eyes sparkled with cruel delight as she took me in.

"I didn't crawl," I said, voice flat.

"You always were dramatic." She drifted closer, finger trailing over my sleeve. "Tell me, what brings the fallen king to my little den of pleasures? Lilith trouble, perhaps?"

"I'm not here about Lilith."

She smiled. "Everyone is here about Lilith."

I stepped closer, crowding her space. "You're going to tell me how the name was removed from the page."

Her brows lifted. "Straight to business. I remember when you used to greet me with more... enthusiasm."

"We were never friends."

"No," she purred, "but we made such interesting enemies."

She slinked back to a chaise, settling in like a queen holding court. "So, you want to know how a name was taken from the Book. How The First Light carved your little mortal lover out of your memory."

"Tell me."

"Names are woven into creation," she said, tracing a circle on the chaise. "You don't erase them. You unmake them. Pull them from the weave and stitch the universe around the hole."

"How did He do it?"

She smiled like a cat with a baby bird. "He used you."

My stomach dropped. "Explain."

Vespera leaned forward, eyes shining. "While you slept, while she slept, He reached into the tether between you, the bond He disapproved of, and snapped it. Then He rewrote your memory around the wound. Elegant, really. Violent, but divine work often is."

I felt my pulse hammering in my throat.

A cold fury slid down my spine. "What else did The First Light do?"

Vespera stopped pacing. Her smile faltered, just a hair.

"Oh. Morningstar." She leaned forward. "You have no idea."

"Try me."

She drifted toward me, slow, graceful, predatory. Her eyes gleamed like amethyst dipped in poison.

"She has lived more lives than you can count," Vespera said. "Each one carrying the echo of what she lost. A pull toward you. A grief she never understood. And every time she came close to remembering, the world bent to stop her."

My pulse kicked hard.

"Accidents. Misfortunes. Illnesses. Death. Whatever it took to sever her path before recognition broke through."

My hands curled into fists.

"And me."

"You were rewritten," she said. "Your instinct to find her. Your recognition of her soul. The part of you that would have known her anywhere. All of it carved out. You walked through centuries numb, and she died through centuries reaching for you."

Breath caught in my throat. Vespera watched me unravel.

"He made her into a story of almosts. And He made you empty enough not to notice."

Her tone softened. "He had planned to take more than just her name."

I stared at her, chest burning.

She smiled, sharp at the edges. "And you should be grateful. Truly. Because this was the merciful version."

My stomach turned. "What the fuck does that mean?"

"I know what He really wants from her."

My jaw clenched. "Say it."

"She is an anomaly. What happened between you two should never have been possible. Yet, it did. And that... strikes His fancy. He doesn't want her gone. He wants her kept."

A cold chill slid through me.

"Kept where."

Vespera's laugh rasped like cracked glass. "In His collection, of course."

"What collection? There is no collection," I snapped. "I was in Heaven. I would know."

"No," she said softly. "You wouldn't. The Beloved are hidden and locked away, especially from angels. They are... creatures He finds interesting. Beings He plucks from worlds you have never seen. Kept out of time. Preserved."

"That's impossible."

"Oh, it's real." She stepped closer. "And Lilith? She gathers them. She moves through realms like smoke. She senses power. She seduces. She delivers. She has spent thousands of years bringing Him the things He covets."

"And you?"

Vespera's smile twisted. "I tended them. I kept them docile. Beautiful. Quiet. I made sure they stayed exactly how He wanted them."

I felt sick. "Why are you here then?"

Her laughter was sharp and bitter. "Because she found you. And suddenly I was unnecessary. Lilith discards what no longer amuses her. She threw me to the ground to make space for you."

Her eyes shone, violet and venomous. "Why do you think I'm running a brothel? It's all I was ever trained for. Tending bodies."

I stared at her, breath shallow.

"And now," she whispered, stepping close, "He wants her. Your little mortal. The soul He has been trying to break for lifetimes."

Her smile was a blade.

"You should be thankful all He did was sever your bond."

For a second, I just stared at her, breath stuck somewhere between my lungs and the pit of my stomach. Her words wrapped around me like barbed wire.

He wants her kept.

My vision narrowed. Vespera smiled slowly, satisfied, like she'd been waiting centuries to watch me come apart. My control snapped like a brittle bone. My hand was on her throat before I could think. Her breath caught, more surprise than fear, and her fingers closed around my wrist. Her pulse hammered against my palm.

"Say it again," I said. My voice sounded wrong, too quiet. Too calm. "Say He wants her."

She let out a broken laugh. "Touched a nerve."

I tightened my grip and slammed her into the wall. The impact rattled glass on the shelves, shook dust from the velvet canopy. Her feet left the floor. Her horns scraped stone.

"Tell me the truth," I said. "All of it."

Her eyes glittered, vicious and delighted. "I already did."

Heat crawled over my vision, gold pricking at the edges. I could break her neck, crush her windpipe.

Rip her fucking head off and end her. Silence her for every lifetime she'd sat on this knowledge and watched me walk blind.

But I didn't. Instead, I let go.

She slid down the wall, coughing, her hand pressing to the red marks rising on her throat. The bruises would bloom later. She'd smile when she saw them—a souvenir.

"Careful, Morningstar," she rasped. "If He felt that little tantrum, He'll be thrilled. Your rage is proof the bond's waking. Proof she's waking. And He wants that."

I couldn't breathe. I couldn't think.

I turned and walked out before I did something I couldn't come back from. The Siren Room's glamour rippled as I passed, every demon in the place holding very, very still. Vespera's laugh followed me through the curtains, low and raw and triumphant.

"Hope He doesn't get to her first," she called.

The night air hit me like a slap. The parking lot tilted under my feet. The glow from the Strip hovered miles off in the distance, neon against the dark desert sky. Out here it was quieter, emptier, the kind of silence that made every breath sound too loud. I braced a hand on the rough brick wall outside, head bowed, breath sawing in and out like my lungs had forgotten how to work.

Centuries. Lifetimes. All the times she'd died. All the times she'd reached for me and found nothing because there was nothing left in me that remembered how to reach back.

He wants her kept. Not lost. Not scattered. Not human. Kept.

My hands shook. Gold flickered at the edges of my vision. Something pulled under my ribs and thrummed like a trapped heartbeat, wild and weak and waking.

Evie. I needed to get to her.

I pushed off the wall and forced myself to move— one step, then another. Something under my ribs wouldn't settle, a strange pull I couldn't shake, like a bruise I couldn't see. Was it her? Was it Him? I didn't know. I only knew I needed to get back to her, now.

I didn't remember crossing the road. I didn't remember the Strip swallowing me in lights and noise. I didn't remember getting into the elevator or jabbing the button hard enough to crack the panel.

All I knew was that by the time I reached the penthouse door, my hands were still shaking. And for the first time in a very, very long time, I was afraid of what I'd find on the other side.

CHAPTER TWENTY-EIGHT

Evie

I woke up slowly, the way you do when your body has been running on fumes for too long. For a second, I didn't even remember falling asleep. The bed was soft, too soft, and everything smelled like him. Warm spice. Smoke. Stormlight.

That should've been comforting. It wasn't. Something felt wrong before I even opened my eyes, like the air had gone still around me. Like the room was holding its breath.

I pushed up on my elbows. Luc wasn't there. The spot beside me was cold.

A tiny tremor fluttered under my ribs. I slid out of the bed, bare feet hitting cool stone. I walked to the door, rubbing the sleep from my eyes, telling myself I was ridiculous. He'd probably gone to get food or torment Topher or brood dramatically in some hallway.

I grabbed the handle. It didn't move. I frowned and tried again, harder this time. Nothing. A soft thrum pulsed against my palm, warm and final. Magic? My stomach dropped so fast I had to put a hand on the wall.

"No," I whispered. "No, no, no."

The room tilted. The shadows stretched. I tried the handle again, frantic now, shaking it so hard the wood rattled in the frame. It didn't budge. I pressed my shoulder into the door, shoved, clawed at the gilded lock, and slammed my palm against it.

The magic flared again. Locked. I was locked in.

Something old and sharp tore open inside me. For a moment, I wasn't in the penthouse. I was twelve again, back in that narrow bedroom with the peeling floral wallpaper and the broken window. I was fourteen, listening to the key turn on the other side, knowing it'd be days before anyone slipped food under the door. I was sixteen, pounding my fists on the wood until they bruised, begging to be let out.

My pulse sped so fast my vision spotted. I stumbled back from the door, hand flying to my mouth. My breath came too quick, too sharp, hitting the back of my throat like glass.

Not again. Not here. Not with him.

I wrapped my arms around myself and tried to breathe. In. Out. Slow. Destiny had taught me the pattern. Four in. Hold. Four out. But my body didn't care. The memories swarmed like flies. The dark. The hunger. The isolation. The sound of my own heartbeat thudding in the quiet until it felt like I was disappearing.

I pressed my back into the wall and slid down until I hit the floor. My hands wouldn't stop shaking. My jaw trembled so hard I had to bite down on it.

Why would he lock me in? Why would he leave? Why would he do that to me?

A helpless sound cracked out of my chest, half sob, half laugh, because wasn't this to be expected?

Of course, the universe would put me in a room I couldn't get out of, right after I finally let myself feel safe enough to fall asleep next to someone.

"Luc," I whispered, voice shaking. "Where are you?" Silence answered.

I pulled my knees in and pressed my forehead to them, trying to make my breathing get smaller, quieter, anything to stop the panic from clawing up my throat. He wouldn't hurt me. He wouldn't. Except he'd locked me in. Just like them.

My eyes burned. I clenched my fists in my t-shirt until my knuckles went white. If he didn't come back soon, I wasn't sure what version of myself would be left. The girl who clawed at doors until her fingers bled? The teen who stopped begging because begging never mattered? The woman who swore she'd never let anyone make her small again?

I stayed there, shaking, trying not to break. Trying not to believe I already had.

I don't know how long I sat there, curled on the floor with my breath jerking in and out like my lungs were malfunctioning. Time felt slippery. Wrong. My throat was raw. My hands wouldn't stop shaking. Every sound in the room made me flinch.

So when the magic finally sighed, and the lock clicked, I froze. The door opened, and Luc stepped inside. He looked... terrible. I'd never seen him like this.

His shirt was rumpled and half untucked, eyes too bright, jaw tight, like he'd sprinted through hellfire. For half a second, relief shot through me so fast it hurt. Then the fear crashed back.

"You locked me in," I said. My voice shook as my breath stuttered. "Why would you do that?"

The question hit him like a physical force. He shut

the door behind him, leaning on it like his legs weren't steady.

"I know," he said quietly. "I'm sorry. I didn't think you'd wake up before I got back."

"What does that matter?" I asked. "Why did you lock me in at all?"

He swallowed like the question scraped on the way down. "I was trying to keep you safe."

"By trapping me?" My laugh came out sharp, broken. "Do you have any idea what that did to me?"

His gaze dragged over my face, slow and pained, taking in my red eyes, the way my shoulders were curled in on themselves, the fact that I was still half crouched against the wall like I expected him to hit me.

His whole body went still. "You woke up and thought I was doing what your father did to you," he said. Not a question. A horrified realization.

"I didn't think," I said, shaking my head as I stood up. "I remembered and... panicked."

He stepped forward. I stepped back. I flinched before I could stop myself, and he froze.

"I wouldn't hurt you," he said, softer than I ever heard him.

"You did," I whispered. "Not like them, but you still did."

Something in him cracked. I saw it. The tightness in his jaw, the tremor in his hands, the way he blinked like he was trying not to fall apart.

"I know," he said again, voice rough. "I'm sorry. I thought the ward would keep you safe. I didn't think it would make you feel trapped." He hesitated. "I didn't think you'd be afraid."

"Then you don't know me at all," I whispered.

His breath hitched, a tiny sound. He looked

wrecked, like I'd just reached in and pulled out something vital.

"I— I'm terrified of losing you," he said. "That's why I did it."

The honesty in his voice knocked something loose in me. I could feel my anger shaking under its weight.

"What happened to you?" I asked. "You didn't leave for no reason."

He looked at the floor like he couldn't bear to meet my eyes. "I needed to talk to someone, and I—I learned something. Something I should have known. Something that..." His voice broke. "I can't carry it alone."

I didn't know who moved first. I only knew my hand lifted. I touched his face gently, fingers brushing his cheekbone.

He flinched, but he leaned into the touch like it meant everything. His breath shuddered out of him. His eyes shut for a heartbeat. When his eyes met mine again, he looked at me like I was something sacred he wasn't sure he was meant to touch.

"Evie," he said, barely audible.

Something tugged low in my chest, deep and insistent, like an invisible thread had been pulled tight between us. I had the strangest feeling that if I moved away, I would feel it snapping.

He reached for my waist at the same moment I fisted my hand in his shirt. And we collided.

The kiss wasn't gentle. It was not careful. It tasted like panic and apology and ten thousand unsaid things. His mouth crashed into mine, and the world dropped out from under my feet.

His hands trembled on my back. Mine curled into his collar and dragged him closer, like I had waited lifetimes for this exact moment. Heat poured through me in a rush. The room, the ward, the past, all of it fell away. There was only the slide of his mouth, the desperate sound he made when I opened for him, the way he groaned like he'd been holding his breath for centuries.

It felt wrong to call this the first time. My body didn't act like this was new. It arched like it remembered the weight of him. My hands knew exactly where to go, the curve of his shoulders, the back of his neck, the spot in his hair that made him shudder. Somewhere under my fear, something deep and instinctive whispered, "Finally."

His hand cupped the back of my neck, fingers sliding into my hair, holding me in place while he kissed me again, deeper, harder. His breath was hot against my lips, uneven, almost frantic.

I gasped, and he used the sound like permission.

His other hand gripped my waist and hauled me closer until my chest hit his, until there wasn't a single inch of space left to breathe. He wasn't gentle. He wasn't pretending to be human. There was nothing human about the way he touched me.

His lips found their way to my shoulder, up my throat.

A shiver ran up my spine. "Luc..." I whispered.

"Say my name again," he said, voice low and ruined against my neck.

I did, and his breath caught hard enough that I felt it. He backed me up until my shoulder blades hit the wall. The impact made my breath hitch, and his eyes flashed—gold, molten, hungry—like the sound did something to him he couldn't hide.

"I shouldn't touch you like this," he said, his forehead pressing to mine, breath shaking. "Tell me to stop."

I didn't. I couldn't.

His fingers slid up my ribs, slow and possessive, his touch burning even through my shirt. He didn't push for more. He didn't rush. He just held me there with his body caging mine, waiting, trembling with how badly he wanted and how hard he was trying not to take.

"You're shaking," I whispered.

"So are you," he said. "You think I don't feel that?"

His lips brushed my jaw, my throat, the place where my pulse hammered far too fast. His mouth didn't open. His teeth didn't graze. But the promise of both hung between us, sharp as a blade.

"You locked me in," My voice cracked. Not accusing. Just honest. Exposed.

His hand slid from my waist to my hip, gripping hard, his thumb pressing into my skin like an apology he didn't know how to say out loud.

"I was scared," he said, voice raw. "Scared of what's coming. Scared of losing you before I even get to understand what you are to me."

I forgot how to breathe. "What am I to you?" I asked. "Really."

His eyes lifted to mine. They weren't blue anymore. His pupils were blown wide, gold flickering like a warning. Or a confession.

"Mine," he growled.

The word hit me like deep water, cold and hot at once. It sucked the air from my lungs, pulled me under. There it was, that sense of being caught in a current I could fight or let take me, but not ignore.

He kissed me again, nothing soft about it. His hand pinned my hip to the wall. His other slid into my hair, tilting my head back so he could take my mouth the way he wanted.

Every bit of dominance he'd been holding back poured out of him in the way he pressed against me, in the way he handled me, in the low growl in the back of his throat when I pulled him closer.

"Tell me you want this," he murmured against my lips. "You want me."

"I do," I said, breathless. "I want you."

That broke him. He lifted me in one smooth movement, his hands gripping my thighs, hauling me up against him like my body belonged there, like it had always belonged there. My legs wrapped around him without thought. His mouth found my throat, his breath hot against my skin, his teeth scraping just enough to make heat pool low and heavy in my belly.

"I've waited so long," he said, voice rough against my neck. "Longer than this life, longer than I can remember properly. I was drowning in it once. In you. I think I still am."

He carried me to the bed. He lay me down and hovered over me, his breath shaking, his eyes wild.

"If I take you," he said, voice ragged, "I won't be able to pretend afterward. I won't be able to put this back where it was. Do you understand that?"

Water, waist-deep. That is what it felt like. We were already in. This was just choosing to stop trying to touch the bottom.

"Who's pretending?" I whispered.

I reached up and slipped his shirt buttons open, one by one. My fingers brushed warm skin, and I pressed a kiss to his chest. That was all it took. His control snapped.

He shrugged out of the shirt in one rough motion and let it fall, then caught my mouth in a kiss like he'd been starving for centuries. His hands slid under my clothes, not tearing, not rushing, just gliding over my skin like he was testing how much I could take.

He traced down my sides, along my hips, over the curve of my thighs, until I felt his breath through the thin fabric of my leggings. He inhaled, low and deliberate, and my legs parted on reflex.

"Luc," I breathed.

He caught the waistband of my leggings and peeled them down slowly, like he had all the time in the world and absolutely no intention of being gentle about any of it later. When he straightened again, he slid a finger under my chin and tilted my face up.

"Look at me."

My eyes fluttered open and locked on his. The hunger there should have scared me. It didn't. It made something in me lean closer.

My shirt slid down my shoulder. He steadied it with a gentle touch, thumb brushing my skin, then took the hem with both hands and lifted it over my head like he was unwrapping something precious. The cool air hit my skin a second before his hands did, warm and possessive.

He glanced down at my underwear, the plain cotton pair I'd put on without thinking, and his mouth curved in a way that was all teeth and promise. He hooked his fingers in the sides and tugged, the fabric giving way with a sharp little rip that made my breath catch.

"I'll buy you a new pair," he murmured against my ear. "These look better in my pocket anyway."

Heat rolled through me.

He drew back just enough to look at me, mapping me with his eyes like he was carving me into memory. Like he was claiming me.

"You're overdressed," I managed.

"Am I?" His voice went low and amused. "Do something about it."

My hands found his belt. The leather was warm from his body, smooth under my fingers. I unbuckled it, the soft clink of metal loud in the quiet room.

I reached for the button, but his hand caught my wrist.

"Let me," he murmured.

He undid the button himself, slowly, watching my face the whole time, like he wanted to see every reaction. The zipper followed with a low rasp that sent a shiver straight down my spine. Then he stepped back just far enough to push his pants down and kick them aside, shedding the last bit of distance between us along with the fabric.

He sank to his knees in front of me.

Lucifer. Kneeling. The King of Hell. That sight alone scrambled my brain. The devil on the floor looking at me like I was something holy. He looked up at me from under his lashes, something dark and hungry in his eyes, then dipped his head.

His hands slid up the backs of my thighs, slow and reverent, and then he leaned in. Heat and breath and the drag of his mouth against that bundle of nerves made my whole body jolt. Whatever sound I made, he swallowed it, completely focused, like there was nothing else in the universe worth his attention.

My hands went to his curls, and heat rolled through me in waves. My heart pounded so hard I thought it might burn out of my chest.

And then... holy fuck. This. This was not like that time in the hallway. This was something else entirely. I felt it flicker. Then, something deep inside me pulsed. A spark. A flare. A pull.

His breath caught. His eyes found mine. He felt it too.

"Evie," he whispered, voice breaking as he climbed over me.

His forehead pressed to mine. His body trembled above me as he entered me in one smooth motion. He slowly began to thrust, and it was like nothing I'd ever experienced. It was like communion. With every thrust, his eyes pulsed gold.

Something ancient and bright and terrifying unfurled between us like a waking flame.

"What is that?" I whispered.

"I don't know. I've never —," he said, shaking his head, eyes wide. "But it feels like... you."

He kissed me again, deeper, his mouth desperate, his body anchoring mine, heat spiraling through every place he touched.

And with every breath, every kiss, every tremor between us, that pull grew stronger, glowing under my ribs like a truth I wasn't supposed to touch. Like something was remembering us before we did. I felt it under my skin, under my ribs, deep in a place I didn't have a name for, like a thread being pulled taut from inside me, stretching, humming, sparking.

Lucifer hovered above me, breath ragged, eyes blown wide. His hands were gripping my hips, his body shaking with a need that scared both of us.

"Evie... Sweetness," he whispered. My name sounded like a prayer he had forgotten he knew, and my stomach fluttered. "Something's happening."

"I know," I breathed. "I feel it."

His thumb stroked my clit in a slow, trembling circle as his lips locked onto my left nipple, stroking, teasing, sucking. And everything inside me climbed higher and higher, hotter and hotter, pressure curling tight around my spine like a fist. It felt like a metamorphosis, and if I just let go, something would change within me.

My heart raced. His matched it, beating against my chest like he was trying to sync with me. Then his tongue swiped against the seam of my mouth, and his lips were on mine again. Not rough this time. Not greedy. Just impossibly deep. Like he was giving me something, or taking it back.

Heat rushed through me so fast my vision blurred. My body arched instinctively, pulling him closer. His hand slid to the back of my neck, holding me to him, his breath shaking into my mouth.

The pressure inside me snapped tighter. It was almost painful—a coil of heat wound low in my body. My fingers dug into his shoulders. I felt myself slipping, tipping over some precipice I couldn't see.

"Luc... please," I gasped. "Something's... I'm..."

His voice was nearly a growl. "Let go."

I shattered. The breath tore out of me, my whole body pulling tight, clenching around him. The sensation felt too big, too bright, too consuming. Heat bloomed low and sharp, spreading fast, like a flower forced open all at once. Everything blurred white at the edges. Sound dropped out. The world narrowed to the heat between us, the pressure breaking open inside me, the way he held me through it.

"Good girl," he murmured.

The words hit almost as hard as the pleasure. And right as my climax crested, he roared my name.

And then— it happened.

The tether woke. A shockwave of gold slammed through my body like lightning. I cried out, not from pain, but from the sheer force of it. It felt like a star igniting under my ribs. Like something ancient and powerful had just recognized me and claimed me. Called something inside him home.

Light burst out of me. I felt it. I saw it.

"Luc!" I screamed.

He gasped, actually gasped, his entire body jerking as if the same fire had ripped through him. Gold flared along his arms where he held me, racing up his chest, catching at his throat. His hands clutched me harder. His forehead pressed to mine. His breath stuttered against my lips.

"Evie," he choked, voice breaking open. "Fucking Hell... I feel you."

The heat didn't fade. It didn't ebb. It spread. Light flared at the edges of my vision, soft and gold and terrifyingly beautiful, curling around us like we were in the center of a sun only we could see.

I saw flashes. Not memories. Not exactly. More like impressions burned into the backs of my eyes. A garden full of warm wind. Hands made of starlight. A voice saying my name like it was sacred. Wings of blinding white unfolding behind him.

Lucifer sucked in a breath, his eyes flying open, pupils blown wide in a ring of molten gold.

"Did you see that?" I whispered, shaking.

"I don't know what I saw," he said, voice rough. "But it was yours."

The tether pulsed between us again. Hard. Deep. Unavoidable. It wasn't a choice anymore. It wasn't lust. It wasn't fear. It wasn't even desire. It was recognition.

He buried his face in my neck, his breath trembling, his voice a broken whisper. "I think we just remembered something we weren't supposed to."

And I realized something, with a clarity that terrified me. We hadn't just crossed a line. We had destroyed one.

CHAPTER TWENTY-NINE

Lucifer

We lay there for a long time, the room still bright in places where the gold had flared out of us, the air was warm with it, humming under my skin like an aftershock. Every time my heart beat, I felt something answer.

It wasn't just in me. It was in her. In both of us. Our bond was alive. Not metaphorically. Not romantically. Literally alive, a thread of heat pulled tight between us, warm and terrifyingly right, like a nerve that had finally been reconnected after lifetimes of being severed.

She was tucked against me, my arm under her head, my other hand resting at her waist. I felt her breathing, soft and human, and every exhale made something in my chest ache in a way I wasn't ready to look at yet.

My thumb traced slow circles on her skin. Familiar. Soothing. But my mind was nowhere near calm. I was thinking too hard. And of course, she noticed.

"Say it," she murmured.

I looked at her. "Say what?"

"You're thinking so loud I'm surprised the lights aren't flickering. What is it?"

I almost smiled. Almost. Instead, I watched her, weighing whether to lie, to soften it, to pretend I wasn't already counting the ways the First Light might try to rip her out of my hands.

I didn't lie.

"He's going to feel it, if he hasn't already," I said quietly. "The First Light. He'll know our bond woke up. He may not understand how we slipped His leash, but He'll have felt whatever that was."

She flinched. The idea of being a "disturbance" in His system bothered her more than she let on.

"How long do we have?" she asked.

"I don't know," I admitted. "He might already know. He's very good at noticing things that should have stayed broken."

Her breath hitched. "So what do we do?" she asked. "Run? Hide? Change our names and move to Idaho?"

One corner of my mouth lifted. "Idaho would not help."

"Then what?" she asked, fiercer now. "Because I'm just not going to sit here waiting for some cosmic hand to pluck me off the board."

I drew in a slow breath. Let it out. It felt like swallowing glass. "There's a thing we could do," I said. "But you're not gonna like the sound of it."

"Try me."

My hand slid from her waist to her collarbone, my thumb brushing the spot where her pulse beat steady and fragile under her skin. I hated how vulnerable she was. I hated that the First Light wanted that vulnerability for Himself. And after what happened in Hell—after my wings tore free and Lilith's stolen crown crumbled to dust—my power was no longer a theory. It was awake. It was mine again. And I could feel the bond humming between us, bright and undeniable.

"He took your name from His Book," I said. "So I'll write it where He can't reach."

"Okay." She gave a shaky little laugh. "That sounds very metal. Where?"

"In Hell," I said. Then I met her eyes. "In me."

Her heart stuttered. And I felt it like a spark under my ribs.

"What does that even mean?"

My fingers curled lightly around her neck, not to restrain, just to hold. To warn. To ask.

"It means I mark you," I said. "With this power that's mine again. Power He didn't expect me to keep. I anchor you to it—anchor you to me. If He tries to take you, and... I think He will, He won't be pulling an unclaimed soul. He'll be ripping you out of Hell's grasp. Out of my grasp."

"That sounds dangerous," she said, "like it could kill me or you or... something."

"It is," I said. "For both of us."

"What does it do to me? Exactly."

I hesitated, choosing every word with the care she deserved.

"It won't change who you are," I said. "You're not going to be damned or turned into some kind of demon. But it'll tie you to me. I think... it might even strengthen this bond between us. I'll feel you more clearly. I'll know if you're hurt. I'll find you no matter where you run. And when anything divine or infernal looks at you, they'll see what's true."

"What's that?" she whispered.

I brushed my thumb over her pulse again, slow, feeling it race under my touch.

"That you're mine."

"Possessive much?" she asked, but her voice had already gone softer, like she knew exactly what that did to me.

I didn't answer. I leaned in and pressed my mouth to that spot, the fluttering beat under her skin. I felt her breath catch, felt the bond flare, gold and hot. And I let my lips linger there, a promise and a warning all at once.

"Get used to it," I murmured against her pulse.

I raised up to look her in the eyes. "If you do this," I said, "it is exactly that. Possessive. Protective. Stupid. Necessary."

"And if we don't?"

"Then when He comes for you," I said, voice low, "there will be nothing between His hand and your throat but me."

I meant it. Every word. And we both knew it still might not be enough.

"How— how would you mark me?" she asked and swallowed hard.

My thumb stroked the side of her neck again, slower.

"Here," I said. "Where they will look first."

Realization hit her. "You're talking about biting me."

I sat up. "Yes," I said.

Her mind ran through a decade of nightmares. I saw every shadow cross her face.

"Are you a..." she tried, but her voice trembled, "a vampire?"

"No," I said quickly. "I'm not like her. She turns what she touches into something hungry. I do not. This is a mark, not a curse like your brand—a sigil. The scar will carry my power. Only the supernatural will see it."

"So angels, demons, gods," she said. "But not the

guy at Starbucks."

"Yes."

"Will it hurt?"

"Yes." No point lying.

"Are you going to..." She trailed off, eyes widening as the implication hit her. She looked away, throat working.

I could guess where that was going. "Drink your blood? No, of course not."

Some of the tension bled out of her shoulders. Her fingers, which had been clenched in the sheet, loosened one by one. She let out a breath she probably didn't realize she'd been holding, the tight line of her mouth softening.

"Will you be able to control me with it?"

My jaw clenched. "I could never control you. But it'll give me influence. I'll feel where you are. I'll know when you're in danger. If you call for me, the mark will make it easier for me to reach you."

"And the part that is not the sales pitch?" she asked.

I huffed a dark laugh. "It will also tell anything that wants you that they will have to kill me to get to you."

She swallowed. "You think that will stop Him?"

"No," I whispered. "But it may slow Him. It may complicate His claim. And if it forces His hand early, it will be on ground I know, not in some hidden sanctum where I can never reach you."

She was quiet for a long moment.

"This is a—a bad idea," she said.

"Yes," I agreed.

"I've made worse."

The words hit me harder than she knew. Something like hope flickered in me.

"Evie."

She took my wrist and pulled my hand back to her neck, pressing my palm to her pulse.

"Do it," she said. "But only if you promise me one thing."

"Anything."

"Do not ever use this mark to make me smaller. If you use it to control me, to cage me, to punish me, I will cut it out myself."

That threat cut deep. I deserved it.

I'd put my teeth to people before. Left my mark on throats and wrists like a signature, like ownership, like I was doing them a favor by choosing them. I'd used it to pull strings I had no right to touch, to make desire feel inevitable, to make no sound like yes, to make bodies obey when hearts didn't want to. I'd taken what I wanted and called it sin, called it nature.

I'd made cages out of touch and called them devotion. So yes, I deserved her warning, every sharp word of it. But the thought of her carving herself open to escape me, of her bleeding because I couldn't be trusted with anything holy, made something in my chest recoil.

I flinched.

"I swear," I said quietly. "On everything I have ever been. That's not what this is."

She held my gaze. Believed me.

"Then, do it."

I searched her eyes one last time for doubt, fear, or any hesitation. All I found was courage she shouldn't have had to earn.

I nodded. "Come here," I said softly.

She climbed into my lap. My hands slid up her sides, my fingers skimming her breasts. Then, up her shoulders to cup her chin. I kissed her slowly, tenderly, then along her cheek, then down her jaw to the place I was about to claim.

"Last chance," I whispered, wrapping my hands around her shoulders.

"Take it."

I exhaled. My mouth found the curve of her neck. Warm. Soft. Mortal in a way that made something inside me go feral.

"This will burn," I warned.

"Good," she breathed. "I hope He feels it."

A growl of pride rose in me. "That's my girl."

Then I sank my teeth in.

Her breath broke. The pain hit her like lightning cascading down the bond to me. Her fingers dug into my shoulders. The gold flared through her again, this time braided with shadow, with Hellfire, with me. I felt it stitching into her.

Not taking. Adding.

I groaned against her skin, the taste of her wrecking me in ways I hadn't felt in eons, if ever. Power rushed out of me and into her, spiraling into a pattern I couldn't fully see, only feel—lines of ancient language burning themselves into place under her skin.

When it was done, I soothed the bite with my tongue, sealing it. She trembled as she pulled back. Beautiful. Alive with my power.

"Does it show?" she asked.

I studied the mark. My vision went gold.

"Yes," I said softly. "To me."

"What does it look like?" she asked.

My eyes narrowed. The shape was the same as her wrist—that inverted triangle at the base, solid and dark, the two loops rising from its corners like horns or curled flames, and the lines below narrowing into a crossed X that suggested a chalice. My sigil—But something else had threaded through it.

Finer lines, almost luminous, wove in and around the triangle and loops, like veins of light running through obsidian, reshaping the whole thing without breaking it.

"It looks like the one on your wrist," I said slowly. "My mark, with something else wrapped through it. I— I don't know what it means, but any supernatural being will see it and know they're touching what belongs to Hell."

"And to you," she said.

"And to me."

Her fingers drifted up to her neck, searching. Mortals weren't supposed to feel it. To them, it was just skin, maybe a little warm, maybe a little tender.

She froze. "Oh," she breathed.

My stomach tightened. "What?"

Her fingertips pressed over the mark, slow, testing. "I can feel it," she said. "It's... raised. Like scar tissue. And hot."

That wasn't possible.

"The skin will be sore," I said automatically. "You're imagining the rest."

She shot me a look. "I know the difference between a bruise and a brand, Luc."

The bond hummed, low and insistent. I reached up and caught her wrist, dragging her hand gently away so I could touch the spot myself. To my senses, the sigil blazed, lines of power etched in fire. Under my fingers, the skin felt faintly ridged. Warm Alive. To human touch, it should've been nothing.

"You shouldn't be able to feel it like that," I said.

She huffed out a breath, eyes flicking away. "Yeah, well... maybe I'm not completely human."

That landed harder than it should've. The corner of my mouth twitched, but the unease didn't go away. If she could feel the mark, then it wasn't just my power sitting under her skin. Something inside her was waking up and answering it.

"Could He undo it?" she asked.

I felt my expression harden. "He can fucking try."

Something fierce lit in her eyes, and I swore her eyes flashed gold so fast I almost missed it. It felt like it answered something in me.

The First Light may have taken her out of His Book, out of existence, but I had carved her somewhere He couldn't reach. Not without her consent. Not without her choice. For the first time since I realized He wanted to add her to His "collection," she didn't look helpless.

She met my gaze.

"All right," she said. "If He wants me, He is going to have to get through both of us."

A slow, deadly smile curved my mouth. "Oh, Sweetness," I said. "I am counting on it."

CHAPTER THIRTY

Evie

His bite throbbed at my neck, hot and strange, not painful exactly, just... present like a new gravity. My skin was still humming, the gold still pulsing between us softer but steady, like a second heartbeat neither of us had ever known we were missing.

Luc was still sitting against the headboard, legs stretched out, his body a wall of heat behind me. I was curled in his lap, my back against his chest, his arms loose around my middle like he didn't quite trust the world not to steal me if he let go. His breathing was steady, but his thoughts were loud, coiled tight, crackling under his skin.

I tipped my head just enough to look back at him. And that's when the entire hotel shook. Not a tremble. Not a rumble. A full-throated, bone-deep shudder that rattled the glass, jolted the mattress, and made the lamp on the nightstand clattering sideways like the building had been slapped by a giant hand.

And just like that, whatever peace we'd found in the aftermath of our truth... shattered.

I jerked upright. "Does Vegas have earthquakes?"

Luc was out of bed in one breath. His whole body went tense, wings flickering under his skin like they wanted out.

"No," he said. No hesitation. No softness. Just no.

He grabbed his boxers off the floor, yanked them on, and was already halfway to the door as I tossed my t-shirt back on.

"Whoa, whoa—hold on," I said, scrambling for my pants. "You can't just—"

"Stay here."

He didn't look at me when he said it. He just snapped the order and shut the door behind him. Which, obviously, meant I opened it immediately. I stepped into the hall just in time to see him whirl back around, clearly two seconds from lecturing me like some ancient, furious PTA mom.

He pinched the bridge of his nose. "Evie."

"What part of 'stay here' sounds reasonable after everything that just happened?"

He exhaled like I was personally ending his immortal life. "Fine. Stay behind me."

Then he kept walking, barefoot, half-dressed, radiating so much power the lights in the hallway flickered as we passed. He pushed open the door to the rooftop patio. Cold desert air whipped at my skin. And then I saw him.

A man—no, not a man—standing at the edge of the rooftop. Tall. Broad. Armor that looked forged in sunlight. Wings that stretched wider than the entire patio, glowing with white fire. His face was carved like he didn't bother with expressions—just righteous fury.

Luc muttered a curse under his breath, old and ugly enough to feel like it had teeth. The angel's eyes snapped to us.

"Morning Star." His voice hit like thunder wrapped in judgment.

"Michael," Luc said dryly. "You're looking very... shiny."

Michael didn't blink. "Where is the girl?"

My stomach dropped. Oh. Cool. So this was it, I guess. The end of all of it.

Luc stepped in front of me so fast I barely saw it. "No."

Michael's jaw flexed. "The First Light demands —"

"And I don't care," Luc cut in. "Not now. Not ever."

Michael's gaze slid past him, landing on me. Not with hatred. With something worse, pity. Like he already knew how this story usually ended and was mildly annoyed we were insisting on a different script.

"The First Light will not be denied," Michael said, voice quieter now, but somehow heavier. "You know what happens when He's crossed, Lucifer. You've gone through it yourself. If you keep her from Him, this won't stop at warnings. Heaven will move. Hell will answer. The world you're hiding in will crack under the weight of it."

Luc's shoulders squared. "He wants what doesn't belong to Him. Tell him to come and ask nicely."

A muscle ticked in Michael's cheek. "You always did confuse defiance with bravery."

"Funny," Luc said, "you always did confuse obedience with faith."

Michael held his stare for a long beat, then looked at me one last time.

"I hope you understand what he's choosing for you," he said. Not cruel. Not kind. Just final.

Then he lifted his hand toward the sky. Light

split the air open with a sound like stone breaking, and he shot upward, wings flaring wide before he vanished into the seam in the clouds. The tear sealed behind him, leaving only dark sky and the faint echo of thunder.

Luc was already moving.

"What was that?" I demanded when he stormed back inside, straight back to the bedroom.

He shook his head, grabbing his shirt off the floor as he walked. "You don't want the answer."

"Try me."

He met my eyes then, something raw flickering behind the gold. "We need to go."

There was no argument in his voice this time. No chance to push back. He was afraid. Lucifer Morningstar was afraid. That alone made my blood run cold.

We threw clothes into bags—well, he threw, I tried to fold, and he told me to stop being adorable —and then he was on the phone with Topher, who picked up on the first ring with a panicked, "What did you do? The sky just cracked open."

"Get the jet," Luc snapped. "Now."

Ten minutes later, I was being hustled through a private elevator, through a back corridor I didn't know existed, to a car, Rafi at the wheel. Fifteen minutes later, we pulled up to a silent hangar lit by emergency lights. My brain still hadn't caught up when the jet door sealed behind us and the engines began to roar.

The cabin lights were low, warm amber against polished wood and leather. Too calm. Too quiet. Like the universe had paused to inhale.

I sank into one of the seats because my legs didn't trust the floor anymore. Adrenaline does that—rips through you, burns out, leaves you hollow.

I looked at Luc. "What now?"

He didn't answer right away. He wasn't looking at me. He stared straight ahead, jaw tight, hands braced on the armrests like he was holding the jet in the air with brute force alone.

"Now?" he finally said. "We sleep."

Sleep. Right. Sure.

The tether pulsed between us at that exact moment, like it disagreed. Like it had very strong feelings about what sleeping in the same enclosed metal tube would lead to. It throbbed through my ribs, warm and heavy, threading under my skin like it belonged there.

A warning. A promise. I couldn't tell the difference anymore.

The engines shook the cabin just enough to remind me that the world was moving whether I was ready or not. We taxied down the runway, the lights of Vegas running in gold streaks, and I tried not to think about the fact that we were running away from a god. Or that a very pissed-off archangel had just ascended through my... whatever Luc was to me's... roof.

He still hadn't unclenched. His wings weren't out, but I could feel them—feel the ghost of their vastness pressed tight under his skin, ready to tear through reality if anything tried to touch me.

Somewhere above the clouds, Michael was telling the First Light that the girl He erased—the girl He wanted, the one He thought was safely broken—was awake. And my stomach knotted at the thought.

Luc closed his eyes like he knew exactly what I was thinking. "Don't," he murmured.

"Don't what?"

"Don't imagine the worst before it's here."

"That's cute," I said. "You assume there's still a 'before.'"

A muscle jumped in his jaw. "Evie."

I knew that tone. It meant he was scared. Which, frankly, did wonders for my nerves.

He unbuckled his seat belt and moved to the sofa lining the cabin wall, dropping onto it like gravity had finally remembered him. He patted the cushion beside him. Not an order. Not a request. More like... inevitability.

I went. Because pretending I wasn't going to end up pressed against him anyway felt stupid. As soon as I sat, his arm wound around my waist, pulling me into his side with a slow exhale that sounded more like defeat than relief, not at me—at everything else.

The tether softened, warmed, like it approved.

He rested his forehead against mine. "Sleep," he repeated. "While we can."

His hand splayed over my ribs. His power thrummed under his skin. The mark on my neck tingled, a faint heat pulsing in time with his heartbeat.

I closed my eyes; even though every part of me was wired and trembling.

Luc and I were in a metal box hurtling into darkness, with no plan except don't die and run faster than God can grab you.

Great. Perfect. Exactly the kind of romantic getaway I'd always dreamed of.

The bond pulsed once more, steady and deep, right under my heart. I yawned, not sure if it was a promise or a warning, as I snuggled against his warmth and fell drowsy.

I woke with a start, blinking into dim cabin light and the low rumble of engines. Someone had draped a blanket over me, tucking it around my legs. A nice touch, if I hadn't immediately remembered that gods, angels, and death wishes were all currently in play.

The jet lurched upward, climbing again. We were taking off. Again.

I pushed myself upright on the narrow couch, the blanket sliding to the floor. Across the aisle, Luc and Topher sat in two leather seats, leaned toward each other, talking in sharp whispers.

Topher's face was tight, mouth pressed into a flat line like he was trying very hard not to say, "You're out of your damn mind." Luc wasn't looking at him. That was how I knew whatever they were discussing wasn't up for debate.

"What's going on?" I asked, voice still sleep-rough.

Both men froze. Topher glanced at Luc as if to say, "You tell her."

Luc exhaled like he'd been delaying the inevitable. "We just landed to refuel," he said. "You were dead asleep. I didn't want to wake you."

"That's ominous," I muttered. "Where are we now?"

"Bogota," Luc said.

I blinked. "As in... Columbia? In South America? How long have I been asleep?"

Luc shrugged, "Eight hours?"

Topher rubbed a hand over his face. "We're not exactly making pit stops in Kansas right now."

"And where are we going from here?" I asked.

Luc's gaze met mine, steady and impenetrable. "La Frontera Sombra."

The tether between us pulsed—once, sharp enough that it almost felt like someone had plucked a string inside my chest.

I frowned. "Okay, dramatic name. What is it?"

Luc shifted in his seat, bracing his elbows on his knees. "It means the Shadow Border. It's near Patagonia. It's a... seam in reality. A place where, eons ago, another universe hit this one. One that wasn't His."

I swallowed. "Meaning the First Light doesn't... see it?"

"Not clearly," Luc said. "It's interference. A blind spot. One of the only ones left."

Topher cut in, voice low. "It's not safe."

Luc shot him a look. "Nothing's safe."

"That place is less safe," Topher said. "And you know it."

A little chill dragged its fingers down my spine. "Why? What's in La Frontera Sombra?"

Topher's eyes met mine, dark and serious. "Things that belong to neither world. The Iemisch still roam the dry riverbeds. They drag anything warm off the edge of the desert, and no one finds bodies, just blood. And Gualicho's real there," he added. "Not just a story. It's a curse that walks, picks a person, and won't let go. It'll bargain with you, tempt you, bleed your luck and your sleep and everyone you love until it gets what it wants."

"Oh," I said faintly. "So like supernatural stalking. Perfect."

Luc ignored the commentary, turning back to me. "It buys us time. Space. A place where He can't pluck you out of the sky with a flick of His wrist."

My skin crawled at the visual.

"Do humans live there?" I asked.

"Some," Luc said. "Not many. The land pushes most people away."

"Great," I said. "So we're going somewhere even humans avoid. Love that."

Topher didn't smile. He just stared at the carpet like it personally offended him.

"How long until we're there?" I asked.

"Four hours," Luc said. "Maybe you should try to get some more sleep?"

I gave him a look. "Last time you said that, an archangel dropped in and tried to collect me like a library book."

Luc's jaw tightened. "Michael won't find you where we're going."

"And if the First Light does?" I pressed.

His eyes darkened. "He won't."

Topher muttered something under his breath in Spanish that sounded suspiciously like "You hope."

Luc shot him another warning look.

"Guys? I'm sitting right here," I said.

Topher finally spoke directly to me, his voice softer than I expected. "Evie... La Frontera Sombra isn't normal. The rules aren't either."

"Fantastic," I said. "Neither am I."

Luc's mouth twitched—just barely—and he stood, crossing to me with that controlled, predatory grace that said he was still thinking about what we did... earlier and still thinking about the bond. The bite. Everything.

He crouched in front of me, hands gentle on my knees. "Rest. I'll explain everything when we're closer."

"Promise?"

His eyes softened. "Yeah. I promise."

The tether pulsed again, warm and steady.

We were flying toward a seam in reality to keep me from a god. And all I could think was— Four hours. Four hours until La Frontera Sombra. Wherever the hell that was. Four hours until we reached a place where another universe collided with this one— and the monsters there already knew the rules better than I did.

I couldn't sleep—too much adrenaline in my veins, too much Luc in my immediate vicinity, too much everything. The leather seat beneath me was softer than my mattress at home, the cabin lights were dimmed to something that should have been soothing, and the jet purred through the sky like the world's fanciest white noise machine.

Didn't matter. My brain was wide awake and pacing.

Luc had buckled himself in across from me, long legs stretched out, eyes closed, fingers tapping on the armrest in an irregular rhythm that made me want to either kiss him or smack his hand away. Maybe both.

"You're fidgeting," he said suddenly, without opening his eyes.

"I'm breathing," I muttered. "Sorry if that offends your royal highness."

One corner of his mouth twitched. "You keep shifting. And sighing. And glaring at me like I dragged you into a confessional instead of onto a private jet."

"You kind of did," I said. "You just used the words prophecy and Hell instead of 'oceanfront property' and 'complimentary brunch.'"

He actually laughed at that, low and genuine. The sound settled over my nerves like a warm blanket, which was rude, considering this entire situation should have been a neon sign flashing: Bad Idea.

Before I could decide if I wanted to keep arguing, he unbuckled with a fluid motion and stood.

"Stay," he said. "I'll fix the insomnia."

"What, you know a lullaby?"

"Better." He stepped past me toward the front of

the cabin. "I know a woman with a cart."

I blinked. "We have a flight attendant?"

He gave me a look over his shoulder like I'd just admitted I believed airplanes flap their wings to stay up. "What did you think, the jet flies itself, and food appears from the Void?"

"With you involved?" I said. "That honestly seemed like an option."

He disappeared through a narrow door I'd assumed was a closet. A soft murmur of voices floated back, a clink of something metal, the low hiss of... I had no idea. I hadn't even seen anyone when we boarded. It had just been me, him, and more expensive leather than a luxury car showroom. I was still trying to figure out how Topher got on board.

I hugged my knees to my chest and stared out the oval window. Night sky, more night sky, a streak of clouds lit from beneath by distant city glows. We could have been anywhere above anywhere.

The door opened again.

A woman stepped out first, tall and composed, wearing a sleek black uniform with a subtle gold pin at her collar. Not a logo I recognized, just a stylized circle around a slash of light. Her blond hair was twisted into a smooth chignon that seemed to defy physics. Her eyes met mine briefly, and for a second, something in my chest stuttered.

Her irises were a strange, clear gray. Not cold, exactly. Just... assessing. Like she saw more than she should in the half-second we made eye contact.

"Miss Grace," she said, with the kind of calm warmth you only heard from professional hostages and customer service. "I apologize, I should have introduced myself earlier. I'm Alina."

"Hi," I said carefully. "But... I'm pretty sure you

weren't here before."

She smiled like that was adorable. "I assure you, I was."

Had she been? Logically, she probably had. I'd been a little preoccupied with not hyperventilating when we took off. Still, something in my brain whispered, No, you'd have noticed her. You'd have noticed anyone.

The cart she pushed would have been normal on any commercial flight, except this one looked like it belonged in a five-star restaurant. White linen draped the top, real silver glinting beneath small metal lids. Steam curled up in lazy ribbons, carrying a scent that hit my empty stomach like a punch.

Grilled meat. Pepper. Butter.

"Steak?" I asked because thinking about the logistics was easier than thinking about how my life had gone from balancing tips and rent to a private jet in under a month. "On a plane?"

Luc slid back into his seat across from me, smoothing his suit jacket like he hadn't just gone into a hidden room and conjured dinner. "You sound skeptical."

"It smells like it came off an actual grill," I said. "Like, a hot, fire, outdoor grill. Not a microwave situation."

Alina lifted the lid from a plate with a practiced flourish. A perfectly cooked steak sat there, crosshatched with fresh grill marks, edging into a glossy pool of resting juices. Next to it, there were roasted potatoes and asparagus spears, flecked with something green.

Steam rose—actual, visible steam. No way.

"Medium rare," she said. "As requested."

My eyebrows shot up and locked somewhere

near my hairline. "Requested by who? Because I don't remember filling out a steak survey, and I definitely don't remember a grill on board."

Luc's eyes were on me, not the food. "Eat, Evie." His voice softened. "You haven't had more than coffee and nervous energy since morning."

I should have pushed. I should have kept asking, should have demanded a tour of this magical airborne kitchen. Instead, my stomach growled loud enough that everyone in the cabin heard it. Alina's lips twitched, the faintest hint of amusement breaking through the professional mask.

Heat flooded my cheeks.

"Fine," I muttered.

The first bite stole my ability to complain anyway. It melted. Warm and salty and perfectly seared, buttery at the center. Whatever seasoning they'd used woke up every taste bud I had.

My brain tried to whisper that this was weird, that this should not be possible at 40,000 feet. My mouth told it to shut up and take the win.

I ate. Luc watched, ignoring his own plate until I pointed my fork at him.

"You're creeping me out," I said. "Eat your spooky Hell steak."

He huffed a laugh and obediently cut into his.

For a few minutes, the tension loosened. The cabin felt smaller, less like a luxury coffin and more like a strange little bubble away from everything, where steak appeared out of nowhere, and devils sat across from you telling you to eat.

Eventually, the plates disappeared, whisked away by Alina in near silence. She asked if I'd like coffee or tea. I chose herbal tea because my anxiety did not need caffeine as a wingman, and when she returned with it, the cup was already the exact shade of "has steeped long enough and not a second more" that I preferred.

"Thank you," I said slowly, watching her. "Do you do mind-reading as an in-flight service, or is that just for special passengers?"

Her gaze flicked to Luc, then back to me. Something unreadable flashed behind her composed expression, there and gone before I could parse it.

"We take good care of our guests," she said simply. "We're approaching descent. Please fasten your seatbelt."

My stomach dropped.

Luc waited until the galley door closed again. Then, quietly, "You alright?"

"No," I said honestly. "But that seems like the correct answer."

He nodded, as if he respected that. Then he buckled in and looked out at the darkness.

The gentle hum beneath us shifted after a while, that almost imperceptible change as the plane began to tip forward and relinquish altitude. Pressure tugged at my ears. I swallowed, staring out the window again.

The distant city glow had vanished. There were no clusters of light beneath us, just an endless, tired black, broken up by occasional pinpricks that might have been small towns or lonely gas stations or something else entirely.

"Where are we landing?" I asked.

"In the desert," he said.

"Yeah, I caught that vibe," I said. "Could you be slightly more specific, or is vague and ominous part of the package?"

"Vague and ominous is my brand," he said, deadpan. "You know that by now."

I shot him a look. "Luc."

He exhaled through his nose, watching the dark. "Technically, it's still a city. Practically, it is nowhere. A private airstrip. Remote. Quiet."

"Is there a reason it has to be remote and quiet?" I asked. "Other than the fact that you clearly enjoy scaring the human girl you dragged into your apocalyptic road trip."

Something in his expression softened, but his jaw tightened. "Because what we are walking into is not for an audience."

Cool. Great. Perfect. Love that for me.

The plane sank lower. My eyes adjusted enough to make out shapes now. A long strip, faintly lit, like someone had dropped a single line of civilization in the middle of a dead world. A cluster of low buildings crouched nearby, square and dark—no sprawling airport, no bright terminal windows, just a skeletal suggestion of infrastructure.

As we touched down, the wheels hit the runway with a jolt that rattled through my bones. The sound was louder out here, without city noise to swallow it. The engines slowed, their pitch dropping into a low, thrumming growl.

I couldn't shake it, the feeling that we were landing somewhere we weren't supposed to be. Like the desert itself was frowning at our intrusion.

The jet rolled to a stop near one of the low buildings. There were no other planes. No baggage carts. No people moving around in reflective vests. Just the deep dark of the desert pressing in on all sides, and the thin wash of floodlights painting the tarmac in harsh white.

A single black SUV waited a short distance away, its headlights off.

"Of course," I whispered. "Of course, you have a mysterious murder car waiting."

Luc unbuckled and stood, shrugging into his jacket. "If I were going to murder you, Evie, I wouldn't need the car."

"Comforting."

Alina appeared again as if conjured, her footsteps soft on the carpet runner. "We have arrived," she said. "The car will take you the rest of the way."

"The rest of the way where?" I asked.

Her gaze skimmed over me, pausing at my face like she wanted to say something and thought better of it. "Be careful," she said instead. Quiet, like it was for me alone.

The tiny hairs on the back of my neck stood up. "Okay," I said slowly. "That didn't sound like a normal customer service line."

She gave me the ghost of a smile. "Safe travels, Miss Grace."

Luc descended the narrow stairs first. I followed, the metal cool under my shoes.

The desert night hit me in the face like a wall. It was colder than I expected, the kind of cold that comes when the heat lets go all at once after sundown. The air smelled like dust and old stone and something faintly metallic.

Above us, the sky was a black bowl, stars thrown across it in a careless scatter. There were more of them than I ever saw over Vegas, bright and sharp. For a heartbeat, it was beautiful. Then the emptiness underneath it elbowed through.

There was no sound.

Not the distant hum of traffic. Not the whine of another plane. Just the ticking of the cooling engines behind us and the soft whisper of wind dragging over sand. The vast open space felt wrong, somehow. Not free. Exposed.

My chest tightened. I wrapped my arms around

myself and turned in a slow circle. The floodlights cast long, screaming shadows across everything, stretching the wheel chocks and the stairs into warped black claws on the concrete.

"You're being dramatic," I told myself. This is just an airstrip in the middle of nowhere. People do this. Celebrities. Rich people. Cartels. Great, brain, thanks.

Luc moved to my side, close enough that his shoulder brushed mine. His presence was warm, solid, an anchor in all that emptiness.

"Feel it?" he asked quietly.

I swallowed. "Feel what, exactly? The urge to run? The urge to throw up?"

"The hush," he said. His eyes were on the horizon, on the black line where the earth met the sky. "Places like this are in between. Neither here nor there. Humans pretend they are just geography, but the world remembers what it was before there were roads and runways. Sometimes it resents you for forgetting."

Okay, yeah, that did not help.

"What are we in between?" I asked because if I didn't keep talking, my brain was going to spiral.

"Worlds," he said. "Doors. Stories."

A shiver ran down my spine. Our tether, that strange, invisible pull between us, pulsed once, like a heartbeat against my skin. The feeling rolled through me, familiar and foreign, like déjà vu with teeth.

For a second, the air felt heavier, charged, like the moments before a storm. The floodlights flickered, just once, a quick glitch that snapped off and on again too fast to be natural.

I froze. "Did you see that?"

"Yes." His voice had gone murderously calm.

"Stay close."

"I'm literally glued to your side," I said, even as I stepped closer, my shoulder pressing into his arm. "Where exactly would I go? There is sand. And more sand. And in case you missed it, additional sand."

The SUV's engine turned over then, breaking the quiet. The headlights flared to life, twin spears of white cutting through the dark toward us.

As it rolled closer, my unease sharpened instead of easing. The windows were tinted so dark I couldn't see inside, not even a hint of a silhouette. The license plate was blank. Not missing. Just... empty. A smooth oblong of metal with no numbers, no state.

"That's not legal," I whispered.

Luc's mouth curved, humorless. "Neither am I."

The car stopped a few feet away. The driver's door opened with a soft click.

A man climbed out, dressed in a plain black suit. No tie, no visible weapon. His face was so average it swung back around to unnerving, the kind of bland that never stayed in anyone's memory—dark hair, nondescript features, eyes that slid over me like I was a piece of luggage.

"Mr. Lux," he said, inclining his head to Luc. His voice was smooth, but empty, as if someone had dusted human inflection over a machine. "We are ready."

We. My skin crawled.

Luc's hand brushed against mine, a simple touch, but my fingers curled around his automatically, like my body was done pretending I wasn't terrified. He squeezed once, firm, grounding.

"Evie," he said quietly, pitched so only I could hear. "You can still walk away. Say the word, and I will put you back on that jet and send you home."

I looked out at the darkness, at the endless desert and the strange airstrip that seemed to have been carved into the world by something that did not particularly like people. I thought about my old life, about cheap apartments and dead-end shifts and the feeling that something was missing, something big and bright and unnamed.

I thought about the way the tether between us had flared when the lights flickered, about the way the world seemed to lean closer every time we were together, listening.

Home no longer felt like a place. It felt like a person.

"Too late," I said, my voice sounding small but steady in the cold air. "You already dragged me into the weird desert portal zone. I'm seeing it through."

His eyes softened, just for a heartbeat. Then he nodded, released my fingers, and pressed his hand to the small of my back instead.

"Then stay with me," he said. "Whatever you feel, however strange this place becomes, stay with me."

The driver watched us with that bland, patient expression, as if it did not matter what we decided, as if he already knew.

A chill slid through me that had nothing to do with the night air.

"Yeah," I said, more to myself than anyone. "What could possibly go wrong?"

We walked toward the waiting car, the desert stretching out around us like an open mouth. And even though the sky was crowded with stars, it still felt like something in the dark was watching us back

CHAPTER THIRTY-ONE

Lucifer

The dirt road wound through the desert like a thin scar, nearly invisible except for the faint glow of the SUV's headlights. Patagonia at night was a different sort of darkness—older, quieter, the kind that didn't just surround you, it pressed against the windows like it wanted in.

Evie slept against my shoulder, her breath slow and soft, like the sleep exhaustion had finally wrung out of her. Topher was in the third row behind me, laptop closed for once, head tipped back. He looked harmless like that. Human. Small. But he wasn't.

The first warning was the wind going still. Not quieter—still. Completely still, like the air seemed to suspend itself, like the whole world had paused to listen. The kind of stillness you're not supposed to feel in a moving car, like the air outside had been scooped out and the world was holding its breath.

Then the sky tore. A slash of gold light cut downward, too fast, too deliberate. A divine descent. It wasn't one of Lilith's crawling little toys. This was Heaven. The First Light sending His dogs.

"Shit," I muttered. "Topher."

He didn't answer with words. His eyes snapped open, pupils blown wide, and he inhaled sharply, like someone had punched him. A faint line of blood already trailed from his nose.

The first creature dove for the car, all razor-edged light and too many wings.

Topher reached. The air bent, and then, the thing's path folded in on itself mid-strike, a violent kink that should have been impossible. It veered sideways, slamming into another streak of gold cutting in from the right. They collided, screaming light exploding across the desert like a sun dying.

Evie jolted awake, clutching my arm. "What—what was that?"

"Heaven being dramatic," I said, though the words tasted like lies. Even I hadn't seen that particular trick before.

More of them dropped, circling, adjusting. Learning.

Topher blinked hard, and suddenly the entire dashboard flickered. GPS dead. Radio silent. The sky above us shimmered like heat off asphalt.

The creatures dove again. And missed. Wildly. Unnaturally.

Topher's voice came low, frayed at the edges. "They can't see us. I pulled the road. Don't—don't make me hold it long."

The SUV shuddered as something massive hit the ground behind us. The driver swore and kept his hands locked on the wheel.

Another attacker descended on us directly, blade-bright. It should have sliced the car open. Instead, mid-dive, its wings spasmed. Its pattern broke. It dropped like a stone, carving a trench through the gravel.

Evie gasped, staring upward out the window.

"Luc—"

"I see it." My stomach sank. Not at the attack. At Topher.

He wasn't meant to do this, not in a mortal shell. His grace had been cut down to embers, and still he was pulling threads out of the world like he'd never stopped.

"Topher," I said sharply. "Enough."

He didn't stop.

Two more creatures descended and suddenly turned on each other, ripping and shrieking. A third flew straight into a cliffside, wings folding wrong. A fourth burned out midair like a dying star, its divine signal collapsing under the weight of whatever Topher was jamming into its channel.

The desert flashed with their unraveling.

Finally, Topher's head dropped forward. His breath hitched. Blood dripped from his chin onto his shirt. His fingers twitched like he was still editing every path he could see.

"Topher," I said again. Firmer. "Release it."

He exhaled shakily. The world snapped back. The sky went silent. Whatever was left of Heaven's attack scattered, retreating into the stars like insects fleeing a flame.

Evie pressed against me, trembling.

The SUV drove on. The road was empty again. But the silence was wrong in a new way now, heavy with what we'd seen. That's when I knew. We couldn't do this alone. The thought lodged itself between my ribs like a splinter. I hated it. I also knew it was true.

Topher wiped his face with a shaking hand. "They'll keep coming," he whispered. "You know they will."

"I know," I said. "We're not staying here long. A

couple of days. Then we go back."

Evie looked up at me. "Back where?"

"Home," I said. "We... need to find those who'll stand with us. Against Him."

Names flickered through my mind.

Vespera. She despised me. But I had a hunch she despised Him even more. And the only reason she wasn't already here was that something else had its claws in her. I'd seen it the night I lost my temper and shoved her into the wall of that velvet-draped brothel she called a business, her dress riding high enough to flash the mark burned into her hip. Not ink, not art. A brand. His. A leash written in light and scar tissue, tying her to her little empire and everyone inside it.

Damien. That two-faced bastard would help break the First Light if he thought it would earn him five minutes of leverage. Sure, he ran with Lilith now and then, but Damien never swore loyalty so much as rented it out. Now that she was without my crown, I was sure that if I dangled the right promise, he'd switch sides mid-sentence and smile while doing it.

And then, Azazael. My chest tightened.

My closest friend in Heaven. Or that's what the edges of my memories insisted, though those edges were still blurred, soft, unstable. I remembered him the way you remember a dream after waking, all shapes and flickers and a warmth in the rib cage that didn't match the version of events I'd been fed.

I'd told Topher that much once. Barely. Late one night, after too much whiskey and not enough restraint, when the world was quiet and whatever mask I usually wore had loosened its grip. I'd admitted the memory was wrong somehow, that something about Azazael's supposed betrayal never sat right in my bones.

Topher hadn't said anything, just stared into his glass and watched me with those tired, all-knowing eyes that made me feel like he saw the cracks before I did.

I knew Azazael had gone to the First Light about... something about me. But in my mind, it lived like a smudged painting, colors without lines. Every time I reached for the specifics, they dissolved, leaving only that déjà vu shiver down my spine that made me feel hunted by my own recollections.

And then the First Light brought him to me after I Fell.

That part was sharp. Too sharp.

Azazael, beaten. Broken. Barely breathing. Wings mangled, half torn from his back. His face was bruised beyond recognition. His words had become a tangle of prophecy and madness, spilling out in fractured loops and impossible images, like The First Light had shattered his mind and left him trying to speak through the pieces. And gods, listening to him, I wished I could remember even half of what he was trying to say.

I had confessed this part to Topher too, though quietly, like the words were knives in my throat. I'd told him how seeing Azazael like that had gutted me, how I couldn't understand why it felt like I'd lost more than a soldier, more than a friend... something bigger. Something sacred.

And yet, idiot that I was, I still wanted to please the First Light back then. Still clung to the belief that my fall was a punishment I deserved, that obedience could earn forgiveness, that if I did everything He asked, I could crawl my way back into grace.

So when He told me Azazael needed to be contained...

I obeyed.

Gods help me, I obeyed.

And even remembering it now made a hard, vicious urge tighten in my jaw. I wanted to wrap my hands around His throat and squeeze the stolen life out of Him.

Now, with my memories drifting back in jagged, disorienting fragments, I wasn't sure I'd ever committed any sins up there at all. Not the ones I'd been blamed for. Not the ones that supposedly warranted a Fall.

And if that was true...

Then maybe I had shoved my best friend into an oubliette for eons on the word of a god who wasn't a god at all. Maybe I'd condemned an innocent angel because a monster wearing a throne told me to.

The thought made something cold and sour slide down my throat.

But what haunted me most wasn't the violence. It wasn't the betrayal. It was the last thing Azazael whispered before I dropped him into that pit.

Find the one who matters.

Fractured. Terrified. No more than a whisper of breath.

Find the one who matters.

I'd dismissed it back then as nonsense, the babbling of a mind crushed under divine punishment—a glitch in a broken choirboy. I'd even told Topher that a few days ago, and he'd just gone very, very still.

Now... Now I wasn't so sure. Was Azazael warning me? Even then? Had he been trying to point me toward Evie? I didn't know. Not yet. But the possibility coiled in my gut with sick, undeniable certainty.

What I did know—what hit me with sudden clarity, harsh as the memory of his blood on my hands—was simple.

I had to get him out of that oubliette. If anyone knew what the First Light was planning... it was him. Had he tried to stop it? Is that why he lost everything, and still, even at the end, tried to warn me? His punishment had been far worse than mine...

Topher slumped sideways, eyelids fluttering. Evie reached back and grabbed his hand. I stared into the dark horizon where the Andes rose like black teeth and felt something cold settle in my chest.

I couldn't send anyone else. I had to go back to Hell and get Azazael myself, even if it was more dangerous now than ever. And Topher was in no condition to come with me. We were running out of time. And I was running from a fucking god. But I would rip open Heaven itself if I had to.

Dawn was creeping fast over the horizon by the time we reached the place I'd prayed was safe. The first thin blade of sunlight cut through the darkness behind us, chasing the night across the desert as if it wanted to make sure we kept moving.

The house emerged from the mountain's open mouth like a secret breathed into stone. Half architecture, half living cavern, impossibly carved straight into the Andes themselves. Marble inlaid with raw rock. Ancient lines meeting modern angles. A sanctuary that shouldn't exist and yet somehow always had.

I'd had it built ages ago. Topher called me insane for pouring time and magic into a hollow place no one else had ever seen. But something in me— something old, something I didn't question back then—had whispered that I'd need it someday. Maybe I'd always known it would come to this.

Wards disguised the place from the outside, wrapping the cave house in the illusion of something ancient and forgotten. From the winding dirt road along the mountain, it looked like an abandoned ruin, all crumbling stone and weather-scarred carvings, the kind of structure indigenous people had built millennia ago, and time had reclaimed—nothing living inside.

And if any human did wander too close, the wards nudged their mind like a quiet suggestion. A sudden urge to turn the car around. A feeling in the gut that said not this way, not today, followed by a clean slice of forgetting. They'd leave believing they'd simply taken a wrong turn, unaware that a sanctuary carved into a scar of the universe had ever breathed behind them.

In reality, the entire front of the cavern had been transformed into a sweeping wall of glass, set into marble and raw rock, bulletproof panes catching the faint starlight and throwing it back in warm gold. Soft arches framed the entrance, their curves carved right out of the cliff face, and the interior glowed like a heartbeat under layers of warm amber lighting. Stalactites hung above polished floors like frozen chandeliers. A balcony walkway spiraled along the inner wall, and the air—the air hummed, faint and low in a different frequency.

We were standing dead center in one of the universe's scars. A wound that had been left in creation long ago. A hollow place that bent perception and signature just enough that His sight slipped right over it.

Here, He was blind. And gods, I needed Him blind.

I carried Topher inside. He was limp in my arms, breathing shallow and uneven, his skin chalk-pale from overusing magic no mortal spine could handle. Evie hovered at my heels the entire walk down the stone hall, her hands wringing like she wasn't sure whether to touch him or steady herself. The driver took care of the rest of our things.

One of the bedrooms was tucked into a hollow chamber to the left, warm with natural stone and soft lamplight. I laid Topher on the bed while Evie knelt and tugged his shoes off. I stripped his jacket, eased him back against the pillows.

He didn't wake.

Evie's voice was small. "Is he going to be alright?"

I studied him. The twitch of his fingers. The faint tremor under his eyelids. The blood crusted under his nose. He looked too breakable in that bed, too human to house what he'd unleashed tonight.

"I think so," I said. Then quietly, darker, "But his earthly body isn't made for his magic."

She swallowed hard, brushing hair off his forehead. There was worry in her touch, and something else—fear, maybe, of what she'd witnessed, what he'd done. What she'd been dragged into.

I stepped out of the room before my thoughts crawled too far in that direction. She followed a few minutes later, closing the door behind her.

The living room opened wide inside the cavern— soaring stone ceilings dripping with formations older than any city, leather sofas arranged around a cavernous hearth, warm light catching the glint of metal fixtures, and the natural shine of the rock. It should have felt safe—a sanctuary tucked deep in the Andes, where the First Light couldn't reach us.

Instead, something inside me was unraveling.

I turned to her. "Are you alright?" I asked.

Her eyes darted over the cave walls, the impossible beauty of it, the impossible truth of everything that had happened. She let out a shaky breath. "I don't know. My world's kinda... shattered. Everything I thought I'd convinced myself was a myth... is real. And now, we're running and... it's crazy. It's all just crazy."

I didn't know what answer I expected. But she wasn't wrong. Yet, something in me buckled anyway—Topher collapsing in the backseat, bleeding from places magic shouldn't reach... and still it had been ages, but Azazael's ruined face haunted by prophecy I'd ignored... the sick suspicion I'd obeyed a monster masquerading as a god... And suddenly all of it spilled over in the wrong direction, sharp and ugly.

"So you're not fine," I said, too cold. "Of course, you're not. Mortals never are when the universe finally shows you its teeth."

She stiffened, jaw tightening, hurt flashing across her face. I'd meant to comfort her. What came out was venom. Because the truth was rattling inside me like something feral. Topher nearly destroyed himself. Azazael... gods, Azazael had been trying to warn me.

And I threw him into a pit, and who fucking knew what he'd been surviving down there all this time. Everything in me was telling me to get him right now. But I couldn't. Not yet. And the guilt was eating me alive.

"Luc," she whispered, confusion threading through her voice. "What's going on with you?"

I dragged a hand across my mouth, fingers trembling with exhaustion and a dread I didn't dare name.

"It's nothing," I snapped, sharper than I meant. "I'm fine."

Her eyes flinched, but she didn't move.

I sighed, the sound rough. "I'm dealing with the aftermath of things I don't want to talk about," I said tightly. "Not everything that happens to me is a conversation you get to have."

She blinked, once, twice, like she was sure she'd misheard. Her mouth parted, a soft, stunned breath catching in her throat. For a heartbeat, she just stared at me, hurt and disbelief tangled together, as if I'd reached out and slammed a door in her face.

In the old days, I would have bled this feeling out the easy way, with teeth and skin and someones whose names I never bothered to learn. Demons, humans, it didn't matter, as long as they were willing to let me drown in them for a night — sin as a pressure valve, bodies as forgetfulness.

Now she was standing there instead, all wide eyes and shaking hands, looking at me like she didn't recognize the man — the monster — in front of her, and I wanted to touch her and run from her in the same breath.

Evie stood in the soft light, small and breakable and real, and I suddenly hated the way my darkness kept brushing against her, staining everything it touched — the urge to flee hit hard and fast. The air felt thick, the cave too close, my thoughts spinning like they were trying to claw their way out of my skull.

I moved before I could think better of it. Two steps and I was in front of her. She tipped her head back to look at me, hurt shining in her eyes, a question trembling on her lips.

My hand came up almost of its own accord. I wrapped my fingers around her throat. Not hard.

Not enough to bruise. Just a firm circle of heat at the base of her jaw, thumb resting over the quick thrum of her pulse. I felt it jump under my touch, a sharp little stutter as she swallowed.

Her breath hitched. Her hands hovered like she couldn't decide whether to push me away or hold on. For a heartbeat, all the noise in my head went quiet. *Mine*, some old part of me thought. The same part that had once led armies and broken worlds and called it devotion.

I leaned in, close enough to feel the warmth of her exhale against my cheek, close enough that one wrong thought could turn this into something else entirely.

"I'm not abandoning you," I said, voice low, rough. "The wards will keep you safe. From Heaven. From Hell. From Him."

"From me," hung unsaid between us.

Her eyes searched my face, wide and disbelieving. "Then… why does it feel like you are?"

Her throat bobbed again under my hand. The guilt landed hard. But I let go. The absence of her skin on my palm felt like stepping off a ledge.

I turned away from her, every step to the door heavier than the last. My hand hit the latch. Cold air knifed in from the outer cavern when I pulled it open.

Without looking back, I said, "There's fresh food in the kitchen. Just… check on Topher until I'm back."

"Luc," she said, voice cracking. "Are you seriously just leaving me here?"

I glanced at her over my shoulder, only for a second. It was enough to see the shock, the hurt, the thin line of fear she was trying to swallow down.

"I'll be back before nightfall," I said.

Then I stepped through the doorway and slammed it behind me, the sound echoing through the scar in the world like a promise I wasn't sure I could keep.

CHAPTER THIRTY-TWO

Evie

I stared at the door for a good five seconds after he slammed it, like maybe it would swing back open and he'd say just kidding, like this was some twisted test I'd passed.

It didn't. The echo of it rattled around in my chest. Like I was a problem he could leave on a shelf.

Anger burned through the shock so fast it almost felt like relief.

"Fine," I muttered into the empty room. "Run, then."

The cave house hummed softly around me, this weird, low vibration I could feel in my teeth. Safe, he'd said. Wards, he'd said. From Heaven, Hell... Not from him, apparently. That motherfucker.

I blew out a breath and forced my legs to move. Being pissed at Luc wasn't going to help the unconscious guy we'd basically thrown into a bed and walked away from. Topher first. Emotional breakdown later.

The bedroom was dark and quiet when I slipped back in. The mountain wall curved protectively around the space, stone and shadow, and that expensive-looking bed Luc had flopped him onto.

Topher lay where we'd left him, on his back, hair mussed, skin too pale against the dark sheets. He hadn't moved. Dried blood streaked from his nose down to his upper lip and along his chin, crusted into the faint scruff there.

Something in my chest pinched. "Okay," I whispered. "Not leaving you looking like a crime scene."

I ducked into the attached bathroom. It was annoyingly gorgeous, of course—a rainfall shower cut into the stone of the cavern. There were soft white towels stacked in perfect little rolls like a hotel ad. I grabbed one, then found a washcloth and ran warm water, watching steam curl as I wrung it out.

Back at the bed, I perched on the edge and gently tilted his face toward me.

"Hey, Topher," I said quietly. "I'm gonna clean you up a little. Don't freak out."

He didn't answer, but his eyelids fluttered at the sound of his name.

I pressed the warm cloth to his nose and mouth, wiping away the blood in careful strokes. Up close, he looked younger, less like the quiet man who hid behind screens and more like someone exhausted down to the soul.

"You did well," I murmured, even though he probably couldn't hear me. "Whatever that was in the car... You did well."

I rinsed the cloth in the bathroom, came back, and finished the job, chasing the last rusty streak along his jaw. By the time I was done, his face looked like his again, not like something broken.

He stirred when I pulled my hand away. A small sound slipped out of him, rough and low. His throat worked around a dry swallow.

"Topher?" I leaned in. "Hey. You with me?"

His lashes flickered, then lifted, unfocused eyes searching the ceiling before finally finding me. For a second, he just stared, as it took him a moment to remember who I was and why I was sitting on his bed with a bloody washcloth.

"Evie," he croaked.

"Yeah," I said. "In the flesh."

He blinked slowly. "Where's... where's Lucifer?"

The question hit me harder than I wanted to admit. Of course, that was what he asked first. I hesitated, then decided I was too tired to sugarcoat anything.

"He left," I said. "Walked out. Said there's food, told me to check on you, promised he'd be back before nightfall, and then slammed the door like a drama king."

Topher's eyes widened, the fog in them clearing fast.

"He what?" His voice came out thin, strained. He tried to push himself up, muscles trembling with the effort.

"Hey, slow down." I reached for his shoulder on instinct. "You're barely conscious, you shouldn't—"

He ignored me and fought to sit anyway, jaw clenched, panic starting to crack through the exhaustion on his face. Then, sagged back against the pillows, trying to sit up, the effort shaking through him. I reached out to steady his shoulder, but before my fingers could touch him, something shifted in the air.

A faint crackle. Then a cool bluish gloss slid over his entire body like someone had poured liquid moonlight across his skin. I froze.

Topher inhaled sharply, like a man dragged up from underwater. His spine straightened. His eyes focused. The pallor vanished from his face. He rolled his shoulders once, then casually popped his neck like he'd just woken from a nap.

Then he swung his feet over the edge of the bed and stood. Just stood like he hadn't nearly bled out of his soul twenty minutes ago.

"What the hell," I whispered, unable to stop it.

He stretched his arms overhead, joints clicking back into place with a kind of relieved sigh. "Oh, good. He's awake."

"He?" I repeated. "Lucifer?"

Topher's gaze flicked to the far wall, unfocused. "No," he murmured. "The other one."

Then he stood as if nothing had happened. He was already moving, searching around the room for his backpack and whatever tech disaster he kept inside it.

I followed him, still reeling, into the kitchen. The place glowed with warm cavern light, marble countertops against carved stone, a fridge that probably cost more than my entire childhood.

Topher dug through his bag, muttering to himself. "Where is it, where is it, where is it, he's going to kill me if I lost it, it was right here..."

"Do you want a grilled cheese?" I blurted when the silence stretched too long. I couldn't cook much, but I could make a delicious grilled cheese, if I did say so myself.

He froze for half a second, then nodded absently. "Sure. Fine. Thank you."

Not exactly heartfelt enthusiasm.

"Cool," I said dryly. "Great chat."

He didn't notice my tone. Whatever.

He was elbow deep in another bag now, rooting around for something, his brow furrowed as the fate of the world hung in the balance of a misplaced flash drive.

I let out an annoyed sigh and opened the fridge, hoping Luc hadn't lied about the food. And… there was actual food in there, like he'd stocked up planning to move here or something. Cheese. Butter. Bread. A jar of tomato soup that looked homemade. Thank God.

I pulled out what I needed and began searching for the pans.

Topher muttered to himself, pulling out cables and little metal gadgets I didn't recognize, spreading them across the kitchen table like he was assembling a bomb or a spaceship or maybe both.

"So what are you looking for?" I asked, flicking my eyes his way as I buttered the bread.

"An uplink key," he said without looking up. "Size of a thumbnail. Gold edges. Lucifer would call it a trinket. I call it my entire job."

"Uh huh." I had no idea what he was talking about.

I dropped the sandwiches in, flipped them when they browned, heated the tomato soup in a little pot I found under the counter, and tried not to obsess over the fact that Luc had walked out on me. Again.

Once everything was done, I plated it all and brought everything over to the table.

Topher looked up like he'd forgotten I existed, then blinked and smiled faintly. "Oh. Wow. Thank you. That looks great."

"It is," I said. "Eat."

He did. And for a minute, we just sat there, sharing grilled cheese and soup in a mountain cavern where the universe couldn't see us, like any of this was remotely normal.

Finally, when he'd stopped inhaling his food like a starved ferret, he wiped his mouth with the back of his hand. "Did he tell you?"

"Tell me what?"

"Lucifer went to get Azazael." Topher nodded as if this were just another item on a to-do list.

I choked on my soup. "He's doing what?"

"He's the only one who can reach him," he said. "He's the one who hid Azazael away, so it has to be him who goes back."

My stomach dropped. "Who's Azazael?"

Topher leaned back in his chair, eyes dark and suddenly very tired again. "Lucifer's oldest friend. His shadow before he had a shadow. The only angel who ever understood him." He traced a finger around the rim of his mug. "And the one he threw into an oubliette because the First Light told him to."

I stared at him. "Luc did that?"

"Back then, he still cared," Topher said softly. "Still wanted to please Him. Wanted to stay in His good graces."

I let that sink in with a slow, twisting ache in my chest.

"He thinks Azazael might know something about you and him."

"Is that why he left?" I asked quietly.

Topher closed his eyes like my question carried more weight than I meant. "That's what he does when it gets bad," he said quietly. "He runs at the problem and away from the people."

His eyes opened again, clearer, calmer than I felt. "But he'll come back. He always does."

"You sound sure."

"I am."

"Why?"

Topher's gaze flicked to me, and for the first time since I'd met him, there was no awkwardness or butler energy behind it. Just certainty. Heavy, old, and tired.

"Because he didn't leave to run away," he said. "He left to save someone he abandoned. And Lucifer always comes back to the people he can't bear to lose."

My throat tightened.

Topher pushed his empty plate away, "Now eat. You'll need your strength before he returns."

"Why?"

He didn't look up from the chaos he was wiring together on the kitchen table, cables snaking around his wrists, the last of that impossible blue shimmer fading slowly from his skin.

"Because whatever Azazael knows," he said, voice low, "is going to change everything."

CHAPTER THIRTY-THREE

Lucifer

I didn't make it far, and yet the walls still felt like they were closing in.

The cavern house hummed behind me, stone singing with wards and that strange pressure from the wound in this world, and all I could think was that I'd left her in there. Again. With the echo of my hand at her throat and my voice in her ears.

Coward. I was a coward, and I walked anyway.

Out through the arched entrance, along the ledge clinging to the mountain's side, past the last carved marble and glass. The wind knifed in from the valley, thin and high and cruel, carrying snow and dust and the taste of old rock.

I kept going until the house was just a shadow behind me, and ahead, there was only stone and sky. The air was cold enough to bite. Mortal lungs would have burned. Mine barely protested. I wanted it to hurt. I wanted something to. I needed to feel it.

I stopped on a flat outcropping and looked up at the jagged spine of the Andes. Peaks stabbed into the clouds, white and merciless. Somewhere beneath all that rock, the air dipped and twisted downward into a place that wasn't entirely of this world. A door. A descent.

But I needed the sky first. I grabbed the hem of my shirt and yanked it over my head, letting it fall into the snow. My shoes went next. Socks, gone. The cold hit my bare feet like teeth, sharp and immediate. Good. Let it.

Then I let the rest of me loose. Wings tore free in a rush of sound and sensation, feathers bursting from my shoulder blades in a spill of gleaming white. The mountain wards shivered at the contact, recognizing my shape, weighing me, tolerating me.

For a heartbeat, I just stood there, weight settling, muscles adjusting to the familiar drag and stretch. Then I stepped off the edge, and the world dropped away. Wind roared up to meet me, carving tears out of my eyes that had nothing to do with grief. I snapped my wings wide, caught the fall, and climbed.

The desert and rock blurred beneath me. The sky opened like it had been waiting. Up here, it was just wind and cold and the pull of my wings, no wards humming, no prophecy, no First Light watching. No Evie looking at me like she needed to save me—like I was worth saving in the first place.

For a few breaths, there was nothing I had to carry but myself. Just air and cold and the faint memory of what it felt like to be something other than tired. All the fucking time.

I flew until the summit of the Cordillera Blanca cut through the clouds, a narrow blade of stone dusted in white. I folded my wings and dropped, landing in a crouch hard enough that the snow cracked under my feet. The cold hit me like a punishment, clean and vicious. I stayed there for a long breath, letting the mountain's indifference sink its teeth into me.

Up here, the world looked small and pointless—just a sprawl of dust and ridges under a bruised sky. The cavern house where I'd left Evie was nothing but a dark notch in a lower peak. Around it, at the edge of my senses, the strange pressure of the scar pulsed... that thin, impossible place in reality where the First Light's sight slipped, where the world seemed to cinch tight and hold its breath. I had no name for what it was—only the unmistakable sense of being watched by something other.

Far in the distance, the Cordillera Vilcabamba was jagged against the horizon. Beneath one of its peaks waited a seam in the earth—small, unremarkable, easy to overlook if you didn't know what you were looking for. But I did. A narrow throat that led down into older dark, where the air tasted stale and wrong.

The path to the River Lethe.

Not the neat little stream mortals imagined in their bedtime myths, but the real thing: a vast, slow-moving current where memory softened at the edges, where names bled into nothing, where everything you refused to face eventually dissolved. I knew the sound of its current. The cold of its mist. The way gravity warped as you descended toward it.

And beyond that river, deeper still, was where I had dumped Azazael. Not a cell. Not a prison. Just a deep hole in the ground carved out of the forgotten corners of Hell, at the far edge of Lethe's shadow—a place you put what you didn't want to remember and where, eventually, it would be forgotten to time.

Snow hissed under me as I sat back on my heels. My wings folded closer, more instinct than comfort. My breath puffed white. Azazael's face rose behind my eyes—broken, bloodied, wings mangled, his voice shredded by madness that had torn itself through him like wire. None of what he said made sense.

He kept saying it over and over as I dragged him toward the hole, the words tumbling out of him like he couldn't stop them, like they were hooked under his ribs. Each time he repeated them, they got louder, sharper, more desperate, until they weren't ravings of a madman so much as a warning he was trying to carve into the air.

"It's all stolen," he rasped. "None of it is His. None of it's real."

Then he lurched and caught my arm, fingers digging in hard enough to bruise, hard enough to anchor himself to something solid. I hissed, but he didn't let go.

"Listen to me," he said, voice cracking on the command. "Find the one who matters."

His eyes were wild, glassy with terror, threaded with whatever the First Light had poured into his mind until it split. But beneath the madness, there was something terrifyingly clear, a focus that landed on me and stayed there, like he wasn't looking at a person, he was looking at the hinge point of a universe.

And I... I ripped my arm free.

I told myself he was broken, that he was dangerous, that it wasn't my job to decode the babbling of a mind that had snapped. I told myself I had bigger problems, bigger wars, bigger sins.

So I shoved him toward the edge and let the dark take him.

I threw him away like he was past the point of return with blood on his mouth and nonsense on his tongue, like his fear couldn't possibly be a warning, like his hands on my arm weren't the last thing he had left.

Even now, the memory burned. Not because he'd frightened me, but because he hadn't. Because somewhere inside the wildness, he'd been trying to save me, and I'd answered him with dismissal and distance and the easiest cruelty, pretending I couldn't hear.

I remembered my own hands on him. My own voice telling him this was for the best. For his own good. For everyone's good. Back when I still believed obedience and goodness were the same goddamned thing.

I'd done that. I'd made that choice. And the guilt sat in me like a stone I couldn't swallow.

Evie's face followed—the shock in her eyes when I told her not everything that happened to me was her burden, the way her throat moved under my hand, the way she still asked if I was all right. I should go back, some saner part of me murmured. Turn around. Apologize. Beg her to let me try again.

I was a fucking monster, not much better than the fucking First Light. My fingers dug into my knees until pain bloomed up my arms. If I went back now, I'd break apart in front of her. I could feel it—the edge too close, the part of me that wanted to burn the entire world down just to stop feeling like this.

She had already given herself up once for me. She'd do it again. And I wasn't going to drag her any closer to the worst thing I'd ever done.

I opened my eyes, staring out over the jagged line of mountains. "I'm going to fix it," I said softly. "Just one thing. One."

The wind didn't reply. I rose, snow clinging to my skin in melting flecks. "Hold on," I muttered—whether to Azazael or myself, I didn't know. "I'm coming."

I spread my wings and stepped off the summit, letting gravity seize me before the wind caught. I shot toward Vilcabamba, toward the mountain that hid the descent. The way down waited. The Lethe waited. Azazael waited. It was time to go back and face what I had left in the dark.

The wind sharpened as I cut south, the peaks splitting beneath me like broken teeth. Air thinned. Pressure changed. My wings burned from the strain. My muscles shook, but I didn't slow. I couldn't. The faster I went, the less room there was for the thoughts clawing up my throat.

I was flying straight toward a river in hell that existed to make things disappear— memories, sins, names, entire lifetimes. And that alone made something cold gather at the base of my spine.

The universe had a sick sense of humor, dragging me back there now, just as the memories I'd been robbed of were finally clawing their way to the surface. What if that place took more from me? What if it hollowed out the wrong memories? What if I came back empty-handed and empty-hearted—forgetting her all over again?

Evie's laugh flashed behind my eyes. The catch of her breath when I touched her. The way she said my name made it seem like it meant something. The thought of losing even one of those things struck harder than the wind in my face.

The land blurred below as the ground dropped away. The sky grew colder, darker. The burn in my shoulders turned sharp, electric, demanding that I stop or fall. I gritted my teeth and pushed harder.

Azazael's face rose in my mind—broken, wild, rambling about things that made no sense. I thought... his mind had been shattered. And I'd dismissed him and automatically obeyed the First Light, throwing him into a place built for erasure.

My wings faltered for half a heartbeat. The air lurched. The world rolled sideways. If he hated me when he saw me—He'd be right.

And beneath that fear, another one simmered, ugly and molten, a future I wanted and had no right to want. A future where the First Light is dethroned and Evie was—

No. I couldn't even let myself finish the thought. Not when I'd left her trembling in a new place, hurt by my hands. I didn't deserve her. I never did.

The air stung my eyes. Or maybe that was something else.

The Vilcabamba range rose ahead—dark, jagged, ancient. My wings trembled from the velocity, aching like overworked nerves. I forced them steady, forced myself to breathe, forced everything in me forward. Lethe waited under those mountains —the place I deserved to drown in.

But Azazael was there. And I would rip open every shadow between here and that river before I let him stay forgotten a moment longer. I dropped lower, cold slicing across my face, my wings beating the air into submission.

"I'm coming," I said to the mountains, to the river, to him.

The mountains of Vilcabamba rose up like they'd been waiting for me. Dark ridges. Stone spires. The kind of terrain mortals called dangerous because they didn't have a better word for don't come here, don't look too long, don't ask what sleeps inside.

I dropped hard, cutting through a crosswind that

nearly tore feathers from my wings, and landed on a narrow ledge halfway up the peak. Snow shattered under my feet. The air felt wrong here, heavier and colder, stale like a crypt that had been sealed too long with something still alive inside.

I scanned the rock wall. It was unremarkable. Perfectly, maddeningly unremarkable. A sheet of stone with nothing to distinguish it from a thousand others.

But I knew this place. I knew the shape of its silence. I stepped closer, letting my hand hover an inch from the surface. The rock quivered—just barely—like something on the other side was waiting with its teeth bared.

"Open," I commanded.

At first, nothing happened. Then the seam revealed itself—not a door, not a crack, not even movement. More like the stone simply lost interest in pretending to be solid. A line unfurled downward in a slow, sinuous sigh, widening just enough for a body to pass through.

The air that spilled out was colder than the snow —a cold that felt like fingertips crawling into my ribs. The smell hit next, sulfur mingling with minerals and dampness, something faintly metallic, with the tang of blood.

Memory. Or the absence of it.

I swallowed, forcing my wings to fold tight against my spine. They didn't like this place. They remembered what I'd done here even when I didn't want to.

The rock pulsed once, like a heartbeat, like recognition, like punishment. And I stepped inside. The mountain swallowed me immediately. The light disappeared in two steps, and the sound outside vanished in three. The world narrowed to stone underfoot and the steady drip of water somewhere ahead.

I wasn't ready to vanish my wings, but they brushed the walls when I wasn't careful. Each touch sent a jolt through me, as if the stone whispered back fragments of the voices it had eaten over the centuries.

I kept going. Down, down, deeper still. The air grew heavier with every turn, like breathing in wet wool. My head buzzed. My thoughts frayed at the edges. Lethe's gravity tugged on everything—my memories, my guilt, my name.

I gritted my teeth and forced myself forward. A faint glow rose ahead, green-white and sickly, illuminating the cavern where the river ran. The Lethe's surface gleamed like glass until you focused too hard—then the motion beneath it writhed and twisted and churned with things better left unspoken.

A shiver raced down my spine. This was where souls who tried to erase themselves from existence were sent—creatures who clawed at their own essence, desperate to be nothing. The river took them gladly, gnawing away identity, hunger, sanity, until what remained was a writhing mass of forgetfulness trying to devour anything warm enough to remind them they once lived. Even I hated looking at them.

I'd crossed this river only once before. For the sake of obedience. For the sake of someone who wasn't worthy of kneeling to. Now I was crossing it again for my friend. His name throbbed behind my sternum.

I stepped up to the river's edge, Lethe's mist curling around my ankles like hands.

I whispered into the cavern, "I'm here."

The river didn't answer. But the dark beyond it shifted—just slightly—like something heard me.

There was an alcove a few hundred yards downstream. I followed the curve of the Lethe, keeping to the rock ledge that hugged its side. The water ran silent here, too quiet, its surface smooth as polished obsidian. Every instinct I had screamed not to let it touch me.

I listened, vanishing my wings and staying close to the wall, fingers grazing jagged stone. The air grew colder the further I went, thick with the copper tang of old magic and something beneath it, older and worse.

I was almost to the alcove when the river moved. Not a gentle ripple. Not some harmless eddy. Something hit the surface from below, hard enough to send a spray of black water arcing toward me.

I flinched back on reflex, teeth bared, but a few drops caught my wrist, cold as knives. For a heartbeat, there was nothing. Then the whispers came. Not words, not exactly, more like impressions crawling under my skin. Souls, bones, I had broken. Faces I had forgotten. The smell of feathers burning. Every regret I had ever tried not to look at, crowding up behind my eyes, begging to be let in.

I snarled and shook my arm violently, flinging the drops off, forcing my mind to hold its shape.

"Not today," I muttered.

The river hissed softly as if disappointed. I didn't look at it again.

The alcove opened ahead, a dark mouth in the cavern wall. I stepped into it, leaving the Lethe at my back, and the sound of the river dropped away like someone had muffled the world.

The stone under my feet changed. Smoother. Worn. There, half hidden in shadow, was the staircase I'd made here. Rough steps carved straight into the rock, narrow and steep, leading down into a throat of darkness. This was not built for comfort.

At the bottom of those stairs was the place I had made for him. The place I had thrown him into. I started down, one hand on the wall to steady myself. The air grew thicker with every step, heavy with damp and rot and something sour that reminded me of promises made to a god who never listened.

The staircase ended in a small chamber carved out of the bedrock, maybe ten feet across, the ceiling low enough that I had to keep ducking. On the far side, where the wall curved in, was the thing I had come for—the hatch.

Just a rough wooden door set into the floor, framed by a ring of stones I had stacked myself. Once, long ago, I had liked the symbolism. Now it just made me want to break my own hands.

I had piled the rocks high when I left him here, a neat cairn over a sin I did not want to think about. They were not so neat now. A few had shifted, as if something beneath them had tried to push up and failed.

I swallowed hard and started tearing them away. Stone scraped skin. My fingers split. I hardly felt it. They'd heal quickly anyway.

When the last rock rolled off, the hatch stared up at me, old wood gray with age, iron hinges orange with rust. I could taste the air leaking from the cracks, spoiled and wrong.

"Azazael," I said under my breath, as if the name itself might brace me.

I grabbed the iron ring and pulled. The hinges screamed, a long, ugly sound that ripped through the chamber, and then the door gave way, swinging up and back.

The smell hit me first. Rot and mold and old blood. The stench of a body that didn't decay properly, held between states too long. My eyes watered. My stomach clenched hard enough that I almost doubled over —the Devil, gagging in his own house.

I forced myself to breathe through my mouth and leaned over the opening, sticking my head into the dark. At first, there was nothing but black. Then my eyes adjusted—chains in pieces across rocks. Shredded feathers scattered like dead leaves. Claw marks scored deep into the stone walls.

And in the center of it, curled in on himself like something left to die in a cage, was Azazael. Or what was left of him. His hair hung long in filthy tangles around his face. His wings were little more than broken, ragged stubs, feathers long since rotted away. His skin clung to bone, pale and thin, stretched tight over a frame that had once flown beside mine.

His eyes were open. And somehow, despite everything I had done, they were still glowing blue.

"Hello, old friend," he croaked, voice rusted from disuse and misery, like the words had been sitting in his throat for centuries waiting for me to show up finally.

CHAPTER THIRTY-FOUR

Evie

Night fell fast here.

One minute, the sky outside the cavern windows was bruised purple; the next, it was just... gone. Nothing but black pressing up against the glass, like the universe had turned the lights off and walked away.

Luc still wasn't back.

Topher had colonized half the dining room table sometime around late afternoon. Now it was a full-blown invasion. Laptops, tablets, a weird little box with more blinking lights than should be legal, wires everywhere.

He leaned forward, eyes flicking between eight different screens, a pair of headphones around his neck, mic attached like he was about to livestream the apocalypse.

I wasn't even sure where those cameras were. It definitely wasn't here. Some showed what looked like distant city streets; one was a shaky aerial shot over a desert; another was just a line of numbers changing too fast to read.

Anxiety gnawed at me. Had been gnawing all

day. Now it was full-on chewing through bone.

Where the fuck was Luc?

I hugged my arms around myself, fingers digging into my biceps. The cavern house was warm enough, but it didn't feel that way. The wards hummed low in the walls, that strange void-pressure cushioning my thoughts at the edges. This place was supposed to be safe. Hidden. Untouchable.

Didn't matter. My brain was doing its own little horror film marathon.

Every half hour or so, I checked my phone like it might magically have service now, like he might've texted, even though that was never his thing.

Nothing.

"Stop pacing," Topher said without looking up.

"I'm not pacing," I lied, mid-turn.

He made a soft, unimpressed sound. "You've done the same route around this table twenty-four times."

"You're counting now?" I snapped.

"I'm bored and mildly OCD," he said. "Let me have my hobbies."

I blew out a breath and sank into one of the chairs, the carved wood cold through my leggings. I rested my elbows on the table, careful not to jostle whatever fragile techno-altar Topher had built.

On one of the screens, something flickered. A map, maybe. Or a network layout. It all looked like math and static to me.

"What are you even watching?" I asked. "Please tell me it's not the celestial equivalent of Reddit."

"Wish." He tapped a key, switching one of the feeds. "I'm scraping for ripples."

"English, Topher."

"Fine." He sighed. "He left through something

that behaves like a fault line in the code of reality. When he comes back, the system's going to twitch. I'm waiting for the twitch."

"So you'll know he's okay," I said.

"So I'll know he's back." He finally glanced at me, eyes softening just a fraction. "Okay is... ambitious."

The words sat heavy in my chest.

Our tether, that strange, invisible thread between us, had gone quiet when he walked out. Not gone, just... muted. Like someone had thrown a blanket over a speaker, every so often I thought I felt a faint pulse, then told myself I was imagining it.

He'd wrapped his hand around my throat before he left. Not hard enough to bruise, but hard enough that I could still feel the phantom pressure if I put my fingers there.

What a fun little souvenir.

I swallowed against the burn in my eyes and looked away from Topher's screens.

"I hate this," I muttered. "The waiting. The not knowing. The... everything."

"Yeah," Topher said. "Welcome to knowing Lucifer."

I glared at him.

He held up a hand. "That wasn't a dig. Just... he does this. Disappears into the parts of the story he thinks belong to him alone. Comes back half-dead with a solution and five new problems."

"And we're just supposed to sit here and hope he doesn't get himself killed?"

"Pretty much. But he is... immortal, just so you know."

I stared at him.

He shrugged, one corner of his mouth twitching. "You're allowed to be mad about it, by the way."

"I am mad," I said. "I'm also... worried. And confused. And still kind of pissed he thought walking out on me was a good coping strategy."

Topher's gaze softened more noticeably this time. He slid the headphones off his neck and let them rest on the table.

"He left because he's drowning," he said quietly. "And because he thinks he has to do everything alone. It's not right. It's just... what he does."

"That's supposed to make me feel better?"

"No." He leaned back, studying me. "It's supposed to make you blame the right person."

"Which is?"

He opened his mouth, started to say "The F—", then flinched—actually flinched—and looked toward the far wall like he expected it to crack open.

He swallowed.

"The one who broke him," Topher said instead. "Not the idiot who's trying to put himself back together while the universe falls apart."

I didn't have an answer for that.

I just sat there, listening to the hum of machines and wards, watching symbols dance across screens I didn't understand, feeling the hollow ache in my chest where Luc should be.

Night pressed harder against the windows.

"Where the fuck are you," I whispered, more to the tether than the room. Somewhere, far away and deep below, something tugged back.

I was halfway through burning—toasting, whatever—another batch of grilled cheeses when Topher suddenly straightened in his chair.

"Got 'em," he breathed.

I nearly dropped the spatula. "What? Got who— what—Topher, what does that mean?"

But he was already typing, fingers flying over the

keys like he was hacking the Pentagon from a dining room table covered in crumbs and cables. One of his screens flickered, then another, lines of code jittering into something sharper, brighter.

I grabbed the plates and ran, nearly tripping over a power cord. I slid a sandwich onto the edge of his nearest free space—barely the size of a book—and shoved it toward him.

He blinked at it. Then at me. "Another grilled cheese?"

Heat rushed up my neck. "Don't say it like that."

"Like what?"

"Like—like I've committed a culinary crime!"

Topher lifted an eyebrow. "Evie. You've made five tonight."

"I know!" I huffed. "It's all I'm good at! And it's comforting! So, eat your fucking sandwich!"

Something like a smile twitched at his mouth. Then the middle monitor spasmed. The smile dropped.

Static burst across the image—loud, sharp—followed by a white flash that flooded the whole screen. The speakers crackled, the lights dipped, and the temperature in the room seemed to plummet ten degrees at once.

Topher's posture changed instantly—gone was the tired hacker, and in his place was someone very awake and very alarmed. His fingers froze above the keys.

"Oh no," he whispered.

My stomach bottomed out. "Topher. What is it? What happened?"

He didn't look at me. He didn't breathe. On the main screen, one of the feeds jumped, the blur of data sharpening into a map threaded with lines of light. A single trail moved across it, bright and steady, like someone had drawn a vein through the dark.

Topher zoomed in. Another line flared into existence right behind it. Thinner. Meaner. Matching every turn a fraction of a second later.

My skin went cold. "What's that?"

Topher's jaw clenched. "That first one is Lucifer," he said quietly. "That second one... that's someone riding his signal."

He swallowed, knuckles white on the edge of the table.

"He's being followed."

Topher's screens flickered in a wave, like a heartbeat hitting too hard against fragile ribs. He zoomed in on two bright threads that pulsed across the map—one jagged and unsteady, the other smoother, riding its wake.

I edged closer. "Tell me that's not Luc."

"That's Lucifer," Topher said tightly. "And... he's got someone with him."

My stomach twisted. "Azazael?"

Topher didn't answer right away, which told me more than yes would have. His face had gone tight around the edges, the way it did when he was calculating bad odds in real time.

But then something else—some instinct I couldn't put words to—rose up under my skin in a warm rush— the tether. That invisible, impossible thread between Luc and me. It hummed suddenly, a low vibration under my ribs, like someone had plucked a string running straight through me.

Luc. He was close. And—hurt? No. Not exactly. More like bruised, exhausted, frayed.

Before I even realized I was doing it, I reached inward. Not physically. Not mentally. Just... toward him. Like leaning over the railing of a dream. A spark answered. Not words, not a picture —more like the impression of motion, stone, pain, Azazael's ragged breath, the strain of wings he shouldn't have been using.

Topher whipped toward me. "Evie. Stop. You're lighting up like a flare."

I gasped, pulling back. The connection snapped shut with a sting, like a rubber band against my heart.

"I—I didn't mean to," I whispered. "I just... knew I could."

"Well, now He knows, too." Topher tapped one of the screens. "That spike? That was you. And if I can see it, Heaven sure as hell can."

I didn't have time to argue. The house shuddered —hard. A resounding boom rolled through the cavern, shaking dust down from the stone ceiling in lazy gray sheets.

I froze, "What the fuck?"

Topher spun back to the screens, cursing under his breath. "Something just hit the wards."

Another pulse lit the map. The second thread— the one following Luc—brightened, sharpened, took on definition. Topher squinted. Then swore. Louder.

"Oh, you've got to be kidding me."

"What?" I demanded.

"That's not Heaven." He leaned in, fingers flying. "That's Damien."

A beat of silence.

"That guy who was with Lilith?" I whispered.

Topher grimaced. "Yeah. The one who led her right to Lucifer when we went down to Hell. And he's either about to help us or rip open this mountain like it's wrapping paper."

The house rumbled again—this one sharper, closer, the lights flickering overhead.

"Decision time," Topher muttered.

"Does he ever just—help?"

Topher gave me a flat look. "Damien only works for Damien."

Outside, another boom echoed, louder than before. Soon, it would hit us directly.

I swallowed hard. "What do we do?"

Topher lifted his hands over the keys, hovering, not touching. "We pick who kills us slower," he said.

And then the tether thrashed inside me—Luc, closer, pain, desperate— and the whole cavern shook again.

Before I could respond, a third, sharper impact hit the mountainside—closer, angrier, intentional. The lights flickered. The wards groaned. And Topher looked at me with something that wasn't fear, wasn't hope, but a terrible mixture of both.

"Evie," he said softly, "I really hope Lucifer gets back before that door comes down."

The next boom wasn't distant. It was right on top of us. The floor bucked under my feet, a crack snaking up one of the stone pillars in the living room. A lamp went over, glass shattering. Somewhere behind the walls, the wards screamed, a sound I felt more in my teeth than in my ears.

Topher swore so violently it might've counted as a minor exorcism. He grabbed my wrist hard enough to bruise.

"Move."

"What about the screens, your system, we can't just—"

"Evie, now."

He hauled me away from the table, down the hallway that led deeper into the cavern. The house around us suddenly became a maze of shadow and emergency light, every surface humming as if it had a heartbeat.

The front door exploded inward.

Not creaked, not opened, just full body slammed off its hinges, stone ringing with the impact. A blast of cold light flooded the entryway, harsh and holy and wrong.

I twisted around on instinct.

Topher yanked me harder. "Don't look back."

Of course, my stupid eyes betrayed me anyway. I saw them in the fractured glance over my shoulder, burned into my brain in one hit.

"Cherubim." He muttered.

Not chubby babies with wings like bad greeting cards, not the gentle, glowing things humans like to paint—monsters of light with swords of flames.

They poured through the doorway like living geometry, three faces stacked and turning, animal and human and something in between, all blazing. Four wings each, feathers made of light so bright it hurt to look at, bodies neither male nor female nor anything I had a word for. Every line of them shone, but the shine wasn't comforting; it was surgical, clinical, like being lit up on an operating table.

One of the faces turned, all three sets of eyes locking straight on me. My lungs forgot how to work. Topher dragged me around the corner.

"Evie," he snapped, "eyes forward."

We sprinted down a narrower hall, feet slapping marble, the roar of the invaded house chasing us. The air felt charged, thin, wrong, like the beginning of a storm that had forgotten how to rain and was just static and fury.

At the very end of the hallway was a nondescript wall panel I'd assumed was a closet.

Topher slapped his palm against the stone beside it and muttered something under his breath. The wall shimmered in a way that made my stomach twist, then slid aside to reveal a metal door set into the rock. Not decorative. Functional. Heavy.

"A panic room?" I wheezed.

"Something like that."

He shoved it open. The inside was small, just big enough for a narrow bench, a low shelf, and a whole lot of very serious-looking sigils carved into every surface.

He pushed me in before I could argue, the air cooler and denser inside, like the room was full of held breath.

"Topher, I am not hiding while you—"

He grabbed something from the shelf and thrust it at me. A sword. Like, an actual sword.

Cold weight hit my palms, nearly dragging my arms down. The metal gleamed faintly in the dim light, inscribed with symbols my brain refused to focus on. I had no idea where it had come from or why it suddenly felt like it belonged in my hands.

"I don't know how to use this," I said, voice pitching high.

"You point the sharp end at the thing trying to kill you," he said. "You're smarter than you look, you'll figure it out."

"Wow, okay, rude, also this is heavy."

The house shook again, a distant roar mixing with something that sounded disturbingly like wings.

Topher's face tightened. He gripped the door frame with one hand and my shoulder with the other.

"Evie," he said, and his voice dropped all the way into serious, "listen to me. Do not open this. No matter what you hear. Not my voice, not Luc's, not anything that sounds like them. You wait until

Lucifer or I physically open this door. You understand?"

My heart hammered against my ribs. "Topher..."

"Say it."

"I won't open the door," I whispered. "No matter what I hear."

Something crashed out in the hall, closer now. Light flashed under the metal lip of the doorway, too bright even from here.

Topher nodded once, tight.

"Good." He released my shoulder and stepped back. "Try not to die in there."

"Topher."

He hesitated just long enough to give me a crooked half smile that didn't reach his eyes. Then he pulled the door shut.

Multiple locks slid home with a heavy finality that made my stomach lurch. The ward symbols along the inside of the room flared to life, casting everything in pale, flickering light.

The silence after Topher slammed the door wasn't actually silent. It throbbed. A low, vibrating pressure through the walls, like the panic room itself was a lung holding breath it didn't want to exhale. I pressed my back to the cold metal and slid down until I hit the bench, the sword across my lap like some medieval therapy animal.

My pulse wouldn't settle. It was too fast, too loud —too everything.

Outside, something slammed against the walls— stone shuddering, sigils flaring, the lights overhead flickering harshly. The Cherubim... or whatever the hell those things were... were still here. Still hunting.

Angels. Actual angels. A laugh escaped me, and it was a sharp, cracked thing that echoed too much in the tiny room.

"Those fucking monsters are actual angels?" I asked out loud, because apparently talking to myself was a thing now. "Real. Great. Awesome."

I stood there, pacing and, wide-eyed, sword dragging at my hands, breathing hard in a metal box carved into the bones of a mountain, while something holy and monstrous tore apart the house outside. I tightened my grip until my fingers ached.

"Okay," I muttered to no one. "This is fine. Totally normal..."

The words snapped in half in my throat, twisting into a sound I couldn't even name—a sob, a laugh, a scream—all tangled together as it ripped out of me. I ran a hand over my face, fingers shaking.

Throughout my whole childhood, I'd been taught they were gentle guardians. Warriors of light. Messengers. All that Hallmark card bullshit. Then I'd shoved the entire idea into the same mental filing cabinet as Santa Claus and soulmates—nice stories that made life suck less.

But the things that tore down the front door weren't nice and weren't stories. They had too many eyes. Too many wings. Too much intention. They radiated purpose. And that purpose felt like doom.

I swallowed hard, my throat tight. "What do they want?" I asked the room, like it might answer me. "To kill me? Drag me to Heaven? Stop me from... from what?"

The sword glinted in the flickering light.

"Why me?" My voice cracked. "Why any of this?"

Another boom rocked the hall outside. Dust shook loose from the seams of the ceiling. Something screeched—metal or stone or something alive, I couldn't tell. My heart kicked against my ribs so hard I thought it might crack something.

"This is insane," I whispered. "This is—this can't be—"

But the tether in my chest pulsed again, stronger and real. Luc. Alive. Moving closer.

Those monsters, the Cherubim, were here for a reason, and it wasn't because they were bored on a Tuesday night.

"Stop him," I murmured to myself, the realization sliding cold and slow into place. "They want to stop him. Or stop... us. Or..."

My vision blurred for a moment, panic washing through me so hard I had to grip the sword to keep from dropping it.

"I'm not ready for this," I whispered into my shaking hands. "I'm not—whatever they think I am. I'm not. I'm just—"

A thunderous crash shook the door so hard I flinched, biting back a scream.

I was just Evie Grace. Just a messy girl with pink hair and combat boots who ran away from home. With no plan and who could barely make grilled cheese without burning something.

But angels—actual biblical nightmares—were trying to rip their way into this place to get to me. I climbed under the bench, wrapping myself into a ball. I squeezed my eyes shut, pressed my forehead to the cold steel, and let the truth sink in like a knife.

"Myths are real," I whispered. "And they're coming for me."

The room trembled again. And for the first time since this all began, I wasn't sure Luc would make it back in time.

CHAPTER THIRTY-FIVE

Lucifer

The second my head was through the hatch, and I called his name, he hit me. Skin and bone and rage, but it was enough. He slammed into me with a sound that was half snarl, half sob, knocking me back against the rock. His eyes glowed that electric, ruined blue, hatred burning so bright it almost made him beautiful again.

He was nothing but angles now. Hollow cheeks, ribs like prison bars, wings half-grown and ragged, feathers molting and scattered on the floor like forgotten prayers. But he ran at me like he still had all his strength, like centuries of rot and isolation meant nothing.

"Azazael—"

His fist cracked across my jaw. I let him.

He let out a strained animal sound. "**You—**" It wasn't a name. It was an accusation sharpened into a syllable.

He got another shot in, knuckles splitting my lip. Then his shoulder hit my ribs hard enough to make them sing. I could have stopped him. I could have pinned him to the wall with a thought, folded him in light, and put him down gently.

I didn't. I stood there and took it, because some sick, buried part of me agreed with him. I had put him in this hole, on the word of a false god. If anyone had earned the right to try and break my bones, it was him.

By the time I finally caught his wrists, I could taste blood and feel the deep ache blooming along my side.

"Enough," I rasped, holding him tight. "I'm not here to hurt you."

"You already did," he hissed, voice sandpaper and broken glass. "You—you threw me away."

"I know." The words felt like they were tearing something out of me. "I know. I'm here to get you out."

He laughed then, a horrible, cracked sound that had nothing to do with humor. He sagged all at once, the fight dropping out of him like a marionette with cut strings, and crumpled at my feet. Unconscious. Or close enough.

I healed the worst of it—sealed the festering wound in his side, shored up the fractures I could feel thrumming in his bones. I didn't have time for more than a patch job on myself. My ribs still throbbed when I drew breath. I scooped him up anyway, wings flaring in the cramped space.

"Come on," I muttered, more to myself than to him. "We're done with this place."

I flew. Up the shaft, away from the stench of the Lethe and rot, away from the pit I never should have used. Every beat of my wings felt heavier. Every inch between me and that hatch felt watched, judged, measured.

By the time I hit the scar and slipped back through, my lungs were burning, my wings aching like they'd been carved down to tendon and willpower.

Dark had fallen above the rim of the world, a sky full of stars glittering like someone had spilled a broken crown across the heavens. I'd meant to be back by nightfall, but time gets slippery when you're in Hell, stretchy and mean, the kind of thing that laughs in your face when you try to hold it still.

We broke out over the mountains, the familiar pressure of the void-wound wrapping around us in a cold shiver, and for one wild second, I almost believed it would be fine that I'd bring him home. That I'd walk into the cavern house and find Evie pacing, furious, alive, hurling questions at me in that voice that always hit me like truth and thunder. That the worst thing I'd have to face tonight was explaining why I left.

But then the air changed. A ripple, faint but unmistakable, brushed along my spine. The kind of shift only something celestial could make, subtle enough a human would never notice, sharp enough it made the feathers at the nape of my wings lift.

Someone was behind us.

Not close enough to see, not foolish enough to reveal themselves, but watching, keeping pace just beyond the veil of night. The stars looked peaceful, soft, quiet... but the sky had teeth tonight, and every instinct I had screamed that we weren't alone up here.

I tightened my grip on Azazael and flew faster, pretending I didn't feel the darkness moving when I did, pretending it wasn't following us home.

Then I saw the door.

The cavern house came into view as I dropped lower, marble and glass carved into the mountain's mouth, wards shimmering faintly along the stone. It should've looked serene, untouched. Mine.

But... the front door was gone. Not open, just gone, hinges twisted, stone around the frame scorched black. Smoke billowed out in ragged bursts, lit from within by the dying glow of ward-light. My stomach dropped so fast my wings stuttered mid-flight.

I landed hard on the ledge, knees bending to absorb the hit, Azazael limp in my arms. I laid him gently on the stone near the wall, inside the weakest edge of the wards but far from the wreckage.

"Stay," I muttered, then snorted at myself. "Idiot."

I straightened, wings half-flared, a dozen terrible possibilities clawing at me. That's when Damien landed behind me, boots scraping the stone as his wings folded with that aristocratic snap he always seemed proud of. He brushed a nonexistent piece of lint off his shoulder like he wasn't arriving at the scene of a celestial massacre.

"You didn't mention your décor was going through a phase," he said mildly.

"Not now," I growled.

He lifted his hands in surrender, stepping aside as smoke curled past us.

The wards hummed weakly under my feet as I moved toward the entrance. The smoke tasted like burned feathers, ozone, and something distinctly not-human. I stepped inside.

The first thing I saw was a smoking pile of light where the coffee table used to be.

Not ash, not exactly. Just... residue. Burnt holiness congealed on the marble. The outline of a body that didn't obey mortal geometry, four wings charred.

Cherubim.

There were four heaps like that scattered around the living room. One half melted into the wall. One slumped where the dining chairs had been. Another sprawled across the ruined doorway, half in, half out.

And Topher.

He came around the corner from the back hall, clothes singed at the edges, hair sticking up like he'd been electrocuted, soot streaked across his face. He was breathing a little too fast, but somehow still upright.

"Hey," he said, like I'd just walked in late to a staff meeting. "You're back."

I crossed the room in three strides.

"Where's my mate?" The words tore out of me, bare and lethal. No snark. No softness. Just need, carved down to bone. I couldn't pull a full breath without the answer. I couldn't think, couldn't see past the edge of it. I only knew the tether was taut somewhere in this building, and if it snapped, something in me would go with it.

Topher's expression shifted, whatever joke he'd been reaching for dying before it was born.

"Alive," he said, immediately. "Shaken. Furious. Armed. Come on."

He led me down the back hallway, past cracks in the stone I knew hadn't been there when I left. At the end, I moved past him, pressing my palm against a section of wall. The stone shivered and slid aside, revealing the metal door I had built into the mountain ages ago.

The panic room.

"She's in there," Topher said. "She's fine. Mostly. Sword might be overkill, but it made her feel better."

I laid my hand flat on the cool metal. The wards

recognized me, flaring briefly beneath my palm, and the locks disengaged with a series of heavy clicks. The door swung inward.

Evie stood in the middle of the small room, bathed in the pallid light of active sigils. Her hair was a tangle, her eyes wild and red-rimmed. Both hands gripped a sword that was clearly too heavy for her, the tip dragging a shallow groove in the floor.

For half a second, she did not move. Her gaze swept over me, from my face to my chest down to my bare feet, like she was cataloguing damage. I had healed most of my wounds on the flight back, but not all. My ribs still ached, but thankfully, there were no outward bruises. I could feel dried blood at the corner of my mouth. Her eyes caught on it, lingered.

Then she dropped the sword. It hit the floor with a clang that echoed off the metal walls, and she was out of the room and into my arms before it stopped ringing. I caught her on instinct.

She slammed into my chest hard enough to jar my bruised ribs, arms wrapping around my neck like she was afraid I might vanish if she let go. I folded her in, my wings cradling around us, my hands spreading over her spine like I was trying to memorize every line.

The bond between us hummed to life, hot and bright. The tether dragged hard, pulling me into her, into the certainty that she was here, she was whole, she was mine. It had been the only thing that kept me from losing my mind in Hell, that constant pull in my sternum every time I reached for her across the distance and felt her answer, steady and alive. Every beat of it out there had been a miracle and a punishment, reminding me exactly what I stood to lose.

Thank every forgotten god she had let me mark her. Without that thread, I would have been flying blind through the dark, guessing, hoping, choking on the idea that she might already be gone while I was still fighting my way back.

She was shaking. So was I. I breathed her in, the scent of smoke and sweat and her shampoo, so stupidly human and grounding, it made something inside me loosen and break at the same time.

Behind us, Topher cleared his throat once, quietly. "I'm gonna go... uh... check on our new guest," he said.

His footsteps retreated down the hall, leaving us in the soft hum of ward-light. Evie wrapped her arms around my bare shoulders, holding on like the world might drop out from under us if she let go.

"You left," she said into my chest, voice raw. Not a dramatic accusation. Just a simple, gutted fact.

The bond pulsed once, hard, like it agreed with her. And the words cut deeper than any hit Azazael had managed to land.

"I'm sorry," I murmured into her hair, the words scraping out of me rough and honest. "I had to go get my friend, my brother. I'd left him..."

The guilt slid into my voice before I could cage it, thick and sour, the kind that lived in the bones.

She leaned back just enough to look at me, her palms still warm against my chest. Her eyes softened the second she saw my face, like she could feel every unspoken thing through the tether.

"Okay," she breathed, not forgiving me because she should, but because she understood me in the places no one ever had.

Her gaze flicked past my shoulder, taking in the cracked walls, the lingering smoke, the faint, ugly shimmer where holier things had died minutes before.

"Where is he?" she asked, concern knitting across her features. "Azazael?"

I swallowed hard, the taste of ash and regret still hanging in my throat.

"Outside," I said. "On the ledge. He's unconscious, but alive. He tried to tear me apart for leaving him."

A humorless sound left me—a breath, a ghost of a laugh. "I let him."

Her eyes widened, pity and horror and something fiercer flickering together.

I brushed my thumb across her cheek, needing the contact more than I cared to admit.

"I'm here now," I told her quietly. "You. Him. I'm not leaving again unless the world ends... and even then, I'm taking you with me."

Her hands slid up to the tops of my shoulders, the bond between us pulsing warm, steady, like a heartbeat shared.

"Show me," she said softly. "Take me to him."

CHAPTER THIRTY-SIX

Evie

Luc carried Azazael into one of the spare bedrooms, his body limp in Luc's arms, wings dragged like ruined banners. I followed close behind, and when he laid him on the bed, the breath left my lungs.

I couldn't believe the damage.

Up close, it was worse. So much worse. Bones pressing sharp beneath parchment-thin skin. A collarbone snapped clean once, maybe twice, and healed wrong. His arm had knitted crookedly, muscle warped around it like his body had given up halfway through remembering how to be whole.

"Who did this?" I whispered, though I already knew.

Luc's jaw tightened. "The First Light."

A cold dread moved through me, slow as poison. I didn't know what had happened to him, not really. I only knew what I could see. The way his body looked wrong in that bed. The hunger-thinness of him. The ragged ruin of his wings. The bruises that didn't belong on something made of light.

My stomach turned. The god I'd been taught to revere, to trust, to fear. The god who'd been painted as all-loving. Merciful. Just.

But nothing about Azazael's shattered body looked like mercy.

If this was what was left of an angel after being in His hands, what would happen if He got Luc back in His grasp?

Would He break him the same way, piece by piece, until all of him went quiet? Would He take the beautiful parts first, the wings, the strength, the certainty, and leave only skin and suffering? Would He do it slowly, carefully, like punishment was a craft He'd perfected?

The terror sat behind my ribs, heavy and sharp.

Rip out his wings? Tear him apart until not even his divinity could mend him? That thought alone scraped something primal inside me raw.

I couldn't let that happen. Not to Luc.

If it came to it, if that was the only way left, I would give myself up first. I would rather walk into the fire than watch Him lay a hand on the man—angel—demon that I—

No. I couldn't even think it. And I absolutely couldn't tell Luc. He'd never let me consider it. He'd burn the heavens before he allowed that.

I dipped a cloth into a bowl of warm water, hands shaking slightly, and began cleaning Azazael's face. Dirt and blood gave way to skin so pale it looked almost translucent. Thousands of years trapped underground, starved of light and hope and everything that made a person real, clung to him like a second skin.

Luc worked beside me, quiet, focused. His fingers moved with care I'd never seen him use on anyone else. He healed Azazael's wings first, palms glowing faintly as he pressed them back into place until they folded and vanished into the lines of his back. Most of the fractures he mended with touch alone, but even healed, Azazael was too thin, too fragile, like a gust might scatter him.

When we finished, we dressed him in clean clothes, soft fabric hanging loose on his frame. His old rags went straight into the trash. He looked younger now, and older, both at once—a boy who had been a soldier far too long.

Luc pulled the blankets up around him, brushing dark hair from his forehead with a tenderness that made my chest ache.

Then he turned to me. His hand found mine, warm and sure, fingers threading through like something he'd always done. He didn't say a word, just tugged gently, guiding me out of the room.

He led me to the primary bedroom. It was dark and wooden, warm and shadowed, reminiscent of his penthouse but older, deeper, as if this were the place he actually slept when the world allowed him to.

I barely had time to take in the space before his hands came to my face, palms cradling my jaw, thumbs stroking once, slow and reverent, like he was memorizing me. And then he kissed me.

The kind of kiss that said I found you, I came back to you, I will burn every throne that tries to take you from me. A kiss that made my knees forget their purpose and my heart remember one. It was desperate and shaking and a little uneven at first, like he had too many things to say and no language left but his mouth on mine.

His lips were warm, tasting like smoke and something sweeter underneath, and my hands went straight to his chest, running my hands up his hard body to his shoulders. Something between us flared, gold rising under my skin, the tether pulling tight, and for a second, it felt like the whole room tilted toward him.

I parted my lips, and he groaned into the kiss, low and rough, like the sound had been carved out of his ribs. His thumb dragged along my jaw, my cheek, the corner of my mouth, as if he needed to reassure himself I was solid and not some illusion The First Light had thrown at him.

"Evie," he breathed against my lips, my name like a prayer and a curse both at once.

I kissed him harder as all that fear from the panic room, the vision of Azazael broken on the bed, imagining Luc in his place, wings torn and bones wrong, it all rose in me in one messy wave. I poured it into him the only way I knew how, fingers sliding up into his hair, pulling him over me, closer, until there was no space left to be afraid in.

His hands left my face and traveled down, skimming my throat, my shoulders, taking inventory as he pulled my shirt and bra off. Every brush of his fingers said you are here, you are whole, you are mine. The tether hummed and thrummed in agreement, a steady pulse beneath my skin.

He broke the kiss just long enough to rest his forehead against mine, breath ragged.

"I thought I was going to lose you," he said quietly. "Up there, I could feel you through the tether, but I could also feel your fear. Someone was following us, and I kept thinking, if I get back and you're gone, I will burn everything He has ever loved to ash."

"Hey," I whispered, fingers curling at the back of his neck. "You didn't lose me."

"Not yet," he said, and I heard the crack in it, the terror he wouldn't name.

I cupped his face, forcing him to look at me. "You are not the only one who gets to be terrified, you know. I saw what He did to Azazael. If He ever lays a hand on you..."

My throat closed up. The vow I had made to myself rose to the surface, heavy and sharp. I swallowed it back down. He could never know.

Luc's eyes went darker, softer, like he heard more than I said. He kissed me again, slower now, like he was trying to memorize the exact shape of my mouth, the way my breath hitched when his teeth grazed my bottom lip.

His hands slid to my hips, guiding me gently back until the backs of my legs hit the bed. He broke the kiss to trail his mouth along my cheek, my jaw, the hollow of my throat, each touch a benediction.

"Stay," he murmured against my skin. "Right here. With me. No more running, Evie."

The word stay did something to me. Maybe because I'd never really had a place that wanted me in it. Maybe because, for the first time, staying didn't feel like a cage.

My fingers tangled in his hair, nails scraping lightly against his scalp. "Then, you have to stay, too," I said. "No more disappearing on me or solo rescue missions without telling me. We do this together. Or not at all."

The tether between us pulsed once, hard, like it was putting its own vote in.

He slid my leggings and panties to the floor and then pulled back just enough to meet my eyes again. Whatever he saw there made his expression go wrecked and reverent all at once.

"Together," he said. "I swear it."

He kissed me then like an oath, like a signature, like a seal, his mouth moving over mine with intent as my fingers tightened on his shoulders and I heard the soft clink of his belt coming undone.

The room narrowed to the slide of lips and the press of his body and the steady, golden hum of our bond. The world outside could wait. Heaven and Hell and all the angels in the sky held at the edge of the warded walls could just fuck right off.

Right now, there was only this—him and me.

His hands framed my hips, and when I tipped backward onto the bed, he followed, caging me in, the mattress dipping under his weight. The mark on my neck burned warm and bright, the tether singing with every breath we shared, and for the first time since the wards in the cavern house had started screaming, I felt something like safe.

He pulled back just enough to look at me, pupils blown wide, every ancient, ruined part of him laid bare in his gaze.

"If I was ever meant for a heaven," he whispered, voice rough and reverent, "it was this. You."

It hit me like a prayer detonating in my chest. The devil, calling me his heaven. A version of sacred I'd never been allowed to believe in, looking at me like I was the only thing left worth saving.

My throat went tight. "Luc…"

He dipped his forehead to mine, lacing both our hands together and bringing them over my head. He breathed me in like I was air after a thousand years underground, then kissed me, slow and deep, sealing the words between us as he slowly pushed into me.

It was perfect. It was ecstasy. It was heavenly. Like he had been made to fit perfectly into my body. We began to move together, our lips never parting.

He swallowed my moan as the tether burned bright, the mark humming in my skin as he started to thrust faster, harder, and so good. I never wanted this to end.

I closed my eyes, the coiling building deep in my belly. The rest of the world fell away until there was only him, only us, and the steady, blazing pull of the bond singing through every part of me.

It was coming fast, like I was charging up for something big. Like I was a phoenix about to burn out and re-emerge as something else. I opened my eyes and looked at him, and he was glowing gold, even his eyes, and I could feel it pulsing through me.

"Oh God, Luc," I gasped between pants. It was about to hit me fast.

His mouth curved against my throat. "Careful," he murmured, voice rough. "He's the one name I don't want in your mouth when I'm the one making you pray."

"Oh... Luc... fuck... please..."

I was almost undone when he rose up and turned me, settling me on my hands and knees like he'd done it a thousand times in his head already. He hauled me back and sank in with one smooth, merciless motion that stole the air from my lungs.

He didn't give me a chance to recover, driving into me again, harder, faster, until all I could do was brace and feel. His chest pressed to my back as he leaned over me, wrapping an arm around my waist, holding me flush to him like he was making sure the universe understood exactly where I belonged.

I whimpered.

He bit into my shoulder, just below the mark, and said in a low voice, "Come for me, Evie. Let go. Let me feel your flutters all over my cock."

And that right there undid me. I couldn't stop it if I wanted to. I pressed back into him, getting him as deep as I could. He hit that spot, and I screamed his name. The world came apart in bright, shuddering pieces colored in gold, pleasure tearing through me so hard my arms almost gave out. If he hadn't been holding me, I would've melted straight into the mattress.

I was still having aftershocks when his rhythm faltered. His breath hit my neck in broken bursts, a rough, hoarse sound leaving his throat as he buried himself deep and finally followed me over the edge. The tether between us flared, flooded with his satisfaction, his relief, that raw, stunned gratitude that I was here, that I was his, that we were both still breathing. For a heartbeat, all that feeling surged outward, and a pulse of gold rolled off us in a slow wave, brushing the walls, the wards, the very air, before sinking back into my skin like it had always belonged there.

He didn't pull away. His arm stayed wrapped firmly around my waist, keeping me close as our bodies slowly went from frantic to just... tired. Spent. Soft. He pressed a kiss to my shoulder, right below the mark, something almost sacred in the way his lips lingered there.

"Come here," he murmured, a vulnerability I hadn't heard before.

He eased out of me carefully, still holding me, and guided us both down, hauling me with him toward the pillows like he refused to let even an inch of space appear between us. I went willingly, boneless, letting him rearrange us until I was tucked in front of him, his chest pressed to my back, his arm still snug around my middle.

He fit himself along my spine like he'd been carved to do it, one leg tangled with mine, his nose buried in my hair. Every exhale tasted like smoke and spice and something that was just... him.

The tether between us settled into a slow, steady thrum that was lulling, the mark on my neck a warm, lazy burn instead of a blaze.

His thumb traced idle circles over my stomach, slower and slower as his breathing evened out. The adrenaline, the fear, the fight, all of it started to drain away, leaving only bone-deep exhaustion and the strange, impossible safety of being held by the devil like I was the most precious thing he'd ever been given.

My eyes grew heavy. The last thing I registered before sleep pulled me under was the weight of his arm around me, the solid line of his body at my back, and the unmistakable scent of him curling around my senses like a blanket.

If there was ever a heaven meant for me, it probably wasn't pearly gates and choirs and all the things I'd been promised as a child. It was this, right here, wrapped in the arms of the one person who made my mind go quiet and my soul stop running. Heaven didn't have to be holy to be home, I realized. It just had to be him.

CHAPTER THIRTY-SEVEN

Lucifer

Evie was still asleep when I slipped out of the bedroom. She was bundled in the blankets like she'd been stitched into the center of my universe. The tether hummed with the quiet reassurance of her breathing, and for the first time in hours, the panic in my chest eased.

Topher was at his makeshift command station—eight monitors, a backlit keyboard, and a mug that had definitely once been mine. Damien lounged beside him, boots on the table, legs crossed, slicing an apple with a dagger and eating the pieces straight off the blade. Last night, my mind had been only on Evie. I'd stupidly forgotten he'd even arrived.

Topher glanced up. "Good morning. I found him last night and put him in a room. Can I—"

"We need to talk," Damien cut in, not even bothering to look up.

My stomach tightened. Last time we'd "talked," he'd walked me straight into a trap, and I wasn't about to forget it.

"Fine," I said. "War room," I jerked my chin

toward the hall.

Damien finally looked at me, his eyebrows shooting up. "You have a... war room here?"

I shrugged. "It came with the mountain."

"You own the mountain?"

He snorted but followed us. The door slid open at my touch, wards glowing faint gold along the frame.

Inside, sigils crawled over every inch of stone—protection, concealment, reinforcement. I'd carved most of them centuries ago, more out of restless instinct than intention. I never really used this room, never thought I'd use it for anything but storage. Now it felt less like a relic and more like the only place in existence big enough for the trouble I was about to invite in.

Damien stepped inside, flicked his dagger closed, and hooked it onto his belt. His expression shifted from lazy to lethal in half a second. "I'm in," he said.

I laughed, humorless and sharp. "Like the last time you were 'in'? When you fed Lilith half my plans and nearly delivered me gift-wrapped to her?"

Damien's jaw flexed. "I deserved that."

"You deserve so much worse."

"Probably," he said, voice rougher now. "But this isn't about me anymore."

Topher crossed his arms, leaning against the wall. "Then what's it about?"

Damien hesitated. Something flickered across his face. A crack. Something raw and unguarded. Then he stepped closer, lowered his voice to a whisper.

"Have you heard of the... Beloved?"

The name fell heavy. Even the sigils along the walls trembled.

I stiffened. "Well, that's interesting, see, because I

just recently heard it mentioned," I said slowly. "Apparently, Lilith had dealings there. But I never saw it. Never heard of it in Heaven. And in all the years I've been in Hell... not one whisper. Not one rumor." I shook my head, "which never happens."

Damien huffed a laugh that was anything but amused. "Yeah."

Topher frowned. "You've seen it?"

"No." Damien's voice dropped even further. "But I've heard... things. From things Lilith's accidentally told me. And from some of the angels who still speak to the Fallen, who forgot to shut up. Who spoke in nightmares. It's supposedly in Heaven, but it's not a paradise. Not a reward. It's his... collection." His gaze darted between us. "A place where The First Light keeps souls he likes. His favorites... The ones he doesn't want to let go of. He freezes them in time. Rewrites them. Plays with them."

A chill licked up my spine.

Topher looked sick. "Why would Lilith care about that?"

Damien's knuckles whitened. "Because it's what she does. She finds the ones He'll want." His gaze flicked up. "She found Elias."

Silence tightened. The wards hummed as if they were listening.

"My lover," Damien said, barely audible. "A prophet. Too honest for his own good. Too gifted. He saw things—futures, endings, collapse. He saw what He wanted." His throat worked. "And I told her one thing. One. Stupid. Thing."

He swallowed hard. "I joked that the First Light would love a soul like that."

Topher winced.

Damien's voice cracked. "She took Elias to Him

herself. Dragged him away from me while I begged her. And she smiled. She just smiled at me as she did it. Then she handed him over."

Anger sparked through my veins. Not just at Lilith. At myself too, for not seeing sooner how deep her rot had spread.

Damien's eyes rimmed with fury and grief. "I haven't heard his voice. Haven't felt him since. I don't think he's dead, but I haven't even found a trace in the lower realms. Because there's only one place He puts souls like that." His voice dropped to a trembling whisper. "I think Elias is there. In the Beloved. Frozen. Rewritten. Waiting for someone who isn't coming. Waiting for me to save him."

The room fell silent. Heavy. Grieving. I knew that sound in a man's voice. Loss hollowing him out. Love lighting him on fire. Desperation forging purpose from ashes. It was the sound of someone who'd cross universes to get their person back.

I stepped closer, meeting his eyes. "You want him back."

He nodded once, sharp, broken, unguarded. "I'll burn the sky for him. I'll burn His fucking throne. I don't care what it takes. I'm with you. For real this time."

Topher let out a low whistle. "Well. That's just... terrifying."

It was.

Damien lifted his chin, voice steady and fierce. "I don't know if we can kill a god, but I want Him out. I want to try. And I want Lilith to choke on the ashes of everything she thinks she controls. "

I stared at him for a long moment, then extended my hand. "All right," I said. "You're in."

Damien took it, grip firm, eyes still burning.

I yanked him closer, until he had to hear me over

his own heartbeat, and hissed, "But if you cross me again, I will rip your fucking head clean off."

He let out a low chuckle, like he liked the threat more than the agreement.

Behind him, Topher exhaled hard and folded his arms, the picture of a man watching a bad idea become a team-building exercise.

Damien asked, "So what now? We storm the throne room? Kick in Heaven's front door? Start another revolt with three guys and a half-conscious angel?"

I shook my head. "We don't start anything. Not yet."

They both looked at me.

"We're not ready," I said. "Right now it's just us. And He's already laid a claim on Evie. We try to move now, we get wiped off the board before we even reach the edge."

Damien grimaced. "So we sit on our hands?"

"We build," I corrected. "We find the ones who hate Him more than they fear Him. Vespera owes me. Azazael will want blood when he can stand on his own again. There are others. The two hundred Fallen who followed me to Hell. Disgraced angels. Things Heaven pretends it never made."

Damien tilted his head. "So you've got ideas?"

"A network," I said. "Something that can move in the cracks He doesn't look at."

Damien's mouth curved. "You mean like the old stories? The Gathering of the Wicked?"

A ghost of a smile tugged at my mouth. "That's not what it was called." I chuckled.

Topher raised a brow. He knew who I was talking about.

I glanced at the sigils along the walls, memories stirring like dust. "The Conventus Maleficorum," I said. "The Council of the Wicked. The Fallen and things worse who decided The First Light wasn't the only voice in the room."

Damien's eyes lit with something sharp and hungry. "I thought that was a myth."

"So did most everyone," I said. "That's what made it work."

Topher pushed off the wall. "So the plan is… find the people crazy enough to join this council of yours, and hope we don't die recruiting them."

"Something like that," I said. My gaze drifted toward the door, my mind picturing Evie still asleep in my bed, power coiled under her skin like a storm waiting for a sky. "We don't touch Him until we have more than rage and a handful of ghosts on our side."

Damien nodded slowly. "Then we start there."

"Yeah," I said. "We start there."

The next day, we fixed the front door, and I sent Damien back to Vegas to collect Vespera while I spent the week caring for Azazael with Evie's help. I'd decided to deal with the Maleficorum later. We had more pressing issues.

Damien had grinned like I'd handed him a playground full of explosives, flipped me off cheerfully, and vanished in a blink of smoke and steel. I didn't worry about him. He thrived when you pointed him at trouble.

Azazael… he was a wreck—skin and bones. Wings tattered. His power was running thin as a thread.

Evie hovered at my side like she'd always been there, handing me towels, steadying bowls, brushing damp curls off his forehead with a tenderness I barely remembered the world having.

He slept for the first two days straight, head

turned toward the wall, sweating and breathing shallow. When he woke, it was only long enough for me to coax broth into him and get a few muttered curses for my trouble. Progress, technically.

"Eat," I murmured, lifting another spoonful toward him.

Azazael groaned. "I hate soup."

"You'll need your strength sooner than you know," I reminded him. "So pick your battles."

Evie snorted behind me, tried to hide it, failed.

The broth helped. Mortal food grounded him — salt, fat, heat, things angels were never meant to savor, but he needed now. I made a special stew the second night that he swore was an assassination attempt. He still finished the bowl.

When his hands stopped shaking, I brought out the Devil's manna — my own version of the First Light's leash, stripped of obedience and laced with infernal strength. A liquid I'd conjured eons ago that glowed faint red-gold, warm as a heartbeat. He sniffed it like it might bite him. Evie offered it to him in a mug.

"It'll help," I said behind her.

"It smells like sin," he rasped.

"So do you," Evie said lightly. "Drink anyway."

He glared at her. Drank it. Coughed so violently his wings, black as night, flickered into existence then vanished again. Good. It meant something was working.

By day three, he could sit up without flinching. Color bled back into his skin. His breathing deepened. He didn't look like someone death had forgotten to collect any more. But the real change wasn't physical. It was the gold.

Our tether — mine and Evie's — kept pulsing in soft waves, like it was simmering on the surface, every time we touched, kissed, stared too long at one another. It was a warmth I could feel in my ribs, my spine, the back of my throat. Every time it flared, Azazael stirred. At first, I thought it was a coincidence, but Evie touched his arm once while the gold shimmered through the air, and he inhaled sharply like someone had poured sunlight straight into his lungs.

"He's absorbing our... gold light," Evie whispered.

I nodded slowly. "Angels lived on manna. Like a divine energy. But this—whatever this is between us, it feels like something older."

She looked down and pressed her hand over her heart as if she felt it there, too. Maybe she did. I felt it all over.

Day four, he was awake more than he was asleep. His voice rasped less. He could stretch his wings, though it hurt him and he didn't like to. He still trembled when he stood, but it wasn't the brittle wobble of a body about to collapse. It was the wobble of someone acclimating themselves to life.

Day five, he was hungry. And if you know anything about angels, real hunger is a miracle. Evie brought him a plate of warm starfire bread and fresh fruit.

Starfire bread looked and smelled like brimstone, yet it was among the Fallen's main sustenance down in Hell, where nothing grew. He gobbled it down, but stared at the fruit as if it might bite him.

"You're going to eat it," she said gently.

Azazael looked at me. "Is this a command?"

I raised a shoulder, "It's a suggestion," I said. "But I've seen what happens when you ignore Evie's suggestions, and I don't recommend it."

Her elbow found my ribs. Lightly. Almost fond.

He ate. Slowly. Cautiously. But he finished all of it.

By the end of the first week, he wasn't healthy, not yet, but he was no longer a dying thing curled in bed like an abandoned bird. He was breathing. Strengthening. Gathering pieces of himself with every bowl of stew, every swallow of Devil's manna, every golden pulse that rolled off the bond between Evie and me.

For the past three days, I'd allowed him to walk the perimeter of the living room several times a day. He'd attempt to raise lightning in his fingers, only to have them smolder black smoke.

But I knew he was on the mend when he started giving me his trademark smart-ass responses to my questions. He was becoming Azazael again. Not the full force of the storm he'd once been. But the rumble of thunder was there. Gathering. Waiting. And gods help the First Light when Azazael finally stood against him.

A few days later, Damien returned with Vespera, and she didn't come alone. Four figures stepped through the wards at her back, and the cavern house shifted around them, like the stone knew exactly what kind of trouble had just walked in.

Damien spread his arms. "Miss me?"

"No," I said. "Who are they?"

Vespera rolled her eyes and pushed past him, the train of her skirt trailing behind her on the floor. "These are some of the most prominent members of the Conventus Maleficorum," she said. "Damien said you needed more than rage and ghosts. These are the ones who didn't flinch when I told them who you wanted to take down."

The wards hummed, curious. The first was an angel, or had been once. One wing was still snow-white, feathers pristine. The other was scorched dark, its edges ragged, as if it had been shoved through a sun and barely pulled back out.

"Seren of the Second Choir," Vespera said. "Officially disgraced an eon after you and yours Fell. He let him roam the earth instead of sending him to you." Her gaze flicked to him. "He set up shop in Europe as an antiquities dealer, selling saints' bones and cursed icons to people who thought they were buying holiness."

Seren's expression didn't change, but his hands — those calm, careful hands — looked like they'd handled things sharp enough to rewrite a life.

"Unofficially," Vespera added, voice turning dry, "he's a relic savant. Put any holy weapon in his grip, and he knows how it wants to be used. That's his little secret. He doesn't fight like a brawler. He fights like someone who's spent centuries learning what every blade, spear, and chain was made to do."

Behind her, a broad-shouldered demon stepped in, horns curved back, coat buttoned to his throat in a way that screamed I could kill you and then argue you signed paperwork to allow it.

"Morran the Pact-Breaker," Vespera continued. "He used to write contracts in the First Light's name."

"Everyone makes mistakes," Morran said mildly. His eyes gleamed. "I'm correcting mine."

The third looked almost human. Almost. A woman with dark curls braided with ash and thread, fingers stained with ink and something that might have been blood. Magic clung to her like smoke.

"Liora Ashwind," Vespera said. "Her bloodline used to serve the Heavenly Artisans. Then someone tried to erase them."

Liora glanced at Evie and then met my eyes without a hint of reverence. "He didn't do a very good job," she said. "I still remember the old patterns. But... your bond is loud. Beautiful, but loud. I can braid it, lock it, make it harder to cut, if He tries."

Evie, still hovering near the hallway, shifted at that, like something inside her had heard its name.

The last one slipped in almost unnoticed. Soft-footed, soft-voiced, the kind of angel Heaven liked to pretend didn't exist. His halo was gone, but the faint burn around his temples said it hadn't left politely.

"Cassiel," Vespera finished. "Former archivist."

He inclined his head. "I kept records," he said. "Names. Histories. Places that were meant to be forgotten. When He started editing the story, I walked out with a few chapters still in my head."

My skin prickled. "Names he erased from the Book of Names?"

"No... that wasn't my department. Mine was more...," his eyes narrowed, "...black projects."

"You know about the Beloved," I said.

His gaze sharpened. "None of us were ever given the whole," he said quietly. "Only pieces, carefully rationed, so we couldn't name the thing we served. Even so... I've seen traces. Enough to believe the Beloved exists."

Damien's jaw clenched at that, but he said nothing.

I let the silence stretch for a beat, taking them in. An angel, the First Light had cast loose but not caged, who'd spent centuries selling relics and learning how holy weapons wanted to kill—a demon who once wrote divine contracts and now specialized in breaking them. A woman descended from the Heavenly Artisans, carrying old patterns in her blood and the skill to braid a bond even a god might struggle to sever. And an archivist who'd worked in the dark corners of Heaven, where stories were altered, erased, and quietly buried.

Vespera arched a brow. "You're wanting to overthrow a god, Lucifer," she said. "Even the Fallen are afraid of Him. This is what you need."

Morran's voice slid in smooth as ink. "There are more in our... gathering," he said. "Bound by blood. Bound by will. They'll answer the Maleficorum when the time comes."

I glanced at him, then back at Vespera. "It'll do," I said. It would have to.

Evie snorted softly behind me. I could feel her through the tether, wary, curious, tired. It hummed low and steady in my chest.

I turned to Damien. Azazael's door was still shut, wards humming gently around the frame. "You're done running errands," I told him. "New task."

He saluted with two fingers. "Hit me."

"Azazael's wings are functional," I said. "Barely. He needs strength. Control. Someone to spar with who won't die when he misjudges a swing."

Damien's grin flashed, sharp and feral. "You want me to train your angel."

"Keep him from falling on his face in the middle of a fight," I corrected. "You break him, I break you."

"Luc," Evie murmured, a warning and a smile all at once.

Damien pressed a hand to his chest, mock-wounded. "I would never."

"Start slow," I said. "Work the wings. Balance. No full grace work yet, his body will rip itself apart."

Damien nodded, the joking gone. "I've got him."

Seren tilted her head. "I can help with form. He

was once of the Host. There are patterns we all learned. I remember them."

"Good," I said. "You're all here now. You want Him dead, you want your people back, you're in my house. That means we start small. We build."

Morran smirked. "You mean we don't die immediately. Refreshing."

Liora glanced toward the bedroom hall. "And her?" she asked. "What does she get to be?"

Evie stiffened slightly beside the doorway.

I looked at her, felt the tether thrum, and everyone could see the gold pulse once, slow and inevitable.

"Target," I said. "For now."

Evie's eyes narrowed.

"Later," I added, "the reason He finally bleeds."

I saw the question in her eyes, the old fear of being used. I met it head-on. Not a sacrifice, I thought. Never that.

The new arrivals exchanged glances—some skeptical, some intrigued, none of them backing out.

That weekend, the cavern house stopped being just a refuge. With Vespera and her four at my table, with Damien heading toward Azazael's room, with Evie's power coiling quiet and bright in the next hall over, it became something else.

Not a war, not yet. But the first pieces of a storm big enough to make a god flinch.

CHAPTER THIRTY-EIGHT

Evie

I asked Luc to send for Destiny. I couldn't contact her myself. None of us could. Topher had made us leave our phones back in Vegas, firm and unapologetic about it. Too easy to track. Too easy to listen through. Another quiet sacrifice to the idea of staying alive.

I hated it anyway.

"But she'll come," I said, more certain than I had any right to be. "She'd want to be here."

Luc studied me for a moment, then nodded. "She will."

She did.

Destiny arrived like a crack in the air, boots on stone, presence loud in a way that had nothing to do with volume. Shaved head now dyed blue, black clothes sharp and intentional, spiderweb tattoo flashing at her elbow when she crossed her arms. Living Dead Girl curved along her upper chest like a declaration. She looked exactly like herself, and the tight knot in my chest finally loosened.

"You look like shit," she said fondly.

"Good to see you, too," I laughed, and she pulled

441

me into a hug that reminded my body where it ended and the world began.

We talked for over an hour over dinner. Plates went cold. Candles burned low. I told her everything she didn't already know, and skipped carefully over the one thing I wasn't ready to say yet. She listened the way she always did, eyes sharp, mouth quiet, filing everything away like she was already planning contingencies.

Partway through, Topher drifted over.

"Hey," he said, hands tucked into his pockets like he hadn't rehearsed this. "Can you help me with something?"

Destiny looked up at him. That buttoned-up jacket, careful posture. A demon who looked like he alphabetized things for comfort. She smiled. Not her usual sharp grin. Something softer. Almost shy.

"Sure," she said, and stood immediately. She followed him without another word.

I watched them disappear down the hall, a strange little tug settling in my chest. Destiny didn't usually follow anyone. And she definitely didn't smile like that at men who looked like walking spreadsheets.

Liora took the empty seat across from me in leather pants and a moto jacket. She didn't speak right away. Just studied me, like she was looking at a half-finished design and deciding where the next line should go.

"Lucifer said something happened in Hell," she said finally. "Something... impressive."

I swallowed. My fingers curled around my mug.

"I was scared," I said. "They were everywhere. Things reaching for him." My voice tightened at the memory. "I didn't plan it. I just felt this pull. Like the ground was listening."

I closed my eyes, seeing it again. "The rocks came up," I whispered. "Hundreds of them. Maybe more. They lifted from the earth and smashed into anything that came close. I wasn't angry. I was terrified."

"And it hasn't happened again," Liora said, gently prompting.

I shook my head. "Nothing like that. I don't even know how I did it."

She went quiet, thoughtful, eyes distant as something clicked into place.

"Fear can open doors," she said at last. "But it's a terrible teacher."

I looked at her. "So what isn't?"

She met my gaze, steady and serious. "Choice. Practice. Understanding what you're touching when you reach."

My heart kicked hard. "You think you can help me?"

"I think I might," she said. "If you want that."

The question settled into me deeper than I expected. Wanting help meant admitting this wasn't a fluke. That whatever had answered me in Hell wasn't finished, that it was part of me.

I took a slow breath. Under my skin, something stirred. Not wild. Not burning. Just present. A quiet strength, coiled and waiting, like it had always been there and I was only just noticing it now.

For the first time in my life, learning to harness my own power felt possible.

"Yes," I said. "I do."

And sitting in a cavern full of angels, demons, and ancient grudges, I felt it clearly. I wasn't just the girl being protected. I could be somebody, a part of them.

A few minutes later, Destiny and Topher walked

back in. He peeled off toward his makeshift command center without looking at either of us, already pulling up screens, fingers moving like he needed the distraction. Destiny lingered near the table, cheeks faintly flushed, eyeliner just a touch smudged like she'd forgotten she was wearing it.

She caught me looking. "What?" she said, too quickly.

I lifted a brow. "Nothing." That was a lie, and we both knew it.

Something had shifted around her, subtle but unmistakable. Not guilt. Not fear. Just... possibility. Whatever she and Topher had been up to, it wasn't casual, and it definitely wasn't something she was ready to unpack out loud.

She leaned in and bumped her shoulder lightly against mine. "Later," she said, low —a promise, not an excuse. I nodded. I could wait.

Liora stood then, smoothing her skirts like she'd made a decision and didn't intend to revisit it. "Meet me just after dawn," she said.

"Where?" I asked.

She tilted her head toward the cavern entrance. "Out front. There's another cavern about half a mile away."

I frowned. "That's... outside the wards."

"Yes," she said calmly. "It is."

My stomach tightened. "Liora—"

"That's the point," she interrupted, not unkindly. "You can't learn control if everything dangerous is kept at arm's length. The wards muffle you. Out there, you'll feel the edges of yourself."

I didn't love that. At all.

"That's what we need to practice," she added, softer now. "Choice. Focus. Calling without panic."

I swallowed and nodded. "I'll talk to him."

Before she could say anything else, a knock echoed through the cavern. Sharp. Deliberate. Every conversation stopped.

The wards flared faintly, translucent light rippling across the stone. Beyond them, shapes stood clustered at the entrance. Too many to be accidental. Too still to be lost.

My pulse spiked. I turned instinctively toward the glow of monitors and half-built magic where Topher stood.

"Topher..." I said.

He was already looking.

Luc was there in a heartbeat. One second, the hallway was empty, the next he was striding toward the front of the cavern, sleeves pushed up like he'd decided this was going to be work. His gaze flicked to me, sharp and assessing, then to Topher, then settled on the door.

Whatever he saw there made his jaw tighten. He didn't touch the wards. They opened anyway. Topher was at his shoulder instantly, Morran falling in on the other side, Seren moving with a quiet, deliberate grace that set my teeth on edge. They looked like a unit without ever having practiced it.

Outside, the world widened.

There had to be fifty people standing on the stone path beyond the wards. Maybe more. They were a mix of everything—demons, half-breeds, fallen angels, things that didn't fit cleanly into any category I knew how to name. All of them watched Luc like gravity had shifted.

The man at the very front stepped forward.

He had jet-black hair braided back from his face, the lines of his posture precise and formal, like ceremony lived in his bones. He bowed his head deeply.

"Morningstar," he said, meeting Luc's eyes only after the bow was complete.

Then, as one, the rest of them bowed. Many dropped to their knees, hands to the stone, heads lowered in something that felt older than religion.

My breath caught.

Luc's voice cut clean through the moment. "You may rise."

They did—but the man at the front froze halfway up. His eyes slid past Luc. Locked. On Seren.

Color drained from his face. He stepped forward again and bowed, this time sharper, more reverent. His hands moved in a strange, precise pattern over his chest—fingers crossing, palms open, then pressed flat over his heart.

"My lord," he said, voice rough with something like awe.

Seren stiffened. He took one measured step forward, placing himself fully in view of the crowd. The reaction was immediate. Every single person repeated the gesture. Hands crossed. Palms open. Heartward.

I glanced at Luc, startled. He looked just as surprised as I felt.

Seren swallowed, clearly hating this part, and inclined his head just enough to acknowledge them. "I am not your lord," he said quietly. "Not anymore."

The man with the braids lifted his head. "No," he agreed. "But you were the first of us to refuse Him. That matters."

Luc's voice cut in, calm but sharp. "Why are you here?"

The man's gaze flicked briefly to Morran, then back to Luc, something fierce burning behind his eyes. "I am Malachi, and we've been waiting," he said. "Some of us for centuries."

Luc's eyes narrowed, calculating. "Waiting for what?"

"Every one of us has been broken by the First Light. Stripped. Used. Corrected. He is no loving god," His mouth twisted. "We didn't come for anything but revenge."

A low murmur rippled through the group. Agreement. Anger. Resolve.

"He calls it order," the man went on. "We call it cruelty. He took our names. Our loves. Our choices." His gaze swept the crowd. "We've buried enough of ourselves to know His reign only ends one way."

Luc studied them, measuring something invisible. "And you think I'm that way?"

"We think," the man said steadily, "that you survived Him. And that makes you dangerous."

Silence stretched.

Morran let out a low, pleased hum. "See?" he murmured. "Blood-bound."

I stood there, heart pounding, and for the first time since all of this began—since gods and Hell and impossible power had cracked my life wide open—I felt something unexpected settle into my chest. Not fear. Hope. Not the fragile kind, either. The kind with weight behind it.

These people weren't here because of me. They weren't here because of Luc alone. They were here because they'd been hurt. Because they remembered. Because they were done kneeling.

For the first time, looking out at that sea of scarred, furious faces, I thought—maybe. Maybe a god could bleed. Maybe a god could fall. And just maybe, we actually had a chance.

The next morning, I walked out the front door

and nearly ran straight into Liora. She was leaning against one of the stone posts like she belonged there, one ankle crossed casually over the other.

She looked... different. Younger, somehow. Her blond hair was pulled back into a tight braid thrown over one shoulder, and she was dressed in fitted leathers that hugged her body like they'd been made with intention, not vanity. Black boots laced high up her calves, the kind that promised speed, balance, and very little mercy.

Then she looked at me.

I was wearing an oversized T-shirt from a very questionable, very well-hung winery I'd thrifted two years ago, stretched soft with age. Jeggings. My hair loose down my back.

She didn't say a word. She just turned, grabbed my wrist, and marched me right back inside.

"No," she said flatly. "That's not going to work."

"I wasn't planning on—"

"No," she repeated, already steering me down the hall toward the bedroom I now shared with Luc.

I hadn't even opened the closet yet. I hadn't needed to. Turns out, I hadn't needed to shop either. One entire side was filled with clothes. All my sizes. Everything from soft knits to fitted jackets to things that looked... tactical. Practical. Dangerous. And right there in the middle, hanging like it had been waiting for me all along, was a set of leathers almost identical to Liora's.

She reached for them without hesitation, tugged them off the hanger, and shoved them into my arms. "Put these on."

Then she bent, rummaged once, and came up with a pair of black athletic boots. Solid. Lightweight. Mean.

"These too."

I stared at her. "You planned this."

She smiled faintly. "No, of course I didn't. I assumed you'd know how to dress for training. Your boyfriend—"

"Mate," I corrected.

"Oh..." She said, looking around the room, confused or stunned. I wasn't sure.

I just smiled and took the clothes into the bathroom and shut the door behind me. When I pulled the leathers on, they fit like a second skin. Not tight in a suffocating way, just... right. Like they'd been waiting for my body to catch up to them.

In the mirror, I barely recognized myself. I looked tired and had dark circles under my eyes, but there were gold flecks in my irises I hadn't noticed before. What was that about?

My dark roots were definitely showing, but instead of fighting them, I pulled my long pink hair up into a high ponytail and let it be what it was. When I stepped back out, Liora was sitting on the edge of the bed.

She looked me over once. Then nodded. She patted the spot beside her and handed me the boots. I sat, laced them up, and stood.

"Now that you're ready," she said, rising smoothly, "we go."

We passed through the main room, and Luc was bent over Topher's makeshift command center, screens glowing across his face. He looked up as we walked by.

His eyebrow arched. Heat rushed straight to my cheeks. His fingers brushed my back as I passed, slow, deliberate, sliding down over my ass like a promise he had no intention of keeping private.

I almost tripped. Behind us, I heard Morran snort.

The kitchen was alive with quiet motion. A few of the people who'd arrived the night before were already at work. A massive pot simmered on the stove as vegetables were tossed in by hand. Someone else kneaded bread at the counter, sleeves rolled up, flour dusting their arms. Another person stood at the sink, washing dishes like this was the most normal thing in the world.

For a second, it felt... possible. Like a future someone could survive. Then Liora pushed open the outer door and stepped into the morning light. I followed her.

We walked for nearly half a mile, the path winding through stone and scrub, until the cavern house disappeared behind us. She led me toward another opening in the rock, smaller but just as deliberate.

The ground beyond it was littered with stones. Thousands of them. Pebbles. Boulders. Jagged shards and smooth, worn rounds, scattered across the desert floor like the aftermath of a forgotten war.

She stopped at the edge and turned to face me. "This," she said calmly, "is where we see what you can do without fear doing the driving."

My pulse kicked hard. I looked out over the sea of stone, felt something deep under my skin stir in recognition, like the ground had been waiting.

For the first time in my life, dressed for it, braced for it, not running or reacting—I felt ready. I could do this.

And then... nothing.

I stood there with my boots planted in the dust, arms loose at my sides, staring at a field of stone just like the one in Hell that had answered me like it had been waiting its whole life to be called. I tried everything I could think of. I closed my eyes. I breathed. I reached, the way I had in Hell, blind and desperate and sure something would catch me.

Nothing did.

Liora tried, too. She shifted tactics, voice calm, precise. Had me ground myself, then unground myself. Had me picture the stones as extensions of my body. Had me picture Luc. Fear. Love. Rage. Control. Let go. Hold tighter. Again. Again.

The rocks stayed on the ground.

After an hour, sweat had soaked through the leathers at my spine. My arms trembled, not from power, just from effort that went nowhere. Liora's brow furrowed, not impatient, just... puzzled like a craftsperson staring at a tool that should work and didn't.

We spent the last hour hiking up toward a cliff that overlooked the scattered desert below. Wind whipped my ponytail against my neck. The drop was steep enough to make my stomach tilt.

"Sometimes peril wakes it," Liora said gently. "Not fear. Awareness."

I stepped closer to the edge anyway. Heart pounding. Pulse loud in my ears. I leaned forward just enough to feel gravity tug at me, daring the world to notice.

It didn't.

I laughed once, sharp and humorless, then pressed my hands to my thighs to keep them from shaking. "I'm sorry," I said, and hated how small my voice sounded.

Liora was quiet for a long moment. Then she exhaled and shook her head, more thoughtful than defeated. "No," she said. "This isn't failure. It's..." Her voice trailed off.

That felt an awful lot like useless.

By the time we turned back, my chest ached with

something heavier than exhaustion. Shame, maybe. Or grief. The kind that sneaks up on you when you think you've finally found a way to matter, and then it slips through your fingers.

I stared at the ground as we walked. I guess I was just... broken.

The thought settled in like a verdict—one miracle, one night in Hell where terror had masqueraded as power, and now nothing. No spark. No echo. Just me, walking back empty-handed in borrowed leathers, pretending I hadn't imagined the whole thing.

Maybe Hell had been a fluke.

My legs felt like lead. Sweat clung to me, dust worked into every seam of the leathers. By the time we stepped inside, my cheeks were streaked with dirt I hadn't bothered to wipe away, like my body knew pretending was pointless.

Luc looked up immediately. I knew he felt the emotions I couldn't stop going down the bond. His gaze swept over me in one sharp pass, clocking everything I was trying not to show. The slump of my shoulders. The way my hands curled like I was holding something that wasn't there anymore.

"How'd it go?" he asked.

I opened my mouth. Nothing came out.

Behind me, Liora lifted a shoulder in a small, unapologetic shrug. "We'll get there," she said evenly. "I'm sure."

The disappointment lodged in my throat like a stone, too heavy to move around. I dropped my eyes, turned away from him before he could read any more of me, and headed down the hallway without answering. I didn't slow down.

I went straight into the bathroom and turned the shower on as hot as it would go. Steam filled the space almost instantly, the air thick and suffocating. I stripped out of the leathers and stepped under the spray, letting the scalding water hit my skin hard enough to sting.

It burned. Good.

Dirt streaked down the drain in muddy ribbons. Sweat. Frustration. I braced my hands against the tile and bowed my head, letting the water pound over me, trying to wash away the feeling that I'd failed at something I hadn't even learned how to try.

In Hell, power had answered fear like it knew my name. Here, in safety, in daylight, in choice, there was only silence. I felt so small.

I squeezed my eyes shut, throat tight, and let the water hide the sound of my breath hitching as I sobbed.

CHAPTER THIRTY-NINE

Lucifer

I knew as soon as she walked in. Not because she said anything, she didn't, but I'd felt the frustration and shame rolling down the bond the last few hours. And Evie carried disappointment like smoke, quiet, clinging, impossible to pretend you didn't smell.

She came through the main room dusty and sweat-streaked, dirt smeared across her cheeks. Her eyes were bright in that dangerous way, not from joy, but from holding herself together by the thinnest thread.

"How'd it go?" I asked.

But she didn't answer. She looked away immediately, like my gaze was too heavy to carry, and she disappeared down the hallway.

Liora lifted one shoulder. "We'll get there," she said, steady as stone. "I'm sure."

A beat later, the bathroom door shut. Then the shower turned on. I heard it in the pipes, that furious rush, like she was trying to burn the feeling off her skin.

Topher glanced sideways at me. Morran

pretended not to. Seren's expression didn't change at all, which somehow made it worse. I pushed away from the command station.

My house had been many things over the centuries. Fortress. Tomb. Sanctuary. Tonight, it felt like a cage with one very small, very human heartbeat trapped inside.

I walked down the hall to the bedroom and stopped outside the bathroom door. I knocked once and turned the handle. It was hot by the time I stepped inside, steam curling along the ceiling, fog softening the edges of everything. The glass shower enclosure was already clouded, a hazy silhouette behind it, shoulders hunched, head bowed.

And the sound. Not loud. Not dramatic. The quiet kind of crying that tried to hide under running water. My chest tightened hard enough to ache.

I crossed to the shower and pressed my palm to the glass, feeling the heat through it. "Evie," I said, low.

Her breath hitched. Her head turned just enough that I caught a glimpse of her profile through the fogged pane, lashes clumped with water, jaw tight like she was furious at herself for making any sound at all.

"I couldn't make it work," she rasped, voice nearly swallowed by the spray. "I tried. I tried everything."

Something ugly and protective rose in me, fast. I didn't argue. I didn't offer logic. This wasn't the moment for lessons. I opened the shower door. The warm, wet air hit me like a wave, thick with soap and salt.

She was braced against the tile, hands splayed, forehead nearly touching the wall, letting the water pummel her like punishment. She looked up when she sensed me, eyes red-rimmed, wide and wrecked.

"Luc, don't," she started, like she was going to apologize, like she was going to try to be smaller. I didn't let her.

I tore my shirt over my head, yanked my belt free, and shoved my pants down in a single rough motion. Boots kicked off. Everything was discarded like it didn't matter, because it didn't. I stepped into the shower naked and closed the glass door behind me, sealing us in with the steam and the thunder of water.

Evie's breath caught.

I reached past her and turned the heat down just enough that it stopped being cruel.

She made a sound of protest. "I need it hot."

"No," I said quietly, firm without meaning to be. "You need to breathe."

She shook her head, tears mixing with the spray. "I did it in Hell," she whispered, voice breaking. "I saved you. I felt it answer me and now... now it's gone. I'm just broken and I—"

"Don't," I cut in, softer this time, and stepped close.

I cupped her face, thumbs brushing the wet tracks on her cheeks like I could wipe away the whole morning. "Look at me."

Her eyes lifted, furious and wounded, like she expected me to agree with her. I didn't.

"You are not 'just' anything," I said, voice rough. "Not to me. Not to this war. Not to the universe that keeps trying to pretend you're small."

Her mouth trembled. "What if it was a fluke?"

"It wasn't," I said immediately.

"You don't know that."

I did. I'd felt it in Hell, the way the world had bent toward her like it recognized her, like she was its maker. The way the gold flared between us, the stone rising like it had been waiting for her voice.

I leaned my forehead to hers, water streaming down our faces, and let the truth settle between us like a vow. "What happened in Hell wasn't an accident," I murmured. "It was you. It was you finally reaching without asking permission."

Her breath shuddered.

"And today," I went on, quieter, "you tried to do it without terror driving you. In daylight. In safety. That isn't failure, Evie. That's the beginning."

Her lashes fluttered. Another tear broke free, swallowed instantly by the spray.

I wrapped my arms around her and pulled her against my chest, holding her like I could anchor her back into herself. Her hands grabbed at me, clinging for dear life, and the sobs broke free. I felt her shaking all the way through.

I kissed the top of her head, tasting soap and salt.

"We'll get there," I said into her wet hair. "I swear it. You're not broken."

Through the tether, I felt it then, faint but real, a stubborn pulse like a heartbeat refusing to quit. Alive and kicking.

I shut the water off myself. The silence afterward was almost shocking. Steam clung to the glass, to our skin, to the moment. Evie sagged into me the second the spray stopped, all that fight draining out at once.

"I've got you," I murmured, and this time she didn't argue.

I reached for a towel, thick and warm, and wrapped it around her, careful and tender. I grabbed another for her hair. I eased her back against my chest, holding her there while her breathing slowed, while the shaking softened into something manageable.

I dried her gently, methodically, like this was a ritual I'd always known and only just remembered. When I wrapped the towel around her hair, she let out a small, broken laugh.

"You don't have to—"

"I want to," I said.

I carried her to the bed, sat behind her with her back against my chest, and began working the knots out of her hair with my fingers. Pink strands slid through my hands, damp and heavy, dark roots showing through like a truth she no longer needed to hide.

I dried it slowly. Patiently. When it was just barely damp, I divided it into sections and braided it down her back, neat and steady, something grounding in the repetition.

She leaned into me, trusting. That alone nearly undid me. When I finished, I pressed a kiss to the crown of her head, breathing her scent in, then another to her temple. She tilted her face just enough that I could kiss her properly, soft and lingering, nothing desperate about it. Just us, breathing the same air again.

I rested my forehead against hers. "Hell forced it out," I said quietly. "It tore the door open and didn't care what it did on the way."

Her breath hitched, but she didn't pull away.

"Now," I went on, brushing my thumb along her jaw, "we teach it to come when you call. Not when you're afraid. Not when you're bleeding. When you decide."

She swallowed. Through the tether, I felt that pulse again, steadier this time. Not flaring. Not fading. Just... there.

"What if I lose it? What if it's already... gone?"

she whispered.

"You won't," I said without hesitation. "I won't let you. And you won't let yourself."

I pulled her closer, wrapped us both in the quiet. In here, there was only this. Her breathing evening out. Her weight against me. Her power resting, not gone, just waiting.

And for the first time since all of this began, I wasn't afraid of what she would become. I was certain.

We'd just settled together in the bed when the wards screamed. Not a tremble, not a warning chime, a full-bodied howl that shook dust from the stone and turned the air metallic. The sigils along the bedroom walls flared bright enough to paint Evie's skin in pale light.

I went still. So did she. I didn't let go of her immediately. I tightened my hold instead, one more second, one more inhale of her, sweet and soap and trembling human warmth.

Then I rose. I wrapped the towel higher around her shoulders, tucked her against the headboard, and kissed her forehead like a promise I intended to keep.

"Stay here," I murmured.

Her fingers caught my wrist. "Luc—"

"I'll handle it," I said, softer. "I always do."

I walked out of the room, pulling on pants, letting my wings flair, already reaching for the weapons I kept hidden in plain sight. The cavern house felt different now, not like shelter, like a throat about to close.

Topher met me in the hall, face pale. Morran and Seren were already moving, quiet as a blade. I didn't ask what it was. I could feel it. Heaven had a signature. Clean, arrogant, bright enough to burn.

We reached the main room, and the wards parted like they'd been ordered to. Outside, the sky had gone wrong. Light spilled across the mountains in a hard white column, as if someone had driven a spear through the clear sky. Wind poured in, sharp and holy, carrying the scent of storms that didn't belong on Earth.

They stood beyond the boundary, just outside the wards. Michael. Gabriel. Archangels, radiant and severe, armor gleaming like it had never known dust. Behind them, a wall of power, Cherubim with their wings spread wide like shields, Seraphim hovering higher, burning with that awful, beautiful intensity that made mortals drop to their knees and beg.

None of them looked at the house. All of them looked at me.

Michael's sword was already out, its edge humming with light, not metal, something older. His eyes flashed the same blue I remembered from a world I no longer belonged to.

He didn't bother with ceremony. He yelled, voice cracking through the canyon like thunder. "LUCIFER," he roared, "IT'S TIME TO FACE JUDGMENT."

The words hit the wards and made them shudder. Gabriel's gaze slid past me, quick as a blade, toward the corridor where Evie was in the bedroom. His jaw tightened like he could taste her presence in the air.

"We are not here for your theatrics," Gabriel said, voice carrying without effort. "We are here for what you're hiding."

Morran's smile turned razor-thin.

Seren's hands flexed once at his sides, like the relic-savant in him was already calculating which holy weapon he'd steal first.

"Well," he said evenly, voice clipped and professional despite the glow of Heaven bearing down on us, "that's a lot of wings."

I stepped forward until the wards' glow licked at my skin, until Heaven's light tried to tell my bones to remember obedience. It didn't work.

I lifted my chin and met Michael's stare. "You don't get to summon me," I said calmly. "Not anymore."

Michael's expression twisted, fury sharpening into something almost personal. "By decree of the Throne—"

"By decree of a liar," I cut in.

The Seraphim behind him flared brighter at that, heat rippling the air. The Cherubim shifted like a single organism, ready to surge.

Gabriel's voice dropped, quieter, sharper. "Step aside, Morningstar. Or we will rip through those wards and take what we came for."

The tether in my chest pulsed once, low and warning, like a beast lifting its head.

I smiled without humor. "You can try."

That was when I felt her. Not panic. Not fear. A shift. A decision.

Power rippled down the tether, steady and deliberate, and footsteps sounded behind me, unhurried but unmistakable. Evie stepped out of the hallway.

She wasn't wrapped in towels or softness now. She wore leathers again, darker than before, fitted like they'd learned her body. The boots Liora had found her were laced tight. Her pink hair was pulled back, braided, and practical, no loose ends. There was something new in her eyes—readiness.

She stopped at my back, close enough that I felt

her heat, her presence solid as a second spine. Not hiding. Not waiting to be shielded. Standing tall.

The Cherubim shifted. The Seraphim flared brighter.

Gabriel's gaze snapped to her, pupils tightening like he'd just seen a variable he hadn't calculated for.

Before anyone could move, the sky broke. Not opened. Cracked. Light tore through the desert air above us, spilling down like a wound instead of a blessing. Heaven was not meant to open here, not like this. But the First Light had never cared about rules, only spectacle. Pain was His favorite stage.

The air warped. Not just heated, but folded.

The ground lurched beneath my feet, space bending like wet parchment, and the cavern house vanished in a blink. No warning. No transition. One breath, we were surrounded by wards and witnesses; the next, we were standing farther down the mountain path, a half mile at least, stone cliffs hemming us in on all sides.

Alone.

I understood immediately. He didn't want them to see Him like this.

Heat rolled across the ground, wrong and suffocating, like the world was trying to crawl out of its own skin.

Then He stepped through. No trumpet. No choir. Just a soft golden radiance pushing the dark aside as easily as breath. He walked into our realm the way a man stepped off a porch, calm, unhurried, already certain of welcome.

I hated that He looked gentle. I hated that He looked like a father. And I hated that, for one traitorous heartbeat, my body still remembered how to kneel.

Evie's breath hitched behind me, but she didn't

retreat. Her fingers curled against me, steadying, and the tether held firm. No sparks this time. No terror. Just a quiet, coiled awareness.

I wanted to reach for her. I didn't. Not with Him here.

The First Light smiled, like He knew. And then His gaze went straight to her, like He'd always known exactly where she would stand when the reckoning finally came.

"Asherah," He said to her, using his pet names for his Heavenly Artisans. A name she hadn't carried in lifetimes, a name that cut her open like a memory she wasn't ready to hold. "My little artisan. You have wandered long enough."

Evie made a choked, broken sound. Her fear beat like sparks down the tether.

I stepped forward, wings flaring, claws pressing against the inside of my bones. "You do not speak to her."

The First Light tilted His head, like a man humoring a stubborn child. "Lucifer," He said softly. "My brightest star. You never did learn your place."

I lunged.

The ground shattered beneath me as I hit Him with everything I was allowed to remember, every ounce of rage, every ancient instinct. Light exploded where my fist met His chest. The shockwave hurled sand into a storm around us.

But when the dust fell, He was untouched.

"You always fight hardest when you are afraid," The First Light said, and reached for her with a hand that glowed like a dying star.

I moved on instinct. His light hit me instead. It didn't feel like being struck. It felt like being corrected, like my body was a sentence he'd decided to edit with fire. The glow slammed into my chest, ripped through my ribs, and kept going, hungry, searching for the parts of me that still remembered Heaven and still refused Him.

Pain tore through me, white hot and blinding, splitting me from the inside out. It raced along bone and muscle and every living feather, like someone had grabbed my wings and lit the marrow beneath them on fire. I hit the ground hard enough to crack stone.

Blood poured out of me, too much, too fast, running down my throat, my stomach, my hips. It slicked the rock beneath my palms. It soaked my feathers, turned white to red to something darker as it cooled, and still the light kept burning, as if my body was a candle, and He'd decided the only mercy was to melt it all the way down.

I tried to breathe. My lungs refused. I tried to move. My limbs didn't answer. I tasted iron and ash, and I couldn't tell which was mine. I could only listen as He walked toward Evie.

She stumbled back, shaking her head. "No," she whispered. "Please."

He touched her cheek like a father soothing a frightened child. "This was always where you were meant to be. You were created to stand at My side. You were never meant to live as a mortal. You were never meant to love him."

Evie's chin trembled. "Stop," she said, voice breaking. "Stop lying."

He smiled. "My dear, I do not lie. Mortals lie. Demons lie. You lie. But I only reshape truth."

I clawed at the ground. My fingers slipped in my own blood. My nails cracked. Stone scraped my skin raw. I dragged myself forward an inch, then another, my ribs grinding like broken glass inside me.

"Evie," I rasped. My voice came out wet. "Run."

The First Light turned toward me, palm open.

His light hit instantly, blinding and holy, burning my skin where it touched. Not just scorching, rewriting, trying to force me into the shape He preferred. The pressure slammed into my spine, into my knees, into the ancient reflex buried in every joint, in every part of me that had once bowed.

My body tried to obey. My wings trembled with the instinct to fold and submit. But I fought it anyway.

I forced myself up. One knee. Then both feet. Then I stood, shaking so violently my vision pulsed in and out like a dying bulb. Blood ran down my side, dripping from my fingers. It hit the stone with soft, steady taps that felt obscene in all that holy noise.

I took a step and tried to turn toward her. My leg buckled. I caught myself on sheer hatred and the tether between us, the one thing in the universe that didn't belong to Him.

Behind me, Evie moved. I felt her before I saw her, felt the tether tighten like a hand closing around my heart. She stepped forward, hands lifting, fingers spreading like she could grab the air itself and snap it into place.

"Stop!" she shouted, voice cracking through the canyon.

The First Light didn't flinch. He only turned his head slowly, like he'd been waiting for her to remember she could speak.

For a heartbeat, his expression softened into something almost kind. Then he smiled. "For you?" he said gently. "Anything."

His gaze slid back to me. And the pressure doubled.

The pain bloomed under my feathers, sharp and bright, as if every quill was a nerve and every nerve was a wick. I felt my wings ignite from the inside out again as old scars split open and fresh blood burst free and ran hot down my back.

My knees tried to fold. I didn't let them. I refused to let them.

Evie's breath hitched. Tears cut clean tracks through the dirt on her face, but she didn't back down. Fear lived in her eyes, yes, but so did love, and something harder than both, the kind of resolve that tastes like salt and steel.

She threw her hands toward the ground. The canyon answered. Or it tried to. The stone beneath us shuddered, a familiar rumble, the same wild surge she'd called in Hell when she'd shattered rock like it was brittle sugar. Dust lifted in a halo around her boots.

For one stunning second, it looked like the world was going to split open for her.

Then, The First Light exhaled, almost bored, and his glow sharpened. The rumble died. The dust fell. The stone stilled like a chastised animal.

Evie's hands stayed outstretched, fingers trembling. She tried again, harder, face straining, shoulders shaking with the effort. The canyon gave her nothing, not even a crack. It was like her power slammed into an invisible wall and returned to her in a cruel recoil that made her gasp.

"No," she whispered, horrified, like she could not believe her own body had betrayed her.

The First Light's smile deepened, soft and pitiless. "You cannot unmake what I am holding," he said, voice gentle as a lullaby.

Evie's eyes snapped to me. I was still standing. Barely.

Blood ran down my torso. It dripped from my nose down to my chin. My wings hung heavy and ruined, feathers clumped together, charred at the edges, trembling like they might fall off. My breaths came in broken pulls that didn't fill anything. My vision tunneled, dark at the corners, the world narrowing to two things, her face and His light.

I tried to take another step toward her. My body swayed. My leg gave. I caught myself again, because the alternative was collapsing, and I couldn't collapse while she was watching. I couldn't be the thing that proved Him right.

The First Light lifted his hand slightly. And I felt it, the threat, not aimed at me this time, but through me, like He was holding my life at the end of a string. A demonstration. A warning. For her.

Evie saw it, too. Her mouth opened, but no sound came out at first. She swallowed hard, like she was trying to force down the terror rising in her throat.

"Stop," she said again, lower now, shaking with the effort of it. "Please."

He looked at her like she was a prayer he'd finally decided to answer. "I will," he said softly. "If you come with me."

Evie froze. The canyon went impossibly quiet, the kind of quiet that happens right before something breaks.

I felt it, the shock, the rage, the instinct in me to lunge, to tear Heaven down with my bare hands, to drag Him into the dirt and make Him bleed like the rest of us. I tried. My body did not cooperate.

My voice came out wrecked. "Evie, don't," I rasped, and the words turned into a cough that sprayed red onto the stone.

Her eyes flashed toward me, wide, devastated.

And there it was beneath everything, beneath the

fear and the grief and the shaking human skin, a flicker of divinity that didn't belong to Him. It rose like a sun behind her eyes, bright and furious, and for a heartbeat, I thought she might do something impossible anyway.

Then, The First Light shifted his hand again. Not even a strike, just a slight curl of his fingers. Agony lanced through me so sharply I saw white. My broken wings jerked reflexively. My throat tore around a sound I couldn't control. My body finally folded, not in obedience, but in failure, hitting the ground hard, blood smearing beneath me like a thrown paintbrush.

Evie made a broken sound. She took one step toward me.

He didn't move. He didn't need to. His light held the space between us like a locked door. Her hands clenched at her sides, empty now, powerless against Him. She looked at me, and I felt the tether tremble like a live wire.

I forced my head up anyway. I met her gaze through the blur and the blood and the dying dark. And with everything I had left, I begged without words, "Please don't do this."

But she was already seeing what I knew in my bones. That there was no version of this where she fought Him and I lived. Not like this. Not with my blood running in rivers, my wings decimated and burning from the inside, my body one breath away from becoming a lesson carved into stone.

Her lips parted. Her chin lifted. And the choice, the terrible, bright thing, settled into her like it had been waiting inside her all along. For me.

"Luc," she whispered. "You can't win this."

"I will," I hissed, blood in my teeth as I began to fold. "Stay with me. Stay. Please."

Her breath hitched, a soft sound that shattered me worse than any blade.

"This is my fate," she said. "It always has been."

"No," I growled. "I found you. I found you again. I'm not losing you."

Her voice shook. "My father was going to give me to a man who wanted to own me. Now it's Him. You can't stop Him from taking me. But I can stop Him from killing you."

She stepped closer to The First Light.

"Evie," I begged. I didn't care that I begged through gritted teeth. "Please. Do. Not. Do. This."

She looked back at me, and in her eyes I saw everything we had been, everything we had lost, everything we were finally on the brink of remembering.

Her voice broke on the words. "I love you."

Then she turned to The First Light. "I'll go with you," she said quietly. "Willingly."

His light flared with satisfaction.

"Good," He murmured. "Come, my Beloved."

And as Evie took the first step toward Him, something inside me screamed, something ancient, something holy, something forbidden.

"No!" It tore out of me like a wound opening. Not a word, a rupture. The sound hit the stone cliffs and came back louder, multiplying, reverberating off rock and sky until it felt like the world itself was shouting with me.

"No," I roared again, voice breaking into raw thunder, and the canyon answered, the echoes chasing her steps like hands reaching for her, like I could stop her if I was loud enough.

The tether between us snapped taut. Not broken. Not cut. Awake. Stronger. It sang through me, a bright, burning line from my chest to hers. Judging by the way Evie's body jerked, she felt it, too. Her hand flew to her heart, eyes going wide, pupils blown black in the glare of His light.

She turned, glancing back at me, and for a heartbeat her whole face changed. A puff of gold light rolled off her like smoke. Recognition hit her like a wave. Like she was seeing me for the first time and the thousandth time, all at once.

Her lips parted. "Luc," she breathed, and the way she said it sounded like heaven.

I reached for her, fingers clawing at empty air, every nerve suddenly alive with her.

"Evie," I broke, "look at me. Stay."

Before I could move, The First Light wrapped an arm around her shoulders, gentle as a father, possessive as a cage. His light folded around her like a curtain. She vanished in it.

They were simply gone, swallowed by radiance, and I had no idea where He had taken her. Only that the tether was still there, burning in my chest, pulling toward a place I had spent an eternity trying to forget.

The sky snapped back to cloudless blue, the echoes of The First Light's presence evaporating like smoke. My knees hit stone. The last traces of His radiance burned through my skin, leaving me shaking, blind, and empty.

The tether in my chest vibrated like a struck wire, a thin bright agony pulling in a direction I couldn't name. She was gone. But not gone. Not dead. Not free.

My body refused to stand. Black blood dripped from my mouth, metallic and bitter. I pressed a hand to the ground to push myself up and almost collapsed again. Something hot and sharp carved through my ribs where His touch had hit me, like

He had branded me with light from the inside.

I choked on a breath.

The mountain above rumbled. Footsteps pounded down a stone trail.

"Lucifer!" Topher shouted, half-panic, half-fury. "Lucifer, where the hell are you?"

I tried to answer, but the sound that came out wasn't a word. It was a broken gasp, torn from a throat scraped raw.

He came skidding around the bend in the mountain path, eyes wild, shirt half untucked, some magic-scanner gadget still blinking uselessly in his hands.

He took one look at the scorched stone, the blood all over me, my wrecked wings. The empty space where Evie should have been.

"Oh, fuck," he breathed.

I didn't look at him.

"Lucifer, talk to me. What happened? What the hell happened?"

Every nerve was lit from the inside by not just the pain, but the tether's pull. Every instinct screamed her name. My vision blurred, gold flickering at the edges like wings trying to tear through mortal skin.

"She's gone," I rasped. "He took her."

Topher froze. "Who?"

My chest seized. "The First Light."

He went, and his eyes darted upward, toward the sky as if expecting that same false holy light to tear it open again.

Then he leaned in, voice low, fierce. "Can you feel where she is?"

"I don't know," I growled, every word scraped from agony. "I can't see it. I can't feel the place. Only her. Only the pull."

Topher swallowed hard. His hands tightened on me as the canyon walls carved into the mountainside around us shook again.

"We need to get out of here," he said, urgency rough in his tone. "This whole place is reacting to whatever the fuck just happened."

I pressed a hand to the ground again and forced myself upright. My limbs trembled, vision swimming. The tether tugged painfully toward a direction I couldn't name.

"She was afraid," I whispered. "And she still went."

"That's Evie," Topher muttered. "Selfless as hell even when she shouldn't be."

The air itself felt wrong, like a storm building that shouldn't.

Topher hauled my arm over his shoulder, lifting half my weight.

"Come on," he said. "We need to leave."

I did not have the strength to argue. The cavern trembled again. Dust rained from above.

Topher pulled me toward the trail he'd come from, staggering beneath my weight.

"We're going to figure this out," he said, not convincing himself, not convincing me, but saying it because silence was worse. "We're going to get her back."

My throat burned.

"She looked at me," I said softly. "She felt it. She remembered. She knew me."

Topher tightened his grip, practically dragging me now.

"Then we find her before He cuts that tether out of both of you a second time," he said.

I let him pull me along the path, the tether burning in my chest like a fuse that could not be snuffed out, not even by God Himself. And for the first time since my Fall, I knew exactly where I was going back to. Whether Heaven survived it or not.

CHAPTER FORTY

Evie

One minute I was in the canyon at the side of the mountain, and the next... I wasn't. The world dissolved and re-formed all at once. Light. Color. Sound. I was alone, and there was a weird, sweet taste on my tongue.

I stumbled as my feet instantly hit marble, polished so smooth it reflected my face at me, small and pale and shaking. The air was warm, scented with gardenias and something sweeter underneath, something cloying that made my skin crawl.

The room around me was vast. Endless. Beautiful in a way that felt wrong. Too perfect. Too still. Rows and rows of alcoves lined the curved walls as far as I could see, each containing a bed draped in silk, soft light glowing from above. Shapes lay in them, sleeping or pretending to sleep, bodies too lovely to be real, too quiet to be alive. Most looked human. Some had wings and faint halos around their heads like dusted gold. Some didn't look human at all. And some had marks on their wrists that glimmered faintly, like bracelets made of light.

I stepped closer to one and froze. The woman's

eyes were open, wide, glass-clear. Empty. Her gaze tracked me, but behind those eyes? There was nothing there.

My stomach dropped like a stone. What was this place? Was it Heaven? This wasn't love or mercy. This wasn't devotion. This was nothing I pictured from Bible stories. This was a cage lined with velvet. A place for pretty things to be stored. A place He wanted to keep... me.

The tether in my chest still pulsed, faint and angry, pulling toward a direction I couldn't reach. Luc. Somewhere far below or far above or far beyond. It hurt not to follow it.

The First Light appeared beside me without sound. His presence filled the hall, warm and suffocating, like a father tucking a child in before locking the door.

"Do not be afraid," He said gently. His voice vibrated through the marble, through the air, through the bones of every creature He kept here. "These are my Beloved. This is where you belong."

"I don't belong here," I whispered, though my voice cracked on the last word.

He brushed a curl of hair away from my face, tender like it was love instead of ownership. He smiled, "Of course you do. You have wandered too long in the chaos of mortals. Here, you will be cherished. Here, nothing will ever harm you again."

His fingers grazed my cheek. I pulled away as my breath hitched. His skin didn't feel warm, it felt polished. Wrong. It made my stomach turn even as my nerves flared, my body reacting to His power, to some instinct to obey.

My entire body screamed. Not in pleasure, but in revolt, every cell trying to crawl away from the place his fingertips had been, like he'd left residue there, like I'd need to scrub my own skin raw to feel clean again.

My father would have handed me over to a man like this. And now a god was finishing the job.

I raised my chin. "Lucifer will come for me," I said, trying to convince myself more than Him, like speaking it would make it true.

Something in His expression flickered. "He will try," The First Light agreed. "But love is a sickness that blinds even the brightest. He will forget you again, just as he has before."

A cold, sick dread slid through my spine.

He stepped behind me and placed a hand at the small of my back, guiding me forward like I was walking down an aisle. Toward a raised dais. Toward a bed carved from ivory and draped in gold.

Recognition hit me like a punch. My stomach dropped to the floor. That was meant for me, where He would lie with me, where He would keep me. Where He would take from me whatever He believed was His right.

"No," I whispered, stumbling back. "Please. Please do not."

I ran right into his chest and turned.

The First Light smiled—a soft, patient smile. "There is nothing to fear. You were made for this."

He reached for me. His fingers brushed my shoulder. My breath shattered. Something inside me snapped open like a flower blooming in reverse.

Not the girl I'd been. Not the name I wore now. Something older, something terrible, something that had never known fear rose up.

The air vibrated. The hall flickered. The light in the room bent around me like it recognized me. I felt my spine straighten without permission. My panic and fear evaporated like steam off a hot stone.

The room shrank. The First Light jerked back a step, His face twisting. Not fear. Not yet. But recognition. But the wrong kind.

"Who are you?" He whispered.

My voice came out layered, deeper, edged in something that did not belong to humanity. "You know. Have you already forgotten?"

He shook His head, stepping back another pace. "No. Not possible. She was sealed out. Gone. Lost to the outer veil."

I smiled, slow and terrible. "If I am lost, why do you tremble?"

His breath hitched. A crack formed in the air behind me, a faint shimmer, a memory of stars spilling from my palms like spilled salt, precise and endless. Then the moment collapsed.

I gasped, stumbling as my knees buckled. The light dimmed. The air stilled. Whatever had risen inside me slammed shut again, leaving me the same small, shaking human.

The First Light stared at me with a new hunger — a new calculation. There was no lust. No love. It was purpose.

"You are more dangerous than I believed," He said softly, almost fondly. "Very well. I will not take you yet." His smile warmed, the way a father's might. "I'll be patient. I'll sand down every sharp edge you've grown, soothe every bruise you insist on calling strength, until surrender feels like relief." His gaze held mine, gentle as a hand on the back of your neck. "Slowly. Completely. And when you kneel for me, you will kneel forever."

He lifted a hand. The nearest alcove unsealed with a soft hiss.

Silk curtains spilled open like the mouth of a

beast, light glowing warm and false inside. The bed within was carved from ivory, smooth and perfect, waiting.

"Rest," He commanded. "This is your home now. You will not want for anything. Not even to leave this hall again."

The walls seemed to lean in as the light dimmed, and He turned away, His presence retreating like a tide that I knew would return soon.

My fear came roaring back. But before the alcove could close, something shifted across the way. A woman lay on the bed directly across from me, her alcove still open. Her body was impossibly still, her skin luminous, her face too beautiful to be real. I had thought her asleep.

Her fingers twitched. Just once. Her eyes slid toward me, glassy and hollow and terrified, and for a fraction of a second, something behind them screamed. No sound came out.

"Are—are you okay?" I asked.

Then both our curtains fell shut. My stomach twisted violently. This wasn't rest. This was a dollhouse. This was storage.

The tether in my chest pulsed again, but different —wrong. Here it was jagged and strained, like a wire pulled too tight through stone. It didn't sing in this place. It scraped. It burned cold, aching toward a direction I couldn't reach.

Luc. His name wasn't a word so much as a wound.

I staggered as the alcove sealed around me, silk brushing my skin, light dimming to a false dusk. The bed was soft beneath my hands, too soft, like it was designed to make you stay.

I didn't lie down. I stayed sitting, boots still on, spine rigid, memorizing everything. The sound of the hall. The pattern of the light. The number of breaths between pulses of power.

The First Light had not touched me again. That alone told me everything. He knew something. He knew what had looked back at Him, even for a heartbeat. He knew what He'd tried to cage.

"You are more dangerous than I believed," He had said. Was I dangerous? To isolate? To soften instead of force? To be broken?

I pressed two fingers to my chest, to the place where the tether burned brightest, like a brand that refused to cool. Somewhere far away, he answered.

Not gently. Not patiently. Rage slammed into me like heat through a door someone had just kicked open, raw and volcanic and only his. It wasn't just anger, it was motion, a wild, feral promise with teeth. The kind of fury that didn't negotiate. The kind that didn't pray.

It lit up every nerve I had. My breath hitched, and to my own surprise, a smile tugged at my mouth, small and sharp. Good. Let him feel it. Let him wallow in his anger.

The tether thrummed, tight as a drawn bowstring. I could feel him through it, pacing the edge of himself, trying not to snap, failing anyway.

"Yeah," I whispered under my breath, like I was speaking to the burn in my chest. "That's it."

Because his rage didn't scare me, it pleased me. It meant he was alive. It meant he was still mine in the only way that mattered, not possession, not ownership, but with the pull of what could not be undone. A force that would cross time and hell-mouths and holy thresholds just to get back to the place I was. I leaned into it, let it flood me, let it curl around my ribs like a hand.

Luc would come for me. He wouldn't stop. Not for

distance. Not for pain. Not for whatever The First Light thought He could demand. I closed my eyes, savoring it like a sip of something strong and sinful.

"Come find me, Luc," I thought, and the tether flared in answer, as if he'd heard the shape of my words even if he couldn't hear my voice. "Come tear the fucking sky open."

Then, the walls hummed, as if settling. The hall grew quiet again, rows upon rows of stolen bodies breathing in unison, a cathedral of sleep and silence and stolen will.

And something inside me, something ancient, whispered, "Not yet. Not like this. But when the time comes... He will learn you are inevitable."

I lifted my chin, alone in a place meant to break me, and let that thought anchor itself. And then I made a vow to myself. I would remember. I would not forget their faces. I would remember their names. I would not let myself be sanded smooth.

He thought He had taken me, added me to his collection. He had only given me more time to find that power again.

CHAPTER FORTY-ONE

Lucifer - Epilogue

Epilogue

The war room felt too small. Too many bodies. Too many eyes. Not nearly enough air. I paced the room like something feral, magic sparking off my skin in uneven bursts. Every breath scraped my ribs raw. Every heartbeat was a hammer. The mountain hummed with my temper, echoing it back like a warning.

"I have to get her back." My voice went lethal. "And I'm going to kill Him, I should've done it a long time ago."

Evie wasn't dragged into Heaven, into wherever He was keeping her. She gave herself up for me. And that was killing me.

They all looked away as soon as I said it, like my desperation was contagious, like if they didn't meet my eyes, they wouldn't have to confess the truth. Morran studied the floor as if it owed him an answer. Seren's jaw flexed once, tight enough to crack stone. Even Topher, usually made of steel and spreadsheets, blinked hard and stared at a dead monitor like it might save him.

Azazael barely stood near the stone map table, holding himself upright. He was still gaunt from the oubliette, wings tucked tight and trembling. Topher was at the far end, hunched over two tablets and a stack of torn notes. The overhead light illuminated his exhausted face. I couldn't remember the last time he slept.

Damien leaned in the shadows, his back against a load-bearing stone pillar, watching me with narrowed, assessing eyes. Vespera lounged on a couch, dangerous amusement curling around her smile.

They all waited silently, waiting for me to break. And I was nearly there.

No one wanted to be the first to say it out loud that we didn't even know where she'd been taken, not really. That the tether could burn a hole through my chest and still not give me a map. That the thing who'd stolen her was not a king or a demon, but a false god who wrote rules like scripture and called it love.

My wings twitched, restless, violent with the need to tear through something. "Look at me," I snapped, voice rough enough to scrape. "You think I can't feel what you're all thinking?"

Silence. It tasted like ash.

"She walked into that place willingly," I rasped, voice shaking so hard it barely held shape. "For me. She traded herself for me. And now she's with him. Alone. In that gilded hell, He built. I should've—"

Topher cut me off, gentle but firm. "Lucifer."

"I'm going to Heaven," I snarled. "Tonight. Now. I'll tear it down brick by brick, angel by angel, until I find her."

"Absolutely not," Damien said, stepping forward.

"He's a fucking god, Morningstar. You go up there in this state, you'll last ten seconds."

"Maybe that's what it takes."

Azazael lifted his head, voice soft but steady. "That is exactly what He wants."

I froze.

He held my gaze—old grief, old love, old wounds flickering there. "He wants you broken. Blind. Raging. He wants you to run to him like a lamb—so he can finish what he started."

My hands shook. My vision went red. "Then what am I supposed to do? Sit here while she— while He—"

"Survive," Azazael said. "Long enough to save her."

Silence tightened like a noose.

Topher finally exhaled, slow and careful, like he was handling explosives. "Lucifer," he said quietly, "it's not that we don't want to. It's that if we go in blind, we probably all die, and then she's trapped there forever."

The words hit like a blade between the ribs. I turned on him, fury flashing hot, then felt it, the faintest tug in my chest, the tether twitching like a living thing. Not a direction. Not an answer. Just... proof. She was still there. Still breathing. Still mine.

I dragged a hand through my hair and forced myself to stop pacing, forced my voice into something colder, sharper. Something that could lead. "Then we don't go blind," I said.

They lifted their heads. Every eye in the room found me, war and fear and hope all tangled together.

"We find a way in," I continued, each word settling into place like a weapon being assembled. "Someone up there has to be unhappy, has to see through His lies, and is willing to turn on him. Then, we gather bodies. The Fallen, angels, humans, anyone with grudges and nothing left to lose."

My gaze cut to Damien. "And we start with everyone who's ever watched Him smile while he ruined them."

And then Vespera laughed—low, rich, serpentine. "All this rage and no imagination," she purred.

She stood and sauntered toward the table, tracing a fingertip along its edge. "You talk of overthrowing a god and killing Him. But no one kills a god outright. You know that, Lucifer." She looked around the room. "We all know that."

I said nothing. I couldn't trust my voice not to crack.

"But," she said, circling us like a predator playing with her prey, "I've heard... things. Old texts. Rituals no one can trace back to a beginning. Inscriptions carved into stone in languages He thought were gone." Her smile sharpened. "And I've heard Him, too, when he forgets who's listening. Things he's said to Lilith that don't fit his little story, like the time He said he had brothers and sisters once."

Topher stiffened. "Vespera—don't start with—"

"What he said was there were Twelve," she said, ignoring Topher, eyes gleaming.

My heart twisted. "You're saying there are others like Him."

"I don't know," she said simply. "Maybe they're long gone. Maybe He made sure of it. But what I do know?"

A shiver ran through the room.

Azazael's half-grown wings twitched, feathers rustling. His eyes widened, recognition flickering. "What about the Oracle? Could she tell us something?"

Vespera's mouth curved like she enjoyed the question. "If she's still alive." She tapped the stone table once. "And if she is, it's because she knows things He never managed to erase."

"Like what?" I demanded.

Vespera's gaze lifted to mine. "Maybe who the Twelve were," she said.

The air tightened.

"Or maybe He was never the First Light. Maybe He was someone else. Never the brightest. Never the true creator," Damien said slowly.

"Maybe," Vespera replied. "Maybe He just wanted it all. No rivals, no witnesses, no shared throne."

Topher swallowed and looked at me. "So this could have been ambition."

Vespera's eyes gleamed as she met my gaze. "The oldest kind. And... I think this was panic. He saw what you two were together, and somehow it frightened Him. That's why He's doing all this. Because you two together... It's something He can't control, and it scares Him."

The tether flared without warning. Not a pulse. Not a tug. A spike.

My breath punched out of me as something sharp and frantic tore through my chest, raw panic flooding the bond so fast it blurred my vision. I staggered, palm slamming into the table hard enough to make the stone ring.

"Lucifer?" Topher snapped.

I barely heard him. Fear poured through me— Evie's fear—immediate and suffocating, the kind that came when there was nowhere left to run. Not confusion. Not doubt. She was cornered.

My wings shuddered, feathers twitching like they

wanted to rip free and fly to her on instinct alone. "No," I breathed, low and broken. "No, no—"

And then, beneath the fear, something else surged. Power.

It rolled through the tether like a tide hitting stone, vast and sudden and wrong in its scale. It wasn't wild or chaotic. It was controlled, like something ancient lifting its head after a very long sleep.

It spilled into my skin. Gold lit beneath my flesh, seeping through every vein and scar until I was glowing. The air around me shimmered. Dust caught the light and turned into stars.

The room went dead still. Every face lifted. Vespera took a step back, her eyes widening. Morran's dagger paused mid-spin. Seren's scorched wing twitched once, as if it recognized a command it hadn't heard in centuries. Even Topher stopped breathing for a beat, like he'd just watched the laws of the world stutter.

No one said a word. They just stared at the gold radiating off my skin, and at the proof written in light, that whatever happened on the other side of that bond had touched me back.

"What was that?" Damien demanded.

I couldn't answer. My heart was slamming so hard it hurt. For one terrifying, electric heartbeat, the fear vanished. In its place was clarity—cold, vast, endless. Not Evie. Something older. Something that didn't need to beg.

The tether burned like a live wire, bright enough to sting tears from my eyes, and then—it slammed shut.

The power vanished, and my skin stopped glowing. The fear rushed back in, ragged and shaking, layered with confusion, like she didn't understand what had just happened either.

I dragged in a breath, hands clenched into fists, blood roaring in my ears.

"She's alive," I said hoarsely, not looking at anyone. "But whatever He's doing to her... it just changed."

Silence spread, thick and uneasy. Vespera was the only one who didn't look frightened.

She looked satisfied. Slowly, thoughtfully, like she'd just watched a god flinch in real time and filed the information away.

Azazael's voice came quieter than before. "We need to find out what the Oracle knows. If there's a way to destroy Him."

Vespera nodded once. "Maybe she knows what He believes would destroy Him if it ever came back."

The mountain hummed beneath our feet, low and ominous.

"And if Evie matters to Him now," Vespera added softly, almost kindly, eyes flicking to my chest where the tether still burned, "it's because she brushed against something He thought was gone forever."

"Then tell me where to find her," I said.

Vespera's smile widened, "Santa Monica. She hides where the veil thins and mortals pretend they don't see magic. Look for a woman everyone avoids."

"I'll find her," I said, voice hard as iron. "Before He decides Evie's disobedience is worth finishing. Because even when she's scared, she's going to defy Him. She's going to refuse him. And that is going to make Him very angry."

I didn't hesitate. I turned for the door, heart pounding, body shaking, fury burning all the way down to bone.

"Lucifer..." Topher's voice followed me, careful. "Are you sure you want to go... alone?"

I stopped with my hand on the stone frame, shoulders rising on a slow breath. The tether in my chest pulsed, faint with fear. How was I supposed to sit here while she was scared?

"I have to," I said without turning around.

Silence held.

Then, quieter, I confessed, "Because it won't just be her. This will continue, and He'll use anyone."

My wings flexed, restless, under my skin.

"And because if this goes wrong," I added, voice gone razor-calm, "it has to be me who pays for it. Not you. Not Azazael. Not anyone who followed me into this war thinking they might still get to live."

Topher didn't answer. I could feel his stare on my back like a weight. I glanced back just enough to catch his eyes.

"Call for the car," I said. "Now. And tell the pilot the plane's wheels don't leave the ground until I'm in my seat, but it needs to be ready like we're running from the end of the world."

Topher swallowed, jaw working once, then nodded, already moving. The mountain hummed again, lower this time, like a vow.

"I'm going to bring her home," I said, voice quiet and lethal. "And if I have to burn Heaven to do it..."

I bared my teeth as my rage burned down the tether. "...so be it. He's going to regret ever calling our love the First Sin."

About the Author

Stephanie Pass hails from a tiny Texas town where she lives with her husband, children, and a Boxer dog who talks more than she does. She writes contemporary romance with magical realism and romantasy. Soon, she will dip her toe into some sci-fi romance. She loves books about love, magic, and high fae. She had her own real-life romance story come true when a chance encounter led her to meet her now husband. When she's not writing romance stories, Stephanie is a mom blogger dancing to Taylor Swift at https://thetiptoefairy.com. But you can often find her at the roller skating rink or dancing at the goth nightclub.

To learn more join Stephanie's email list - https://thetiptoefairy.myflodesk.com/join-romance-list

THE END

Thank you so much for reading The First Sin, book 1 in the Hell of a Time dark romantasy series.

I hope you enjoyed it! If you did...

1. Help other people find this book by writing a review.
2. Sign up for my email list so you can know when the next book is coming out.
3. Come follow me on Instagram, TikTok, or Facebook.
4. Use the QR code below to visit my website:

Sneak Peek at The Second Coming

Book 2, **The Second Coming**, starts
where love turns feral. Evie is gone,
stolen into The First Light's Beloved like
she's a pretty thing on a shelf, and
Lucifer is unraveling thread by thread,
all teeth and prayer and rage. He's out of
time and out of options. If you're here
for desperate devotion, divine danger,
and a love that refuses to stay buried,
here's your first bite.

Lucifer

It took three days to get her to speak
to me. Three days of walking the length
of the pier, up the salt-worn planks, past
the neon vendors and shrieking gulls,
searching for a presence that felt like a
wrinkle in the air.

And there she was. A hunched old
woman with stringy hair, pushing a
grocery cart overflowing with trash—
mismatched shoes, busted radios, dirty
blankets, newspaper bundles so soaked
with seawater they'd fossilized into
shapes.

The string lights overhead warped as
I approached her, their glow bending
inward as if they were being quietly
swallowed, without dimming, not
flickering. Correcting. The shadow

beneath her cart stretched the wrong way, angling toward the ocean instead of away from it, as if the pier itself couldn't agree on where she belonged.

Magic does that when it's being strangled, when something ancient is pretending to be small. I slowed without meaning to.

She muttered to herself, scolded passing pigeons, and barked at the ocean like it had personally offended her. Her muttering wasn't nonsense. It was unfinished. Sentences without verbs. Names that stopped halfway out of her mouth. Words swallowed hard, like they hurt to hold too long.

Mortals gave her a wide berth, eyes skipping over her like she wasn't real. But I could see the air bent around her. It bent the way magic does when it's trying very hard not to be noticed.

"Can you help me?" I asked.

But that first day, she didn't even look at me.

"Go away," she snapped, waving a crooked hand. "You're too tall and too dramatic. Shoo."

On the second day, the pier was a mouthful of noise: arcade bells, distant laughter, the ocean breathing beneath it all, like something enormous pretending to sleep. Neon smeared across the fog. Sugar clung to the air.

I found her on a bench facing the water, wrapped in mismatched layers, hair wild as seafoam, a paper boat of churros in her lap like an offering she'd never consented to make. She didn't look up when I stopped in front of her.

She just kept eating, slow, unimpressed, as if the end of the world wasn't worth pausing for. Then, she paused mid-chew, as if she'd almost said something and thought better of it. Her jaw tightened. The word stayed locked behind her teeth.

"I think I need you," I said.

"Everybody needs somebody," she muttered. "Go find a therapist."

"I need an oracle."

That did it. She looked up, eyes cutting straight through the suit, straight through the skin I wore like a lie.

"You don't need an oracle," she said. "You need a nap. And possibly a hobby."

My patience was already a thin wire, fraying. "Tell me how to kill a god."

For a heartbeat, the boardwalk seemed to hush around us, like even the ocean leaned in.

Then she snorted, like I'd asked her the time.

"Kill a god," she repeated, tasting the words like they were stale. "Sweetheart, you can't even kill your ego."

I took a step closer. The air around

me felt wrong, charged, but she didn't move an inch.

"What's your price?" I asked, voice low. "What do you want?"

She snapped off a piece of churro, took one bite, then flicked the remaining chunk at my chest like she was swatting a fly.

It struck my lapel and burst, sugar crystals scattering, clinging to the black of my suit jacket like tiny, glittering accusations. A few caught in the weave near my collar, stubborn as salt.

The piece dropped between us. A seagull screamed. But for half a second after the churro hit the boards, there was no sound—not quiet. Just missing. Like the world had swallowed a syllable it wasn't allowed to say.

I barely had time to blink before a white blur dive-bombed the boards, wings slapping air, beak snapping. It went for the churro, missed, and turned its wrath on the nearest warm body—Me.

The bird lunged at my face like it had a personal grudge. I jerked back, hand coming up on instinct, suit sleeve slicing through fog, dignity collapsing in real time. Another seagull swooped in, then another, a sudden cyclone of feathers and fury, shrieking so loud it made my teeth ache.

I backpedaled, swatting and snarling

while tourists laughed and someone's kid pointed like I was the entertainment.

The oracle didn't even flinch. She sat there, calm as a tidepool, watching me get nearly pecked to death over a pastry I hadn't asked for.

When the birds finally tore the churro to crumbs and scattered, I stood there breathing hard, hair out of place, sugar crystals all over my fingers, and rage bright behind my eyes.

She waved both hands at me like I was a stray cat creeping toward her food.

"I said GO," she crowed, loud enough to carry over the pier. "Persistent men are exhausting!"

I stared at her, stunned in a way I hadn't been in centuries. Not because of the insult, I'd been insulted by better, but because she'd said it like I was nothing, like I was just another man who wouldn't take no for an answer. Like she didn't feel the old darkness in my bones at all.

I tried again, slower. Dangerous, even. "You know who I am."

She barked a laugh, sharp and merciless. "Oh, I know exactly who you are."

Then she leaned forward, eyes narrowing, and pointed down the boardwalk like she was directing traffic.

"And I also know you can walk," she said. "So walk. Go haunt somebody else's bench."

I didn't move.

She reached into her paper boat, snapped off another piece of churro, and held it up like a threat. "Last warning," she said, cheerful as a guillotine. "I can feed you to the birds all night."

For the first time since Evie vanished, something almost unfamiliar flickered in my chest. I'd been numb for days. But this wasn't fear. It was... humiliation. And beneath it, the tiniest, sharpest spark of hope.

Because if she could chase me off like I was nobody, then maybe she wasn't afraid of gods either. Maybe she knew how to break one.

By the third day, the pier felt tired, just worn thin, like even the fog had stayed up too late and regretted it. The Ferris wheel turned slowly and patiently, counting nothing. The ocean kept breathing, indifferent to my timing.

As I stepped onto the planks, the air tightened behind my eyes, a pressure I couldn't shake. The Ferris wheel's lights haloed too brightly, like the universe was overexposing itself. Something here didn't want to be named.

She was on the same bench. Same paper boat. Still watching the water. The light bent around her again, more noticeably now, as if the seal was tired of pretending she wasn't a problem.

This was beginning to feel pointless. She wasn't ever going to help me. I stopped a few steps away and said nothing. I'd learned that much.

But I couldn't give up. I would never give up. I needed to get Evie back. So this time... this time, I didn't ask for her help. I didn't ask about Evie. I didn't even ask how to kill a god. I just walked over and sat down next to her.

She didn't look at me. "If you ask me how to kill Him," she said mildly, "I'm throwing food again. The birds liked you."

"I'm not here to kill Him," I said.

That earned me a glance—one sharp eye, measuring.

"I'm here to get her back." I tried to hide the catch in my throat.

She snorted. "Of course, you are."

"She's being kept," I said, my jaw tight. "Like she belongs to Him."

"Mm," she hummed, noncommittal.

"I need to know how to break His hold," I said. "What kind of god does that? What does He fear?"

She finally turned fully toward me. All of her attention settled, heavy as weather.

"You think he did this once," she said.

The words didn't register at first. "I think He took her," I replied carefully.

She tilted her head. "And you believe she was the first?"

Something cold slid down my spine. "There are rumors He has others," I said. "The Beloved. I know that."

She laughed then, short and sharp, like a bark. "Oh, Little Star. That's not an answer. That's a shelf."

My hands curled. "Then tell me what I'm missing."

She leaned forward, elbows on her knees, eyes locking onto mine like she meant to pin me in place.

"You're staring at the bruise," she said, "and refusing to look at the body."

My pulse picked up. "Speak plainly."

"You're treating this like a riddle. It isn't. It's a lock, and I'm missing teeth." Her mouth twitched, like she hadn't meant to say that much. One of her hands rose and pressed two fingers to her lips, as if holding something in.

I exhaled and then looked over at her, "What did He steal?"

Everything stilled. The ocean froze mid-crash. The air tightened like it held its breath. Even the gulls stopped in place, suspended in the air.

Slowly, she turned. Her clouded eyes

cleared into something vast and ancient —light cutting through them like twin blades. Her back straightened. Her skin shimmered, blue as deep ocean. Her rags peeled away into jeweled armor. Multiple arms unfurled like wings made of fire and memory. Some bent the wrong way at the joint. Others flickered, phasing in and out, like the universe couldn't agree they were allowed to exist.

She was beautiful in the way storms are beautiful. In the way monsters are beautiful. Awe-inspiring, but... dangerous and something... something was wrong in the way broken instruments are wrong—still powerful, but unable to play a clean note.

And she smiled at me. "Everything," she said. "And you finally remembered to ask the only question that matters."

My breath caught. "Oracle."

She nodded once. "You want to know how to stop Him," she said. "How to topple that Lamp?"

One of her hands began to raise, flickering out of view. "He keeps them close," she continued, "because proximity makes the lie feel holy. Makes theft feel like devotion."

My chest tightened. "You're saying—"

"I'm saying your girl isn't special because she was chosen," the oracle said gently, and for the first time, not cruelly.

"She's special because she's an anomaly."

Anger flared, hot and immediate. "Watch your mouth."

She raised a brow. "You asked."

I glanced at her and forced myself to breathe. "Anomaly?"

She straightened, six hands lifting slowly, like a glitch, like she was arranging something invisible between us.

"He takes what reminds Him, He's incomplete," she said. "Beauty. Will. Creation. Things that answer back when touched."

The ocean crashed harder, as if punctuating the thought.

"He keeps them still," she went on. "Because if they move freely, the truth leaks."

My voice came out rough. "The truth of what?"

"That He isn't the source. He is the creator of nothing," she replied. "Only the Spotlight."

I stared at her, the shape of it starting to form, ugly and enormous.

"You think you're fighting a jailer," she said softly. "You're fighting a curator."

Silence stretched. The Ferris wheel creaked.

"How do I get her out?" I asked. Not

loud. Not pleading. Focused. "Because if He's done this before, then there's a system. And systems break."

Her lips curved. "There you are."

She stood, movements unhurried, and stepped closer than she had before. The air shifted, not threatening, just aware.

"You can't break this alone," she said. "Not because you're weak, but because He didn't build it alone."

My brow furrowed. "Explain."

"He didn't always act unchecked," she said. "Others watched Him. Others went in after Him, wearing borrowed lives, waiting for the moment they could pull the thread."

"How many?" I asked.

"You keep thinking in twelves," she said. "It will begin with just two, and then eight." Her gaze flicked, sharp. Measuring me.

"Two." My heart thudded once, hard. "Where are they? H—how do I find them?"

"Sleeping," she said. "Inside the world you walk through every day. Forgetting why they ever cared."

"And they can help me," I said. Not a question.

"They're the only reason help still exists," she replied.

I swallowed. "How do I wake them?"

She shook her head. "Wrong question."

Frustration surged, but I forced it down. Tried again. "What wakes them," I said, slower, "when nothing else has?"

Her smile was small. Earned.

"Contradiction," she said. "Moments where the lie fails. Where theft is named. Where something stolen refuses to stay still."

My thoughts went immediately, painfully, to Evie.

"And her?" I asked.

The oracle's expression softened, just a fraction, like the world had briefly remembered mercy.

"She'll make it," she said quietly. "She'll come back to you."

A beat. Her gaze slid away, toward the black water, toward the place where secrets go to drown.

"She will... loosen things," she added, careful with every word, like she was handling glass. "For them, it will be easier."

My throat tightened. "And for her?"

The oracle swallowed. When she looked back at me, her eyes were gentler than the truth.

"Sometimes," she murmured, "what keeps you alive is the same thing that leaves a crack."

Something hot tore through my ribs. No... a crack. In her.

My hands curled without permission, nails biting into my palms as if pain could anchor me. My vision tunneled, the pier falling away until there was only Evie, only the idea of her dragged through something sharp and holy-looking and wrong, the wrong that smiles while it ruins you.

"Protect her, protect her, protect her," my mind screamed, useless and frantic.

And underneath it, darker, louder, older, the part of me that remembered thrones and punishment and what it felt like to make the world afraid whispered one clear thing:

If he has touched her, I will burn his light out of the sky.

The thought burned hot and fast, threatening to split me open if I let it. I drew it in instead, packed it down where fury has always lived best, dense and contained, a blade rather than a blaze. Rage could wait. Evie couldn't.

I lifted my head. "What do I do first?"

She stepped back, the distance between us returning like a held breath released.

"Wake the two," she said. "One who knows how to open what's sealed. One who can tell the difference between what's real and what's bright."

I met her eyes. "And then?"

She glitched back into the old woman, the transformation stuttering, armor tearing into rags mid-motion, as if her true form couldn't hold under the weight of being seen. She picked up her paper boat, already turning away.

"Then," she said lightly, "you stop thinking this is about rescuing one woman."

She glanced over her shoulder, her stringy hair blowing in the wind with a black-toothed grin sharp as glass as she slowly pushed her cart away.

The fog rolled in thicker, swallowing the bench, and she was gone. And the pier felt much, much smaller than it had three days ago.

www.ingramcontent.com/pod-product-compliance
Lightning Source LLC
Chambersburg PA
CBHW060810120726
47909CB00006B/1859